P9-DEZ-856

TANTALIZING LOCKED ROOM MYSTERIES

TANTALIZING LOCKED ROOM MYSTERIES

Edited by
Isaac Asimov, Charles G. Waugh,
and Martin Harry Greenberg

WALKER AND COMPANY
NEW YORK

First published in the United States of America in 1982 by the Walker Publishing Company, Inc.

Published simultaneously in Canada by John Wiley & Sons Canada, Limited, Rexdale, Ontario.

ISBN: 0-8027-0680-0
Library of Congress Catalog Card Number: 80-54817

Printed in the United States of America
Book design by Ganis & Harris, Inc.
10 9 8 7 6 5 4 3 2 1

ACKNOWLEDGEMENTS

Kantor, MacKinlay. Copyright © 1930 by MacKinlay Kantor. Copyright renewed. Reprinted by permission of Paul R. Reynolds, Inc.

Woolrich, Cornell. Copyright © 1937 by Cornell Woolrich. Copyright renewed 1965. First published in *Dime Detective Magazine*. Reprinted by permission of the agents for the author's estate, the Scott Meredith Literary Agency, Inc., 845 Third Avenue, New York, New York 10022.

Gardner, Erle Stanley. Copyright © 1941 by Red Star News Company. Copyright renewed © 1968 by Earl Stanley Gardner. First published in *Detective Fiction Weekly Magazine*. Used by permission of Jean Gardner for the estate of Earl Stanley Gardner.

Perowne, Barry. Copyright © 1945 by Barry Perowne. Reprinted by permission of A.P. Watt Ltd. Literary Agents.

Arthur, Robert. Copyright © 1951 by Robert Arthur. Reprinted by permission of the agents for the author's estate, the Scott Meredith Literary Agency, 845 Third Avenue, New York 10022.

March, William. Copyright © 1954 by Merchants National Bank of Mobile, Alabama. First published in *Ellery Queen's Mystery Magazine*. Reprinted by permission of Harold Ober Associates, Inc.

Wodhams, Jack. Copyright © 1970 by Conde Nast Publications, Inc. Reprinted by permission of the author and his agents, Cory & Collins.

Hoch, Edward D. Copyright © 1971 by Edward D. Hoch. First published in *Ellery Queen's Mystery Magazine*. Reprinted by permission of the author and Larry Sternig Literary Agency.

Pronzini, Bill and Michael Kurland. Copyright © 1975 by H.D.S. Publications, Inc. First published in *Alfred Hitchcock's Mystery Magazine*. Reprinted by permission of the authors.

Contents

NO ONE DONE IT!

Isaac Asimov

Everyone with a spark of mental agility loves a puzzle. I myself am deficient in puzzle-solving genes (or whatever it is that makes one see a solution) and can never see the ending in a mystery story unless I write the story myself and therefore know the answer to begin with—but I love puzzles all the more for that reason. I love being surprised. I love to get to the answer slowly—slowly—no peeking—not even trying to outguess the author—and then being ravished by the revelation.

No wonder Agatha Christie is by far my favorite mystery writer. Who else can manage to obscure the clues as she could? Who else could hide the solution as neatly? Who else could spring the solution as suddenly and unexpectedly? And whenever I haven't read a particular Agatha Christie for five years or so (there's no such thing as a new one for me, since I have them all and have read them all) I can read it again and be surprised again.

Naturally, the more puzzling a mystery is, the more pleased I am, and since I honestly think I am the most run-of-the-mill person ever invented, and the most nearly average (except, perhaps, for a bit of writing talent) I assume all this is characteristic of everyone.

In that case, since we are all agreed thus far, let us ask ourselves what kind of mystery is the most puzzling and, therefore, the most satisfying. The answer is clear: the one to which there is patently no solution at all.

Let me give you an example from that somewhat complicated and unending variety of mystery tale called scientific research.

There are three ways, and precisely three ways in which the Moon could have come to inhabit our sky as it does; circling the Earth and accompanying our planet in its endless journey about the Sun.

1) The Moon could once have been part of the Earth itself. For some reason, a portion of the Earth broke loose, but that portion, still held by Earth's gravity, won only partial freedom and became the Moon. It has circled Earth ever since and the Earth/Moon relationship is that of mother and daughter.

2) The Moon was never actually part of the Earth itself, but when the original cloud of dust and gas condensed to form Earth, a portion of it condensed about a smaller nucleus and formed the Moon. The two worlds have been associated ever since and the Earth/Moon association is that of brother and sister.

3) The Moon was formed elsewhere in the solar system and was an independent planet to begin with. At some past epoch in Earth's history, however, it was captured. Since then, the two worlds have been associated and the Earth/Moon association is at best, that of cousin and cousin.

Unfortunately, as it happens, strong arguments can be advanced against each of these three theories; so strong that each theory can be ruled out as wrong. Yet there is no natural alternative.

One astronomer, after having considered each hypothesis carefully, pro and con, announced dolefully that the only solution is to suppose that the Moon is simply *not there.*

Well, of course there *is* a fourth possibility beyond nature. Astronomers can simply shrug their shoulders and say: "That's how God arranged it."

That, however, is giving up the game, and scientists are not allowed to do that. Somewhere there is an answer that involves only the laws of nature and it will someday be found. That is the scientists' faith. The delight will be in the finding and in the justification of that faith. The fact that it seems an impossible puzzle now will make the eventual delight in the eventual finding all the more intense.

Back, then, to the mystery story proper, the kind with an invented universe that is more orderly and more controllable than the real one; where we will never have to leave the delight of finding to a future generation, but where we need wait only 250 suspense-filled pages at most—and perhaps only 25.

The best puzzle in that case is not merely a mysterious crime but, like the Moon's existence, an *impossible* one—the kind where the murder takes place in a locked room, or in an unapproachable place, or at a non-existent time, or under conditions when there are no possible suspects.

Here, too, there is always the forbidden possibility: that somehow the solution lies beyond nature.

The true mystery writer is not allowed that solution anymore than the scientist is. The universe of the mystery story must be logical. Somewhere, however impossible the crime seems to be, there must be an answer that involves only logic and the natural world. That is the faith of the mystery aficionado. And, again, the delight is in finding the solution and in the justification of that faith.

The closer the mystery writer can come to suggesting the supernatural without falling into the pit, the better. The more forcefully he pushes the reader into despair, the greater the reader's delight at finding the universe of logic intact and unharmed.

The history of impossible crimes is just about coeval with the history of the mystery story.

The very first of the modern mystery stories, complete with talented amateur detective, and untalented bosom buddy, was *The Murders in the Rue Morgue* by Edgar Allan Poe, published in 1841, and, behold, it was an impossible crime!

The Sherlock Holmes story which most aficionados would agree was the best (and Conan Doyle himself agreed) is *The Adventure of the Speckled Band* and, behold, it, too, was an impossible crime!

One of Agatha Christie's closest rivals for my undying love is John Dickson Carr, and, indeed, impossible-crime novels were his specialty. (What a pity we don't have room in the book for one of his novels!)

Well, confining ourselves to shorter pieces, we still have a long collection of impossible crimes for your delectation and delight. Read on!

THE MURDERS IN THE RUE MORGUE

(1841)

Edgar Allan Poe

Edgar Allan Poe

Soldier, literary critic, editor, poet, and short story writer, Edgar Allan Poe (1809–1849) accomplished a great deal during his relatively brief life, even though he was an essentially tragic and self-destructive figure who drank himself to death. He popularized science fiction and psychological terror and invented the detective story in 1841 with "The Murders in the Rue Morgue." This brilliant story also introduced the first locked room detective story and the first series detective, Auguste Dupin. Ironically, however, it has never appeared in a locked room anthology until now.

THE MURDERS IN THE RUE MORGUE

> What song the Syrens sang, or what name Achilles assumed when he hid himself among women, although puzzling questions, are not beyond *all* conjecture.
>
> Sir Thomas Browne

The mental features discoursed of as the analytical, are, in themselves, but little susceptible of analysis. We appreciate them only in their effects. We know of them, among other things, that they are always to their possessor, when inordinately possessed, a source of the liveliest enjoyment. As the strong man exults in his physical ability, delighting in such exercises as call his muscles into action, so glories the analyst in that moral activity which *disentangles*. He derives pleasure from even the most trivial occupations bringing his talent into play. He is fond of enigmas, of conundrums, hieroglyphics: exhibiting in his solutions of each a degree of *acumen* which appears to the ordinary apprehension preternatural. His results, brought about by the very soul and essence of method, have, in truth, the whole air of intuition.

The faculty of re-solution is possibly much invigorated by mathematical study, and especially by that highest branch of it which, unjustly, and merely on account of its retrograde operations, has been called, as if *par excellence*, analysis. Yet to calculate is not in itself to analyze. A chess-player, for example, does the one, without effort at the other. It follows that the game of chess, in its effects upon mental character, is greatly misunderstood. I am not now writing a treatise, but simply prefacing a somewhat peculiar narrative by observations very much at random; I will, therefore, take occasion to assert that the higher powers of the reflective intellect are more decidedly and more usefully tasked by the unostentatious game of draughts than by all the elaborate frivolity of chess. In this latter, where the pieces have different and *bizarre* motions, with various and variable values, what is only complex, is mistaken (a not unusual error) for what is profound. The *attention* is here called powerfully into play. If it flag for an instant, an oversight is committed, resulting in injury or defeat. The possible moves being not only manifold, but involute, the chances of such oversights are multiplied; and in nine cases out of ten, it is the more concentrative rather than the more acute player who conquers. In draughts, on the contrary, where the moves are *unique* and have but little variation, the probabilities of inadvertence are diminished, and the mere attention being left comparatively unemployed, what advantages, are obtained by either party are obtained by superior *acumen*. To be less abstract, let us suppose a game of draughts where the pieces are reduced to four kings, and where, of course, no oversight is to be expected. It is obvious that here the victory can be decided (the players being at all equal) only by some *recherché* movement, the result of some strong exertion of the intellect. Deprived of ordinary resources, the analyst throws himself into the spirit of his opponent, identifies himself therewith, and not unfrequently sees thus, at a glance, the sole methods (sometimes indeed absurdly simple ones) by which he may seduce into error or hurry into miscalculation.

Whist has long been known for its influence upon what is termed the calculating power; and men of the highest order of intellect have been known to take an apparently unaccountable delight in it, while eschewing chess as frivolous. Beyond doubt there is nothing of a similiar nature so greatly tasking the faculty of analysis. The best chess-player in Christendom *may* be little more than the best player of chess; but proficiency in whist implies capacity for success in all these more important undertakings where mind struggles with mind. When I say proficiency, I mean that perfection in the game which includes a comprehension of *all* the sources whence legitimate advantage may be derived. These are not only manifold, but multiform, and lie frequently among recesses of thought altogether inaccessible to the ordinary understanding. To observe attentively is to remember distinctly; and, so far, the concentrative chess-player will do very well at whist; while the rules of Hoyle (themselves based upon the mere mechanism of the game) are sufficiently and generally comprehensible. Thus to have a retentive memory, and proceed by "the book" are points commonly regarded as the sum total of good playing. But it is in matters beyond the limits of mere rule that the skill of the analyst is evinced. He makes, in silence, a host of observations and inferences. So, perhaps, do his companions; and the difference in the extent of the information obtained, lies not so much in the validity of the inference as in the quality of the observation. The necessary knowledge is that of *what* to observe. Our player confines himself not at all; nor, because the game is the object, does he reject deductions from things external to the game. He examines the countenance of his partner, comparing it carefully with that of each of his opponents. He considers the mode of assorting the cards in each hand; often counting trump by trump, and honor by honor, through the glances bestowed by their holders upon each. He notes every variation of face as the play progresses, gathering a fund of thought from the differences in the expression of certainty, of surprise, of triumph, or chagrin. From the manner of gathering up a trick he judges whether the person taking it, can make another in the suit. He recognizes what is played through feint, by the manner with which it is thrown upon the table. A casual or inadvertent word; the accidental dropping or turning of a card, with the accompanying anxiety or carelessness in regard to its concealment; the counting of the tricks, with the order of their arrangement; embarrassment, hesitation, eagerness, or trepidation—all afford, to his apparently intuitive perception, indications of the true state of affairs. The first two or three rounds having been played, he is in full possession of the contents of each hand, and thenceforward puts down his cards with as absolute a precision of purpose as if the rest of the party had turned outward the faces of their own.

The analytical power should not be confounded with simple ingenuity; for while the analyst is necessarily ingenious, the ingenious man is often remarkably incapable of analysis. The constructive or combining power, by which ingenuity is usually manifested, and to which the phrenologists (I believe erroneously) have assigned a separate organ, supposing it a primitive faculty, has been so frequently seen in those whose intellect bordered otherwise upon idiocy, as to have attracted general observation among writers on morals. Between ingenuity and the analytic ability there exists a difference far greater, indeed, than that between the fancy and the imagination, but of a character very strictly analogous. It will be found, in fact, that the ingenious are always fanciful, and the *truly* imaginative never otherwise than analytic.

The narrative which follows will appear to the reader somewhat in the light of a commentary upon the propositions just advanced.

Residing in Paris during the spring and part of the summer of 18———, I there became acquainted with a Monsieur C. Auguste Dupin. This young gentleman was of an excellent, indeed of an illustrious family, but, by a variety of untoward events, had been reduced to such poverty that the energy of his character succumbed beneath it, and he ceased to bestir himself in the world, or to care for the retrieval of his fortunes. By courtesy of his creditors, there still remained in his possession a small remnant of his patrimony; and, upon the income arising from this, he managed, by means of a rigorous economy, to procure the necessities of life, without troubling himself about its superfluities. Books, indeed, were his sole luxuries, and in Paris these are easily obtained.

Our first meeting was at an obscure library in the Rue Montmartre, where the accident of our both being in search of the same very rare and very remarkable volume, brought us into closer communion. We saw each other again and again. I was deeply interested in the little family history which he detailed to me with all that candor which a Frenchman indulges whenever mere self is the theme. I was astonished, too, at the vast extent of his reading; and, above all, I felt my soul enkindled within me by the wild fervor, and the vivid freshness of his imagination. Seeking in Paris the objects I then sought, I felt that the society of such a man would be to me a treasure beyond price; and this feeling I frankly confided to him. It was at length arranged that we should live together during my stay in the city; and as my worldly circumstances were somewhat less embarrassed than his own, I was permitted to be at the expense of renting, and furnishing in a style which suited the rather fantastic gloom of our common temper, a time-eaten and grotesque mansion, long deserted through superstitions into which we did not inquire, and tottering to its fall in a retired and desolate portion of the Faubourg St. Germain.

Had the routine of our life at this place been known to the world, we should have been regarded as madmen—although, perhaps, as madmen of a harmless nature. Our seclusion was perfect. We admitted no visitors. Indeed the locality of our retirement had been carefully kept a secret from my own former associates; and it had been many years since Dupin had ceased to know or be known in Paris. We existed within ourselves alone.

It was a freak of fancy in my friend (for what else shall I call it?) to be enamored of the night for her own sake; and into this *bizarrerie*, as into all his others, I quietly fell; giving myself up to his wild whims with a perfect *abandon*. The sable divinity would not herself dwell with us always; but we could counterfeit her presence. At the first dawn of the morning we closed all the mossy shutters of our old building; lighted a couple of tapers which, strongly perfumed, threw out only the ghastliest and feeblest of rays. By the aid of these we then busied our souls in dreams—reading, writing, or conversing, until warned by the clock of the advent of true Darkness. Then we sallied forth into the streets, arm in arm, continuing the topics of the day, or roaming far and wide until a late hour, seeking, amid the wild lights and shadows of the populous city, that infinity of mental excitement which quiet observation can afford.

At such times I could not help remarking and admiring (although from his rich ideality I had been prepared to expect it) a peculiar analytic ability in Dupin. He seemed, too, to take an eager delight in its exercise—if not exactly in its display—and did not hesitate to confess the pleasure thus derived. He boasted to me, with a low chuckling laugh, that most men, in respect to himself, wore windows in their bosoms, and was wont to follow up such assertions by direct and very startling proofs of his intimate knowledge of my own. His manner at these moments was frigid and abstract; his eyes were vacant in expression; while his voice, usually a rich tenor, rose into a treble which would have sounded petulant but for the deliberateness and entire distinctness of the enunciation. Observing him in these moods, I often dwelt meditatively upon the old philosophy of the Bi-Part Soul, and amused myself with the fancy of a double Dupin—the creative and the resolvent.

Let it not be supposed, from what I have just said, that I am detailing any mystery, or penning any romance. What I have described in the Frenchman was merely the result of an excited, or perhaps of a diseased intelligence. But of the character of his remarks at the periods in question an example will best convey the idea.

We were strolling one night down a long dirty street, in the vicinity of the Palais Royal. Being both, apparently, occupied with thought, neither of us had spoken a syllable for fifteen minutes at least. All at once Dupin broke forth with these words:

"He is a very little fellow, that's true, and would do better for the *Théâtre des Variétés*."

"There can be no doubt of that," I replied, unwittingly, and not at first observing (so much had I been absorbed in reflection) the extraordinary manner in which the speaker had chimed in with my meditations. In an instant afterward I recollected myself, and my astonishment was profound.

"Dupin," said I, gravely, "this is beyond my comprehension. I do not hesitate to say that I am amazed, and can scarcely credit my senses. How was it possible you should know I was thinking of—?" Here I paused, to ascertain beyond a doubt whether he really knew of whom I thought.

"—of Chantilly," said he, "why do you pause? You were remarking to yourself that his diminutive figure unfitted him for tragedy."

This was precisely what had formed the subject of my reflections. Chantilly was a *quondam* cobbler of the Rue St. Denis, who, becoming stage-mad, had attempted the *rôle* of Xerxes, in Crébillon's tragedy so called, and been notoriously Pasquinaded for his pains.

"Tell me, for Heaven's sake," I exclaimed, "the method—if method there is—by which you have been enabled to fathom my soul in this matter." In fact, I was even more startled than I would have been willing to express.

"It was the fruiterer," replied my friend, "who brought you to the conclusion that the mender of soles was not of sufficient height for Xerxes *et id genus omne*."

"The fruiterer!—you astonish me—I know no fruiterer whomsoever."

"The man who ran up against you as we entered the street—it may have been fifteen minutes ago."

I now remembered that, in fact, a fruiterer, carrying upon his head a large basket of apples, had nearly thrown me down, by accident, as we passed from the Rue C——— into the thoroughfare where we stood; but what this had to do with Chantilly I could not possibly understand.

There was not a particle of *charlatânerie* about Dupin. "I will explain," he said, "and that you may comprehend all clearly, we will first retrace the course of your meditations, from the moment in which I spoke to you until that of the *rencontre* with the fruiterer in question. The larger links of the chain run thus—Chantilly, Orion, Dr. Nichols, Epicurus, Stereotomy, the street stones, the fruiterer."

There are few persons who have not, at some period of their lives, amused themselves in retracing the steps by which particular conclusions of their own minds have been attained. The occupation is often full of interest; and he who attempts it for the first time is astonished by the apparently illimitable distance and incoherence between the starting-point and the goal. What, then, must have been my amazement, when I heard the Frenchman speak what he had just spoken, and when I could not help acknowledging that he had spoken the truth. He continued:

"We had been talking of horses, if I remember aright, just before leaving the Rue C———. This was the last subject we discussed. As we crossed into this street, a fruiterer, with a large basket upon his head, brushing quickly past us, thrust you upon a pile of paving-stones collected at a spot where the causeway is undergoing repair. You stepped upon one of the loose fragments, slipped, slightly strained your ankle, appeared vexed or sulky, muttered a few words, turned to look at the pile, and then proceeded in silence. I was not particularly attentive to what you did; but observation has become with me, of late, a species of necessity.

"You kept your eyes upon the ground—glancing, with a petulant expression, at the holes and ruts in the pavement (so that I saw you were still thinking of the stones), until we reached the little alley called Lamartine, which has been paved, by way of experiment, with the overlapping and riveted blocks. Here your countenance brightened up, and, perceiving your lips move, I could not doubt that you murmured the word 'stereotomy,' a term very affectedly applied to this species of pavement. I knew that you could not say to yourself 'stereotomy' without being brought to think of atomies, and thus of the theories of Epicurus; and since, when we discussed this subject not very long ago, I mentioned to you how singularly, yet with how little notice, the vague guesses of that noble Greek had met with confirmation in the late nebular cosmogony, I felt that you could not avoid casting your eyes upward to the great *nebula* in Orion, and I certainly expected that you would do so. You did look up; and I was now assured that I had correctly followed your steps. But in that bitter *tirade* upon Chantilly, which appeared in yesterday's '*Musée*,' the satirist, making some disgraceful allusions to the cobbler's change of name upon assuming the buskin, quoted a Latin line about which we have often conversed. I mean the line

Perdidit antiquum litera prima sonum.

I had told you that this was in reference to Orion, formerly written Urion; and, from certain pungencies connected with this explanation, I was aware that you could not have forgotten it. It was clear, therefore, that you would not fail to combine the two ideas of Orion and Chantilly. That you did combine them I saw by the character of the smile which passed over your lips. You thought of the poor cobbler's immolation. So far, you had been stooping in your gait; but now I saw you draw yourself up to your full height. I was then sure that you reflected upon the diminutive figure of Chantilly. At this point I interrupted your meditations to remark that as, in fact, he *was* a very little fellow—that Chantilly—he would do better at the *Théâtre des Variétés.*"

Not long after this, we were looking over an evening edition of the *Gazette des Tribunaux* when the following paragraphs arrested our attention.

"EXTRAORDINARY MURDERS.—This morning, about three o'clock, the inhabitants of the Quartier St. Roch were roused from sleep by a succession of terrific shrieks, issuing, apparently, from the fourth story of a house in the Rue Morgue, known to be in the sole occupancy of one Madame L'Espanaye, and her daughter, Mademoiselle Camille L'Espanaye. After some delay, occasioned by a fruitless attempt to procure admission in the usual manner, the gateway was broken in with a crowbar, and eight or ten of the neighbors entered, accompanied by two *gendarmes.* By this time the cries had ceased; but, as the party rushed up the first flight of stairs, two or more rough voices, in angry contention, were distinguished, and seemed to proceed from the upper part of the house. As the second landing was reached, these sounds, also, had ceased, and every thing remained perfectly quiet. The party spread themselves, and hurried from room to room. Upon arriving at a large back chamber in the fourth story (the door of which, being found locked, with the key inside, was forced open), a spectacle presented itself which struck every one present not less with horror than with astonishment.

"The apartment was in the wildest disorder—the furniture broken and thrown about in all directions. There was only one bedstead; and from this the bed had been removed, and thrown into the middle of the floor. On a chair lay a razor, besmeared with blood. On the hearth were two or three long and thick tresses of gray human hair, also dabbled with blood, and seeming to have been pulled out by the roots. Upon the floor were found four Napoleons, an earring of topaz, three large silver spoons, three smaller of *métal d'Alger,* and two bags containing nearly four thousand francs in gold. The drawers of a *bureau,* which stood in one corner, were open, and had been, apparently, rifled, although many articles still remained in them. A small iron safe was discovered under the *bed* (not under the bedstead). It was open, with the key still in the door. It had no contents beyond a few old letters, and other papers of little consequence.

"Of Madame L'Espanaye no traces were here seen; but an unusual quantity of soot being observed in the fire-place, a search was made in the chimney, and (horrible to relate!) the corpse of the daughter, head downward, was dragged therefrom; it having been thus forced up the narrow aperture for a considerable distance. The body was quite warm. Upon examining it, many excoriations were perceived, no doubt occasioned by the violence with which it had been thrust up and disengaged. Upon the face were many severe scratches, and, upon the throat, dark bruises, and deep indentations of finger nails, as if the deceased had been throttled to death.

"After a thorough investigation of every portion of the house without farther discovery, the party made its way into a small paved yard in the rear of the building, where lay the corpse of the old lady, with her throat so entirely cut that, upon an attempt to raise her, the head fell off. The body, as well as the head, was fearfully mutilated—the former so much so as scarcely to retain any semblance of humanity.

"To this horrible mystery there is not as yet, we believe, the slightest clue."

The next day's paper had these additional particulars:

"*The Tragedy in the Rue Morgue.*—Many individuals have been examined in relation to this most extraordinary and frightful affair," (the word *'affaire'* has not yet, in France, that levity of import which it conveys with us) "but nothing whatever has transpired to throw light upon it. We give below all the material testimony elicited.

"*Pauline Dubourg,* laundress, deposes that she has known both the deceased for three years, having washed for them during that period. The old lady and her daughter seemed on good terms—very affectionate toward each other. They were excellent pay. Could not speak in regard to their mode or means of living. Believe that Madame L. told fortunes for a living. Was reputed to have money put by. Never met any person in the house when she called for the clothes or took them home. Was sure that they had no servant in employ. There appeared to be no furniture in any part of the building except in the fourth story.

"*Pierre Moreau,* tobacconist, deposes that he has been in the habit of selling small quantities of tobacco and snuff to Madame L'Espanaye for nearly four years. Was born in the neighborhood, and has always resided there. The deceased and her daughter had occupied the house in which the corpses were found, for more than six years. It was formerly occupied by a jeweller, who under-let the upper rooms to various persons. The house was the property of Madame L. She became dissatisfied with the abuse of the premises by her tenant, and moved into them herself, refusing to let any portion. The old lady was childish. Witness had seen the daughter some five or six times during the six years. The two lived an exceedingly retired life—were reputed to have money. Had heard it said among the neighbors that Madame L. told fortunes—did not believe it. Had never seen any person enter the door except the old lady and her daughter, a porter once or twice, and a physician some eight or ten times.

"Many other persons, neighbors, gave evidence to the same effect. No one was spoken of as frequenting the house. It was not known whether there were any living connections of Madame L. and her daughter. The shutters of the front windows were seldom opened. Those in the rear were always closed, with the exception of the large back room, fourth story. The house was a good house—not very old.

"*Isidore Musèt, gendarme,* deposes that he was called to the house about three o'clock in the morning, and found some twenty or thirty persons at the gateway, endeavoring to gain admittance. Forced it open, at length, with a bayonet—not with a crowbar. Had but little difficulty in getting it open, on account of its being a double or folding gate, and bolted neither at bottom nor top. The shrieks were continued until the gate was forced—and suddenly ceased. They seemed to be screams of some person (or persons) in great agony—were loud and drawn out, not short and quick. Witness led the way up stairs. Upon reaching the first landing, heard two voices in loud and angry contention—the one a gruff voice, the other much shriller—a very strange voice. Could distinguish some words of the former, which was that of a Frenchman. Was positive that it was not a woman's voice. Could distinguish the words "*sacré*' and '*diable*'. The shrill voice was that of a foreigner. Could not be sure whether it was the voice of a man or a woman. Could not make out what was said, but believed the language to be Spanish. The state of the room and of the bodies was described by this witness as we described them yesterday.

"*Henri Duval,* a neighbor, and by trade a silver-smith, deposes that he was one of the party who first entered the house. Corroborates the testimony of Musèt in general. As soon as they forced an entrance, they reclosed the door, to keep out the crowd, which collected very fast, notwithstanding the lateness of the hour. The shrill voice, this witness thinks, was that of an Italian. Was certain it was not French. Could not be sure that it was a man's voice. It might have been a woman's. Was not acquainted with the Italian language. Could not distinguish the words, but was convinced by the intonation that the speaker was an Italian. Knew Madame L. and her daughter. Had conversed with both frequently. Was sure that the shrill voice was not that of either of the deceased.

"———Odenheimer, restaurateur.—This witness volunteered his testimony. Not speaking French, was examined through an interpreter. Is a native of Amsterdam. Was passing the house at the time of the shrieks. They lasted for several minutes—probably ten. They were long and loud—very awful and distressing. Was one of those who entered the building. Corroborated the previous evidence in every respect but one. Was sure that the shrill voice was that of a man—of a Frenchman. Could not distinguish the words uttered. They were loud and quick—unequal—spoken apparently in fear as well as in anger. The voice was harsh—not so much shrill as harsh. Could not call it a shrill voice. The gruff voice said repeatedly, '*sacré,*' '*diable,*' and once '*mon Dieu.*'

"*Jules Mignaud,* banker, of the firm of Mignaud et Fils, Rue Deloraine. Is the elder Mignaud. Madame L'Espanaye had some property. Had opened an account with his banking house in the spring of the year ——— (eight years previously). Made frequent deposits in small sums. Had checked for nothing until the third day before her death, when she took out in person the sum of 4,000 francs. This sum was paid in gold, and a clerk sent home with the money.

"*Adolphe Le Bon,* clerk to Mignaud et Fils, deposes that on the day in question, about noon, he accompanied Madame L'Espanaye to her residence with the 4,000 francs, put up in two bags. Upon the door being opened, Mademoiselle L. appeared and took from his hands one of the bags, while the old lady relieved him of the other. He then bowed and departed. Did not see any person in the street at the time. It is a by-street—very lonely.

"*William Bird,* tailor, deposes that he was one of the party who entered the house. Is an Englishman. Has lived in Paris two years. Was one of the first to ascend the stairs. Heard the voices in contention. The gruff voice was that of a Frenchman. Could make out several words, but cannot now remember all. Heard distinctly '*sacré*' and '*mon Dieu.*' There was a sound at the moment as if of several persons struggling—a scraping and scuffling sound. The shrill voice was very loud—louder than the gruff one. Is sure that it was not the voice of an Englishman. Appeared to be that of a German. Might have been a woman's voice. Does not understand German.

"Four of the above-named witnesses, being recalled, deposed that the door of the chamber in which was found the body of Mademoiselle L. was locked on the inside when the party reached it. Everything was perfectly silent—no groans or noises of any kind. Upon forcing the door no person was seen. The windows, both of the back and front room, were down and firmly fastened from within. A door between the two rooms was closed but not locked. The door leading from the front room into the passage was locked, with the key on the inside. A small room in the front of the house, on the fourth story, at the head of the passage, was open, the door being ajar. This room was crowded with old beds, boxes, and so forth. These were carefully removed and searched. There was not an inch of any portion of the house which was not carefully searched. Sweeps were sent up and down the chimneys. The house was a four-story one, with garrets *(mansardes).* A trap door on the room was nailed down very securely—did not appear to have been opened for years. The time elapsing between the hearing of the voices in contention and the breaking open of the room door was variously stated by the witnesses. Some made it as short as three minutes—some as long as five. The door was opened with difficulty.

"*Alfonzo Garcio,* undertaker, deposes that he resides in the Rue Morgue. Is a native of Spain. Was one of the party who entered the house. Did not proceed up stairs. Is nervous, and was apprehensive of the consequences of agitation. Heard the voices in contention. The gruff voice was that of a Frenchman. Could not distinguish what was said. The shrill voice was that of an Englishman—is sure of this. Does not understand the English language, but judges by the intonation.

"*Alberto Montani,* confectioner, deposes that he was among the first to ascend the stairs. Heard the voices in question. The gruff voice was that of a Frenchman. Distinguished several words. The speaker appeared to be expostulating. Could not make out the words of the shrill voice. Spoke quick and unevenly. Thinks it the voice of a Russian. Corroborates the general testimony. Is an Italian. Never conversed with a native of Russia.

"Several witnesses, recalled, here testified that the chimneys of all the rooms on the fourth story were too narrow to admit the passage of a human being. By 'sweeps' were meant cylindrical sweeping-brushes, such as are employed by those who clean chimneys. These brushes were passed up and down every flu in the house. There is no back passage by which any one could have descended while the party proceeded up stairs. The body of Mademoiselle L'Espanaye was so firmly wedged in the chimney that it could not be got down until four or five of the party united their strength.

"*Paul Dumas,* physician, deposes that he was called to view the bodies about daybreak. They were both then lying on the sacking of the bedstead in the chamber where Mademoiselle L. was found. The corpse of the young lady was much bruised and excoriated. The fact that it had been thrust up the chimney would sufficiently account for these appearances. The throat was greatly chafed. There were several deep scratches just below the chin, together with a series of livid spots which were evidently the impression of fingers. The face was fearfully discolored, and the eyeballs protruded. The tongue had been partially bitten through. A large bruise was discovered upon the pit of the stomach, produced, apparently, by the pressure of a knee. In the opinion of M. Dumas, Mademoiselle L'Espanaye had been throttled to death by some person or persons unknown. The corpse of the mother was horribly mutilated. All the bones of the right leg and arm were more or less shattered. The left *tibia* much splintered, as well as all the ribs of the left side. Whole body dreadfully bruised and discolored. It was not possible to say how the injuries had been inflicted. A heavy club of wood, or a broad bar of iron—a chair—any large, heavy, and obtuse weapon would have produced such results, if wielded by the hands of a very powerful man. No woman could have inflicted the blows with any weapon. The head of the deceased, when seen by witness, was entirely separated from the body, and was also greatly shattered. The throat had evidently been cut with some very sharp instrument—probably with a razor.

"*Alexandre Etienne,* surgeon, was called with M. Dumas to view the bodies. Corroborated the testimony, and the opinions of M. Dumas.

"Nothing further of importance was elicited, although several other persons were examined. A murder so mysterious, and so perplexing in all its particulars, was never before committed in Paris—if indeed a murder has been committed at all. The police are entirely at fault—an unusual occurrence in affairs of this nature. There is not, however, the shadow of a clew apparent."

The evening edition of the paper stated that the greatest excitement still continued in the Quartier St. Roch—that the premises in question had been carefully re-searched, and fresh examinations of witnesses instituted, but all to no purpose. A postscript, however, mentioned that Adolphe Le Bon had been arrested and imprisoned—although nothing appeared to criminate him beyond the facts already detailed.

Dupin seemed singularly interested in the progress of this affair—at least so I judged from his manner, for he made no comments. It was only after the announcement that Le Bon had been imprisoned, that he asked me my opinion respecting the murders.

I could merely agree with all Paris in considering them an insoluble mystery. I saw no means by which it would be possible to trace the murderer.

"We must not judge of the means," said Dupin, "by this shell of an examination. The Parisian police, so much extolled for *acumen,* are cunning, but no more. There is no method in their proceedings, beyond the method of the moment. They make a vast parade of measures; but, not unfrequently, these are so ill-adapted to the objects proposed, as to put us in mind of Monsieur Jourdain's calling for his *robe-de-chambre—pour mieux entendre la musique.* The results attained by them are not unfrequently surprising, but, for the most part, are brought about by simple diligence and activity. When these qualities are unavailing, their schemes fail. Vidocq, for example, was a good guesser, and a persevering man. But, without educated thought, he erred continually by the very intensity of his investigations. He impaired his vision by holding the object too close. He might see, perhaps, one or two points with unusual clearness, but in so doing he, necessarily, lost sight of the matter as a whole. Thus there is such a thing as being too profound. Truth is not always in a well. In fact, as regards the more important knowledge, I do believe that she is invariably superficial. The depth lies in the valleys where we seek her, and not upon the mountain-tops where she is found. The modes and sources of this kind of error are well typified in the contemplation of the heavenly bodies. To look at a star by glances—to view it in a side-long way, by turning toward it the exterior portions of the *retina* (more susceptible of feeble impressions of light than the interior), is to behold the star distinctly—is to have the best appreciation of its lustre—a lustre which grows dim just in proportion as we turn our vision *fully* upon it. A greater number of rays actually fall upon the eye in the latter case, but in the former, there is the more refined capacity for comprehension. By undue profundity we perplex and enfeeble thought; and it is possible to make even Venus herself vanish from the firmament by a scrutiny too sustained, too concentrated, or too direct.

"As for these murders, let us enter into some examinations for ourselves, before we make up an opinion respecting them. An inquiry will afford us amusement," (I thought this an odd term, so applied, but said nothing) "and besides, Le Bon once rendered me a service for which I am not ungrateful. We will go and see the premises with our own eyes. I know G———, the Prefect of Police, and shall have no difficulty in obtaining the necessary permission."

The permission was obtained, and we proceeded at once to the Rue Morgue. This is one of those miserable thoroughfares which intervene between the Rue Richelieu and the Rue St. Roch. It was late in the afternoon when we reached it, as this quarter is at a great distance from that in which we resided. The house was readily found; for there were still many persons gazing up at the closed shutters, with an objectless curiosity, from the opposite side of the way. It was an ordinary Parisian house, with a gateway, on one side of which was a glazed watch-box, with a sliding panel in the window, indicating a *loge de concierge.* Before going in we walked up the street, turned down an alley, and then, again turning, passed in the rear of the building—Dupin, meanwhile, examining the whole neighborhood, as well as the house, with a minuteness of attention for which I could see no possible object.

Retracing our steps we came again to the front of the dwelling, rang, and, having shown our credentials, were admitted by the agents in charge. We went up stairs—into the chamber where the body of

Mademoiselle L'Espanaye had been found, and where both the deceased still lay. The disorders of the room had, as usual, been suffered to exist. I saw nothing beyond what had been stated in the *Gazette des Tribunaux*. Dupin scrutinized every thing—not excepting the bodies of the victims. We then went into the other rooms, and into the yard; a *gendarme* accompanying us throughout. The examination occupied us until dark, when we took our departure. On our way home my companion stepped in for a moment at the office of one of the daily papers.

I have said that the whims of my friend were manifold, and that *Je les ménageais:*—for this phrase there is no English equivalent. It was his humor, now, to decline all conversation on the subject of the murder until about noon the next day. He then asked me, suddenly, if I had observed any thing *peculiar* at the scene of the atrocity.

There was something in his manner of emphasizing the word "*peculiar,*" which caused me to shudder, without knowing why.

"No, nothing *peculiar,*" I said: "nothing more, at least, than we both saw stated in the paper."

"The *Gazette,*" he replied, "has not entered, I fear, into the unusual horror of the thing. But dismiss the idle opinions of this print. It appears to me that this mystery is considered insoluble, for the very reason which should cause it to be regarded as easy of solution—I mean for the *outré* character of its features. The police are confounded by the seeming absence of motive—not for the murder itself—but for the atrocity of the murder. They are puzzled, too, by the seeming impossibility of reconciling the voices heard in contention, with the facts that no one was discovered upstairs but the assassinated Mademoiselle L'Espanaye, and that there were no means of egress without the notice of the party ascending. The wild disorder of the room; the corpse thrust, with the head downward, up the chimney; the frightful mutilation of the old lady; these considerations, with those just mentioned, and others which I need not mention, have sufficed to paralyze the powers, by putting completely at fault the boasted *acumen,* of the government agents. They have fallen into the gross but common error of confounding the unusual with the abstruse. But it is by these deviations from the plane of the ordinary, that reason feels its way, if at all, in its search for the true. In investigations such as we are now pursuing, it should not be so much asked 'what has occurred,' as 'what has occurred that has never occurred before.' In fact, the facility with which I shall arrive, or have arrived, at the solution of this mystery, is in the direct ratio of its apparent insolubility in the eyes of the police."

I stared at the speaker in mute astonishment.

"I am now awaiting," continued he, looking toward the door of our apartment—"I am now awaiting a person who, although perhaps not the perpetrator of these butcheries, must have been in some measure implicated in their perpetration. Of the worst portion of the crimes committed, it is probable that he is innocent. I hope that I am right in this supposition; for upon it I build my expectation of reading the entire riddle. I look for the man here—in this room—every moment. It is true that he may not arrive; but the probability is that he will. Should he come, it will be necessary to detain him. Here are pistols; and we both know how to use them when occasion demands their use."

I took the pistols, scarcely knowing what I did, or believing what I heard, while Dupin went on, very much as if in a soliloquy. I have already spoken of his abstract manner at such times. His discourse was addressed to myself; but his voice, although by no means loud, had that intonation which is commonly employed in speaking to some one at a great distance. His eyes, vacant in expression, regarded only the wall.

"That the voices heard in contention," he said, "by the party upon the stairs, were not the voices of the women themselves, was fully proved by the evidence. This relieves us of all doubt upon the question whether the old lady could have first destroyed the daughter, and afterward have committed suicide. I speak of this point chiefly for the sake of method; for the strength of Madame L'Espanaye would have been utterly unequal to the task of thrusting her daughter's corpse up the chimney as it was found; and the nature of the wounds upon her own person entirely precludes the idea of self-destruction. Murder, then, has been committed by some third party; and the voices of this third party were those heard in contention. Let me now advert—not to the whole testimony respecting these voices—but to what was *peculiar* in that testimony. Did you observe any thing peculiar about it?"

I remarked that, while all the witnesses agreed in supposing the gruff voice to be that of a Frenchman, there was much disagreement in regard to the shrill, or, as one individual termed it, the harsh voice.

"That was the evidence itself," said Dupin, "but it was not the peculiarity of the evidence. You have observed nothing distinctive. Yet there *was* something to be observed. The witnesses, as you remark, agreed about the gruff voice; they were here unanimous. But in regard to the shrill voice, the peculiarity is—not that they disagreed—but that, while an Italian, an Englishman, a Spaniard, a Hollander, and a Frenchman attempted to describe it, each one spoke of it as that *of a foreigner.* Each is sure that it was not the voice of one of his own countrymen. Each likens it—not to the voice of an individual of any nation with whose language he is conversant—but the converse. The Frenchman supposes it the voice of a Spaniard, and 'might have distinguished some words *had he been acquainted with the Spanish.'* The Dutchman maintains it to have been that of a Frenchman; but we find it stated that *'not understanding French this witness was examined through an interpreter.'* The Englishman thinks it the voice of a German, and *'does not understand Geman.'* The Spaniard 'is sure' that it was that of an Englishman, but 'judges by the intonation' altogether, *'as he has no knowledge of the English.'* The Italian believes it the voice of a Russian, but *'has never conversed with a native of Russia.'* A second Frenchman differs, moreover with the first, and is positive that the voice was that of an Italian; but *not being cognizant of that tongue,* is like the Spaniard, 'convinced by the intonation.' Now, how strangely unusual must that voice have really been, about which such testimony as this *could* have been elicited!—in whose *tones,* even denizens of the five great divisions of Europe could recognize nothing familiar! You will say that it might have been the voice of an Asiatic—of an African. Neither Asiatics nor Africans abound in Paris; but, without denying the inference, I will now merely call your attention to three points. The voice is termed by one witness 'harsh rather than shrill.' It is represented by two others to have been 'quick and *unequal.'* No words—no sounds resembling words—were by any witness mentioned as distinguishable.

"I know not," continued Dupin, "what impression I may have made, so far, upon your own understanding; but I do not hesitate to say that legitimate deductions even from this portion of the testimony—the portion respecting the gruff and shrill voices—are in themselves sufficient to engender a suspicion which should give direction to all farther progress in the investigation of the mystery. I said 'legitimate deductions'; but my meaning is not thus fully expressed. I designed to imply that the deductions are the *sole* proper ones, and that the suspicion arises *inevitably* from them as a single result. What the suspicion is, however, I will not say just yet. I merely wish you to bear in mind that, with myself, it was sufficiently forcible to give a definite form—a certain tendency—to my inquiries in the chamber.

"Let us now transport ourselves, in fancy, to this chamber. What shall we first seek here? The means of egress employed by the murderers. It is not too much to say that neither of us believes in preternatural events. Madame and Mademoiselle L'Espanaye were not destroyed by spirits. The doers of the deed were material and escaped materially. Then how? Fortunately there is but one mode of reasoning upon the point, and that mode *must* lead us to a definite decision. Let us examine, each by each, the possible means of egress. It is clear that the assassins were in the room where Mademoiselle L'Espanaye was found, or at least in the room adjoining, when the party ascended the stairs. It is, then, only from these two apartments that we have to seek issues. The police have laid bare the floors, the ceiling, and the masonry of the walls, in every direction. No *secret* issues could have escaped their vigilance. But, not trusting to *their* eyes, I examined with my own. There were, then, *no* secret issues. Both doors leading from the rooms into the passage were securely locked, with the keys inside. Let us turn to the chimneys. These, although of ordinary width for some eight or ten feet above the hearths, will not admit, throughout their extent, the body of a large cat. The impossibility of egress, by means already stated, being thus absolute, we are reduced to the windows. Through those of the front room no one could have escaped without notice from the crowd in the street. The murderers *must* have passed, then, through those of the back room. Now, brought to this conclusion in so unequivocal a manner as we are, it is not our part, as reasoners, to reject it on account of apparent impossibilities. It is only left for us to prove that these apparent 'impossibilities' are, in reality, not such.

"There are two windows in the chamber. One of them is unobstructed by furniture, and is wholly visible. The lower portion of the other is hidden from view by the head of the unwieldy bedstead which is thrust close up against it. The former was found securely fastened from within. It resisted the utmost force of those who endeavored to raise it. A large gimlet-hole had been pierced in its frame to the left, and a very stout nail was found fitted therein, nearly to the head. Upon examining the other window, a similar nail was seen similarly fitted in it; and a vigorous attempt to raise this sash failed also. The police were now entirely satisfied that egress had not been in these directions. And, *therefore,* it was thought a matter of supererogation to withdraw the nails and open the windows.

"My own examination was somewhat more particular, and was so for the reason I have just given—because here it was, I knew, that all apparent impossibilities *must* be proved to be not such in reality.

"I proceeded to think thus—*a posteriori.* The murderers *did* escape from one of these windows. This being so, they could not have refastened the sashes from the inside, as they were found fastened;—the consideration which put a stop, through its obviousness, to the scrutiny of the police in this quarter. Yet the sashes *were* fastened. They *must,* then, have the power of fastening themselves. There was no escape from this conclusion. I stepped to the unobstructed casement, withdrew the nail with some difficulty, and attempted to raise the sash. It resisted all my efforts, as I had anticipated. A concealed spring must, I now knew, exist; and this corroboration of my idea convinced me that my premises, at least, were correct, however mysterious still appeared the circumstances attending the nails. A careful search soon brought to light the hidden spring. I pressed it, and, satisfied with the discovery, forbore to upraise the sash.

"I now replaced the nail and regarded it attentively. A person passing out through this window might have reclosed it, and the spring would have caught—but the nail could not have been replaced. The conclusion was plain, and again narrowed in the field of my investigations. The assassins *must* have escaped through the other window. Supposing, then, the springs upon each sash to be the same, as was probable, there *must* be found a difference between the nails, or at least between the modes of their fixture. Getting upon the sacking of the bedstead, I looked over the headboard minutely at the second casement. Passing my hand down behind the board, I readily discovered and pressed the spring, which was, as I had supposed, identical in character with its neighbor. I now looked at the nail. It was as stout as the other, and apparently fitted in the same manner—driven in nearly up to the head.

"You will say that I was puzzled; but, if you think so, you must have misunderstood the nature of the inductions. To use a sporting phrase, I had not been once 'at fault.' The scent had never for an instant been lost. There was no flaw in any link of the chain. I had traced the secret to its ultimate result,—and that result was *the nail.* It had, I say, in every respect, the appearance of its fellow in the other window; but this fact was an absolute nullity (conclusive as it might seem to be) when compared with the consideration that here, at this point, terminated the clew. 'There *must* be something wrong,' I said, 'about the nail.' I touched it; and the head, with about a quarter of an inch of the shank, came off in my fingers. The rest of the shank was in the gimlet-hole, where it had been broken off. The fracture was an old one (for its edges were incrusted with rust), and had apparently been accomplished by the blow of a hammer, which had partially imbedded, in the top of the bottom sash, the head portion of the nail. I now carefully replaced this head portion in the indentation whence I had taken it, and the resemblance to a perfect nail was complete—the fissure was invisible. Pressing the spring, I gently raised the sash for a few inches; the head went up with it, remaining firm in its bed. I closed the window, and the semblance of the whole nail was again perfect.

"This riddle, so far, was now unriddled. The assassin had escaped through the window which looked upon the bed. Dropping of its own accord upon his exit (or perhaps purposely closed), it had become fastened by the spring; and it was the retention of this spring which had been mistaken by the police for that of the nail,—farther inquiry being thus considered unnecessary.

"The next question is that of the mode of descent. Upon this point I had been satisfied in my walk with you around the building. About five feet and a half from the casement in question there runs a lightning-rod. From this rod it would have been impossible for any one to reach the window itself, to say nothing of entering it. I observed, however, that the shutters of the fourth story were of the peculiar kind called by Parisian carpenters *ferrades*—a kind rarely employed at the present day, but frequently seen upon very old mansions at Lyons and Bordeaux. They are in the form of an ordinary door (a single, not a folding door), except that the lower half is latticed or worked in open trellis—thus affording an excellent hold for the hands. In the present instance these shutters are fully three feet and a half broad. When we saw them from the rear of the house, they were both about half open—that is to say they stood off at right angles from the wall. It is probable that the police, as well as myself, examined the back of the tenement; but, if so, in looking at these *ferrades* in the line of their breadth (as they must have done), they did not perceive this great breadth itself, or, at all events, failed to take it into due consideration. In fact, having once satisfied themselves that no egress could have been made in this quarter, they would naturally bestow here a very cursory examination. It was clear to me, however, that the shutter belonging to the window at the head of the bed, would, if swung fully back to the wall, reach to within two feet of the lightning-rod. It was also evident that, by exertion of a very unusual degree of activity and courage, an entrance into the window, from the rod, might have been thus effected. By reaching to the distance of two feet and a half (we now suppose the shutter open to its whole extent) a robber might have taken a firm grasp upon the trellis-work. Letting go, then, his hold upon the rod, placing his feet securely against the wall, and springing boldly from it, he might have swung the shutter so as to close it, and, if we imagine the window open at the time, might even have swung himself into the room.

"I wish you to bear especially in mind that I have spoken of a *very* unusual degree of activity as requisite to success in so hazardous and so difficult a feat. It is my design to show you first, that the thing might possibly have been accomplished:—but, secondly and *chiefly*, I wish to impress upon your understanding the *very extraordinary*—the almost preternatural character of that agility which could have accomplished it.

"You will say, no doubt, using the language of the law, that 'to make out my case, I should rather undervalue than insist upon a full estimation of the activity required in this matter.' This may be the practice in law, but it is not the usage of reason. My ultimate object is only the truth. My immediate purpose is to lead you to place in juxtaposition, that *very unusual* activity of which I have just spoken, with that *very peculiar* shrill (or harsh) and *unequal* voice, about whose nationality no two persons could be found to agree, and in whose utterance no syllabification could be detected."

At these words a vague and half-formed conception of the meaning of Dupin flitted over my mind. I seemed to be upon the verge of comprehension, without power to comprehend—as men, at times, find themselves upon the brink of remembrance, without being able, in the end, to remember. My friend went on with his discourse.

"You will see," he said, "that I have shifted the question from the mode of egress to that of ingress. It was my design to convey the idea that both were effected in the same manner, at the same point. Let us now revert to the interior of the room. Let us survey the appearances here. The drawers of the bureau, it is said, had been rifled, although many articles of apparel still remained within them. The conclusion here is absurd. It is a mere guess—a very silly one—and no more. How are we to know that the articles found in the drawers were not all these drawers had originally contained? Madame L'Espanaye and her daughter lived an exceedingly retired life—saw no company—seldom went out—had little use for numerous changes of habiliment. Those found were at least of as good quality as any likely to be possessed by these ladies. If a thief had taken any, why did he not take the best—why did he not take all? In a word, why did he abandon four thousand francs in gold to encumber himself with a bundle of linen? The gold *was* abandoned. Nearly the whole sum mentioned by Monsieur Mignaud, the banker, was discovered, in bags, upon the floor. I wish you therefore, to discard from your thoughts the blundering idea of *motive,* engendered in the brains of the police by that portion of the evidence which speaks of money delivered at the door of the house. Coincidences ten times as remarkable as this (the delivery of the money, and murder committed within three days upon the party receiving it), happen to all of us every hour of our lives, without attracting even momentary notice. Coincidences, in general, are great stumbling-blocks in the way of that class of thinkers who have been educated to know nothing of the theory of probabilities—that theory to which the most glorious objects of human research are indebted for the most glorious of illustration. In the present instance, had the gold been gone, the fact of its delivery three days before would have formed something more than a coincidence. It would have been corroborative of this idea of motive. But, under the real circumstances of the case, if we are to suppose gold the motive of this outrage, we must also imagine the perpetrator so vacillating an idiot as to have abandoned his gold and his motive together.

"Keeping now steadily in mind the points to which I have drawn your attention—that peculiar voice, that unusual agility, and that startling absence of motive in a murder so singularly atrocious as this—let us glance at the butchery itself. Here is a woman strangled to death by manual strength, and thrust up a chimney head downward. Ordinary assassins employ no such mode of murder as this. Least of all, do they thus dispose of the murdered. In the manner of thrusting the corpse up the chimney, you will admit that there was something *excessively outré*—something altogether irreconcilable with our common notions of human action, even when we suppose the actors the most depraved of men. Think, too, how great must have been that strength which could have thrust the body *up* such an aperture so forcibly that the united vigor of several persons was found barely sufficient to drag it *down!*

"Turn, now, to other indications of the employment of a vigor most marvellous. On the hearth were thick tresses—very thick tresses—of gray human hair. These had been torn out by the roots. You are aware of the great force necessary in tearing thus from the head even twenty or thirty hairs together. You saw the locks in question as well as myself. Their roots (a hideous sight!) were clotted with fragments of the flesh of the scalp—sure token of the prodigious power which had been exerted in uprooting perhaps half a million of hairs at a time. The throat of the old lady was not merely cut, but the head absolutely severed from the body: the instrument was a mere razor. I wish you also to look at the *brutal* ferocity of these deeds. Of the bruises upon the body of Madame L'Espanaye I do not speak. Monsieur Dumas, and his worthy coadjutor Monsieur Etienne, have pronounced that they were inflicted by some obtuse instrument; and so far these gentlemen are very correct. The obtuse instrument was clearly the stone pavement in the yard, upon which the victim had fallen from the window which looked in upon the bed. This idea, however simple it may now seem, escaped the police for the same reason that the breadth of the shutters escaped them—because, by the affair of the nails, their perceptions had been hermetically sealed against the possibility of the windows having ever been opened at all.

"If now, in addition to all these things, you have properly reflected upon the odd disorder of the chamber, we have gone so far as to combine the ideas of an agility astounding, a strength superhuman, a ferocity brutal, a butchery without motive, a *grotesquerie* in horror absolutely alien from humanity, and a voice foreign in tone to the ears of men of many nations, and devoid of all distinct or intelligible syllabification. What result, then, has ensued? What impression have I made upon your fancy?"

I felt a creeping of the flesh as Dupin asked me the question. "A madman," I said, "has done this deed—some raving maniac, escaped from a neighboring *Maison de Santé.*"

"In some respects," he replied, "your idea is not irrelevant. But the voices of madmen, even in their wildest paroxysms, are never found to tally with that peculiar voice heard upon the stairs. Madmen are of some nation, and their language, however incoherent in its words, has always the coherence of syllabification. Besides, the hair of a madman is not such as I now hold in my hand. I disentangled this little tuft from the rigidly clutched fingers of Madame L'Espanaye. Tell me what you can make of it."

"Dupin!" I said, completely unnerved; "this hair is most unusual —this is no *human* hair."

"I have not asserted that it is," said he; "but, before we decide this point, I wish you to glance at the little sketch I have here traced upon this paper. It is a *facsimile* drawing of what has been described in one portion of the testimony as 'dark bruises and deep indentations of finger nails' upon the throat of Mademoiselle L'Espanaye, and in another (by Messrs. Dumas and Etienne) as a 'series of livid spots, evidently the impression of fingers.'

"You will perceive," continued my friend, spreading out the paper upon the table before us, "that this drawing gives the idea of a firm and fixed hold. There is no *slipping* apparent. Each finger has retained—possibly until the death of the victim—the fearful grasp by which it originally imbedded itself. Attempt, now, to place all your fingers, at the same time, in the respective impressions as you see them."

I made the attempt in vain.

"We are possibly not giving this matter a fair trial," he said. "The paper is spread out upon a plane surface; but the human throat is cylindrical. Here is a billet of wood, the circumference of which is about that of the throat. Wrap the drawing around it, and try the experiment again."

I did so; but the difficulty was even more obvious than before. "This," I said, "is the mark of no human hand."

"Read now," replied Dupin, "this passage from Cuvier."

It was a minute anatomical and generally descriptive account of the large fulvous Ourang-Outang of the East Indian Islands. The gigantic stature, the prodigious strength and activity, the wild ferocity, and the imitative propensities of these mammalia are sufficiently well known to all. I understood the full horrors of the murder at once.

"The description of the digits," said I, as I made an end of the reading, "is in exact accordance with this drawing. I see that no animal but an Ourang-Outang, of the species here mentioned, could have impressed the indentations as you have traced them. This tuft of tawny hair, too, is identical in character with that of the beast of Cuvier. But I cannot possibly comprehend the particulars of this frightful mystery. Besides, there were *two* voices heard in contention, and one of them was unquestionably the voice of a Frenchman."

"True; and you will remember an expression attributed almost unanimously, by the evidence, to this voice,—the expression, *'mon Dieu!'* This, under the circumstances, has been justly characterized by one of the witnesses (Montani, the confectioner) as an expression of remonstrance or expostulation. Upon these two words, therefore, I have mainly built my hopes of a full solution of the riddle. A Frenchman was cognizant of the murder. It is possible—indeed it is far more than probable—that he was innocent of all participation in the bloody transactions which took place. The Ourang-Outang may have escaped from him. He may have traced it to the chamber; but, under the agitating circumstances which ensued, he could never have recaptured it. It is still at large. I will not pursue these guesses—for I have no right to call them more—since the shades of reflection upon which they are based are scarcely of sufficient depth to be appreciable by my own intellect, and since I could not pretend to make them intelligible to the understanding of another. We will call them guesses, then, and speak of them as such. If the Frenchman in question is indeed, as I suppose, innocent of this atrocity, this advertisement, which I left last night, upon our return home, at the office of *Le Monde* (a paper devoted to the shipping interest, and much sought by sailors), will bring him to our residence."

He handed me a paper, and I read thus:

"CAUGHT—In the Bois de Boulogne, early in the morning of the ——— inst. (the morning of the murder), a very large, tawny Ourang-Outang of the Bornese species. The owner (who is ascertained to be a sailor, belonging to a Maltese vessel) may have the animal again, upon identifying it satisfactorily, and paying a few charges arising from its capture and keeping. Call at No. ——— Rue ———, Faubourg St. Germain—au troisième."

"How was it possible," I asked, "that you should know the man to be a sailor, and belonging to a Maltese vessel?"

"I do *not* know it," said Dupin. "I am not *sure* of it. Here, however, is a small piece of ribbon, which from its form, and from its greasy appearance, has evidently been used in tying the hair in one of those long *queues* of which sailors are so fond. Moreover, this knot is one which few besides sailors can tie, and is peculiar to the Maltese. I picked the ribbon up at the foot of the lightning-rod. It could not have belonged to either of the deceased. Now if, after all, I am wrong in my induction from this ribbon, that the Frenchman was a sailor belonging to a Maltese vessel, still I can have done no harm in saying what I did in the advertisement. If I am in error, he will merely suppose that I have been misled by some circumstance into which he will not take the trouble to inquire. But if I am right, a great point is gained. Cognizant although innocent of the murder, the Frenchman will naturally hesitate about replying to the advertisement—about demanding the Ourang-Outang. He will reason thus:—'I am innocent; I am poor; my Ourang-Outang is of great value—to one in my circumstance a fortune of itself—why should I lose it through idle apprehensions of danger? Here it is, within my grasp. It was found in the Bois de Boulogne—at a vast distance from the scene of that butchery. How can it ever be suspected that a brute beast should have done the deed? The police are at fault—they have failed to procure the slightest clew. Should they even trace the animal, it would be impossible to prove me cognizant of the murder, or to implicate me in guilt on account of that cognizance. Above all, *I am known.* The advertiser designates me as the possessor of the beast. I am not sure to what limit his knowledge may extend. Should I avoid claming a property of so great value, which it is known that I possess, I will render the animal at least, liable to suspicion. It is not my policy to attract attention either to myself or to the beast. I will answer the advertisement, get the Ourang-Outang, and keep it close until this matter has blown over.'"

At this moment we heard a step upon the stairs.

"Be ready," said Dupin, "with your pistols, but neither use them nor show them until at a signal from myself."

The front door of the house had been left open, and the visitor had entered, without ringing, and advanced several steps upon the staircase. Now, however, he seemed to hesitate. Presently we heard him descending. Dupin was moving quickly to the door, when we again heard him coming up. He did not turn back a second time, but stepped up with decision, and rapped at the door of our chamber.

"Come in," said Dupin, in a cheerful and hearty tone.

A man entered. He was a sailor, evidently,—a tall, stout, and muscular-looking person, with a certain dare-devil expression of countenance, not altogether unprepossessing. His face, greatly sunburnt, was more than half hidden by whisker and *mustachio.* He had with him a huge oaken cudgel, but appeared to be otherwise unarmed. He bowed awkwardly, and bade us "good evening," in

French accents, which, although somewhat Neufchâtelish, were sufficiently indicative of a Parisian origin.

"Sit down, my friend," said Dupin. "I suppose you have called about the Ourang-Outang. Upon my word, I almost envy you the possession of him; a remarkably fine, and no doubt a very valuable animal. How old do you suppose him to be?"

The sailor drew a long breath, with the air of a man relieved of some intolerable burden, and then replied, in an assured tone:

"I have no way of telling—but he can't be more than four or five years old. Have you got him here?"

"Oh, no; we had no conveniences for keeping him here. He is at a livery stable in the Rue Dubourg, just by. You can get him in the morning. Of course you are prepared to identify the property?"

"To be sure I am, sir."

"I shall be sorry to part with him," said Dupin.

"I don't mean that you should be at all this trouble for nothing, sir," said the man. "Couldn't expect it. Am very willing to pay a reward for the finding of the animal—that is to say, any thing in reason."

"Well," replied my friend, "that is all very fair, to be sure. Let me think!—what should I have? Oh! I will tell you. My reward shall be this. You shall give me all the information in your power about these murders in the Rue Morgue."

Dupin said the last words in a very low tone, and very quietly. Just as quietly, too, he walked toward the door, locked it, and put the key in his pocket. He then drew a pistol from his bosom and placed it, without the least flurry, upon the table.

The sailor's face flushed up as if he were struggling with suffocation. He started to his feet and grasped his cudgel; but the next moment he fell back into his seat, trembling violently, and with the countenance of death itself. He spoke not a word. I pitied him from the bottom of my heart.

"My friend," said Dupin, in a kind tone, "you are alarming yourself unnecessarily—you are indeed. We mean you no harm whatever. I pledge you the honor of a gentleman, and of a Frenchman, that we intend you no injury. I perfectly well know that you are innocent of the atrocities in the Rue Morgue. It will not do, however, to deny that you are in some measure implicated in them. From what I have already said, you must know that I have had means of information about this matter—means of which you could never have dreamed. Now the thing stands thus. You have done nothing which you could have avoided—nothing, certainly, which renders you culpable. You were not even guilty of robbery, when you might have robbed with impunity. You have nothing to conceal. You have no reason for concealment. On the other hand, you are bound by every principle of honor to confess all you know. An innocent man is now imprisoned, charged with that crime of which you can point out the perpetrator."

The sailor had recovered his presence of mind, in a great measure, while Dupin uttered these words; but his original boldness of bearing was all gone.

"So help me God!" said he, after a brief pause, "I *will* tell you all I know about this affair;—but I do not expect you to believe one half I say—I would be a fool indeed if I did. Still, I *am* innocent, and I will make a clean breast if I die for it."

What he stated was, in substance, this. He had lately made a voyage to the Indian Archipelago. A party, of which he formed one, landed at Borneo, and passed into the interior on an excursion of pleasure. Himself and a companion had captured the Ourang-Outang. This companion dying, the animal fell into his own exclusive possession. After great trouble, occasioned by the intractable ferocity of his captive during the home voyage, he at length succeeded in lodging it safely at his own residence in Paris, where, not to attract toward himself the unpleasant curiosity of his neighbors, he kept it carefully secluded, until such time as it should recover from a wound in the foot, received from a splinter on board ship. His ultimate design was to sell it.

Returning home from some sailors' frolic on the night, or rather in the morning, of the murder, he found the beast occupying his own bedroom, into which it had broken from a closet adjoining, where it had been, as was thought, securely confined. Razor in hand, and fully lathered, it was sitting before a looking-glass, attempting the operation of shaving, in which it had no doubt previously watched its master through the keyhole of the closet. Terrified at the sight of so dangerous a weapon in the possession of an animal so ferocious, and so well able to use it, the man, for some moment, was at a loss what to do. He had been accustomed, however, to quiet the creature, even in its fiercest moods, by the use of a whip, and to this he now resorted.

Upon sight of it, the Ourang-Outang sprang at once through the door of the chamber, down the stairs, and thence, through a window, unfortunately open, into the street.

The Frenchman followed in despair; the ape, razor still in hand, occasionally stopping to look back and gesticulate at his pursuer, until the latter had nearly come up with it. It then again made off. In this manner the chase continued for a long time. The streets were profoundly quiet, as it was nearly three o'clock in the morning. In passing down an alley in the rear of the Rue Morgue, the fugitive's attention was arrested by a light gleaming from the open window of Madame L'Espanaye's chamber, in the fourth story of her house. Rushing to the building, it perceived the lightning-rod, clambered up with inconceivable agility, grasped the shutter, which was thrown fully back against the wall, and, by its means, swung itself directly upon the headboard of the bed. The whole feat did not occupy a minute. The shutter was kicked open again by the Ourang-Outang as it entered the room.

The sailor, in the meantime, was both rejoiced and perplexed. He had strong hopes of now recapturing the brute, as it could scarcely escape from the trap into which it had ventured, except by the rod, where it might be intercepted as it came down. On the other hand, there was much cause for anxiety as to what it might do in the house. This latter reflection urged the man still to follow the fugitive. A lightning-rod is ascended without difficulty, especially by a sailor; but, when he had arrived as high as the window, which lay far to his left, his career was stopped; the most that he could accomplish was to reach over so as to obtain a glimpse of the interior of the room. At this glimpse he nearly fell from his hold through excess of horror. Now it was that those hideous shrieks arose upon the night, which had startled from slumber the inmates of the Rue Morgue. Madame L'Espanaye and her daughter, habited in their night clothes, had apparently been occupied in arranging some papers in the iron chest already mentioned, which had been wheeled into the middle of the room. It was open, and its contents lay beside it on the floor. The victims must have been sitting with their backs toward the window; and, from the time elapsing between the ingress of the beast and the screams, it seems probable that it was not immediately perceived. The flapping-to of the shutter would naturally have been attributed to the wind.

As the sailor looked in, the gigantic animal had seized Madame

L'Espanaye by the hair (which was loose, as she had been combing it), and was flourishing the razor about her face, in imitation of the motions of a barber. The daughter lay prostrate and motionless; she had swooned. The screams and struggles of the old lady (during which the hair was torn from her head) had the effect of changing the probably pacific purposes of the Ourang-Outang into those of wrath. With one determined sweep of its muscular arm it nearly severed her head from her body. The sight of blood inflamed its anger into phrensy. Gnashing its teeth, and flashing fire from its eyes, it flew upon the body of the girl, and imbedded its fearful talons in her throat, retaining its grasp until she expired. Its wandering and wild glances fell at this moment upon the head of the bed, over which the face of its master, rigid with horror, was just discernible. The fury of the beast, who no doubt bore still in mind the dreaded whip, was instantly converted into fear. Conscious of having deserved punishment, it seemed desirous of concealing its bloody deeds, and skipped about the chamber in an agony of nervous agitation; throwing down and breaking the furniture as it moved, and dragging the bed from the bedstead. In conclusion, it seized first the corpse of the daughter, and thrust it up the chimney, as it was found; then that of the old lady, which it immediately hurled through the window headlong.

As the ape approached the casement with its mutilated burden, the sailor shrank aghast to the rod, and, rather gliding than clambering down it, hurried at once home—dreading the consequences of the butchery, and gladly abandoning, in his terror, all solicitude about the fate of the Ourang-Outang. The words heard by the party upon the staircase were the Frenchman's exclamations of horror and affright, commingled with the fiendish jabberings of the brute.

I have scarcely any thing to add. The Ourang-Outang must have escaped from the chamber, by the rod, just before the breaking of the door. It must have closed the window as it passed through it. It was subsequently caught by the owner himself, who obtained for it a very large sum at the *Jardin des Plantes.* Le Bon was instantly released, upon our narration of the circumstances (with some comments from Dupin) at the *bureau* of the Prefect of Police. This functionary, however, well disposed to my friend, could not altogether conceal his chagrin at the turn which affairs had taken, and was fain to indulge in a sarcasm or two about the propriety of every person minding his own business.

"Let him talk," said Dupin, who had not thought it necessary to reply. "Let him discourse; it will ease his conscience. I am satisfied with having defeated him in his own castle. Nevertheless, that he failed in the solution of this mystery, is by no means that matter for wonder which he supposes it; for, in truth, our friend the Prefect is somewhat too cunning to be profound. In his wisdom is no *stamen.* It is all head and no body, like the pictures of the Goddess Laverna—or, at best, all head and shoulders, like a codfish. But he is a good creature after all. I like him especially for one master stroke of cant, by which he has attained his reputation for ingenuity. I mean the way he has '*de nier ce qui est, et d'expliquer ce qui n'est pas.*' "[1]

[1]Rousseau—*Nouvelle Héloise.*

THE ADVENTURE OF THE SPECKLED BAND

(1892)

Sir Arthur Conan Doyle

Sir Arthur Conan Doyle

The four novels and numerous short stories of Sir Arthur Conan Doyle (1859–1930) featuring Sherlock Holmes are known all over the world and are as admired and beloved today as they were when they were written. Indeed, a high-quality fan club exists in the form of the Baker Street Irregulars to further the great detective's memory, and he has been the subject of many films and television productions. His creator was almost as interesting, a doctor who at the end of his life was a firm believer in the occult. Doyle was also an outstanding science fiction writer and fantasist, a mainstream novelist of some dozen noncrime books, and the scholarly author (for which he won his title) of dozens of nonfiction works.

THE ADVENTURE OF THE SPECKLED BAND

[Friday, April 6, 1883]

In glancing over my notes of the seventy odd cases in which I have during the last eight years studied the methods of my friend Sherlock Holmes, I find many tragic, some comic, a large number merely strange, but none commonplace; for, working as he did rather for the love of his art than for the acquirement of wealth, he refused to associate himself with any investigation which did not tend towards the unusual, and even the fantastic. Of all these varied cases, however, I cannot recall any which presented more singular features than that which was associated with the well-known Surrey family of the Roylotts of Stoke Moran. The events in question occurred in the early days of my association with Holmes, when we were sharing rooms as bachelors, in Baker Street. It is possible that I might have placed them upon record before, but a promise of secrecy was made at the time, from which I have only been freed during the last month by the untimely death of the lady to whom the pledge was given. It is perhaps as well that the facts should now come to light, for I have reasons to know there are widespread rumours as to the death of Dr. Grimesby Roylott which tend to make the matter even more terrible than the truth.

It was early in April, in the year '83, that I woke one morning to find Sherlock Holmes standing, fully dressed, by the side of my bed. He was a late riser as a rule, and, as the clock on the mantelpiece showed me that it was only a quarter past seven, I blinked up at him in some surprise, and perhaps just a little resentment, for I was myself regular in my habits.

"Very sorry to knock you up, Watson," said he, "but it's the common lot this morning. Mrs. Hudson has been knocked up, she retorted upon me, and I on you."

"What is it, then? A fire?"

"No, a client. It seems that a young lady has arrived in a considerable state of excitement, who insists upon seeing me. She is waiting now in the sitting-room. Now; when young ladies wander about the metropolis at this hour of the morning, and knock sleepy people up out of their beds, I presume that it is something very pressing which they have to communicate. Should it prove to be an interesting case, you would, I am sure, wish to follow it from the outset. I thought at any rate that I should call you, and give you the chance."

"My dear fellow, I would not miss it for anything."

I had no keener pleasure than in following Holmes in his professional investigations, and in admiring the rapid deductions, as swift as intuitions, and yet always founded on a logical basis, with which he unravelled the problems which were submitted to him. I rapidly threw on my clothes, and was ready in a few minutes to accompany my friend down to the sitting-room. A lady dressed in black and heavily veiled, who had been sitting in the window, rose as we entered.

"Good morning, madam," said Holmes cheerily.
"My name is Sherlock Holmes. This is my intimate friend and associate, Dr. Watson, before whom you can speak as freely as before myself. Ha, I am glad to see that Mrs. Hudson has had the good sense to light the fire. Pray draw up to it, and I shall order you a cup of hot coffee, for I observe that you are shivering."

"It is not cold which makes me shiver," said the woman in a low voice, changing her seat as requested.

"What then?"

"It is fear, Mr. Holmes. It is terror." She raised her veil as she spoke, and we could see that she was indeed in a pitiable state of agitation, her face all drawn and grey, with restless, frightened eyes, like those of some hunted animal. Her features and figure were those of a woman of thirty, but her hair was shot with premature grey, and her expression was weary and haggard. Sherlock Holmes ran her over with one of his quick, all-comprehensive glances.

"You must not fear," said he soothingly, bending forward and patting her forearm. "We shall soon set matters right, I have no doubt. You have come in by train this morning, I see."

"You know me, then?"

"No, but I observe the second half of a return ticket in the palm of your left glove. You must have started early, and yet you had a good drive in a dog-cart, along heavy roads, before you reached the station."

The lady gave a violent start, and stared in bewilderment at my companion.

"There is no mystery, my dear madam," said he, smiling. "The left arm of your jacket is spattered with mud in no less than seven places. The marks are perfectly fresh. There is no vehicle save a dog-cart which throws up mud in that way, and then only when you sit on the left-hand side of the driver."

"Whatever your reasons may be, you are perfectly correct," said she. "I started from home before six, reached Leatherhead at twenty past, and came in by the first train to Waterloo. Sir, I can stand this strain no longer, I shall go mad if it continues. I have no one to turn to—none, save only one, who cares for me, and he, poor fellow, can be of little aid. I have heard of you, Mr. Holmes; I have heard of you from Mrs. Farintosh, whom you helped in the hour of her sore need. It was from her that I had your address. Oh, sir, do you not think you could help me too, and at least throw a little light through the dense darkness which surrounds me? At present it is out of my power to reward you for your services, but in a month or two I shall be married, with the control of my own income, and then at least you shall not find me ungrateful."

Holmes turned to his desk, and unlocking it, drew out a small case-book which he consulted.

"Farintosh," said he. "Ah, yes, I recall the case; it was concerned with an opal tiara. I think it was before your time, Watson. I can only say, madam, that I shall be happy to devote the same care to your case as I did to that of your friend. As to reward, my profession is its reward; but you are at liberty to defray whatever expenses I may be put to, at the time which suits you best. And now I beg that you will lay before us everything that may help us in forming an opinion upon the matter."

"Alas!" replied our visitor. "The very horror of my situation lies in the fact that my fears are so vague, and my suspicions depend so entirely upon small points, which might seem trivial to another, that even he to whom of all others I have a right to look for help and advice looks upon all that I tell him about it as the fancies of a nervous woman. He does not say so, but I can read it from his soothing answers and averted eyes. But I have heard, Mr. Holmes, that you can see deeply into the manifold wickedness of the human heart. You may advise me how to walk amid the dangers which encompass me."

"I am all attention, madam."

"My name is Helen Stoner, and I am living with my stepfather, who is the last survivor of one of the oldest Saxon families in England, the Roylotts of Stoke Moran, on the western border of Surrey."

Holmes nodded his head. "The name is familiar to me," said he.

"The family was at one time among the richest in England, and the estate extended over the borders into Berkshire in the north, and Hampshire in the west. In the last century, however, four successive heirs were of a dissolute and wasteful disposition, and the family ruin was eventually completed by a gambler, in the days of the Regency. Nothing was left save a few acres of ground and the two-hundred-year-old house, which is itself crushed under a heavy mortgage. The last squire dragged out his existence there, living the horrible life of an aristocratic pauper; but his only son, my stepfather, seeing that he must adapt himself to the new conditions, obtained an advance from a relative, which enabled him to take a medical degree, and went out to Calcutta, where, by his professional skill and his force of character, he established a large practice. In a fit of anger, however, caused by some robberies which had been perpetrated in the house, he beat his native butler to death, and narrowly escaped a capital sentence. As it was, he suffered a long term of imprisonment, and afterwards returned to England a morose and disappointed man.

"When Dr. Roylott was in India he married my mother, Mrs. Stoner, the young widow of Major-General Stoner, of the Bengal Artillery. My sister Julia and I were twins, and we were only two years old at the time of my mother's re-marriage. She had a considerable sum of money, not less than a thousand a year, and this she bequeathed to Dr. Roylott entirely whilst we resided with him, with a provision that a certain annual sum should be allowed to each of us in the event of our marriage. Shortly after our return to England my mother died—she was killed eight years ago in a railway accident near Crewe. Dr. Roylott then abandoned his attempts to establish himself in practice in London, and took us to live with him in the ancestral house at Stoke Moran. The money which my mother had left was enough for all our wants, and there seemed no obstacle to our happiness.

"But a terrible change came over our stepfather about this time. Instead of making friends and exchanging visits with our neighbours, who had at first been overjoyed to see a Roylott of Stoke Moran back in the old family seat, he shut himself up in his house, and seldom came out save to indulge in ferocious quarrels with whoever might cross his path. Violence of temper approaching to mania has been hereditary in the men of the family, and in my stepfather's case it had, I believe, been intensified by his long residence in the tropics. A series of disgraceful brawls took place, two of which ended in the police-court, until at last he became the terror of the village, and the folks would fly at his approach, for he is a man of immense strength, and absolutely uncontrollable in his anger.

"Last week he hurled the local blacksmith over a parapet into a stream and it was only by paying over all the money that I could gather together that I was able to avert another public exposure. He had no friends at all save the wandering gipsies, and he would give these vagabonds leave to encamp upon the few acres of bramble-covered land which represent the family estate, and would accept in return the hospitality of their tents, wandering away with them sometimes for weeks on end. He has a passion also for Indian animals, which are sent over to him by a correspondent, and he has at this moment a cheetah and a baboon, which wander freely over his grounds, and are feared by the villagers almost as much as their master.

"You can imagine from what I say that my poor sister Julia and I had no great pleasure in our lives. No servant would stay with us, and for a long time we did all the work of the house. She was but thirty at the time of her death, and yet her hair had already begun to whiten, even as mine has."

"Your sister is dead, then?"

"She died just two years ago, and it is of her death that I wish to speak to you. You can understand that, living the life which I have described, we were little likely to see anyone of our own age and position. We had, however, an aunt, my mother's maiden sister, Miss Honoria Westphail, who lives near Harrow, and we were occasionally allowed to pay short visits at this lady's house. Julia went there at Christmas two year ago, and met there a half-pay Major of Marines, to whom she became engaged. My stepfather learned of the engagement when my sister returned, and offered no objection to the marriage; but within a fortnight of the day which had been fixed for the wedding, the terrible event occurred which has deprived me of my only companion."

Sherlock Holmes had been leaning back in his chair with his eyes closed, and his head sunk in a cushion, but he half opened his lids now, and glanced across at his visitor.

"Pray be precise as to details," said he.

"It is easy for me to be so, for every event of that dreadful time is seared into my memory. The manor house is, as I have already said, very old, and only one wing is now inhabited. The bedrooms in this wing are on the ground floor, the sitting-rooms being in the central block of the buildings. Of these bedrooms, the first is Dr. Roylott's, the second my sister's, and the third my own. There is no communication between them, but they all open out into the same corridor. Do I make myself plain?"

"Perfectly so."

"The windows of the three rooms open out upon the lawn. That fatal night Dr. Roylott had gone to his room early, though we knew that he had not retired to rest, for my sister was troubled by the smell of the strong Indian cigars which it was his custom to smoke. She left her room, therefore, and came into mine, where she sat for some time, chatting about her approaching wedding. At eleven o'clock she rose to leave me, but she paused at the door and looked back.

"'Tell me, Helen,' said she, 'have you ever heard anyone whistle in the dead of the night?'

"'Never,' said I.

"'I suppose that you could not possibly whistle yourself in your sleep?'

"'Certainly not. But why?'

"'Because during the last few nights I have always, about three in the morning, heard a low clear whistle. I am a light sleeper, and it has awakened me. I cannot tell where it came from—perhaps from the next room, perhaps from the lawn. I thought that I would just ask you whether you had heard it.'

"'No, I have not. It must be those wretched gipsies in the plantation.'

"'Very likely. And yet if it were on the lawn I wonder that you did not hear it also.'

"'Ah, but I sleep more heavily than you.'

"'Well, it is of no great consequence, at any rate,' she smiled back at me, closed my door, and a few moments later I heard her key turn in the lock."

"Indeed," said Holmes. "Was it your custom always to lock yourselves in at night?"

"Always."

"And why?"

"I think that I mentioned to you that the Doctor kept a cheetah and a baboon. We had no feeling of security unless our doors were locked."

"Quite so. Pray proceed with your statement."

"I could not sleep that night. A vague feeling of impending misfortune impressed me. My sister and I, you will recollect, were twins, and you know how subtle are the links which bind two souls which are so closely allied. It was a wild night. The wind was howling outside, and the rain was beating and splashing against the windows. Suddenly, amidst all the hubbub of the gale, there burst forth the wild scream of a terrified woman. I knew that it was my sister's voice. I sprang from my bed, wrapped a shawl round me, and rushed into the corridor. As I opened my door I seemed to hear a low whistle, such as my sister described, and a few moments later a clanging sound, as if a mass of metal had fallen. As I ran down the passage my sister's door was unlocked, and revolved slowly upon its hinges. I stared at it horror-stricken, not knowing what was about to issue from it. By the light of the corridor lamp I saw my sister appear at the opening, her face blanched with terror, her hands groping for help, her whole figure swaying to and fro like that of a drunkard. I ran to her and threw my arms round her, but at that moment her knees seemed to give way and she fell to the ground. She writhed as one who is in terrible pain, and her limbs were dreadfully convulsed. At first I thought that she had not recognized me, but as I bent over her she suddenly shrieked out in a voice which I shall never forget, 'O, my God! Helen! It was the band! The speckled band!' There was something else which she would fain have said, and she stabbed with her finger into the air in the direction of the Doctor's room, but a fresh convulsion seized her and choked her words. I rushed out, calling loudly for my stepfather, and I met him hastening from his room in his dressing-gown. When he reached my sister's side she was unconscious, and though he poured brandy down her throat, and sent for medical aid from the village, all efforts were in vain, for she slowly sank and died without having recovered her consciousness. Such was the dreadful end of my beloved sister."

"One moment," said Holmes; "are you sure about this whistle and metallic sound? Could you swear to it?"

"That was what the county coroner asked me at the inquiry. It is my strong impression that I heard it, and yet among the crash of the gale, and the creaking of an old house, I may possibly have been deceived."

"Was your sister dressed?"

"No, she was in her nightdress. In her right hand was found the charred stump of a match, and in her left a matchbox."

"Showing that she had struck a light and looked about her when the alarm took place. That is important. And what conclusions did the coroner come to?"

"He investigated the case with great care, for Dr. Roylott's conduct had long been notorious in the county, but he was unable to find any satisfactory cause of death. My evidence showed that the door had been fastened upon the inner side, and the windows were blocked by old-fashioned shutters with broad iron bars, which were secured every night. The walls were carefully sounded, and were shown to be quite solid all round, and the flooring was also thoroughly examined, with the same result. The chimney is wide, but is barred up by four large staples. It is certain, therefore, that my sister was quite alone when she met her end. Besides, there were no marks of any violence upon her."

"How about poison?"

"The doctors examined her for it, but without success."

"What do you think that this unfortunate lady died of, then?"

"It is my belief that she died of pure fear and nervous shock, though what it was which frightened her I cannot imagine."

"Were there gipsies in the plantation at the time?"

"Yes, there are nearly always some there."

"Ah, and what did you gather from this allusion to a band—a speckled band?"

"Sometimes I have thought that it was merely the wild talk of delirium, sometimes that it may have referred to some band of people, perhaps to these very gipsies in the plantation. I do not know whether the spotted handkerchiefs which so many of them wear over their heads might have suggested the strange adjective which she used."

Holmes shook his head like a man who is far from being satisfied.

"These are very deep waters," said he; "pray go on with your narrative."

"Two years have passed since then, and my life has been until lately lonelier than ever. A month ago, however, a dear friend, whom I have known for many years, has done me the honour to ask my hand in marriage. His name is Armitage—Percy Armitage—the second son of Mr. Armitage, of Crane Water, near Reading. My stepfather has offered no opposition to the match, and we are to be married in the course of the spring. Two days ago some repairs were started in the west wing of the building, and my bedroom wall has been pierced, so that I have had to move into the chamber in which my sister died, and to sleep in the very bed in which she slept. Imagine, then, my thrill of terror when last night, as I lay awake, thinking over her terrible fate, I suddenly heard in the silence of the night the low whistle which had been the herald of her own death. I sprang up and lit the lamp, but nothing was to be seen in the room. I was too shaken to go to bed again, however, so I dressed, and as soon as it was daylight I slipped down, got a dog-cart at the Crown Inn, which is opposite, and drove to Leatherhead, from whence I have come on this morning, with the one object of seeing you and asking your advice.'

"You have done wisely," said my friend. "But have you told me all?"

"Yes, all."

"Miss Stoner, you have not. You are screening your stepfather."

"Why, what do you mean?"

For answer Holmes pushed back the frill of black lace which fringed the hand that lay upon our visitor's knee. Five little livid spots, the marks of four fingers and a thumb, were printed upon the white wrist.

"You have been cruelly used," said Holmes.

The lady coloured deeply, and covered over her injured wrist. "He is a hard man," she said, "and perhaps he hardly knows his own strength."

There was a long silence, during which Holmes leaned his chin upon his hands and stared into the crackling fire.

"This is very deep business," he said at last. "There are a thousand details which I should desire to know before I decide upon our course of action. Yet we have not a moment to lose. If we were to come to Stoke Moran to-day, would it be possible for us to see over these rooms without the knowledge of your stepfather?"

"As it happens, he spoke of coming into town to-day upon some most important business. It is probable that he will be away all day, and that there would be nothing to disturb you. We have a housekeeper now, but she is old and foolish, and I could easily get her out of the way."

"Excellent. You are not averse to this trip, Watson?"

"By no means."

"Then we shall both come. What are you going to do yourself?"

"I have one or two things which I would wish to do now that I am in town. But I shall return by the twelve o'clock train, so as to be there in time for your coming."

"And you may expect us early in the afternoon. I have myself some small business matters to attend to. Will you not wait and breakfast?"

"No, I must go. My heart is lightened already since I have confided my trouble to you. I shall look forward to seeing you again this afternoon." She dropped her thick black veil over her face, and glided from the room.

"And what do you think of it all, Watson?" asked Sherlock Holmes, leaning back in his chair.

"It seems to me to be a most dark and sinister business."

"Dark enough and sinister enough."

"Yet if the lady is correct in saying that the flooring and walls are sound, and that the door, window, and chimney are impassable, then her sister must have been undoubtedly alone when she met her mysterious end."

"What becomes, then, of these nocturnal whistles, and what of the very peculiar words of the dying woman?"

"I cannot think."

"When you combine the ideas of whistles at night, the presence of a band of gipsies who are on intimate terms with this old doctor, the fact that we have every reason to believe that the doctor has an interest in preventing his stepdaughter's marriage, the dying allusion to a band, and finally, the fact that Miss Helen Stoner heard a metallic clang, which might have been caused by one of those metal bars which secured the shutters falling back into their place, I think there is good ground to think that the mystery may be cleared along those lines."

"But what, then, did the gipsies do?"

"I cannot imagine."

"I see many objections to any such a theory."

"And so do I. It is precisely for that reason that we are going to Stoke Moran this day. I want to see whether the objections are fatal, or if they may be explained away. But what, in the name of the devil!"

The ejaculation had been drawn from my companion by the fact that our door had been suddenly dashed open, and that a huge man framed himself in the aperture. His costume was a peculiar mixture of the professional and of the agricultural, having a black top-hat, a long frock-coat, and a pair of high gaiters, with a hunting-crop swinging in his hand. So tall was he that his hat actually brushed the cross-bar of the doorway, and his breadth seemed to span it across from side to side. A large face, seared with a thousand wrinkles, burned yellow with the sun, and marked with every evil passion, was turned from one to the other of us, while his deep-set, bile-shot eyes, and the high thin fleshless nose, gave him somewhat the resemblance to a fierce old bird of prey.

"Which of you is Holmes?" asked this apparition.

"My name, sir, but you have the advantage of me," said my companion quietly.

"I am Dr. Grimesby Roylott, of Stoke Moran."

"Indeed, Doctor," said Holmes blandly. "Pray take a seat."

"I will do nothing of the kind. My stepdaughter has been here. I have traced her. What has she been saying to you?"

"It is a little cold for the time of the year," said Holmes.

"What has she been saying to you?" screamed the old man furiously.

"But I have heard that the crocuses promise well," continued my companion imperturbably.

"Ha! You put me off, do you?" said our new visitor, taking a step forward, and shaking his hunting-crop. "I know you, you scoundrel! I have heard of you before. You are Holmes the meddler."

My friend smiled.

"Holmes the busybody!"

His smile broadened.

"Holmes the Scotland Yard jack-in-office."

Holmes chuckled heartily. "Your conversation is most entertaining," said he. "When you go out close the door, for there is a decided draught."

"I will go when I have had my say. Don't you dare to meddle with my affairs. I know that Miss Stoner has been here—I traced her! I am a dangerous man to fall foul of! See here." He stepped swiftly forward, seized the poker, and bent it into a curve with his huge brown hands.

"See that you keep yourself out of my grip," he snarled, and hurling the twisted poker into the fireplace, he strode out of the room.

"He seems a very amiable person," said Holmes, laughing. "I am not quite so bulky, but if he had remained I might have shown him that my grip was not much more feeble than his own." As he spoke he picked up the steel poker, and with a sudden effort straightened it out again.

"Fancy his having the insolence to confound me with the official detective force! This incident gives zest to our investigation, however, and I only trust that our little friend will not suffer from her imprudence in allowing this brute to trace her. And now, Watson, we shall order breakfast, and afterwards I shall walk down to Doctors' Commons, where I hope to get some data which may help us in this matter."

It was nearly one o'clock when Sherlock Holmes returned from his excursion. He held in his hand a sheet of blue paper, scrawled over with notes and figures.

"I have seen the will of the deceased wife," said he. "To determine its exact meaning I have been obliged to work out the present prices of the investments with which it is concerned. The total income, which at the time of the wife's death was little short of £1,100, is now through the fall in agricultural prices not more than £750. Each daughter can claim an income of £250, in case of marriage. It is evident, therefore, that if both girls had married this beauty would have had a mere pittance, while even one of them would cripple him to a serious extent. My morning's work has not been wasted, since it has proved that he has the very strongest motives for standing in the way of anything of the sort. And now, Watson, this is too serious for dawdling, especially as the old man is aware that we are interesting ourselves in his affairs, so if you are ready we shall call a cab and drive to Waterloo. I should be very much obliged if you would slip your revolver into your pocket. An Eley's No. 2 is an excellent argument with gentlemen who can twist steel pokers into knots. That and a tooth-brush are, I think, all that we need."

At Waterloo we were fortunate in catching a train for Leatherhead, where we hired a trap at the station inn, and drove for four or five miles through the lovely Surrey lanes. It was a perfect day, with a bright sun and a few fleecy clouds in the heavens. The trees and wayside hedges were just throwing out their first green shoots, and the air was full of the pleasant smell of the moist earth. To me at least there was a strange contrast between the sweet promise of the spring and this sinister quest upon which we were engaged. My companion sat in front of the trap, his arms folded, his hat pulled down over his eyes, and his chin sunk upon his breast, buried in the deepest thought. Suddenly, however, he started, tapped me on the shoulder, and pointed over the meadows.

"Look there!" said he.

A heavily timbered park stretched up in a gentle slope, thickening into a grove at the highest point. From amidst the branches there jutted out the grey gables and high rooftree of a very old mansion.

"Stoke Moran?" said he.

"Yes, sir, that be the house of Dr. Grimesby Roylott," remarked the driver.

"There is some building going on there," said Holmes; "that is where we are going."

"There's the village," said the driver, pointing to a cluster of roofs some distance to the left; "but if you want to get to the house, you'll find it shorter to go over this stile, and so by the footpath over the fields. There it is, where the lady is walking."

"And the lady, I fancy, is Miss Stoner," observed Holmes, shading his eyes. "Yes, I think we had better do as you suggest."

We got off, paid our fare, and the trap rattled back on its way to Leatherhead.

"I thought it as well," said Holmes, as we climbed the stile, "that this fellow should think we had come here as architects, or on some definite business. It may stop his gossip. Good afternoon, Miss Stoner. You see that we have been as good as our word."

Our client of the morning had hurried forward to meet us with a face which spoke her joy. "I have been waiting so eagerly for you," she cried, shaking hands with us warmly. "All has turned out splendidly. Dr. Roylott has gone to town, and it is unlikely that he will be back before evening."

"We have had the pleasure of making the Doctor's acquaintance," said Holmes, and in a few words he sketched out what had occurred. Miss Stoner turned white to the lips as she listened.

"Good heavens!" she cried, "he has followed me, then."

"So it appears."

"He is so cunning that I never know when I am safe from him. What will he say when he returns?"

"He must guard himself, for he may find that there is someone more cunning than himself upon his track. You must lock yourself from him to-night. If he is violent, we shall take you away to your aunt's at Harrow. Now, we must make the best use of our time, so kindly take us at once to the rooms which we are to examine."

The building was of grey, lichen-blotched stone, with a high central portion, and two curving wings, like the claws of a crab, thrown out on each side. In one of these wings the windows were broken, and blocked with wooden boards, while the roof was partly caved in, a picture of ruin. The central portion was in little better repair, but the right-hand block was comparatively modern, and the blinds in the windows, with the blue smoke curling up from the chimneys, showed that this was where the family resided. Some scaffolding had been erected against the end wall, and the stonework had been broken into, but there were no signs of any workmen at the moment of our visit. Holmes walked slowly up and down the ill-trimmed lawn, and examined with deep attention the outsides of the windows.

"This, I take it, belongs to the room in which you used to sleep, the centre one to your sister's, and the one next to the main building to Dr. Roylott's chamber?"

"Exactly so. But I am now sleeping in the middle one."

"Pending the alterations, as I understand. By the way, there does not seem to by any very pressing need for repairs at that end wall."

"There were none. I believe that it was an excuse to move me from my room."

"Ah! that is suggestive. Now, on the other side of this narrow wing runs the corridor from which these three rooms open. There are windows in it, of course?"

"Yes, but very small ones. Too narrow for anyone to pass through."

"As you both locked your doors at night, your rooms were unapproachable from that side. Now, would you have the kindness to go into your room, and to bar your shutters."

Miss Stoner did so, and Holmes, after a careful examination through the open window, endeavoured in every way to force the shutter open, but without success. There was no slit through which a knife could be passed to raise the bar. Then with his lens he tested the hinges, but they were of solid iron, built firmly into the massive masonry. "Hum!" said he, scratching his chin in some perplexity, "my theory certainly presents some difficulties. No one could pass these shutters if they were bolted. Well, we shall see if the inside throws any light upon the matter."

A small side-door led into the whitewashed corridor from which the three bedrooms opened. Holmes refused to examine the third chamber, so we passed at once to the second, that in which Miss Stoner was now sleeping, and in which her sister had met her fate. It was a homely little room, with a low ceiling and a gaping fireplace, after the fashion of old country houses. A brown chest of drawers stood in one corner, a narrow white-counterpaned bed in another, and a dressing-table on the left-hand side of the window. These articles, with two small wickerwork chairs, made up all the furniture in the room, save for a square of Wilton carpet in the centre. The boards round and the panelling of the walls were brown, wormeaten oak, so old and discoloured that it may have dated from the original building of the house. Holmes drew one of the chairs into a corner and sat silent, while his eyes travelled round and round and up and down, taking in every detail of the apartment.

"Where does that bell communicate with?" he asked at last, pointing to a thick bell-rope which hung down beside the bed, the tassel actually lying upon the pillow.

"It goes to the housekeeper's room."

"It looks newer than the other things?"

"Yes, it was only put there a couple of years ago."

"Your sister asked for it, I suppose?"

"No, I never heard of her using it. We used always to get what we wanted for ourselves."

"Indeed, it seemed unnecessary to put so nice a bellpull there. You will excuse me for a few minutes while I satisfy myself as to this floor." He threw himself down upon his face with his lens in his hand, and crawled swiftly backwards and forwards, examining minutely the cracks between the boards. Then he did the same with the woodwork with which the chamber was panelled. Finally he walked over to the bed and spent some time in staring at it, and in running his eye up and down the wall. Finally he took the bell-rope in his hand and gave it a brisk tug.

"Why, it's a dummy," said he.

"Won't it ring?"

"No, it is not even attached to a wire. This is very interesting. You can see now that it is fastened to a hook just above where the little opening of the ventilator is."

"How very absurd! I never noticed that before."

"Very strange!" muttered Holmes, pulling at the rope.

"There are one or two very singular points about this room. For example, what a fool a builder must be to open a ventilator in another room, when, with the same trouble, he might have communicated with the outside air!"

"That is also quite modern," said the lady.

"Done about the same time as the bell-rope," remarked Holmes.

"Yes, there were several little changes carried out about that time."

"They seem to have been of a most interesting character—dummy bell-ropes, and ventilators which do not ventilate. With your permission, Miss Stoner, we shall now carry our researches into the inner apartment."

Dr. Grimesby Roylott's chamber was larger than that of his stepdaughter, but was as plainly furnished. A camp bed, a small wooden shelf full of books, mostly of a technical character, an arm-chair beside the bed, a plain wooden chair against the wall, a round table, and a large iron safe were the principal things which met the eye. Holmes walked slowly round and examined each and all of them with the keenest interest.

"What's in here?" he asked, tapping the safe.

"My stepfather's business papers."

"Oh! you have seen inside, then?"

"Only once, some years ago. I remember that it was full of papers."

"There isn't a cat in it, for example?"

"No. What a strange idea!"

"Well, look at this!" He took up a small saucer of milk which stood on the top of it.

"No; we don't keep a cat. But there is a cheetah and a baboon."

Ah, yes, of course! Well, a cheetah is just a big cat, and yet a saucer of milk does not go very far in satisfying its wants, I daresay. There is one point which I should wish to determine." He squatted down in front of the wooden chair, and examined the seat of it with the greatest attention.

"Thank you. That is quite settled," said he, rising and putting his lens in his pocket. "Hullo! here is something interesting!"

The object which had caught his eye was a small dog lash hung on one corner of the bed. The lash, however, was curled upon itself, and tied so as to make a loop of whipcord.

"What do you make of that, Watson?"

"It's a common enough lash. But I don't know why it should be tied."

"That is not quite so common, is it? Ah, me! it's a wicked world, and when a clever man turns his brain to crime it is the worst of all. I think that I have seen enough now, Miss Stoner, and, with your permission, we shall walk out upon the lawn."

I had never seen my friend's face so grim, or his brow so dark, as it was when we turned from the scene of this investigation. We had walked several times up and down the lawn, neither Miss Stoner nor myself liking to break in upon his thoughts before he roused himself from his reverie.

"It is very essential, Miss Stoner," said he," that you should absolutely follow my advice in every respect."

"I shall most certainly do so."

"The matter is too serious for any hesitation. Your life may depend upon your compliance."

"I assure you that I am in your hands."

"In the first place, both my friend and I must spend the night in your room."

Both Miss Stoner and I gazed at him in astonishment.

"Yes, it must be so. Let me explain. I believe that that is the village inn over there?"

"Yes, that is the 'Crown.'"

"Very good. Your windows would be visible from there?"

"Certainly."

"You must confine yourself to your room, on pretence of a headache, when your stepfather comes back. Then when you hear him retire for the night, you must open the shutters of your window, undo the hasp, put your lamp there as a signal to us, and then withdraw with everything which you are likely to want into the room which you used to occupy. I have no doubt that, in spite of the repairs, you could manage there for one night."

"Oh, yes, easily."

"The rest you will leave in our hands."

"But what will you do?"

"We shall spend the night in your room, and we shall investigate the cause of this noise which has disturbed you."

"I believe, Mr. Holmes, that you have already made up your mind," said Miss Stoner, laying her hand upon my companion's sleeve.

"Perhaps I have."

"Then for pity's sake tell me what was the cause of my sister's death."

"I should prefer to have clearer proofs before I speak."

"You can at least tell me whether my own thought is correct, and if she died from some sudden fright."

"No, I do not think so. I think that there was probably some more tangible cause. And now, Miss Stoner, we must leave you, for if Dr. Roylott returned and saw us, our journey would be in vain. Good-bye, and be brave, for if you will do what I have told you, you may rest assured that we shall soon drive away the dangers that threaten you."

Sherlock Holmes and I had no difficulty in engaging a bedroom and sitting-room at the Crown Inn. They were on the upper floor, and from our window we could command a view of the avenue gate, and of the inhabited wing of Stoke Moran Manor House. At dusk we saw Dr. Grimesby Roylott drive past, his huge form looming up beside the little figure of the lad who drove him. The boy had some slight difficulty in undoing the heavy iron gates, and we heard the hoarse roar of the Doctor's voice, and saw the fury with which he shook his clenched fists at him. The trap drove on, and a few minutes later we saw a sudden light spring up among the trees as the lamp was lit in one of the sitting-rooms.

"Do you know, Watson," said Holmes, as we sat together in the gathering darkness, "I have really some scruples as to taking you to-night. There is a distinct element of danger."

"Can I be of assistance?"

"Your presence might be invaluable."

"Then I shall certainly come."

"It is very kind of you."

"You speak of danger. You have evidently seen more in these rooms than was visible to me."

"No, but I fancy that I may have deduced a little more. I imagine that you saw all that I did."

"I saw nothing remarkable save the bell-rope, and what purpose that could answer I confess is more than I can imagine."

"You saw the ventilator, too?"

"Yes, but I do not think that it is such a very unusual thing to have a small opening between two rooms. It was so small that a rat could hardly pass through."

"I knew that we should find a ventilator before ever we came to Stoke Moran."

"My dear Holmes!"

"Oh, yes, I did. You remember in her statement she said that her sister could smell Dr. Roylott's cigar. Now, of course that suggests at once that there must be a communication between the two rooms. It could only be a small one, or it would have been remarked upon at the coroner's inquiry. I deduced a ventilator."

"But what harm can there be in that?"

"Well, there is at least a curious coincidence of dates. A ventilator is made, a cord is hung, and a lady who sleeps in the bed dies. Does not that strike you?"

"I cannot as yet see any connection."

"Did you observe anything very peculiar about that bed?"

"No."

"It was clamped to the floor. Did you ever see a bed fastened like that before?"

"I cannot say that I have."

"The lady could not move her bed. It must always be in the same relative position to the ventilator and to the rope—for so we may call it, since it was clearly never meant for a bell-pull."

"Holmes," I cried, "I seem to see dimly what you are hitting at. We are only just in time to prevent some subtle and horrible crime."

"Subtle enough and horrible enough. When a doctor does go wrong he is the first of criminals. He has nerve and he has knowledge. Palmer and Pritchard were among the heads of their profession. This man strikes even deeper, but I think, Watson, that we shall be able to strike deeper still. But we shall have horrors enough before the night is over: for goodness' sake let us have a quiet pipe, and turn our minds for a few hours to something more cheerful."

About nine o'clock the light among the trees was extinguished, and all was dark in the direction of the Manor House. Two hours passed slowly away, and then, suddenly, just at the stroke of eleven, a single bright light shone out right in front of us.

"That is our signal," said Holmes, springing to his feet; "it comes from the middle window."

As we passed out he exchanged a few words with the landlord, explaining that we were going on a late visit to an acquaintance, and that it was possible that we might spend the night there. A moment later we were out on the dark road, a chill wind blowing in our faces, and one yellow light twinkling in front of us through the gloom to guide us on our sombre errand.

There was little difficulty in entering the grounds, for unrepaired breaches gaped in the old park wall. Making our way among the trees, we reached the lawn, crossed it, and were about to enter through the window, when out from a clump of laurel bushes there darted what seemed to be a hideous and distorted child, who threw itself on the grass with writhing limbs, and then ran swiftly across the lawn into the darkness.

"My God!" I whispered, "did you see it?"

Holmes was for the moment as startled as I. His hand closed like a vice upon my wrist in his agitation. Then he broke into a low laugh, and put his lips to my ear.

"It is a nice household," he murmured, "that is the baboon."

I had forgotten the strange pets which the Doctor affected. There was a cheetah, too; perhaps we might find it upon our shoulders at any moment. I confess that I felt easier in my mind when, after following Holmes' example and slipping off my shoes, I found myself inside the bedroom. My companion noiselessly closed the shutters, moved the lamp on to the table, and cast his eyes round the room. All was as we had seen it in the day-time. Then creeping up to me and making a trumpet of his hand, he whispered into my ear again so gently that it was all that I could do to distinguish the words:

"The least sound would be fatal to our plans."

I nodded to show that I had heard.

"We must sit without a light. He would see it through the ventilator."

I nodded again.

"Do not go to sleep; your very life may depend upon it. Have your pistol ready in case we should need it. I will sit on the side of the bed, and you in that chair."

I took out my revolver and laid it on the corner of the table.

Holmes had brought up a long thin cane, and this he placed upon the bed beside him. By it he laid the box of matches and the stump of a candle. Then he turned down the lamp and we were left in darkness.

How shall I ever forget that dreadful vigil? I could not hear a sound, not even the drawing of a breath, and yet I knew that my companion sat open-eyed, within a few feet of me, in the same state of nervous tension in which I was myself. The shutters cut off the least ray of light, and we waited in absolute darkness. From outside came the occasional cry of a night-bird, and once at our very window a long drawn, cat-like whine, which told us that the cheetah was indeed at liberty. Far away we could hear the deep tones of the parish clock, which boomed out every quarter of an hour. How long they seemed, those quarters! Twelve o'clock, and one, and two, and three, and still we sat waiting silently for whatever might befall.

Suddenly there was the momentary gleam of a light up in the direction of the ventilator, which vanished immediately, but was succeeded by a strong smell of burning oil and heated metal. Someone in the next room had lit a dark lantern. I heard a gentle sound of movement, and then all was silent once more, though the smell grew stronger. For half an hour I sat with straining ears. Then suddenly another sound became audible—a very gentle, soothing sound, like that of a small jet of steam escaping continually from a kettle. The instant that we heard it, Holmes sprang from the bed, struck a match, and lashed furiously with his cane at the bell-pull.

"You see it, Watson?" he yelled. "You see it?"

But I saw nothing. At the moment when Holmes struck the light I heard a low, clear whistle, but the sudden glare flashing into my weary eyes made it impossible for me to tell what it was at which my friend lashed so savagely. I could, however, see that his face was deadly pale, and filled with horror and loathing.

He had ceased to strike, and was gazing up at the ventilator, when suddenly there broke from the silence of the night the most horrible cry to which I have ever listened. It swelled up louder and louder, a hoarse yell of pain and fear and anger all mingled in the one dreadful shriek. They say that away down in the village, and even in the distant parsonage, that cry raised the sleepers from their beds. It struck cold to our hearts, and I stood gazing at Holmes, and he at me, until the last echoes of it had died away into the silence from which it rose.

"What can it mean?" I gasped.

"It means that it is all over," Holmes answered. "And perhaps, after all, it is for the best. Take your pistol, and we shall enter Dr. Roylott's room."

With a grave face he lit the lamp, and led the way down the corridor. Twice he struck at the chamber door without any reply from within. Then he turned the handle and entered, I at his heels, with the cocked pistol in my hand.

It was a singular sight which met our eyes. On the table stood a dark lantern with the shutter half open, throwing a brilliant beam of light upon the iron safe, the door of which was ajar. Beside this table, on the wooden chair, sat Dr. Grimesby Roylott, clad in a long grey dressing-gown, his bare ankles protruding beneath, and his feet thrust into red heelless Turkish slippers. Across his lap lay the short stock with the long lash which we had noticed during the day. His chin was cocked upwards, and his eyes were fixed in a dreadful rigid stare at the corner of the ceiling. Round his brow he had a peculiar yellow band, with brownish speckles, which seemed to be bound tightly round his head. As we entered he made neither sound nor motion.

"The band! the speckled band!" whispered Holmes.

I took a step forward. In an instant his strange headgear began to move, and there reared itself from among his hair the squat diamond-shaped head and puffed neck of a loathsome serpent.

"It is a swamp adder!" cried Holmes—"the deadliest snake in India. He has died within ten seconds of being bitten. Violence does, in truth, recoil upon the violent, and the schemer falls into the pit which he digs for another. Let us thrust this creature back into its den, and we can then remove Miss Stoner to some place of shelter, and let the county police know what has happened."

As he spoke he drew the dog whip swiftly from the dead man's lap, and throwing the noose round the reptile's neck, he drew it from its horrid perch, and, carrying it at arm's length, threw it into the iron safe, which he closed upon it.

Such are the true facts of the death of Dr. Grimesby Roylott, of Stoke Moran. It is not necessary that I should prolong a narrative which has already run to too great a length, by telling how we broke the sad news to the terrified girl, how we conveyed her by the morning train to the care of her good aunt at Harrow, of how the slow process of official inquiry came to the conclusion that the Doctor met his fate while indiscreetly playing with a dangerous pet. The little which I had yet to learn of the case was told me by Sherlock Holmes as we travelled back next day.

"I had," said he, "come to an entirely erroneous conclusion, which shows, my dear Watson, how dangerous it always is to reason from insufficient data. The presence of the gipsies, and the use of the word 'band', which was used by the poor girl, no doubt, to explain the appearance which she had caught a horrid glimpse of by the light of her match, were sufficient to put me upon an entirely wrong scent. I can only claim the merit that I instantly reconsidered my position when, however, it became clear to me that whatever danger threatened an occupant of the room could not come either from the window or the door. My attention was speedily drawn, as I have already remarked to you, to this ventilator, and to the bell-rope which hung down to the bed. The discovery that this was a dummy, and that the bed was clamped to the floor, instantly gave rise to the suspicion that the rope was there as a bridge for something passing through the hole, and coming to the bed. The idea of a snake instantly occurred to me, and when I coupled it with my knowledge that the Doctor was furnished with a supply of creatures from India, I felt that I was probably on the right track. The idea of using a form of poison which could not possibly be discovered by any chemical test was just such a one as would occur to a clever and ruthless man who had had an Eastern training. The rapidity with which such a poison would take effect would also, from his point of view, be an advantage. It would be a sharp-eyed coroner indeed who could distinguish the two little dark punctures which would show where the poison fangs had done their work. Then I thought of the whistle. Of course, he must recall the snake before the morning light revealed it to the victim. He had trained it, probably by the use of the milk which we saw, to return to him when summoned. He would put it through the ventilator at the hour that he thought best, with the certainty that it would crawl down the rope, and land on the bed. It might or might not bite the occupant, perhaps she might escape every night for a week, but sooner or later she must fall a victim.

"I had come to these conclusions before ever I had entered his room. An inspection of his chair showed me that he had been in the habit of standing on it, which, of course, would be necessary in order that he should reach the ventilator. The sight of the safe, the saucer of milk, and the loop of whipcord were enough to finally dispel any doubts which may have remained. The metallic clang heard by Miss Stoner was obviously caused by her father hastily closing the door of his safe upon its terrible occupant. Having once made up my mind, you know the steps which I took in order to put the matter to the proof. I heard the creature hiss, as I have no doubt that you did also, and I instantly lit the light and attacked it."

"With the result of driving it through the ventilator."

"And also with the result of causing it to turn upon its master at the other side. Some of the blows of my cane came home, and roused its snakish temper, so that it flew upon the first person it saw. In this way I am no doubt indirectly responsible for Dr. Grimesby Roylott's death, and I cannot say that it is likely to weigh very heavily upon my conscience."

THE PROBLEM OF CELL 13

(1905)

Jacques Futrelle

Jacques Futrelle

A newspaper reporter for the Boston American, *Jacques Futrelle (1875–1912) perished as a passenger on the Titanic. He is best remembered for his stories about Professor S. F. X. Van Dusen, "The Thinking Machine," one of the world's most famous analytic detectives. A good collection of these tales is* Best "Thinking Machine" Detective Stories *(1973). Strangely enough it is even possible that the near future may see additional Van Dusen manuscripts recovered from the bottom of the ocean if and when the Titanic's wreck is located. Two of his other notable crime novels are* The Diamond Master *(1909) and* My Lady's Garter *(1912).*

THE PROBLEM OF CELL 13

Practically all those letters remaining in the alphabet after Augustus S. F. X. Van Dusen was named were afterward acquired by that gentleman in the course of a brilliant scientific career, and, being honorably acquired, were tacked on to the other end. His name, therefore, taken with all that belonged to it, was a wonderfully imposing structure. He was a Ph.D., and LL.D., an F.R.S., an M.D., and an M.D.S. He was also some other things—just what he himself couldn't say—through recognition of his ability by various foreign educational and scientific institutions.

In appearance he was no less striking than in nomenclature. He was slender with the droop of the student in his thin shoulders and the pallor of a close, sedentary life on his clean-shaven face. His eyes wore a perceptual, forbidding squint—the squint of a man who studies little things—and when they could be seen at all through his thick spectacles, were mere slits of watery blue. But above his eyes was his most striking feature. This was a tall, broad brow, almost abnormal in height and width, crowned by a heavy shock of bushy, yellow hair. All these things conspired to give him a peculiar, almost grotesque, personality.

Professor Van Dusen was remotely German. For generations his ancestors had been noted in the sciences; he was the logical result, the mastermind. First and above all he was a logician. At least thirty-five years of the half century or so of his existence had been devoted exclusively to providing that two and two always equal four, except in unusual cases, where they equal three or five, as the case may be. He stood broadly on the general proposition that all things that start must go somewhere, and was able to bring the concentrated mental force of his forefathers to bear on a given problem. Incidentally it may be remarked that Professor Van Dusen wore a No. 8 hat.

The world at large had heard vaguely of Professor Van Dusen as The Thinking Machine. It was a newspaper catchphrase applied to him at the time of a remarkable exhibition at chess; he had demonstrated then that a stranger to the game might, by the force of inevitable logic, defeat a champion who had devoted a lifetime to its study. The Thinking Machine! Perhaps that more nearly described him than all his honorary initials, for he spent week after week, month after month, in the seclusion of his small laboratory from which had gone forth thoughts that staggered scientific associates and deeply stirred the world at large.

It was only occasionally that The Thinking Machine had visitors, and these were usually men who, themselves high in the sciences, dropped in to argue a point and perhaps convince themselves. Two of these men, Dr. Charles Ransome and Alfred Fielding, called one evening to discuss some theory which is not of consequence here.

"Such a thing is impossible," declared Dr. Ransome emphatically, in the course of the conversation.

"Nothing is impossible," declared The Thinking Machine with equal emphasis. He always spoke petulantly. "The mind is master of all things. When science fully recognizes that fact a great advance will have been made."

"How about the airship?" asked Dr. Ransome.

"That's not impossible at all," asserted The Thinking Machine. "It will be invented some time. I'd do it myself, but I'm busy."

Dr. Ransome laughed tolerantly.

"I've heard you say such things before," he said. "But they mean nothing. Mind may be master of matter, but is hasn't yet found a way to apply itself. There are some things that can't be *thought* out of existence, or rather which would not yield to any amount of thinking."

"What, for instance?" demanded The Thinking Machine.

Dr. Ransome was thoughtful for a moment as he smoked.

"Well, say prison walls," he replied. "No man can *think* himself out of a cell. If he could, there would be no prisoners."

"A man can so apply his brain and ingenuity that he can leave a cell, which is the same thing," snapped The Thinking Machine.

Dr. Ransome was slightly amused.

"Let's suppose a case," he said, after a moment. "Take a cell where prisoners under sentence of death are confined—men who are desperate and, maddened by fear, would take any chance to escape—suppose you were locked in such a cell. Could you escape?"

"Certainly," declared The Thinking Machine.

"Of course," said Mr. Fielding, who entered the conversation for the first time, "you might wreck the cell with an explosive—but inside, a prisoner, you couldn't have that."

"There would be nothing of that kind," said The Thinking Machine. "You might treat me precisely as you treated prisoners under sentence of death, and I would leave the cell."

"Not unless you entered it with tools prepared to get out," said Dr. Ransome.

The Thinking Machine was visibly annoyed and his blue eyes snapped.

"Lock me in any cell in any prison anywhere at any time, wearing only what is necessary, and I'll escape in a week," he declared, sharply.

Dr. Ransome sat up straight in the chair, interested. Mr. Fielding lighted a new cigar.

"You mean you could actually *think* yourself out?" asked Dr. Ransome.

"I would get out," was the response.

"Are you serious?"

"Certainly I am serious."

Dr. Ransome and Mr. Fielding were silent for a long time.

"Would you be willing to try it?" asked Mr. Fielding, finally.

"Certainly," said Professor Van Dusen, and there was a trace of irony in his voice. "I have done more asinine things than that to convince other men of less important truths."

The tone was offensive and there was an undercurrent strongly resembling anger on both sides. Of course it was an absurd thing, but Professor Van Dusen reiterated his willingness to undertake the escape and it was decided upon.

"To begin now," added Dr. Ransome.

"I'd prefer that it begin to-morrow," said The Thinking Machine, "because—"

"No, now," said Mr. Fielding, flatly. "You are arrested, figuratively, of course, without any warning locked in a cell with no chance to communicate with friends, and left there with identically the same care and attention that would be given to a man under sentence of death. Are you willing?"

"All right, now, then," said The Thinking Machine, and he arose.

"Say, the death cell in Chisholm Prison."

"The death cell in Chisholm Prison."

"And what will you wear?"

"As little as possible," said The Thinking Machine. "Shoes, stockings, trousers and a shirt."

"You will permit yourself to be searched, of course?"

"I am to be treated precisely as all prisoners are treated," said The Thinking Machine. "No more attention and no less."

There were some preliminaries to be arranged in the matter of obtaining permission for the test, but all three were influential men and everything was done satisfactorily by telephone, albeit the prison commissioners, to whom the experiment was explained on purely scientific grounds, were sadly bewildered. Professor Van Dusen would be the most distinguished prisoner they had ever entertained.

When The Thinking Machine had donned those things which he was to wear during his incarceration, he called the little old woman who was his housekeeper, cook and maidservant all in one.

"Martha," he said, "it is now twenty-seven minutes past nine o'clock. I am going away. One week from to-night, at half past nine, these gentlemen and one, possibly two, others will take supper with me here. Remember Dr. Ransome is very fond of artichokes."

The three men were driven to Chisholm Prison, where the warden was awaiting them, having been informed of the matter by telephone. He understood merely that the eminent Professor Van Dusen was to be his prisoner, if he could keep him, for one week; that he had committed no crime, but that he was to be treated as all other prisoners were treated.

"Search him," instructed Dr. Ransome.

The Thinking Machine was searched. Nothing was found on him; the pockets of the trousers were empty; the white, stiff-bosomed shirt had no pocket. The shoes and stockings were removed, examined, then replaced. As he watched all these preliminaries, and noted the pitiful, childlike physical weakness of the man—the colorless face, and the thin, white hands—Dr. Ransome almost regretted his part in the affair.

"Are you sure you want to do this?" he asked.

"Would you be convinced if I did not?" inquired The Thinking Machine in turn.

"No."

"All right. I'll do it."

What sympathy Dr. Ransome had was dissipated by the tone. It nettled him, and he resolved to see the experiment to the end; it would be a stinging reproof to egotism.

"It will be impossible for him to communicate with anyone outside?" he asked.

"Absolutely impossible," replied the warden. "He will not be permitted writing materials of any sort."

"And your jailers, would they deliver a message from him?"

"Not one word, directly or indirectly," said the warden.

"You may rest assured of that. They will report anything he might say or turn over to me, anything he might give them."

"That seems entirely satisfactory," said Mr. Fielding, who was frankly interested in the problem.

"Of course, in the event he fails," said Dr. Ransome, "and asks for his liberty, you understand you are to set him free?"

"I understand," replied the warden.

The Thinking Machine stood listening, but had nothing to say until this was all ended, then:

"I should like to make three small requests. You may grant them or not, as you wish."

"No special favors, now," warned Mr. Fielding.

"I am asking none," was the stiff response. "I should like to have some tooth powder—buy it yourself to see that it is tooth powder—and I should like to have one five-dollar and two ten-dollar bills."

Dr. Ransome, Mr. Fielding and the warden exchanged astonished glances. They were not surprised at the request for tooth powder, but were at the request for money.

"Is there any man with whom our friend would come in contact that he could bribe with twenty-five dollars?"

"Not for twenty-five hundred dollars," was the positive reply.

"Well, let him have them," said Mr. Fielding. "I think they are harmless enough."

"And what is the third request?" asked Dr. Ransome.

"I should like to have my shoes polished."

Again the astonished glances were exchanged. This last request was the height of absurdity, so they agreed to it. These things all being attended to, The Thinking Machine was led back into the prison from which he had undertaken to escape.

"Here is Cell 13," said the warden, stopping three doors down the steel corridor. "This is where we keep condemned murderers. No one can leave it without my permission; and no one in it can communicate with the outside. I'll stake my reputation on that. It's only three doors back of my office and I can readily hear any unusual noise."

"Will this cell do, gentlemen?" asked The Thinking Machine. There was a touch of irony in his voice.

"Admirably," was the reply.

The heavy steel door was thrown open, there was a great scurrrying and scampering of tiny feet, and The Thinking Machine passed into the gloom of the cell. Then the door was closed and double locked by the warden.

"What is that noise in there?" asked Dr. Ransome, through the bars.

"Rats—dozens of them," replied The Thinking Machine, tersely.

The three men, with final good nights, were turning away when The Thinking Machine called:

"What time is it exactly, Warden?"

"Eleven-seventeen," replied the warden.

"Thanks. I will join you gentlemen in your office at half past eight o'clock one week from to-night," said The Thinking Machine.

"And if you do not?"

"There is no 'if' about it."

Chisholm Prison was a great, spreading structure of granite, four stories in all, which stood in the center of acres of open space. It was surrounded by a wall of solid masonry eighteen feet high, and so smoothly finished inside and out as to offer no foothold to a climber, no matter how expert. Atop of this fence, as a further precaution, was a five-foot fence of steel rods, each terminating in a keen point. This fence in itself marked an absolute deadline between freedom and imprisonment, for, even if a man escaped from his cell, it would seem impossible for him to pass the wall.

The yard, which on all sides of the prison building was twenty-five feet wide, that being the distance from the building to the wall, was by day an exercise ground for those prisoners to whom was granted the boon of occasional semi-liberty. But that was not for those in Cell 13.

At all times of the day there were armed guards in the yard, four of them, one patrolling each side of the prison building.

By night the yard was almost as brilliantly lighted as by day. On each of the four sides was a great arc light which rose above the prison wall and gave to the guards a clear sight. The lights, too, brightly illuminated the spiked top of the wall. The wires which fed the arc lights ran up the side of the prison building on insulators and from the top story led out to the poles supporting the arc lights.

All these things were seen and comprehended by The Thinking Machine, who was only enabled to see out his closely barred cell window by standing on his bed. This was on the morning following his incarceration. He gathered, too, that the river lay over there beyond the wall somewhere, because he heard faintly the pulsation of a motor boat and high up in the air saw a river bird. From that same direction came the shouts of boys at play and the occasional crack of a batted ball. He knew then that between the prison wall and the river was an open space, a playground.

Chisholm Prison was regarded as absolutely safe. No man had ever escaped from it. The Thinking Machine, from his perch on the bed, seeing what he saw, could readily understand why. The walls of the cell, though built he judged twenty years before, were perfectly solid, and the window bars of new iron had not a shadow of rust on them. The window itself, even with the bars out, would be a difficult mode of egress because it was small.

Yet, seeing these things, The Thinking Machine was not discouraged. Instead, he thoughtfully squinted at the great arc light—there was bright sunlight now—and traced with his eyes the wire which led from it to the building. That electric wire, he reasoned, must come down the side of the building not a great distance from his cell. That might be worth knowing.

Cell 13 was on the same floor with the offices of the prison—that is, not in the basement, nor yet upstairs. There were only four steps up to the office floor, therefore the level of the floor must be only three or four feet above the ground. He couldn't see the ground directly beneath his window, but he could see it further out toward the wall. It would be an easy drop from the window. Well and good.

Then The Thinking Machine fell to remembering how he had come to the cell. First, there was the outside guard's booth, a part of the wall. There were two heavily barred gates there, both of steel. At this gate was one man always on guard. He admitted persons to the prison after much clanking of keys and locks, and let them out when ordered to do so. The warden's office was in the prison building, and in order to reach that official from the prison yard one had to pass a gate of solid steel with only a peephole in it. Then coming from that inner office to Cell 13, where he was now, one must pass a heavy wooden door and two steel doors into the corridors of the prison; and always there was the double-locked door of Cell 13 to reckon with.

There were then, The Thinking Machine recalled, seven doors to be overcome before one could pass from Cell 13 into the outer world, a free man. But against this was the fact that he was rarely interrupted. A jailer appeared at his cell door at six in the morning with a breakfast of prison fare; he would come again at noon, and again at six in the afternoon. At nine o'clock at night would come the inspection tour. That would be all.

"It's admirably arranged, this prison system," was the mental tribute paid by The Thinking Machine. "I'll have to study it a little when I get out. I had no idea there was such great care exercised in the prisons."

There was nothing, positively nothing, in his cell, except his iron bed, so firmly put together that no man could tear it to pieces save with sledges or a file. He had neither of these. There was not even a chair, or a small table, or a bit of tin or crockery. Nothing! The jailer stood by when he ate, then took away the wooden spoon and bowl which he had used.

One by one these things sank into the brain of The Thinking Machine. When the last possibility had been considered he began an examination of his cell. From the roof, down the walls on all sides, he examined the stones and the cement between them. He stamped over the floor carefully time after time, but it was cement, perfectly solid. After the examination he sat on the edge of the iron bed and was lost in thought for a long time. For Professor Augustus S. F. X. Van Dusen, The Thinking Machine, had something to think about.

He was disturbed by a rat, which ran across his foot, then scampered away into a dark corner of the cell, frightened at its own daring. After a while The Thinking Machine, squinting steadily into the darkness of the corner where the rat had gone, was able to make out in the gloom many little beady eyes staring at him. He counted six pair, and there were perhaps others; he didn't see very well.

Then The Thinking Machine, from his seat on the bed, noticed for the first time the bottom of his cell door. There was an opening there of two inches between the steel bar and floor. Still looking steadily at this opening, The Thinking Machine backed suddenly into the corner where he had seen the beady eyes. There was a great scampering of tiny feet, several squeaks of frightened rodents, and then silence.

None of the rats had gone out the door, yet there were none in the cell. Therefore there must be another way out of the cell, however small. The Thinking Machine, on hands and knees, started a search for this spot, feeling in the darkness with his long, slender fingers.

At last his search was rewarded. He came upon a small opening in the floor, level with the cement. It was perfectly round and somewhat larger than a silver dollar. This was the way the rats had gone. He put his fingers deep into the opening; it seemed to be a disused drainage pipe and was dry and dusty.

Having satisfied himself on this point, he sat on the bed again for an hour, then made another inspection of his surroundings through the small cell window. One of the outside guards stood directly opposite, beside the wall, and happened to be looking at the window of Cell 13 when the head of The Thinking Machine appeared. But the scientist didn't notice the guard.

Noon came and the jailer appeared with the prison dinner of repulsively plain food. At home The Thinking Machine merely ate to live; here he took what was offered without comment. Occasionally he spoke to the jailer who stood outside the door watching him.

"Any improvements made here in the last few years?" he asked.

"Nothing particularly," replied the jailer. "New wall was built four years ago."

"Anything done to the prison proper?"

"Painted the woodwork outside, and I believe about seven years ago a new system of plumbing was put in."

"Ah!" said the prisoner. "How far is the river over there?"

"About three hundred feet. The boys have a baseball ground between the wall and the river."

The Thinking Machine had nothing further to say just then, but when the jailer was ready to go he asked for some water.

"I get very thirsty here," he explained. "Would it be possible for you to leave a little water in a bowl for me?"

"I'll ask the warden," replied the jailer, and he went away.

Half an hour later he returned with water in a small earthen bowl.

"The warden says you may keep this bowl," he informed the

prisoner. "But you must show it to me when I ask for it. If it is broken, it will be the last."

"Thank you," said The Thinking Machine. "I shan't break it."

The jailer went on about his duties. For just the fraction of a second it seemed that The Thinking Machine wanted to ask a question, but he didn't.

Two hours later this same jailer, in passing the door of Cell No. 13, heard a noise inside and stopped. The Thinking Machine was down on his hands and knees in a corner of the cell, and from that same corner came several frightened squeaks. The jailer looked on interestedly.

"Ah, I've got you," he heard the prisoner say.

"Got what?" he asked, sharply.

"One of these rats," was the reply. "See?" And between the scientist's long fingers the jailer saw a small gray rat struggling. The prisoner brought it over to the light and looked at it closely.

"It's a water rat," he said.

"Ain't you got anything better to do than to catch rats?" asked the jailer.

"It's disgraceful that they should be here at all," was the irritated reply. "Take this one away and kill it. There are dozens more where it came from."

The jailer took the wriggling, squirmy rodent and flung it down on the floor violently. It gave one squeak and lay still. Later he reported the incident to the warden, who only smiled.

Still later that afternoon the outside armed guard on the Cell 13 side of the prison looked up again at the window and saw the prisoner looking out. He saw a hand raised to the barred window and then something white fluttered to the ground, directly under the window of Cell 13. It was a little roll of linen, evidently of white shirting material, and tied around it was a five-dollar bill. The guard looked up at the window again, but the face had disappeared.

With a grim smile he took the little linen roll and the five-dollar bill to the warden's office. There together they deciphered something which was written on it with a queer sort of ink, frequently blurred. On the outside was this:

"Finder of this please deliver to Dr. Charles Ransome."

"Ah," said the warden, with a chuckle, "Plan of escape number one has gone wrong." Then, as an afterthought: "But why did he address it to Dr. Ransome?"

"And where did he get the pen and ink to write with?" asked the guard.

The warden looked at the guard and the guard looked at the warden. There was no apparent solution of that mystery. The warden studied the writing carefully, then shook his head.

"Well, let's see what he was going to say to Dr. Ransome," he said at length, still puzzled, and he unrolled the inner piece of linen.

"Well, if that—what—what do you think of that?" he asked dazed.

The guard took the bit of linen and read this:—

"Epa cseot d'net niiy awe htto n'si sih. T."

The warden spent an hour wondering what sort of a cipher it was, and half an hour wondering why his prisoner should attempt to communicate with Dr. Ransome, who was the cause of his being there. After this the warden devoted some thought to the question of where the prisoner got writing materials, and what sort of writing materials he had. With the idea of illuminating this point, he examined the linen again. It was a torn part of a white shirt and had ragged edges.

Now it was possible to account for the linen, but what the prisoner had used to write with was another matter. The warden knew it would have been impossible for him to have either pen or pencil, and, besides, neither pen nor pencil had been used in this writing. What, then? The warden decided to investigate personally. The Thinking Machine was his prisoner; he had orders to hold his prisoners; if this one sought to escape by sending cipher messages to persons outside, he would stop it, as he would have stopped it in the case of any other prisoner.

The warden went back to Cell 13 and found The Thinking Machine on his hands and knees on the floor, engaged in nothing more alarming than catching rats. The prisoner heard the warden's step and turned to him quickly.

"It's disgraceful," he snapped, "these rats. There are scores of them."

"Other men have been able to stand them," said the warden. "Here is another shirt for you—let me have the one you have on."

"Why?" demanded The Thinking Machine, quickly. His tone was hardly natural, his manner suggested actual perturbation.

"You have attempted to communicate with Dr. Ransome," said the warden severely. "As my prisoner, it is my duty to put a stop to it."

The Thinking Machine was silent for a moment.

"All right," he said, finally. "Do your duty."

The warden smiled grimly. The prisoner arose from the floor and removed the white shirt, putting on instead a striped convict shirt the warden had brought. The warden took the white shirt eagerly, and then and there compared the pieces of linen on which was written the cipher with certain torn places in the shirt. The Thinking Machine looked on curiously.

"The guard brought *you* those, then?" he asked.

"He certainly did," replied the warden triumphantly. "And that ends your first attempt to escape."

The Thinking Machine watched the warden as he, by comparison, established to his own satisfaction that only two pieces of linen had been torn from the white shirt.

"What did you write this with?" demanded the warden.

"I should think it a part of your duty to find out," said The Thinking Machine, irritably.

The warden started to say some harsh things, then restrained himself and made a minute search of the cell and of the prisoner instead. He found absolutely nothing; not even a match or toothpick which might have been used for a pen. The same mystery surrounded the fluid with which the cipher had been written. Although the warden left Cell 13 visibly annoyed, he took the torn shirt in triumph.

"Well, writing notes on a shirt won't get him out, that's certain," he told himself with some complacency. He put the linen scraps into his desk to await developments. "If that man escapes from that cell I'll—hang it—I'll resign."

On the third day of his incarceration The Thinking Machine openly attempted to bribe his way out. The jailer had brought his dinner and was leaning against the barred door, waiting, when The Thinking Machine began the conversation.

"The drainage pipes of the prison lead to the river, don't they?" he asked.

"Yes," said the jailer.

"I suppose they are very small."

"Too small to crawl through, if that's what you're thinking about," was the grinning response.

There was silence until The Thinking Machine finished his meal. Then:

"You know I'm not a criminal, don't you?"

"Yes."

"And that I've a perfect right to be freed if I demand it?"

"Yes."

"Well, I came here believing that I could make my escape," said the prisoner, and his squint eyes studied the face of the jailer. "Would you consider a financial reward for aiding me to escape?"

The jailer, who happened to be an honest man, looked at the slender, weak figure of the prisoner, at the large head with its mass of yellow hair, and was almost sorry.

"I guess prisons like these were not built for the likes of you to get out of," he said, at last.

"But would you consider a proposition to help me get out?" the prisoner insisted, almost beseechingly.

"No," said the jailer, shortly.

"Five hundred dollars," urged The Thinking Machine. "I am not a criminal."

"No," said the jailer.

"A thousand?"

"No," again said the jailer, and he started away hurriedly to escape further temptation. Then he turned back. "If you should give me ten thousand dollars I couldn't get you out. You'd have to pass through seven doors, and I only have the keys to two."

Then he told the warden all about it.

"Plan number two fails," said the warden, smiling grimly. "First a cipher, then bribery."

When the jailer was on his way to Cell 13 at six o'clock, again bearing food to The Thinking Machine, he paused, startled by the unmistakable scrape, scrape of steel against steel. It stopped at the sound of his steps, then craftily the jailer, who was beyond the prisoner's range of vision, resumed his tramping, the sound being apparently that of a man going away from Cell 13. As a matter of fact he was in the same spot.

After a moment there came again the steady scrape, scrape, and the jailer crept cautiously on tiptoes to the door and peered between the bars. The Thinking Machine was standing on the iron bed working at the bars of the little window. He was using a file, judging from the backward and forward swing of his arms.

Cautiously the jailer crept back to the office, summoned the warden in person, and they returned to Cell 13 on tiptoes. The steady scrape was still audible. The warden listened to satisfy himself and then suddenly appeared at the door.

"Well?" he demanded, and there was a smile on his face.

The Thinking Machine glanced back from his perch on the bed and leaped suddenly to the floor, making frantic efforts to hide something. The warden went in, with hand extended.

"Give it up," he said.

"No," said the prisoner, sharply.

"Come, give it up," urged the warden. "I don't want to have to search you again."

"No," repeated the prisoner.

"What was it—a file?" asked the warden.

The Thinking Machine was silent and stood squinting at the warden with something very nearly approaching disappointment on his face—nearly, but not quite. The warden was almost sympathetic.

"Plan number three fails, eh?" he asked, good-naturedly. "Too bad, isn't it?"

The prisoner didn't say.

"Search him," instructed the warden.

The jailer searched the prisoner carefully. At last, artfully concealed in the waistband of the trousers, he found a piece of steel about two inches long, with one side curved like a half moon.

"Ah," said the warden, as he received it from the jailer. "From your shoe heel," and he smiled pleasantly.

The jailer continued his search and on the other side of the trousers waistband found another piece of steel identical with the first. The edges showed where they had been worn against the bars of the window.

"You couldn't saw a way through those bars with these," said the warden.

"I could have," said The Thinking Machine firmly.

"In six months, perhaps," said the warden, good-naturedly.

The warden shook his head slowly as he gazed into the slightly flushed face of his prisoner.

"Ready to give it up?" he asked.

"I haven't started yet," was the prompt reply.

Then came another exhaustive search of the cell. Carefully the two men went over it, finally turning out the bed and searching that. Nothing. The warden in person climbed upon the bed and examined the bars of the window where the prisoner had been sawing. When he looked he was amused.

"Just made it a little bright by hard rubbing," he said to the prisoner, who stood looking on with a somewhat crestfallen air. The warden grasped the iron bars in his strong hands and tried to shake them. They were immovable, set firmly in the solid granite. He examined each in turn and found them all satisfactory. Finally he climbed down from the bed.

"Give it up, Professor," he advised.

The Thinking Machine shook his head and the warden and jailer passed on again. As they disappeared down the corridor The Thinking Machine sat on the edge of the bed with his head in his hands.

"He's crazy to try to get out of that cell," commented the jailer.

"Of course he can't get out," said the warden. "But he's clever. I would like to know what he wrote that cipher with."

It was four o'clock next morning when an awful, heartracking shriek of terror resounded through the great prison. It came from a cell, somewhere about the center, and its tone told a tale of horror, agony, terrible fear. The warden heard and with three of his men rushed into the long corridor leading to Cell 13.

As they ran there came again that awful cry. It died away in a sort of wail. The white faces of prisoners appeared at cell doors upstairs and down, staring out wonderingly, frightened.

"It's that fool in Cell 13," grumbled the warden.

He stopped and stared in as one of the jailers flashed a lantern. "That fool in Cell 13 " lay comfortably on his cot, flat on his back with his mouth open, snoring. Even as they looked there came again the piercing cry, from somewhere above. The warden's face blanched a little as he started up the stairs. There on the top floor he found a man in Cell 43, directly above Cell 13, but two floors higher, cowering in a corner of his cell.

"What's the matter?" demanded the warden.

"Thank God you've come," exclaimed the prisoner, and he cast himself against the bars of his cell.

"What is it?" demanded the warden again.

He threw open the door and went in. The prisoner dropped on his knees and clasped the warden about the body. His face was white with terror, his eyes were widely distended, and he was shuddering. His hands, icy cold, clutched at the warden's.

"Take me out of this cell, please take me out," he pleaded.

"What's the matter with you, anyhow?" insisted the warden, impatiently.

"I heard something—something," said the prisoner, and his eyes roved nervously around the cell.

"What did you hear?"

"I—I can't tell you," stammered the prisoner. Then, in a sudden burst of terror: "Take me out of this cell—put me anywhere—but take me out of here."

The warden and the three jailers exchanged glances.

"Who is this fellow? What's he accused of?" asked the warden.

"Joseph Ballard," said one of the jailers. "He's accused of throwing acid in a woman's face. She died from it."

"But they can't prove it," gasped the prisoner. "They can't prove it. Please put me in some other cell."

He was still clinging to the warden, and that official threw his arms off roughly. Then for a time he stood looking at the cowering wretch, who seemed possessed of all the wild, unreasoning terror of a child.

"Look here, Ballard," said the warden, finally, "if you heard anything, I want to know what it was. Now tell me."

"I can't, I can't," was the reply. He was sobbing.

"Where did it come from?"

"I don't know. Everywhere—nowhere. I just heard it."

"What was it—a voice?"

"Please don't make me answer," pleaded the prisoner.

"You must answer," said the warden, sharply.

"It was a voice—but—but it wasn't human," was the sobbing reply.

"Voice, but not human?" repeated the warden, puzzled.

"It sounded muffled and—and far away—and ghostly," explained the man.

"Did it come from inside or outside the prison?"

"It didn't seem to come from anywhere—it was just here, here, everywhere. I heard it. I heard it."

For an hour the warden tried to get the story, but Ballard had become suddenly obstinate and would say nothing—only pleaded to be placed in another cell, or to have one of the jailers remain near him until daylight. These requests were gruffly refused.

"And see here," said the warden, in conclusion, "if there's any more of this screaming I'll put you in the padded cell."

Then the warden went his way, a sadly puzzled man. Ballard sat at his cell door until daylight, his face, drawn and white with terror, pressed against the bars, and looked out into the prison with wide, staring eyes.

That day, the fourth since the incarceration of The Thinking Machine, was enlivened considerably by the volunteer prisoner, who spent most of his time at the little window of his cell. He began proceedings by throwing another piece of linen down to the guard, who picked it up dutifully and took it to the warden. On it was written:

"Only three days more."

The warden was in no way surprised at what he read; he understood that The Thinking Machine meant only three days more of his imprisonment, and he regarded the note as a boast. But how was the thing written? Where had The Thinking Machine found this new piece of linen? Where? How? He carefully examined the linen. It was white, of fine texture, shirting material. He took the shirt which he had taken and carefully fitted the two original pieces of the linen to the torn places. This third piece was entirely superfluous; it didn't fit anywhere, and yet it was unmistakably the same goods.

"And where—where does he get anything to write with?" demanded the warden of the world at large.

Still later on the fourth day The Thinking Machine, through the window of his cell, spoke to the armed guard outside.

"What day of the month is it?" he asked.

"The fifteenth," was the answer.

The Thinking Machine made a mental astronomical calculation and satisfied himself that the moon would not rise until after nine o'clock that night. Then he asked another question:

"Who attends to those arc lights?"

"Man from the company."

"You have no electricians in the building?"

"No."

"I should think you could save money if you had your own man."

"None of my business," replied the guard.

The guard noticed The Thinking Machine at the cell window frequently during that day, but always the face seemed listless and there was a certain wistfulness in the squint eyes behind the glasses. After a while he accepted the presence of the leonine head as a matter of course. He had seen other prisoners do the same thing; it was the longing for the outside world.

That afternoon, just before the day guard was relieved, the head appeared at the window again, and The Thinking Machine's hand held something out between the bars. It fluttered to the ground and the guard picked it up. It was a five-dollar bill.

"That's for you," called the prisoner.

As usual, the guard took it to the warden. That gentleman looked at it suspiciously; he looked at everything that came from Cell 13 with suspicion.

"He said it was for me," explained the guard.

"It's a sort of a tip, I suppose," said the warden. "I see no particular reason why you shouldn't accept—"

Suddenly he stopped. He had remembered that The Thinking Machine had gone into Cell 13 with one five-dollar bill and two ten-dollar bills; twenty-five dollars in all. Now a five-dollar bill had been tied around the first pieces of linen that came from the cell. The warden still had it, and to convince himself he took it out and looked at it. It was five dollars; yet here was another five dollars, and The Thinking Machine had only had ten-dollar bills.

"Perhaps somebody changed one of the bills for him," he thought at last, with a sigh of relief.

But then and there he made up his mind. He would search Cell 13 as a cell was never before searched in this world. When a man could write at will, and change money, and do other wholly inexplicable things, there was something radically wrong with his prison. He planned to enter the cell at night—three o'clock would be an excellent time. The Thinking Machine must do all the weird things he did sometime. Night seemed the most reasonable.

Thus it happened that the warden stealthily descended upon Cell 13 that night at three o'clock. He paused at the door and listened. There was no sound save the steady, regular breathing of the prisoner. The keys unfastened the double locks with scarcely a clank, and the warden entered, locking the door behind him. Suddenly he flashed his dark lantern in the face of the recumbent figure.

If the warden had planned to startle The Thinking Machine he was mistaken, for that individual merely opened his eyes quietly, reached for his glasses and inquired, in a most matter-of-fact tone: "Who is it?"

It would be useless to describe the search that the warden made. It was minute. Not one inch of the cell or the bed was overlooked. He found the round hole in the floor, and with a flash of inspiration thrust his thick fingers into it. After a moment of fumbling there he drew up something and looked at it in the light of his lantern.

"Ugh!" he exclaimed.

The thing he had taken out was a rat—a dead rat. His inspiration fled as a mist before the sun. But he continued the search. The Thinking Machine, without a word, arose and kicked the rat out of the cell into the corridor.

The warden climbed on the bed and tried the steel bars in the tiny window. They were perfectly rigid; every bar of the door was the same.

Then the warden searched the prisoner's clothing, beginning at the shoes. Nothing hidden in them! Then the trousers waistband. Still nothing! Then the pockets of the trousers. From one side he drew out some paper money and examined it.

"Five one-dollar bills," he gasped.

"That's right," said the prisoner.

"But the—you had two tens and a five—what the—how do you do it?"

"That's my business," said The Thinking Machine.

"Did any of my men change this money for you—on your word of honor?"

The Thinking Machine paused just a fraction of a second.

"No," he said.

"Well, do you make it?" asked the warden. He was prepared to believe anything.

"That's my business," again said the prisoner.

The warden glared at the eminent scientist fiercely. He felt—he knew—that this man was making a fool of him, yet he didn't know how. If he were a real prisoner he would get the truth—but, then, perhaps, those inexplicable things which had happened would not have been brought before him so sharply. Neither of the men spoke for a long time, then suddenly the warden turned fiercely and left the cell, slamming the door behind him. He didn't dare to speak then.

He glanced at the clock. It was ten minutes to four. He had hardly settled himself in bed when again came that heart-breaking shriek through the prison. With a few muttered words, which, while not elegant, were highly expressive, he relighted his lantern and rushed through the prison again to the cell on the upper floor.

Again Ballard was crushing himself against the steel door, shrieking, shrieking at the top of his voice. He stopped only when the warden flashed his lamp in the cell.

"Take me out, take me out," he screamed. "I did it, I did it, I killed her. Take it away."

"Take what away?" asked the warden.

"I threw the acid in her face—I did it—I confess. Take me out of here."

Ballard's condition was pitiable; it was only an act of mercy to let him out into the corridor. There he crouched in a corner, like an animal at bay, and clasped his hands to his ears. It took half an hour to calm him sufficiently for him to speak. Then he told incoherently what had happened. On the night before at four o'clock he had heard a voice—a sepulchral voice, muffled and wailing in tone.

"What did it say?" asked the warden, curiously.

"Acid—acid—acid!" gasped the prisoner. "It accused me. Acid! I threw the acid, and the woman died. Oh!" It was a long, shuddering wail of terror.

"Acid?" echoed the warden, puzzled. The case was beyond him.

"Acid. That's all I heard—that one word, repeated several times. There were other things, too, but I didn't hear them."

"That was last night, eh?" asked the warden. "What happened to-night—what frightened you just now?"

"It was the same thing," gasped the prisoner. "Acid—acid—acid!" He covered his face with his hands and sat shivering. "It was acid I used on her, but I didn't mean to kill her. I just heard the words. It was something accusing me—accusing me." He mumbled, and was silent.

"Did you hear anything else?"

"Yes—but I couldn't understand—only a little bit—just a word or two."

"Well, what was it?"

"I heard 'acid' three times, then I heard a long, moaning sound, then—then—I heard 'No. 8 hat.' I heard that twice."

"No. 8 hat," repeated the warden. "What the devil—No. 8 hat? Accusing voices of conscience have never talked about No. 8 hats, so far as I ever heard."

"He's insane," said one of the jailers, with an air of finality.

"I believe you," said the warden. "He must be. He probably heard something and got frightened. He's trembling now. No. 8 hat! What the—"

When the fifth day of The Thinking Machine's imprisonment rolled around the warden was wearing a hunted look. He was anxious for the end of the thing. He could not help but feel that his distinguished prisoner had been amusing himself. And if this were so, The Thinking Machine had lost none of his sense of humor. For on this fifth day he flung down another linen note to the outside guard, bearing the words: "Only two days more." Also he flung down half a dollar.

Now the warden knew—he *knew*—that the man in Cell 13 didn't have any half dollars—he *couldn't* have any half dollars, no more than he could have pen and ink and linen, and yet he did have them. It was a condition, not a theory; that is one reason why the warden was wearing a hunted look.

That ghastly, uncanny thing, too, about "Acid" and "No. 8 hat" clung to him tenaciously. They didn't mean anything, of course, merely the ravings of an insane murderer who had been driven by fear to confess his crime, still there were so many things that "didn't mean anything" happening in the prison now since The Thinking Machine was there.

On the sixth day the warden received a card stating that Dr. Ransome and Mr. Fielding would be at Chisholm Prison on the following evening, Thursday, and in the event Professor Van Dusen had not yet escaped—and they presumed he had not because they had not heard from him—they would meet him there.

"In the event he had not yet escaped!" The warden smiled grimly. Escaped!

The Thinking Machine enlivened this day for the warden with three notes. They were on the usual linen and bore generally on the appointment at half past eight o'clock Thursday night, which appointment the scientist had made at the time of his imprisonment.

On the afternoon of the seventh day the warden passed Cell 13 and glanced in. The Thinking Machine was lying on the iron bed, apparently sleeping lightly. The cell appeared precisely as it always did from a casual glance. The warden would swear that no man was going to leave it between that hour—it was then four o'clock—and half past eight o'clock that evening.

On his way back past the cell the warden heard the steady breathing again, and coming close to the door looked in. He wouldn't have done so if The Thinking Machine had been looking, but now—well, it was different.

A ray of light came through the high window and fell on the face of the sleeping man. It occurred to the warden for the first time that his prisoner appeared haggard and weary. Just then The Thinking Machine stirred slightly and the warden hurried on up the corridor guiltily. That evening after six o'clock he saw the jailer.

"Everything all right in Cell 13?" he asked.

"Yes, sir," replied the jailer. "He didn't eat much, though."

It was with a feeling of having done his duty that the warden received Dr. Ransome and Mr. Fielding shortly after seven o'clock. He intended to show them the linen notes and lay before them the full story of his woes, which was a long one. But before this came to pass the guard from the river side of the prison yard entered the office.

"The arc light in my side of the yard won't light," he informed the warden.

"Confound it, that man's a hoodoo," thundered the official. "Everything has happened since he's been here."

The guard went back to his post in the darkness, and the warden phoned to the electric light company.

"This is Chisholm Prison," he said through the phone. "Send three or four men down here quick, to fix an arc light."

The reply was evidently satisfactory, for the warden hung up the receiver and passed out into the yard. While Dr. Ransome and Mr. Fielding sat waiting, the guard at the outer gate came in with a special-delivery letter. Dr. Ransome happened to notice the address, and, when the guard went out, looked at the letter more closely.

"By George!" he exclaimed.

"What is it?" asked Mr. Fielding.

Silently the doctor offered the letter. Mr. Fielding examined it closely.

"Coincidence," he said. "It must be."

It was nearly eight o'clock when the warden returned to his office. The electricians had arrived in a wagon, and were now at work. The warden pressed the buzz-button communicating with the man at the outer gate in the wall.

"How many electricians came in?" he asked, over the short phone. "Four? Three workmen in jumpers and overalls and the manager? Frock coat and silk hat? All right. Be certain that only four go out. That's all."

He turned to Dr. Ransome and Mr. Fielding.

"We have to be careful here—particularly," and there was broad sarcasm in his tone, "since we have scientists locked up."

The warden picked up the special delivery letter carelessly, and then began to open it.

"When I read this I want to tell you gentlemen something about how—Great Caesar!" he ended, suddenly, as he glanced at the letter. He sat with mouth open, motionless, from astonishment.

"What is it?" asked Mr. Fielding.

"A special delivery letter from Cell 13," gasped the warden. "An invitation to supper."

"What?" and the two others arose, unanimously.

The warden sat dazed, staring at the letter for a moment, then called sharply to a guard outside the corridor.

"Run down to Cell 13 and see if that man's in there."

The guard went as directed, while Dr. Ransome and Mr. Fielding examined the letter.

"It's Van Dusen's handwriting; there's no question of that," said Dr. Ransome. "I've seen too much of it."

Just then the buzz on the telephone from the outer gate sounded, and the warden, in a semi-trance, picked up the receiver.

"Hello! Two reporters, eh? Let 'em come in." He turned suddenly to the doctor and Mr. Fielding. "Why; the man *can't* be out. He must be in his cell."

Just at that moment the guard returned.

"He's still in his cell, sir," he reported, "I saw him. He's lying down."

"There, I told you so," said the warden, and he breathed freely again. "But how did he mail that letter?"

There was a rap on the steel door which led from the jail yard into the warden's office.

"It's the reporters," said the warden. "Let them in," he instructed the guard; then to the two other gentlemen: "Don't say anything about this before them, because I'd never hear the last of it."

The door opened, and the two men from the front gate entered.

"Good-evening, gentlemen," said one. that was Hutchinson Hatch; the warden knew him well.

"Well?" demanded the other, irritably. "I'm here."

That was The Thinking Machine.

He squinted belligerently at the warden, who sat with mouth agape. For the moment that official had nothing to say. Dr. Ransome and Mr. Fielding were amazed, but they didn't know what the warden knew. They were only amazed; he was paralyzed. Hutchinson Hatch, the reporter, took in the scene with greedy eyes.

"How—how—how did you do it?" gasped the warden, finally.

"Come back to the cell," said The Thinking Machine, in the irritated voice which his scientific associates knew so well.

The warden, still in a condition bordering on trance, led the way.

"Flash your light in there," directed The Thinking Machine.

The warden did so. There was nothing unusual in the appearance of the cell, and there—there on the bed lay the figure of The Thinking Machine. Certainly! There was the yellow hair! Again the warden looked at the man beside him and wondered at the strangeness of his own dreams.

With trembling hands he unlocked the cell door and The Thinking Machine passed inside.

"See here," he said.

He kicked at the steel bars in the bottom of the cell door and three of them were pushed out of place. A fourth broke off and rolled away in the corridor.

"And here, too," directed the erstwhile prisoner as he stood on the bed to reach the small window. He swept his hand across the opening and every bar came out.

"What's this in bed?" demanded the warden, who was slowly recovering.

"A wig," was the reply. "Turn down the cover."

The warden did so. Beneath it lay a large coil of strong rope, thirty feet or more, a dagger, three files, ten feet of electric wire, a thin, powerful pair of steel pliers, a small tack hammer with its handle, and—and a derringer pistol.

"How did you do it?" demanded the warden.

"You gentlemen have an engagement to supper with me at half past nine o'clock," said The Thinking Machine. "Come on, or we shall be late."

"But how did you do it?" insisted the warden.

"Don't ever think you can hold any man who can use his brain," said The Thinking Machine. "Come on; we shall be late."

It was an impatient supper party in the rooms of Professor Van Dusen and a somewhat silent one. The guests were Dr. Ransome, Alfred Fielding, the warden, and Hutchinson Hatch, reporter. The meal was served to the minute, in accordance with Professor Van Dusen's instructions of one week before; Dr. Ransome found the artichokes delicious. At last the supper was finished and The Thinking Machine turned on Dr. Ransome and squinted at him fiercely.

"Do you believe it now?" he demanded.

"I do," replied Dr. Ransome.

"Do you admit that it was a fair test?"

"I do."

With the others, particularly the warden, he was waiting anxiously for the explanation.

"Suppose you tell us how—" began Mr. Fielding.

"Yes, tell us how," said the warden.

The Thinking Machine readjusted his glasses, took a couple of preparatory squints at his audience, and began the story. He told it from the beginning logically; and no man ever talked to more interested listeners.

"My agreement was," he began, "to go into a cell, carrying nothing except what was necessary to wear, and to leave that cell within a week. I had never seen Chisholm Prison. When I went into the cell I asked for tooth powder, two ten- and one five-dollar bills, and also to have my shoes blacked. Even if these requests had been refused it would not have mattered seriously. But you agreed to them.

"I knew there would be nothing in the cell which you thought I might use to advantage. So when the warden locked the door on me I was apparently helpless, unless I could turn three seemingly innocent things to use. They were things which would have been permitted any prisoner under sentence of death, were they not, warden?"

"Tooth powder and polished shoes, yes, but not money," replied the warden.

"Anything is dangerous in the hands of a man who knows how to use it," went on The Thinking Machine. "I did nothing that first night but sleep and chase rats." He glared at the warden. "When the matter was broached I knew I could do nothing that night, so suggested next day. You gentlemen thought I wanted time to arrange an escape with outside assistance, but this was not true. I knew I could communicate with whom I pleased, when I pleased."

The warden stared at him a moment, then went on smoking solemnly.

"I was aroused next morning at six o'clock by the jailer with my breakfast," continued the scientist. "He told me dinner was at twelve and supper at six. Between these times, I gathered, I would be pretty much to myself. So immediately after breakfast I examined my outside surroundings from my cell window. One look told me it would be useless to try to scale the wall, even should I decide to leave my cell by the window, for my purpose was to leave not only the cell, but the prison. Of course, I could have gone over the wall, but it would have taken me longer to lay my plans that way. Therefore, for the moment, I dismissed all idea of that.

"From this first observation I knew the river was on that side of the prison, and that there was also a playground there. Subsequently these surmises were verified by a keeper. I knew then one important thing—that anyone might approach the prison wall from that side if necessary without attracting any particular attention. That was well to remember. I remembered it.

"But the outside thing which most attracted my attention was the feed wire to the arc light which ran within a few feet—probably three or four—of my cell window. I knew that would be valuable in the event I found it necessary to cut off that arc light."

"Oh, you shut it off to-night, then?" asked the warden.

"Having learned all I could from that window," resumed The Thinking Machine, without heeding the interruption, "I considered the idea of escaping through the prison proper. I recalled just how I had come into the cell, which I knew would be the only way. Seven doors lay between me and the outside. So, also for the time being, I gave up the idea of escaping that way. And I couldn't go through the solid granite walls of the cell."

The Thinking Machine paused for a moment and Dr. Ransome lighted a new cigar. For several minutes there was silence, then the scientific jailbreaker went on:

"While I was thinking about these things a rat ran across my foot. It suggested a new line of thought. There were at least half a dozen rats in the cell—I could see their beady eyes. Yet I had noticed none come under the cell door. I frightened them purposely and watched the cell door to see if they went out that way. They did not, but they were gone. Obviously they went another way. Another way meant another opening.

"I searched for this opening and found it. It was an old drain pipe, long unused and partly choked with dirt and dust. But this was the way the rats had come. They came from somewhere. Where? Drain pipes usually lead outside prison grounds. This one probably led to the river, or near it. The rats must therefore come from that direction. If they came a part of the way, I reasoned that they came all the way, because it was extremely unlikely that a solid iron or lead pipe would have any hole in it except at the exit.

"When the jailer came with my luncheon he told me two important things, although he didn't know it. One was that a new system of plumbing had been put in the prison seven years before; another that the river was only three hundred feet away. Then I knew positively that the pipe was a part of an old system; I knew, too, that it slanted generally toward the river. But did the pipe end in the water or on land?

"This was the next question to be decided. I decided it by catching several of the rats in the cell. My jailer was surprised to see me engaged in this work. I examined at least a dozen of them. They were perfectly dry; they had come through the pipe, and, most important of all, they were *not house rats, but field rats*. The other end of the pipe was on land, then, outside the prison walls. So far, so good.

"Then, I knew that if I worked freely from this point I must attract the warden's attention in another direction. You see, by telling the warden that I had come there to escape you made the test more severe, because I had to trick him by false scents."

The warden looked up with a sad expression in his eyes.

"The first thing was to make him think I was trying to communicate with you, Dr. Ransome. So I wrote a note on a piece of linen I tore from my shirt, addressed it to Dr. Ransome, tied a five-dollar bill around it and threw it out the window. I knew the guard would take it to the warden, but I rather hoped the warden would send it as addressed. Have you that first linen note, warden?"

The warden produced the cipher.

"What the deuce does it mean, anyhow?" he asked.

"Read it backward, beginning with the "T" signature and disregard the division into words," instructed The Thinking Machine.

The warden did so. *T-h-i-s,* this," he spelled, studied it for a moment, then read it off, grinning:

"This is not the way I intend to escape."

"Well, now what do you think o' that?" he demanded, still grinning.

"I knew that would attract your attention, just as it did," said The Thinking Machine, "and if you really found out what it was it would be a sort of gentle rebuke."

"What did you write it with?" asked Dr. Ransome, after he had examined the linen and passed it to Mr. Fielding.

"This," said the erstwhile prisoner, and he extended his foot. On it was the shoe he had worn in prison, though the polish was gone—scraped off clean. "The shoe blacking, moistened with water, was my ink; the metal tip of the shoe lace made a fairly good pen."

The warden looked up and suddenly burst into a laugh, half of relief, half of amusement.

"You're a wonder," he said, admiringly. "Go on."

"That precipitated a search of my cell by the warden, as I had intended," continued The Thinking Machine. "I was anxious to get the warden into the habit of searching my cell, so that finally, constantly finding nothing, he would get disgusted and quit. This at last happened, practically."

The warden blushed.

"He then took my white shirt away and gave me a prison shirt. He was satisfied that those two pieces of the shirt were all that was missing. But while he was searching my cell I had another piece of that same shirt, about nine inches square, rolled up into a small ball in my mouth."

"Nine inches of that shirt?" demanded the warden. "Where did it come from?"

"The bosoms of all stiff white shirts are of triple thickness," was the explanation. "I tore out the inside thickness, leaving the bosom only two thicknesses. I knew you wouldn't see it. So much for that."

There was a little pause, and the warden looked from one to another of the men with a sheepish grin.

"Having disposed of the warden for the time being by giving him something else to think about, I took my first serious step toward freedom," said Professor Van Dusen. "I knew, within reason, that the pipe led somewhere to the playground outside; I knew a great many boys played there; I knew the rats came into my cell from out there. Could I communicate with some one outside with these things at hand?

"First was necessary, I saw, a long and fairly reliable thread, so— but here," he pulled up his trousers legs and showed that the tops of both stockings, of fine, strong lisle, were gone. "I unraveled those— after I got them started it wasn't difficult—and I had easily a quarter of a mile of thread that I could depend on.

"Then on half of my remaining linen I wrote, laboriously enough I assure you, a letter explaining my situation to this gentleman here," and he indicated Hutchinson Hatch. "I knew he would assist me—for the value of the newspaper story. I tied firmly to this linen letter a ten-dollar bill—there is no surer way of attracting the eye of anyone—and wrote on the linen: 'Finder of this deliver to Hutchinson Hatch, *Daily American,* who will give another ten dollars for the information.'

"The next thing was to get this note outside on that playground where a boy might find it. There were two ways, but I chose the best. I took one of the rats—I became adept in catching them—tied the linen and money firmly to one leg, fastened my lisle thread to another, and turned him loose in the drain pipe. I reasoned that the natural fright of the rodent would make him run until he was outside the pipe and then out on earth he would probably stop to gnaw off the linen and money.

"From the moment the rat disappeared into that dusty pipe I became anxious. I was taking so many chances. The rat might gnaw the string, of which I held one end; other rats might gnaw it; the rat might run out of the pipe and leave the linen and money where they would never be found; a thousand other things might have happened. So began some nervous hours, but the fact that the rat ran on until only a few feet of the string remained in my cell made me think he was outside the pipe. I had carefully instructed Mr. Hatch what to do in case the note reached him. The question was: Would it reach him?

"This done, I could only wait and make other plans in case this one failed. I openly attempted to bribe my jailer, and learned from him that he held the keys to only two of seven doors between me and freedom. Then I did something else to make the warden nervous. I took the steel supports out of the heels of my shoes and made a pretense of sawing the bars of my cell window.The warden raised a pretty row about that. He developed, too, the habit of shaking the bars of my cell window to see if they were solid. They were—then."

Again the warden grinned. He had ceased being astonished.

"With this one plan I had done all I could and could only wait to see what happened," the scientist went on. "I couldn't know whether my note had been delivered or even found, or whether the mouse had gnawed it up. And I didn't dare to draw back through the pipe that one slender thread which connected me with the outside.

"When I went to bed that night I didn't sleep, for fear there would come the slight signal twitch at the thread which was to tell me that Mr. Hatch had received the note. At half past three o'clock, I judge, I felt this twitch, and no prisoner actually under sentence of death ever welcomed a thing more heartily."

The Thinking Machine stopped and turned to the reporter.

"You'd better explain just what you did," he said.

"The linen note was brought to me by a small boy who had been playing baseball," said Mr. Hatch. "I immediately saw a big story in it, so I gave the boy another ten dollars, and got several spools of silk, some twine, and a roll of light, pliable wire. The professor's note suggested that I have the finder of the note show me just where it was picked up, and told me to make my search from there, beginning at two o'clock in the morning. If I found the other end of the thread, I was to twitch it gently three times, then a fourth.

"I began the search with a small-bulb electric light. It was an hour and twenty minutes before I found the end of the drain pipe, half hidden in weeds. The pipe was very large there, say twelve inches across. Then I found the end of the lisle thread, twitched it as directed and immediately I got an answering twitch.

"Then I fastened the silk to this and Professor Van Dusen began to pull it into his cell. I nearly had heart disease for fear the string would break. To the end of the silk I fastened the twine, and when that had been pulled in I tied on the wire. Then that was drawn into the pipe and we had a substantial line, which rats couldn't gnaw, from the mouth of the drain into the cell."

The Thinking Machine raised his hand and Hatch stopped.

"All this was done in absolute silence," said the scientist. "But when the wire reached my hand I could have shouted. Then we tried another experiment, which Mr. Hatch was prepared for. I tested the pipe as a speaking tube. Neither of us could hear very clearly, but I dared not speak loud for fear of attracting attention in the prison. At last I made him understand what I wanted immediately. He seemed to have great difficulty in understanding when I asked for nitric acid, and I repeated the word 'acid' several times.

"Then I heard a shriek from a cell above me. I knew instantly that someone had overheard, and when I heard you coming, Mr. Warden, I feigned sleep. If you had entered my cell at that moment that whole plan of escape would have ended there. But you passed on. That was the nearest I ever came to being caught.

"Having established this improvised trolley it is easy to see how I got things in the cell and made them disappear at will. I merely dropped them back into the pipe. You, Mr. Warden, could not have reached the connecting wire with your fingers; they are too large. My fingers, you see, are longer and more slender. In addition I guarded the top of that pipe with a rat—you remember how."

"I remember," said the warden, with a grimace.

"I thought that if anyone were tempted to investigate that hole the rat would dampen his ardor. Mr. Hatch could not send me anything useful through the pipe until next night, although he did send me change for ten dollars as a test, so I proceeded with other parts of my plan. Then I evolved the method of escape which I finally employed.

"In order to carry this out successfully it was necessary for the guard in the yard to get accustomed to seeing me at the cell window. I arranged this by dropping linen notes to him, boastful in tone, to make the warden believe, if possible, one of his assistants was communicating with the outside for me. I would stand at my window for hours gazing out, so the guard could see, and occasionally I spoke to him. In that way I learned that the prison had no electricians of its own, but was dependent upon the lighting company if anything should go wrong.

"That cleared the way to freedom perfectly. Early in the evening of the last day of my imprisonment, when it was dark, I planned to cut the feed wire which was only a few feet from my window, reaching it with an acid-tipped wire I had. That would make that side of the prison perfectly dark while the electricians were searching for the break. That would also bring Mr. Hatch into the prison yard.

"There was only one more thing to do before I actually began the work of setting myself free. This was to arrange final details with Mr. Hatch through our speaking tube. I did this within half an hour after the warden left my cell on the fourth night of my imprisonment. Mr.

Hatch again had serious difficulty in understanding me, and I repeated the word 'acid' to him several times, and later on the words: 'No.8 hat'—that's my size—and these were the things which made a prisoner upstairs confess to murder, so one of the jailers told me next day.This prisoner heard our voices, confused of course, through the pipe, which also went to his cell. The cell directly over me was not occupied, hence no one else heard.

"Of course the actual work of cutting the steel bars out of the window and door was comparatively easy with nitric acid, which I got through the pipe in tin bottles, but it took time. Hour after hour on the fifth and sixth and seventh days the guard below was looking at me as I worked on the bars of the window with the acid on a piece of wire. I used the tooth powder to prevent the acid spreading. I looked away abstractedly as I worked and each minute the acid cut deeper into the metal. I noticed that the jailers always tried the door by shaking the upper part, never the lower bars, therefore I cut the lower bars, leaving them hanging in place by thin strips of metal. But that was a bit of daredeviltry. I could not have gone that way so easily."

The Thinking Machine sat silent for several minutes.

"I think that makes everything clear," he went on. "Whatever points I have not explained were merely to confuse the warden and jailers. These things in my bed I brought in to please Mr. Hatch, who wanted to improve the story. Of course, the wig was necessary in my plan. The special-delivery letter I wrote and directed in my cell with Mr. Hatch's fountain pen, then sent it out to him and he mailed it. That's all, I think."

"But your actually leaving the prison grounds and then coming in through the outer gate to my office?" asked the warden.

"Perfectly simple," said the scientist. "I cut the electric light wire with acid, as I said, when the current was off. Therefore when the current was turned on the arc didn't light. I knew it would take some time to find out what was the matter and make repairs. When the guard went to report to you the yard was dark. I crept out the window—it was a tight fit, too—replaced the bars by standing on a narrow ledge and remained in a shadow until the force of electricians arrived. Mr. Hatch was one of them.

"When I saw him I spoke and he handed me a cap, a jumper and overalls, which I put on within ten feet of you, Mr. Warden, while you were in the yard. Later Mr. Hatch called me, presumably as a workman, and together we went out the gate to get something out of the wagon. The late guard let us pass out readily as two workmen who had just passed in. We changed our clothing and reappeared, asking to see you. We saw you. That's all."

There was silence for several minutes. Dr. Ransome was first to speak.

"Wonderful!" he exclaimed. "Perfectly amazing."

"How did Mr. Hatch happen to come with the electricians?" asked Mr. Fielding.

"His father is manager of the company," replied The Thinking Machine.

"But what if there had been no Mr. Hatch outside to help?"

"Every prisoner has one friend outside who would help him escape if he could."

"Suppose—just suppose—there had been no old plumbing system there?" asked the warden, curiously.

"There were two other ways out," said The Thinking Machine, enigmatically.

Ten minutes later the telephone bell rang. It was a request for the warden.

"Light all right, eh?" the warden asked, through the phone. "Good. Wire cut beside Cell 13? Yes, I know. One electrician too many? What's that? Two came out?"

The warden turned to the others with a puzzled expression.

"He only let in four electricians, he has let out two and says there are three left."

"I was the odd one," said The Thinking Machine.

"Oh," said the warden. "I see." Then through the phone: "Let the fifth man go. He's all right."

THE LIGHT AT THREE O'CLOCK

(1930)

MacKinlay Kantor

MacKinlay Kantor

MacKinlay Kantor (1904–) is best known as the author of the Pulitzer Prize-winning novel of the Civil War, Andersonville *(1955), but most readers are unaware of his contributions to crime fiction which are considerable. These include the novel* Midnight Lace *(1948) which was effectively if not faithfully brought to the screen in 1960; the excellent police procedural novel* Signal Thirty-two *(1950); and a number of strong short stories, some of which were collected as* It's About Crime *in 1960. Particularly noteworthy among his shorter crime pieces is the oft-reprinted 1935 story "Rogue's Gallery."*

THE LIGHT AT THREE O'CLOCK

Above the switchboard a little clock ticked nervously away.

There was a certain hesitation in its chatter, as if after each catch of minute cogs it was waiting for something to happen. As if the clock had advance information on something relentless and implacable, and much more portentous than the black water dripping outside.

Its little white hands registered 2:53. The clock was the only active mechanism, apparently, in all that room. Below it, the black surface of the switchboard dozed, unbroken by any gleam of bulbs. Soon, of course, the bulbs would gleam. A woman would need a doctor for her baby. A man would call up his mistress. A long-distance call would come in from Milwaukee. People somewhere in the Allan Court would be living, even at this hour of the night, and even in this cold rain.

Unlike the clock, Shultz wasn't functioning. Mr. Shultz had fallen asleep, leaning back in his chair, the metal band of the headphone gleaming tightly across his slick black hair. Mr. Shultz was very young and romantic, and just at this moment he was dreaming of a certain ruddy waitress with slender ankles. . . . The job being what it was—night operator and office boy in a large Sheridan Road apartment hotel—Mr. Shultz did not receive any enormous stipend. But he could sleep—and dream.

Suddenly, one red circle exploded amid the waiting rows of flat bulbs. The buzzer sounded, long and insistently. . . . Still the operator slept, stubbornly refusing to turn away from the romance in his dream. *Guzzzzzzzz* said the buzzer. The sound grew louder in its insistency; the office seemed to be alive with it, and its exasperation was almost visible.

Eddie Shultz came back to the Allan Court with a frantic bound. He blinked, jerked forward, and pawed hurriedly at a switch. His foggy hand found a plug, rammed it in. The red circle winked into blackness.

"Office."

The board waited blankly. Above, the clock chattered and scurried on its ceaseless round.

"Office," said Mr. Shultz.

No answer. Then—it might have been his imagination—there was the sound of a receiver going back on its hook. The red bulb glowed instantly. Very much annoyed, Eddie withdrew the plug, and cursed.

Then, with a quick tightening of his muscles, he bent forward and looked searchingly at the offending light and its accompanying hole. . . . He could hear his own breath, alarmingly close and alarmingly loud. And he could feel an uncomfortable and cool irritation all up and down the back of his neck.

"God!" he thought. "That was 22! At least, I guess—but probably it was 20. Yes, it musta been 20." He leaned back and sighed with relief.

Guzzzzzz.

The little red bulb was gleaming again. And this time there was no mistaking the location. The typewritten numerals in the slot beneath were all too visible: 22.

It might readily be admitted that Eddie Shultz's hand was cold and shaking. Eddie Shultz himself gulped and strangled. But there was nothing else to do; there was that red glow, that waiting connection, and there was the sound of the buzzer.

With one mad lunge, he stuffed in the plug and tore open the switch. The bulb winked out, quickly. Shultz found his voice. He roared, "Office!"

Through the headphone clamped against his ear came one sound—a slight sound, but one which filled him with icy horror. It was the sound of some unseen person *swallowing*. Then the switch clicked, and the red glare of an uncompleted connection showed before his eyes.

He drew out the plug and rose slowly to his feet. His eyes were riveted on that calm row of electric bulbs. His dry lips shaped the whispered words. "22. Goddamn it . . . 22 . . ."

A moaning gust of wind swept around the corner past the basement window. The dark rain sprayed against it as it flung from some menacing hand. There wasn't any traffic out in the street, not even the welcome sound of one lone car. The neighborhood was dead. And in Apartment 22 . . .

Two fifty-eight was what the hands of the clock registered. He had spent a most uncomfortable five minutes. The job was lousy, anyway. Didn't get much money. And these calls . . .

Eddie sighed, and sat down very slowly. Had to stay, that was all. . . . Hell, he oughtn't to be so nervous. He'd quit drinking gin, that's what he'd do. Probably that was what ailed him. There wasn't any such thing as a ghost; any fool would know that. When people were dead, they were done for. Even on a black night in that great U-shaped building, with the oily rain sweeping down in sheets, with—

Guzzzzzz.

He shrieked in his mind: I won't look! By God, I don't have to look. It isn't so! That place is . . . " But his eyes twisted in their sockets, led by a hideous fascination. There, in the middle of the row, that same little flat lamp was registering its rosy gleam.

Eddie's lips were as white as his cheeks. He faltered, then nerved himself with one final spurt. It wouldn't be hard. The switch was right there, and the plug. Open it. Stick it in. There! The light was gone. It was easy. It—

And that same ghastly whisper came to him, seeming nearer than before. Gargling, choking, like breath come back into the frozen throat of a corpse. He screamed madly: "Office! Answer. Office!" And the switch closed, and the light winked, and . . .

Eddie had had enough. He leaped up, ripping off the head clamp and flinging it down. He plunged across the shadowy little office and opened the front door. The rain poured down at him in a black, blinding spray. He turned up the collar of his coat, then falterd. No, no. He couldn't go out. Run around the corner and down through the court in the rain? No! It was too much. He didn't have the nerve, that was all. He didn't care who knew it.

His eyes were wide and staring as he groped his way back to the switchboard. Hurriedly he thrust a plug into the hole marked 4 and opened a switch. His fingers pushed painfully on the red lever. *Ring.* Again. *Ring.* This was too much for anybody in the world to bear alone.

Eddie lifted the headphone. A startled sleepy voice was saying: "Hello, there. Hello. Hello—"

"Mr. Edwards."

"Well?"

"This is Shultz. . . . " He strangled for a moment.

"Well, what is it?"

And then the barriers were swept down in one fearful flood. "My God, Mr. Edwards, I'm quitting! I tell you I'm quitting! I don't want this job. It ain't right for me to go through this. Mr. Edwards, come down here right now, or I'll beat it and leave the board, and go home. No, I'm not crazy. Listen here: you come down . . . It's Apartment 22! Something's up there. Three times it's rung in here, and each time it hangs up when I answer. But it sort of chokes and swallows first. . . . My God! It's the truth, I tell you! . . . Yes, I know there ain't any person up there. But . . . Yes, I know Mr. Duncan's dead, too. But it was just about this time last night that he got killed. . . . Mr. Edwards . . . *That light's on again!*"

Hatless, his topcoat and trousers drawn loosely over pajamas, Matt Edwards stood in the office and scowled at the pale and twitching Shultz.

"Now, what's all this damn hullabaloo about?"

"Nothing, Mr. Edwards, I mean . . . Well, the light. It keeps coming on. And you know . . . "

The manager, slim and debonair—in spite of his strange attire—went over to the switchboard and bent to examine the row of bulbs. "It isn't on now."

"No, it stopped registering just before you came. But wait. It'll come on again."

"Who's this talking right now? Is 45 hooked up with Outside? And 38 hooked up with 7?" Quickly he opened first one switch, then the other. A man's voice saying calmly: "Well, heat a little water and give it to her in a teaspoon if she won't take her bottle—" And one woman saying vengefully: ". . . if you go out to any more poker games for a month, my dear sir! All right, stay there and lose—" Edwards made a wry face and clicked the switches.

He turned to Shultz. "Nothing there. You're—you're sure you weren't mistaken?"

"Guess I know one light from another," protested the operator.

Edwards frowned, tapping his white hand on the back of the chair.

"Look here. The apartment was locked tightly inside—every door and window—when we broke in there with the police last night. I mean, at three o'clock yesterday morning. Duncan's key was on the inside of the front door. We had to break it open. I had a new lock put on the door afterward, and I've got the *only* key in my pocket. The back door is bolted and has the safety chain on. How could anybody—"

"There may be something else," whispered Shultz. His face was white as a scaled fish.

"Ghosts? Bunk!"

"It registered, Mr. Edwards. The light was on. Four different times it came on and buzzed."

The silence was broken only by the splash of water outside—a hollow, lonely drip that somehow reminded one of water seeping out of an old burial vault. In spite of himself, the young manager strove desperately to keep from shuddering.

"We'll sit down here, and rest, and watch that board. I don't want to doubt your word, Shultz, but . . . If that light comes on again, and I see it with my own eyes, we'll go up to the apartment."

Shultz huddled in a settee by the inner door. His employer sat down in the chair by the switchboard, an unlighted cigarette between his lips. His brow creased painfully as he reviewed the events of the succeeding twenty-four hours, trying to arrive at some explanation.

Duncan, the tenant in Apartment 22, had lived at the Allan Court three years—a man of evident wealth and refinement, though something of a recluse. He belonged to no clubs, attended but few theaters, and drove an imported roadster. Few people ever called at his apartment; all his tastes seemed ordinary, not to say conventional. He was an ardent collector of old flasks and glassware, and was said to be an authority on early American glass. The management had permitted him, at his own expense, to install many cupboards and cabinets for the housing of his treasures. Tall, gray-haired and slender, he was the perfect picture of a sedate gentleman.

Some time before three o'clock on the previous morning, adjacent tenants had been aroused by a shot. The sound seemed to come from Mr. Duncan's apartment. The building was old, although remodeled and modernized, the thick walls prevented voices in one apartment from being heard in another. . . . A few minutes later the woman in the flat above heard a large automobile drive down the alley.

The manager was notified. When repeated calls to Apartment 22 failed to elicit any response, Edwards summmoned the police. The door of the apartment was locked, with Duncan's key inside, and it was impossible to use a passkey. The officers forced the door, and entered the rooms. There was, at first glance, no trace of Duncan. Though every closet and cubbyhole in the place was ransacked, the tenant could not be found.

Every window was solidly fastened. The lights were burning. The back door was locked, with its inner safety chain in place. The unused kitchen (Duncan took his meals in restaurants) offered no clue. Only the parlor proved what had occurred. . . . There was a bullet hole in the wall, and Sergeant Sherris dug out a .45-caliber bullet. There were fresh bloodstains, in quantity, over the rugs—and one splotch of yellowish-white, sickening and unmistakable.

So Duncan was dead—he had been murdered. But where was his body? And what was the motive? The rich stores of Stiegel glass and curios were untouched; there were diamond studs and platinum cuff links on the dresser in the bedroom.

A terrified janitor came hammering at the door. He had been attending to boiler fires in the building next door, and his attention was drawn to some minor disturbance in the alley outside. He came out to find several men hoisting the inert body of another man into a big sedan.

"What's the matter?" he asked.

"Sick man," said one of them ominously. "Get back inside that door, and get back quick!"

He had fled, and they had driven away. No, he hadn't seen the license number—he was too frightened. No, he didn't know how many men there were—maybe three or four. . . .

So Duncan had been murdered, and his body taken away in that unidentified car. But how did the murderers leave the apartment? Every door and every window locked inside.

Sergeant Sherris nodded and looked wise. Every so often, for several years, some prominent or wealthy man had been kidnapped. Sometimes they got back alive—blindfolded and unable to relate any clues. Sometimes they didn't come back at all; the money hadn't been sent as directed. There had been Page, the hair tonic king. And Rosenbaum, the hotel man. And Justessen, that rich Dane visiting at the Drake Hotel. All kidnapped by extortionists. . . . It was possible that the same gang had come after Duncan. He had resisted. He had been shot. They had taken his body out of the apartment. But—how? And—why?

Edwards twisted uncomfortably in his chair. No denying it—that was where the spooks came in . . . at least, a mystery. And now, this strange call, this lighting of Apartment 22's switchboard lamp, when nobody was in the place . . . when he had the only key to the new lock—*Guzzzzzz.*

"Look there!" cried Shultz. "See it? *The light's on!*"

The rain tore clammily at them while they hurried down the court, as if unseen hands, ghastly and intent, were bent on holding them back from those dark rooms. Edwards lifted his eyes as they passed the last concrete flower bed. The windows of 22 were blank and ominous. . . . He didn't want to go. No. Of course, there weren't any ghosts. But in that room—that stained rug where the blood had soaked, and that other place. . . . His senses were screaming at him: *Stop, stop! Go back before it's too late. . . .*

"Come on," he said brusquely, as Shultz halted irresolutely at the vestibule door.

The night operator turned a greenish face to him. "By God, Mr. Edwards, I don't want to go."

"No more do I," growled the manager. "But we're both going."

Their steps shuddered softly on the carpeted stairway. It was impossible to believe that the opposite door of that first landing opened on an ordinary apartment occupied by ordinary people—a man, his wife, their daughters. Apartment 21. There were human beings, there. But across the hall, in 22 . . .

Edwards fumbled in his pocket for the key. That new lock gleamed hideously on the damaged door.

Shultz whispered icily, "You got a—a—gun?"

"No, I haven't." And Edwards had a spinning, helpless sensation. "But, listen here. There's nothing to hurt us. Nothing . . . "

The door whined as it turned on its hinges.

Edwards felt along the wall for the light switch. The pressure of his finger flooded the hall with yellow light. As if twisted in their sockets by an invincible suction, the eyes of both men turned toward the telephone stand. And there was no one beside it, or anywhere else within sight.

The telephone stand was of the cabinet type, narrow and high, of carved walnut. A small stool had been placed beside it. One door of the cabinet swung partly ajar.

Slowly, Edwards walked toward the phone; it seemed as if years passed before he reached it, and looked inside, and saw the instrument reposing in the shadows. He lifted the bracket; the connection clicked; yes, the phone was in working order. But no one . . .

"Nobody here," said Shultz. He stood close behind; Edwards could feel his nervous breath.

"We'll turn on the lights," the manager said. They advanced into the living room, the dining room, the bedrooms. Fearfully, they peered under the beds and opened closet doors. Nothing.

In the kitchen they stared at the outer door, locked and bolted, its heavy safety chain snugly in place. Nobody there. Nobody in the pantry. A vacant apartment—a ghoulish, threatening place—with locked windows, locked doors, and still the thought of something inside.

Once more they toured the rooms, turning on the lights with prodigal haste. The dining room and one bedroom had been refurnished by Duncan to act as galleries for his rare collections. Electricity gleamed softly on rows of dark flasks, blown glass, vases. There were tall cupboards along the walls, each containing its fund of glistening treasure. Nothing had been disturbed. Only that ragged hole in the plaster, and the dark stains on the rugs, told what had happened there. . . . The police had told Edwards to leave everything just as it was. They wanted to "investigate further." All right, let them investigate. See if they could find anything.

Edwards and Shultz made a last examination. They poked beneath the davenports, peered into the hamper in the bathroom. No tracks. No marks of any human being.

As they retreated into the hallway, the manager once more opened the telephone cabinet and lifted the instrument. No, his ears had not deceived him. He could hear that *click*. The phone was in working order.

"We haven't found anything," he said to Schultz. He tried to laugh. The sound was eerie and startling in those deserted rooms. "I'm afraid it was just—just something the matter with the switchboard. We might as well go." He reached into his pocket for the key, and brought it out—a shining fragment of metal.

"Mr. Edwards!" The voice of Shultz was deadened with a cold, listless horror. "Look at your hand! You've got blood . . . all over your hand!"

For a full twenty seconds Edwards stared down at those telltale marks on his right hand. It seemed to him that he could hear his own heart, thundering in that oppressive silence all about. . . . Outside, the rain came down, blackly, dripping, dripping on damp ledges.

Then Edwards straightened. There was a tense, quick tightening of his mouth.

"Turn off the rest of those lights," he said. His voice was unnecessarily loud, perhaps from fear. . . . He waited in the open door, wiping his hand on a handkerchief. Shultz leaped back out of the parlor, his lips trembling. "Let's get out of here," said Edwards, "for good."

At the doorway, one finger on the light switch, he motioned for the operator to go ahead of him. Then, with a lightning gesture, he had pressed the key into Shultz's hand.

His voice was a hard whisper:

"There's something here. I'm going to stay. You turn out that light and slam the door; I'll hide here in the corner. If the light shows on the board again, you call the police and come up here, and come in! I don't know where it's hidden; I don't even know what it is. But that blood on my hand came off the telephone! Something's here. Now, beat it!"

The electric switch snapped out the one remaining light. Darkness. With a thud, the door slammed shut. Quietly, Edwards tiptoed across the hall and slid into a corner opposite the telephone cabinet. He crouched there in the quibbering darkness, choking breath down, waiting, waiting.

The minutes passed like heavy bats, circling low, unwilling to alight.

It seemed an hour before Edwards heard the downstairs door shut, and knew that Shultz was in the court, hurrying toward the office. The constant fury of rain was somewhat abated; water still came down outside, but in an intermittent dribble. Far away, the siren of a fire truck screeched with a horrid earnestness, but in the apartment there was a bated silence as if unguessed monsters were only biding their time—waiting to spring out.

He was crouched in the further corner of the hall, opposite the outside door, between the opening into the bedroom and the wider doorway which gave on the living room. No person—no thing—could come from any direction without his seeing it. Lights from the alley and from the court shone in, faintly and bitterly, yet strong enough for Edwards to discern the bulk of furniture.

That telephone! The first time he picked it up, he had not placed his hands on the standard. The second time he had done so. And immediately afterward, Shultz had cried out his awful news. . . . The blood—the fresh wet stain—of something. . . .

Far away, in one of the other rooms, there was a sound. It was unmistakable—the creak of wood, of an opening door. Edwards waited, swallowing fearfully. Something had moved. He was not alone!

Creak. Once more. Then, the tinkle of glass. A sound of footsteps, creeping slowly and heavily.

It was coming. It was moving nearer, out of the dining room into the living room. Its body thudded softly against some piece of furniture; there was a horrid sound, half human and half animal, a muffled cough and growl. . . . Edwards shrank closer against the wall. His fists were clenched tightly; the nails bit into his palms.

Nearer, nearer. It moved between him and the court window, a thin shape like a clothed skeleton. Yes, it was coming to the telephone again. It couldn't stay away. It must call, call on the telephone! . . . It was in the doorway now, black and gruesome, an arm's length away. Edwards heard that same choking sound, and a spasm of strained breathing. The door of the telephone cabinet banged open. That faint click and sputter—the lifting.

Edwards plunged forward. His clawing hands encountered flesh, damp and clammy. He was grappling with the thing—he had it in his arms. With a thud, the phone was on the floor.

But this creature, ghost or murderer, made no sound—no resistance. Quite suddenly and hideously, it had collapsed against him there in the close blackness. He struggled out into the living room, dragging his terrible burden. And the light from the court shone in its face—the white skin and staring eyes of Duncan, the man who had been murdered.

With a scream, Edwards leaped back. There was the heavy thud of a falling body. The manager felt his own hands raking the wall for a switch. And then, mercifully enough, his fingers encountered metal. He squeezed down. The room was flooded with light.

Duncan lay before him on the floor, clad in pajamas. Stained towels, ghastly and encrusted, were wound around his neck.

"Duncan!" cried Edwards. "It's . . . are you dead? Are you . . . "

Trembling, he dropped down and lifted the shape in his arms.

Duncan's eyes were staring, his lips moved soundlessly. He was alive—he seemed conscious.

"What was it?" Edwards gasped. "What happened? Where were you?"

The head of the injured man moved slowly. His eyes seemed seeking beyond the hotel manager, beseeching some object. The other man turned. On the table behind him lay a small bronze-covered notebook and ornate pencil. He seized them and lifted Duncan to the couch, pressing the book and the pencil into his hands. On a side table was a decanter of whiskey. He forced a few drops between the man's blue lips.

"Write it," he said. "Write it, if you can. You're going to . . . "

Falteringly, the pencil slid over the notebook in a weak scrawl:

> They came in back way as always. LeCron got arguing about his split. We had trouble. Baletto cut me with his knife but I shot him. They took him away in car and I was afraid

Edwards tore off the sheet of paper. The pencil still moved, its words barely legible:

> police would come hearing shot I knew so I hid in my place. Lost much blood and tonight thought I would give up and send for police and doctor. Tried phone but could not talk and lost my nerve. When you came I hid again. Thought I might get out alive and get away but it started bleed again and I came out to phone again

The pencil wavered and dropped from his stiffening fingers. His head lolled back, jerked; there was a choking sob. His eyes stared glassily upward.

Outside, feet trampled in the hall. Men pressed against the door, noisily, fiercely.

"What I don't see," said Shultz, "is where he was hid."

The sergeant straightened up. "We can find that out in a minute. Wonder he lived as long as he did, his throat was almost cut in two."

"If you want to look now," Edwards said, "I think we can find it, and get to the bottom of this thing. When he came out, I heard glass tinkling."

They covered the body with a scarf, and Edwards led the way into the refurnished dining room, Shultz and the officers pressing close behind him.

The manager bent down and inspected the cabinets of glassware with great care. On the bottom shelf of the last cabinet, he found an irregular red circle. "This must be it."

It took them some time to ascertain the combination. At length Edwards fumbled with one old flask which seemed cemented on the shelf. Glassware and all, the big bureau began to turn slowly in its place, disclosing a narrow closet behind the shelves. In the compartment behind were a few cushions, an automatic pistol, a big briefcase stuffed with papers, and the traces that showed all too well how Duncan had weakened and suffered during the hours he lay in hiding.

The red-faced detective sergeant needed only a few minutes' perusal of the papers in the briefcase to tell him what he wanted to know. "I was partly right and partly wrong," he admitted. "Looks as if he had made that cubbyhole when he installed the cabinets, figuring he would need a hideaway for his stuff, and maybe for himself. We can get the rest of the gang from the names he wrote in that notebook, Mr. Edwards. But I was wrong on this: here I thought he had been murdered by that kidnapping gang which has raised so much hell for three years, and all the time he was the brains of the mob. Look at these papers and clippings."

Shultz heaved a vast sigh, and turned to his employer. "Just the same, I think I'll quit my job, Mr. Edwards. I'd go nuts if I was on the board tonight and another call came in from Apartment 22."

MURDER AT THE AUTOMAT

(1937)

Cornell Woolrich

Cornell Woolrich

Often called the twentieth century Poe, Cornell Woolrich (1903–1968) was noted for background, a driving narrative, suspense, style, and an atmosphere of ironic fatalism. From 1934 to 1948 he produced 11 novels and over 150 shorter stories of suspense, love, crime, and the fantastic. The mass media loved him: films were made of twenty-two of his works and many were adapted for radio or TV. But ironically, as the money rolled in, personal problems seemed to rob him of his will to write, and he spent the last few years of his life as a pathetic recluse, gradually wasting away.

MURDER AT THE AUTOMAT

Nelson pushed through the revolving-door at twenty to one in the morning, his squadmate, Sarecky, in the compartment behind him. They stepped clear and looked around. The place looked funny. Almost all the little white tables had helpings of food on them, but no one was at them eating. There was a big black crowd ganged up over in one corner, thick as bees and sending up a buzz. One or two were standing up on chairs, trying to see over the heads of the ones in front, rubbering like a flock of cranes.

The crowd burst apart, and a cop came through. "Now, stand back. Get away from this table, all of you," he was saying. "There's nothing to see. The man's dead—that's all."

He met the two dicks halfway between the crowd and the door. "Over there in the corner," he said unnecessarily. "Indigestion, I guess." He went back with them.

They split the crowd wide open again, this time from the outside. In the middle of it was one of the little white tables, a dead man in a chair, an ambulance doctor, a pair of stretcher-bearers, and the automat manager.

"He gone?" Nelson asked the interne.

"Yep. We got here too late." He came closer so the mob wouldn't overhear. "Better send him down to the morgue and have him looked at. I think he did the Dutch. There's a white streak on his chin, and a half-eaten sandwich under his face spiked with some more of it, whatever it is. That's why I got in touch with you fellows. Good night," he wound up pleasantly and elbowed his way out of the crowd, the two stretcher-bearers tagging after him. The ambulance clanged dolorously outside, swept its fiery headlights around the corner, and whined off.

Nelson said to the cop: "Go over to the door and keep everyone in here, until we get the three others that were sitting at this table with him."

The manager said: "There's a little balcony upstairs. Couldn't he be taken up there, instead of being left down here in full sight like this?"

"Yeah, pretty soon," Nelson agreed, "but not just yet."

He looked down at the table. There were four servings of food on it, one on each side. Two had barely been touched. One had been finished and only the soiled plates remained. One was hidden by the prone figure sprawled across it, one arm out, the other hanging limply down toward the floor.

"Who was sitting here?" said Nelson, pointing to one of the unconsumed portions. "Kindly step forward and identify yourself." No one made a move. "No one," said Nelson, raising his voice, "gets out of here until we have a chance to question the three people that were at this table with him when it happened."

Someone started to back out of the crowd from behind. The woman who had wanted to go home so badly a minute ago pointed accusingly. "*He* was—that man there! I remember him distinctly. He bumped into me with his tray just before he sat down."

Sarecky went over, took him by the arm, and brought him forward again. "No one's going to hurt you," Nelson said, at sight of his pale face. "Only don't make it any tougher for yourself than you have to."

"I never even saw the guy before," wailed the man, as if he had already been accused of murder, "I just happened to park my stuff at the first vacant chair I—" Misery liking company, he broke off short and pointed in turn. "*He* was at the table, too! Why doncha hold him, if you're gonna hold me?"

"That's just what we're going to do," said Nelson dryly. "Over here, you," he ordered the new witness. "Now, who was eating spaghetti on his right here? As soon as we find that out, the rest of you can go home."

The crowd looked around indignantly in search of the recalcitrant witness that was the cause of detaining them all. But this time no one was definitely able to single him out. A white-uniformed busman finally edged forward and said to Nelson: "I think he musta got out of the place right after it happened. I looked over at this table a minute before it happened, and he was already through eating, picking his teeth and just holding down the chair."

"Well, he's not as smart as he thinks he is," said Nelson. "We'll catch up with him, whether he got out or didn't. The rest of you clear out of here now. And don't give fake names and addresses to the cop at the door, or you'll only be making trouble for yourselves."

The place emptied itself like magic, self-preservation being stronger than curiosity in most people. The two table-mates of the dead man, the manager, the staff, and the two dicks remained inside.

An assistant medical-examiner arrived, followed by two men with the usual basket, and made a brief preliminary investigation. While this was going on, Nelson was questioning the two witnesses, the busman, and the manager. He got an illuminating composite picture.

The man was well known to the staff by sight, and was considered an eccentric. He always came in at the same time each night, just before closing time, and always helped himself to the same snack—coffee and a bologna sandwich. It hadn't varied for six months now. The remnants that the busman removed from where the man sat each time were always the same. The manager was able to corroborate this. He, the dead man, had raised a kick one night about a week ago, because the bologna-sandwich slots had all been emptied before he came in. The manager had had to remind him that it's first come, first served, at an automat, and you can't reserve your food ahead of time. The man at the change-booth, questioned by Nelson, added to the old fellow's reputation for eccentricity. Other, well-dressed people came in and changed a half-dollar, or at the most a dollar bill. He, in his battered hat and derelict's overcoat, never failed to produce a ten and sometimes even a twenty.

"One of these misers, eh?" said Nelson. "They always end up behind the eight-ball, one way or another."

The old fellow was removed, also the partly consumed sandwich. The assistant examiner let Nelson know: "I think you've got something here, brother. I may be wrong, but that sandwich was loaded with cyanide."

Sarecky, who had gone through the man's clothes, said: "The

name was Leo Avram, and here's the address. Incidentally, he had seven hundred dollars, in C's, in his right shoe and three hundred in his left. Want me to go over there and nose around?"

"Suppose I go," Nelson said. "You stay here and clean up."

"My pal," murmured the other dick dryly.

The waxed paper from the sandwich had been left lying under the chair. Nelson picked it up, wrapped it in a paper-napkin, and put it in his pocket. It was only a short walk from the automat to where Avram lived, an outmoded, walk-up building, falling to pieces with neglect.

Nelson went into the hall and there was no such name listed. He thought at first Sarecky had made a mistake, or at least been misled by whatever memorandum it was he had found that purported to give the old fellow's address. He rang the bell marked *Superintendent,* and went down to the basement-entrance to make sure. A stout blond woman in an old sweater and carpet-slippers came out.

"Is there anyone named Avram living in this building?"

"That's my husband—he's the superintendent. He's out right now, I expect him back any minute."

Nelson couldn't understand, himself, why he didn't break it to her then and there. He wanted to get a line, perhaps, on the old man's surroundings while they still remained normal. "Can I come in and wait a minute?" he said.

"Why not?" she said indifferently.

She led him down a barren, unlit basement-way, stacked with empty ashcans, into a room green-yellow with a tiny bud of gaslight. Old as the building upstairs was, it had been wired for electricity, Nelson had noted. For that matter, so was this basement down here. There was cord hanging from the ceiling ending in an empty socket. It had been looped up out of reach. "The old bird sure was a miser," thought Nelson. "Walking around on one grand and living like this!" He couldn't help feeling a little sorry for the woman.

He noted to his further surprise that a pot of coffee was boiling on a one-burner gas stove over in the corner. He wondered if she knew that he treated himself away from home each night. "Any idea where he went?" he asked, sitting down in a creaking rocker.

"He goes two blocks down to the automat for a bite to eat every night at this time," she said.

"How is it," he asked curiously, "he'll go out and spend money like that, when he could have coffee right here where he lives with you?"

A spark of resentment showed in her face, but a defeated resentment that had long turned to resignation. She shrugged. "For himself, nothing's too good. He goes there because the light's better, he says. But for me and the kids, he begrudges every penny."

"You've got kids, have you?"

"They're mine, not his," she said dully.

Nelson had already caught sight of a half-grown girl and a little boy peeping shyly out at him from another room. "Well," he said, getting up, "I'm sorry to have to tell you this, but your husband had an accident a little while ago at the automat, Mrs. Avram. He's gone."

The weary stolidity of her face changed very slowly. But it did change—to fright. "Cyanide—what's that?" she breathed, when he'd told her.

"Did he have any enemies?"

She said with utter simplicity. "Nobody loved him. Nobody hated him that much, either."

"Do you know of any reason he'd have to take his own life?"

"Him? Never! He held on tight to life, just like he did to his money."

There was some truth in that, the dick had to admit. Misers seldom commit suicide.

The little girl edged into the room fearfully, holding her hands behind her. "Is—is he dead, Mom?"

The woman just nodded, dry-eyed.

"Then, can we use this now?" She was holding a fly-blown electric bulb in her hands.

Nelson felt touched, hard-boiled dick though he was. "Come down to headquarters tomorrow, Mrs. Avram. There's some money there you can claim. G'night." He went outside and clanged the basement-gate shut after him. The windows alongside him suddenly bloomed feebly with electricity, and the silhouette of a woman standing up on a chair was outlined against them.

"It's a funny world," thought the dick with a shake of his head, as he trudged up to sidewalk-level.

It was now two in the morning. The automat was dark when Nelson returned there, so he went down to headquarters. They were questioning the branch-manager and the unseen counterman who prepared the sandwiches and filled the slots from the inside.

Nelson's captain said: "They've already telephoned from the chem lab that the sandwich is loaded with cyanide crystals. On the other hand, they give the remainder of the loaf that was used, the leftover bologna from which the sandwich was prepared, the breadknife, the cutting-board, and the scraps in the garbage-receptacle—all of which we sent over there—a clean bill of health. There was clearly no slip-up or carelessness in the automat-pantry. Which means that cyanide got into that sandwich on the consumer's side of the apparatus. He committed suicide or was deliberately murdered by one of the other customers."

"I was just up there," Nelson said. "It wasn't suicide. People don't worry about keeping their light bills down when they're going to take their own lives."

"Good psychology," the captain nodded. "My experience is that miserliness is simply a perverted form of self-preservation, an exaggerated clinging to life. The choice of method wouldn't be in character, either. Cyanide's expensive, and it wouldn't be sold to a man of Avram's type, just for the asking. It's murder, then. I think it's highly important you men bring in whoever the fourth man at that table was tonight. Do it with the least possible loss of time."

A composite description of him, pieced together from the few scraps that could be obtained from the busman and the other two at the table, was available. He was a heavy-set, dark-complected man, wearing a light-tan suit. He had been the first of the four at the table, and already through eating, but had lingered on. Mannerisms—had kept looking back over his shoulder, from time to time, and picking his teeth. He had had a small black satchel, or sample-case, parked at his feet under the table. Both survivors were positive on this point. Both had stubbed their toes against it in sitting down, and both had glanced to the floor to see what it was.

Had he reached down toward it at any time, after their arrival, as if to open it or take anything out of it?

To the best of their united recollections—no.

Had Avram, *after* bringing the sandwich to the table, gotten up again and left it unguarded for a moment?

Again, no. In fact the whole thing had been over with in a flash. He had noisily unwrapped it, taken a huge bite, swallowed without chewing, heaved convulsively once or twice, and fallen prone across the tabletop.

"Then it must have happened right outside the slot—I mean the inserting of the stuff—and not at the table, at all," Sarecky told Nelson privately. "Guess he laid it down for a minute while he was drawing his coffee."

"Absolutely not!" Nelson contradicted. "You're forgetting it was all wrapped up in wax-paper. How could anyone have opened, then closed it again, without attracting his attention? And if we're going to suspect the guy with the satchel—and the cap seems to want us to—he was already *at* the table and all through eating when Avram came over. How could he know ahead of time which table the old guy was going to select?"

"Then how did the stuff get on it? Where did it come from?" the other dick asked helplessly.

"It's little things like that we're paid to find out," Nelson reminded him dryly.

"Pretty large order, isn't it?"

"You talk like a layman. You've been on the squad long enough by now to know how damnably unescapable little habits are, how impossible it is to shake them off, once formed. The public at large thinks detective work is something miraculous like pulling rabbits out of a silk-hat. They don't realize that no adult is a free agent—that they're tied hand and foot by tiny, harmless little habits, and held helpless. This man has a habit of taking a snack to eat at midnight in a public place. He has a habit of picking his teeth after he's through, of lingering on at the table, of looking back over his shoulder aimlessly from time to time. Combine that with a stocky build, a dark complexion, and you have him! What more d'a want—a spotlight trained on him?"

It was Sarecky, himself, in spite of his misgivings, who picked him up forty-eight hours later in another automat, sample-case and all, at nearly the same hour as the first time, and brought him in for questioning! The busman from the former place, and the two customers, called in, identified him unhesitatingly, even if he was now wearing a gray suit.

His name, he said, was Alexander Hill, and he lived at 215 Such-and-such a street.

"What business are you in?" rapped out the captain.

The man's face got livid. His Adam's apple went up and down like an elevator. He could barely articulate the words. "I'm—I'm a salesman for a wholesale drug concern," he gasped terrifiedly.

"Ah!" said two of his three questioners expressively. The sample-case, opened, was found to contain only tooth-powders, aspirins, and headache remedies.

But Nelson, rummaging through it, thought: "Oh, nuts, it's too pat. And he's too scared, too defenseless, to have really done it. Came in here just now without a bit of mental build-up prepared ahead of time. The real culprit would have been all primed, all rehearsed, for just this. Watch him go all to pieces. The innocent ones always do."

The captains's voice rose to a roar. "How is it everyone else stayed in the place that night, but you got out in such a hurry?"

"I—I don't know. It happened so close to me, I guess I—I got nervous."

That wasn't necessarily a sign of guilt, Nelson was thinking. It was his duty to take part in the questioning, so he shot out at him: "You got nervous, eh? What reason d'you have for getting nervous? How'd *you* know it wasn't just a heart-attack or malnutrition—unless you were the cause of it?"

He stumbled badly over that one. "No! No! I don't handle that stuff! I don't carry anything like that—"

"So you know what it was? How'd you know? We didn't tell you," Sarecky jumped on him.

"I—I read it in the papers next morning," he wailed.

Well, it had been in all of them, Nelson had to admit.

"You didn't reach out in front of you—toward him—for anything that night? You kept your hands to yourself?" Then, before he could get a word out, "*What about sugar?*"

The suspect went from bad to worse. "I don't use any!" he whimpered.

Sarecky had been just waiting for that. "Don't lie to us!" he yelled, and swung at him. "I watched you for ten full minutes tonight before I went over and tapped your shoulder. You emptied half the container into your cup!" His fist hit him a glancing blow on the side of the jaw, knocked him and the chair he was sitting on both off-balance. Fright was making the guy sew himself up twice as badly as before.

"Aw, we're just barking up the wrong tree," Nelson kept saying to himself. "It's just one of those fluke coincidences. A drug salesman happens to be sitting at the same table where a guy drops from cyanide poisoning!" Still, he knew that more than one guy had been strapped into the chair just on the strength of such a coincidence and nothing more. You couldn't expect a jury not to pounce on it for all it was worth.

The captain took Nelson out of it at this point, somewhat to his relief, took him aside and murmured: "Go over there and give his place a good cleaning while we're holding him here. If you can turn up any of that stuff hidden around there, that's all we need. He'll break down like a stack of cards." He glanced over at the cowering figure in the chair. "We'll have him before morning," he promised.

"That's what I'm afraid of," thought Nelson, easing out. "And then what'll we have? Exactly nothing." He wasn't the kind of a dick that would have rather had a wrong guy than no guy at all, like some of them. He wanted the right guy—or none at all. The last he saw of the captain, he was stripping off his coat for action, more as a moral threat than a physical one, and the unfortunate victim of circumstances was wailing, "I didn't do it, I didn't do it," like a record with a flaw in it.

Hill was a bachelor and lived in a small, one-room flat on the upper West Side. Nelson let himself in with the man's own key, put on the lights, and went to work. In half an hour, he had investigated the place upside-down. There was not a grain of cyanide to be found, nor anything beyond what had already been revealed in the sample-case. This did not mean, of course, that he couldn't have obtained some either through the firm he worked for, or some of the retail druggists whom he canvassed. Nelson found a list of the latter and took it with him to check over the following day.

Instead of returning directly to headquarters, he detoured on an impulse past the Avram house, and, seeing a light shining in the basement windows, went over and rang the bell.

The little girl came out, her brother behind her. "Mom's not in," she announced.

"She's out with Uncle Nick," the boy supplied.

His sister whirled on him. "She told us not to tell anybody that, didn't she!"

Nelson could hear the instructions as clearly as if he'd been in the room at the time, "If that same man comes around again, don't you tell him I've gone out with Uncle Nick, now!"

Children are after all very transparent. They told him most of what he wanted to know without realizing they were doing it. "He's not really your uncle, is he?"

A gasp of surprise. "How'd you know that?"

"Your ma gonna marry him?"

They both nodded approvingly. "He's gonna be our new Pop."

"What was the name of your real Pop—the one before the last?"

"Edwards," they chorused proudly.

"What happened to him?"

"He died."

"In Dee-troit," added the little boy.

He only asked them one more question. "Can you tell me his full name?"

"Albert J. Edwards," they recited.

He gave them a friendly push. "All right, kids, go back to bed."

He went back to headquarters, sent a wire to the Bureau of Vital Statistics in Detroit, on his own hook. They were still questioning Hill down to the bone, meanwhile, but he hadn't caved in yet. "Nothing," Nelson reported. "Only this account-sheet of where he places his orders."

"I'm going to try framing him with a handful of bicarb of soda, or something—pretend we got the goods on him. I'll see if that'll open him up," the captain promised wrathfully. "He's not the push-over I expected. You start in at seven this morning and work your way through this list of retail druggists. Find out if he ever tried to contract them for any of that stuff."

Meanwhile, he had Hill smuggled out the back way to an outlying precinct, to evade the statute governing the length of time a prisoner can be held before arraignment. They didn't have enough of a case against him yet to arraign him, but they weren't going to let him go.

Nelson was even more surprised than the prisoner at what he caught himself doing. As they stood Hill up next to him in the corridor, for a minute, waiting for the Black Maria, he breathed over his shoulder, "Hang on tight, or you're sunk!"

The man acted too far gone even to understand what he was driving at.

Nelson was present the next morning when Mrs. Avram showed up to claim the money, and watched her expression curiously. She had the same air of weary resignation as the night he had broken the news to her. She accepted the money from the captain, signed for it, turned apathetically away, holding it in her hand. The captain, by prearrangement, had pulled another of his little tricks—purposely withheld one of the hundred-dollar bills to see what her reaction would be.

Halfway to the door, she turned in alarm, came hurrying back. "Gentlemen, there must be a mistake! There's—there's a hundred-dollar bill here on top!" She shuffled through the roll hastily. "They're all hundred-dollar bills!" she cried out aghast. "I knew he had a little money in his shoes—he slept with them under his pillow at nights—but I thought maybe, fifty, seventy dollars—"

"There was a thousand in his shoes," said the captain, "and another thousand stitched all along the seams of his overcoat."

She let the money go, caught the edge of the desk he was sitting behind with both hands, and slumped draggingly down it to the floor in a dead faint. They had to hustle in with a pitcher of water to revive her.

Nelson impatiently wondered what the heck was the matter with him, what more he needed to be convinced she hadn't known what she was coming into? And yet, he said to himself, how are you going to tell a real faint from a fake one? They close their eyes and they flop, and which is it?

He slept three hours, and then he went down and checked at the wholesale-drug concern Hill worked for. The firm did not handle cyanide or any other poisonous substance, and the man had a very good record there. He spent the morning working his way down the list of retail druggists who had placed their orders through Hill, and again got nowhere. At noon he quit, and went back to the automat where it had happened—not to eat but to talk to the manager. He was really working on two cases simultaneously—an official one for his captain and a private one of his own. The captain would have had a fit if he'd known it.

"Will you lemme have that busman of yours, the one we had down at headquarters the other night? I want to take him out of here with me for about half an hour."

"You're the Police Department," the manager smiled acquiescently.

Nelson took him with him in his streetclothes. "You did a pretty good job of identifying Hill, the fourth man at that table," he told him. "Naturally, I don't expect you to remember every face that was in there that night. Especially, with the quick turnover there is in an automat. However, here's what you do. Go down this street here to Number One-twenty-one—you can see it from here. Ring the superintendent's bell. You're looking for an apartment, see? But while you're at it, you take a good look at the woman you'll see, and then come back and tell me if you remember seeing her face in the automat that night or any other night. Don't stare now—just size her up."

It took him a little longer than Nelson had counted on. When he finally rejoined the dick around the corner, where the latter was waiting, he said: "Nope, I've never seen her in our place, that night or any other, to my knowledge. But don't forget—I'm not on the floor every minute of the time. She could have been in and out often without my spotting her."

"But not," thought Nelson, "without Avram seeing her, if she went anywhere near him at all." She hadn't been there, then. That was practically certain. "What took you so long?" he asked him.

"Funny thing. There was a guy there in the place with her that used to work for us. He remembered me right away."

"Oh, yeah?" The dick drew up short. "Was *he* in there that night?"

"Naw, he quit six months ago. I haven't seen him since."

"What was he, sandwich-maker?"

"No, busman like me. He cleaned up the tables."

Just another coincidence, then. But, Nelson reminded himself, if one coincidence was strong enough to put Hill in jeopardy, why should the other be passed over as harmless? Both cases—his and the captain's—now had their coincidences. It remained to be seen which was just that—a coincidence and nothing more—and which was the McCoy.

He went back to headquarters. No wire had yet come from Detroit in answer to his, but he hadn't expected any this soon—it took time. The captain, bulldog-like, wouldn't let Hill go. They had spirited him away to still a third place, were holding him on some technicality or other that had nothing to do with the Avram case. The bicarbonate of soda trick hadn't worked, the captain told Nelson ruefully.

"Why?" the dick wanted to know. "Because he caught on just by looking at it that it wasn't cyanide—is that it? I think that's an important point, right there."

"No, he thought it was the stuff all right. But he hollered blue murder it hadn't come out of his room."

"Then if he doesn't know the difference between cyanide and

bicarb of soda at sight, doesn't that prove he didn't put any on that sandwich?"

The captain gave him a look. "Are you for us or against us?" he wanted to know acidly. "You go ahead checking that list of retail druggists until you find out where he got it. And if we can't dig up any other motive, unhealthy scientific curiosity will satisfy me. He wanted to study the effects at first hand, and picked the first stranger who came along."

"Sure, in an automat—the most conspicuous, crowded public eating-place there is. The one place where human handling of the food is reduced to a minimum."

He deliberately disobeyed orders, a thing he had never done before—or rather, postponed carrying them out. He went back and commenced a one-man watch over the basement-entrance of the Avram house.

In about an hour, a squat, foreign-looking man came up the steps and walked down the street. This was undoubtedly "Uncle Nick," Mrs. Avram's husband-to-be, and former employee of the automat. Nelson tailed him effortlessly on the opposite side, boarded the same bus he did but a block below, and got off at the same stop. "Uncle Nick" went into a bank, and Nelson into a cigar-store across the way that had transparent telephone-booths commanding the street through the glass front.

When he came out again, Nelson didn't bother following him any more. Instead, he went into the bank himself. "What'd that guy do—open an account just now? Lemme see the deposit-slip."

He had deposited a thousand dollars cash under the name of Nicholas Krassin, half of the sum Mrs. Avram had claimed at headquarters only the day before. Nelson didn't have to be told that this by no means indicated Krassin and she had had anything to do with the old man's death. The money was rightfully hers as his widow, and, if she wanted to divide it with her groom-to-be, that was no criminal offense. Still, wasn't there a stronger motive here than the "unhealthy scientific curiosity" the captain had pinned on Hill? The fact remained that she wouldn't have had possession of the money had Avram still been alive. It would have still been in his shoes and coat-seams where she couldn't get at it.

Nelson checked Krassin at the address he had given at the bank, and, somewhat to his surprise, found it to be on the level, not fictitious. Either the two of them weren't very bright, or they were innocent. He went back to headquarters at six, and the answer to his telegram to Detroit had finally come. "Exhumation order obtained as per request stop Albert J. Edwards deceased January 1936 stop death certificate gives cause fall from steel girder while at work building under construction stop—autopsy—"

Nelson read it to the end, folded it, put it in his pocket without changing his expression.

"Well, did you find out anything?" the captain wanted to know.

"No, but I'm on the way to," Nelson assured him, but he may have been thinking of that other case of his own, and not the one they were all steamed up over. He went out again without saying where.

He got to Mrs. Avram's at quarter to seven, and rang the bell. The little girl came out to the basement-entrance. At sight of him, she called out shrilly, but without humorous intent, "Ma, that man's here again."

Nelson smiled a little and walked back to the living-quarters. A sudden hush had fallen thick enough to cut with a knife. Krassin was there again, in his shirt-sleeves, having supper with Mrs. Avram and the two kids. They not only had electricity now but a midget radio as well, he noticed. You can't arrest people for buying a midget radio. It was silent as a tomb, but he let the back of his hand brush it, surreptitiously, and the front of the dial was still warm from recent use.

"I'm not butting in, am I?" he greeted them cheerfully.

"N-no, sit down," said Mrs. Avram nervously. "This is Mr. Krassin, a friend of the family. I don't know your name—"

"Nelson."

Krassin just looked at him watchfully.

The dick said: "Sorry to trouble you. I just wanted to ask you a couple questions about your husband. About what time was it he had the accident?"

"You know that better than I," she objected. "You were the one came here and told me."

"I don't mean Avram, I mean Edwards, in Detroit—the riveter that fell off the girder."

Her face went a little gray, as if the memory were painful. Krassin's face didn't change color, but only showed considerable surprise.

"About what time of day?" he repeated.

"Noon," she said almost inaudibly.

"Lunch-time," said the dick softly, as if to himself. "Most workmen carry their lunch from home in a pail—" He looked at her thoughtfully. Then he changed the subject, wrinkled up his nose appreciatively. "That coffee smells good," he remarked.

She gave him a peculiar, strained smile. "Have a cup, Mr. Detective," she offered. He saw her eyes meet Krassin's briefly.

"Thanks, don't mind if I do," drawled Nelson.

She got up. Then, on her way to the stove, she suddenly flared out at the two kids for no apparent reason: "What are you hanging around here for? Go in to bed. Get out of here now, I say!" She banged the door shut on them, stood before it with her back to the room for a minute. Nelson's sharp ears caught the faint but unmistakable click of a key.

She turned back again, purred to Krassin: "Nick, go outside and take a look at the furnace, will you, while I'm pouring Mr. Nelson's coffee? If the heat dies down, they'll all start complaining from upstairs right away. Give it a good shaking up."

The hairs at the back of Nelson's neck stood up a little as he watched the man get up and sidle out. But he'd asked for the cup of coffee, himself.

He couldn't see her pouring it—her back was turned toward him again as she stood over the stove. But he could hear the splash of the hot liquid, see her elbow-motions, hear the clink of the pot as she replaced it. She stayed that way a moment longer, after it had been poured, with her back to him—less than a moment, barely thirty seconds. One elbow moved slightly. Nelson's eyes were narrow slits. It was thirty seconds too long, one elbow-motion too many.

She turned, came back, set the cup down before him. "I'll let you put your own sugar in, yes?" she said almost playfully. "Some like a lot, some like a little." There was a disappearing ring of froth in the middle of the black steaming liquid.

Outside somewhere, he could hear Krassin raking up the furnace.

"Drink it while it's hot," she urged.

He lifted it slowly to his lips. As the cup went up, her eyelids went down. Not all the way, not enough to completely shut out sight, though.

He blew the steam away. "Too hot—burn my mouth. Gotta give it a minute to cool," he said. "How about you—ain't you having any? I couldn't drink alone. Ain't polite."

"I had mine," she breathed heavily, opening her eyes again. "I don't think there's any left."

"Then I'll give you half of this."

Her hospitable alarm was almost overdone. She all but jumped back in protest. "No, no! Wait, I'll look. Yes, there's more, there's plenty!"

He could have had an accident with it while her back was turned a second time, upset it over the floor. Instead, he took a kitchen-match out of his pocket, broke the head off short with his thumbnail. He threw the head, not the stick, over on top of the warm stove in front of which she was standing. It fell to one side of her without making any noise, and she didn't notice it. If he'd thrown stick and all, it would have clicked as it dropped and attracted her attention.

She came back and sat down opposite him. Krassin's footsteps could be heard shuffling back toward them along the cement corridor outside.

"Go ahead. Don't be bashful—drink up," she encouraged. There was something ghastly about her smile, like a death's-head grinning across the table from him.

The match-head on the stove, heated to the point of combustion, suddenly flared up with a little spitting sound and a momentary gleam. She jumped a little, and her head turned nervously to see what it was. When she looked back again, he already had his cup to his lips. She raised hers, too, watching him over the rim of it. Krassin's footfalls had stopped somewhere just outside the room door, and there wasn't another sound from him, as if he were standing there, waiting.

At the table, the cat-and-mouse play went on a moment longer. Nelson started swallowing with a dry constriction of the throat. The woman's eyes, watching him above her cup, were greedy half-moons of delight. Suddenly, her head and shoulders went down across the table with a bang, like her husband's had at the automat that other night, and the crash of the crushed cup sounded from underneath her.

Nelson jumped up watchfully, throwing his chair over. The door shot open, and Krassin came in, with an ax in one hand and an empty burlap-bag in the other.

"I'm not quite ready for cremation yet," the dick gritted, and threw himself at him.

Krassin dropped the superfluous burlap-bag, the ax flashed up overhead. Nelson dipped his knees, down in under it before it could fall. He caught the shaft with one hand, midway between the blade and Krassin's grip, and held the weapon teetering in mid-air. With his other fist he started imitating a hydraulic drill against his assailant's teeth. Then he lowered his barrage suddenly to solar-plexus level, sent in two bodyblows that caved his opponent in—and that about finished it.

Out in the wilds of Corona, an hour later, in a sub-basement locker-room, Alexander Hill—or at least what was left of him—was saying: "And you'll lemme sleep if I do? And you'll get it over real quick, send me out of my misery?"

"Yeah, yeah!" said the haggard captain, flicking ink out of a fountain pen and jabbing it at him. "Why dincha do this days ago, make it easier for us all?"

"Never saw such a guy," complained Sarecky, rinsing his mouth with water over in a corner.

"What's the man signing?" exploded Nelson's voice from the stairs.

"Whaddye think he's signing?" snarled the captain. "And where you been all night, incidentally?"

"Getting poisoned by the same party that croaked Avram!" He came the rest of the way down, and Krassin walked down alongside at the end of a short steel link.

"Who's this guy?" they both wanted to know.

Nelson looked at the first prisoner, in the chair. "Take him out of here a few minutes, can't you?" he requested. "He don't have to know all our business."

"Just like in the story-books," muttered Sarecky jealously. "One-Man Nelson walks in at the last minute and cops all the glory."

A cop led Hill upstairs. Another cop brought down a small brown-paper parcel at Nelson's request. Opened, it revealed a small tin that had once contained cocoa. Nelson turned it upside down and a few threads of whitish substance spilled lethargically out, filling the close air of the room with a faint odor of bitter almonds.

"There's your cyanide," he said. "It came off the shelf above Mrs. Avram's kitchen-stove. Her kids, who are being taken care of at headquarters until I can get back there, will tell you it's roach-powder and they were warned never to go near it. She probably got it in Detroit, way back last year."

"She did it?" said the captain. "How could she? It was on the automat-sandwich, not anything he ate at home. *She* wasn't at the automat that night, she was home, you told us that yourself."

"Yeah, she was home, but she poisoned him at the automat just the same. Look, it goes like this." He unlocked his manacle, refastened his prisoner temporarily to a plumbing-pipe in the corner. He took a paper-napkin out of his pocket, and, from within that, the carefully preserved wax-paper wrapper the death-sandwich had been done in.

Nelson said: "This has been folded over twice, once on one side, once on the other. You can see that, yourself. Every crease in it is double-barreled. Meaning what? The sandwich was taken out, doctored, and rewrapped. Only, in her hurry, Mrs. Avram slipped up and put the paper back the other way around.

"As I told Sarecky already, there's death in little habits. Avram was a miser. Bologna is the cheapest sandwich that automat sells. For six months straight, he never bought any other kind. This guy here used to work there. He knew at what time the slots were refilled for the last time. He knew that was just when Avram always showed up. And, incidentally the old man was no fool. He didn't go there because the light was better—he went there to keep from getting poisoned at home. Ate all his meals out.

"All right, so what did they do? They got him, anyway—like this. Krassin, here, went in, bought a bologna sandwich, and took it home to her. She spiked it, rewrapped it, and, at eleven-thirty, he took it back there in his pocket. The sandwich-slots had just been refilled for the last time. They wouldn't put any more in till next morning. There are three bologna-slots. He emptied all three, to make sure the victim wouldn't get any but the lethal sandwich. After they're taken out, the glass slides remain ajar. You can lift them and reach in without inserting a coin. He put his death-sandwich in, stayed by it so no one else would get it. The old man came in. Maybe he's near sighted and didn't recognize Krassin. Maybe he didn't know him at all—I haven't cleared that point up yet. Krassin eased out of the place. The old man is a miser. He sees he can get a sandwich for nothing, thinks something went wrong with the mechanism, maybe. He grabs it up twice as quick as anyone else would have. There you are.

"What was in his shoes is this guy's motive. As for her, that was only partly her motive. She was a congenital killer, anyway, outside of that. He would have married her, and it would have happened to him in his turn some day. She got rid of her first husband, Edwards, in Detroit that way. She got a wonderful break. He ate the poisoned lunch she'd given him way up on the crossbeams of a building under contstruction, and it looked like he'd lost his balance and toppled to his death. They exhumed the body and performed an autopsy at my request. This telegram says they found traces of cyanide poisoning even after all this time.

"I paid out rope to her tonight, let her know I was onto her. I told her her coffee smelled good. Then I switched cups on her. She's up there now, dead. I can't say that I wanted it that way, but it was me or her. You never would have gotten her to the chair, anyway. She was unbalanced of course, but not the kind that's easily recognizable. She'd have spent a year in an institution, been released, and gone out and done it all over again. It grows on 'em, gives 'em a feeling of power over their fellow human beings.

"This louse, however, is *not* insane. He did it for exactly one thousand dollars and no cents—and he knew what he was doing from first to last. So I think he's entitled to a chicken-and-ice-cream-dinner in the death-house, at the state's expense."

"The Sphinx," growled Sarecky under his breath, shrugging into his coat. "Sees all, knows all, keeps all to himself."

"Who stinks?" corrected the captain, misunderstanding. "If anyone does, it's you and me. He brought home the bacon!"

THE EXACT OPPOSITE

(1939)

Erle Stanley Gardner

Erle Stanley Gardner

A lawyer who began to publish in his early thirties, Erle Stanley Gardner (1889–1970) produced a tremendous body of pulp fiction in the detective, science fiction, and western fields before achieving wider recognition with the publication of the first of the Perry Mason books (The Case of the Velvet Claws, *1933). This series became one of the most popular and widely read in the world, and the eighty-two novels that ended with* The Case of the Postponed Murder *(1973) are still selling well today. Between 1939 and 1970 Gardner also published twenty-nine "A. A. Fair" mystery novels about the firm of Lam and Cool. A major project to reprint many of Gardner's approximately 600 shorter works (which have been shamefully neglected) has begun and the first volumes are* Erle Stanley Gardner's Whispering Sands *and* The Human Zero (1981).

THE EXACT OPPOSITE

There was a glint of amusement in the eyes of Lester Leith as he lazily surveyed the valet, who was in reality no valet at all, but a police undercover operative sent by Seargeant Ackley to spy upon him.

"And so you don't like fanatical East Indian priests, Scuttle?"

"No, sir," he said. "I should hate to have them on *my* trail."

Lester Leith took a cigarette from the humidor and flicked his lighter.

"Scuttle," he said, "why the devil should Indian priests be on anyone's trail?"

"If I were to tell you, sir, you'd think that I was trying to interest you in another crime. As a matter of fact, sir, it *was* a crime which caused me to voice that sentiment about East Indian priests."

"Indeed?" said Lester Leith.

"Yes, sir," he said. "I was thinking about the murder of George Navin."

Lester Leith looked reproachfully at the spy.

"Scuttle," he said, "is it possible that you are trying to interest me in *that* crime?"

"No, sir, not at all," the spy made haste to reassure him. "Although if you *were* interested in the crime, sir, I am satisfied that this is a case made to order for you."

Lester Leith shook his head.

"No, Scuttle," he said. "Much as I like to dabble in crime problems, I don't care to let myself go on them. You see, Scuttle, it's a mental pastime with me. I like to read newspaper accounts of crimes and speculate on what might be a solution."

"Yes, sir," said the spy. "This is just the sort of a crime that you used to like to speculate about, sir."

Lester Leith sighed. "No, Scuttle," he said. "I really don't dare to do it. You see, Scuttle, Seargeant Ackley learned about that fad of mine, and he insists that I am some sort of a super-criminal who goes about hijacking robbers out of their ill-gotten spoils. There's nothing that I can do to convince the man that he is wrong. Therefore, I have found it necessary to give up my fad."

"Well," said the valet, "of course, sir, Sergeant Ackley doesn't need to know everything that happens in the privacy of your own apartment, sir."

Lester Leith shook his head sadly. "One would think so, Scuttle, and yet Sergeant Ackley seems to have some uncanny knowledge of what I am thinking about."

"Yes, sir," he said. "Have you read anything about the murder of George Navin?"

Lester Leith frowned. "Wasn't he mixed up with some kind of a gem robbery, Scuttle?"

"Yes, sir," said the spy eagerly. "He was an explorer, and he had explored extensively in the Indian jungle. Perhaps you've heard something about those jungle temples, sir?"

"What about them, Scuttle?"

"India," the spy said, "is a land of wealth, of gold and rubies. In some of the primitive jungle districts the inhabitants lavish their wealth on idols. Back in a hidden part of the jungle, in a sect known as the Sivaites, there was a huge temple devoted to Vinayaka, the Prince of Evil Spirits, and in that temple was a beautiful ruby, the size of a pigeon egg, set in a gold border which had Sanskrit letters carved in it."

Lester Leith said: "Scuttle, you're arousing my curiosity."

"I'm sorry, sir."

Leith said: "Well, we won't discuss it any more, Scuttle. The way these things go, one thing leads to another, and then—But tell me one thing: is George Navin supposed to have had that gem?"

"Yes, sir. He managed to get it from the temple, although he never admitted it, but in one of his books dealing with some of the peculiar religious sects in India, there's a photographic illustration of this gem—and authorities claim that it would have been absolutely impossible to have photographed it in the temple, that Navin must have managed to get possession of the ruby and brought it to this country."

Lester Leith said: "Wasn't that illustration reproduced in one of the newspapers after Navin's death?"

"Yes, sir. I have it here, sir."

The spy reached inside the pocket of his coat and pulled out a clipping.

Leith hesitated, then reluctantly took it. "I shouldn't look at this. But I'm going to, Scuttle. After that, don't tell me any more about it."

"Very well, sir."

Leith looked at the newspaper illustration. "There'd be a better reproduction in Navin's book, Scuttle?"

"Oh, yes, sir—a full-sized photograph."

Leith said: "And, as I gather it, Scuttle, the Hindu priests objected to the spoliation of the temple?"

"Very much, sir. It seems they attached some deep religious significance to the stone. You may remember four or five months ago, shortly after the book was published, there was an attempted robbery of Navin's house. Navin shot a man with a .45 automatic."

"An East Indian?"

"Yes, sir," said the spy. "A Hindu priest of the particular sect which had maintained the jungle temple."

Leith said: "Well, that's enough, Scuttle. I don't want to hear anything more about it. You'd have thought Navin would have taken precautions."

"Oh, but he did, sir. He hired a bodyguard—a chap named Arthur Blaire and a detective, Ed Springer. They were with him all the time."

"Just the three of them in the house?" Lester Leith asked.

"No, sir. There were four. There was a Robert Lamont, a confidential secretary."

"Accompanying Navin on his travels?" Leith asked.

The spy nodded.

"Any servants?" Leith asked.

"Only a housekeeper who came in and worked by the day."

Leith frowned and then said: "Scuttle, don't answer this if it's going to arouse my curiosity any more. But how the devil could a man get murdered if he had two bodyguards and his secretary with him all the time?"

"That, sir, is the thing the police can't understand. Mr. Navin slept in a room which was considered virtually burglar-proof. There were steel shutters on the windows, and a door which locked with a combination, and there was a guard on duty outside of the door all night."

"How did he get ventilation?"

"Through some ventilating system which was installed, and which permitted a circulation of air but wouldn't permit anyone to gain access to the room, sir."

"Don't go on, Scuttle," he said. "I simply mustn't hear about it."

"But, sir," said the spy wheedlingly, "you have heard so much now that it certainly wouldn't hurt to go on and have your natural curiosity satisfied."

Leith sighed. "Very well, Scuttle," he said. "What happened?"

The spy spoke rapidly. "Navin went to bed, sir. Blaire and Springer, the bodyguards, made the rounds of the room, making certain that the steel shutters were locked on the inside, and that the windows were closed and locked. That was about ten o'clock at night. About ten forty Bob Lamont, the secretary, received an important telegram which he wanted to take up to Mr. Navin. He had the bodyguards open the door, and call Navin softly to find out if he was asleep. Navin was sitting up in bed reading.

"They were in there for fifteen or twenty minutes. The guards don't know exactly what happened, because they sat outside on guard, but apparently it was, as Lamont says, just an ordinary business conference. Then Lamont came out, and the guards closed the door. About midnight Arthur Blaire retired, and Ed Springer kept the first watch until four o'clock in the morning. At four, Blaire came on and relieved Springer, and at nine o'clock the secretary came in with the morning mail.

"That was part of the custom, sir. The secretary was the first to go into the room with the morning mail, and he discussed it while Mr. Navin tubbed and shaved.

"The guard opened the door, and Lamont went in.

"The guard heard him say, 'Good morning,' to Mr. Navin, and walk across the room to open the shutters. Then suddenly he heard Lamont give an exclamation.

"George Navin had been murdered by having his throat cut. Everything in the room had been ransacked; even the furniture had been taken to pieces."

Lester Leith made no attempt to disguise his interest now.

"What time was the crime committed, Scuttle?" he asked. "The autopsy surgeon could tell that."

"Yes, sir," said the spy. "At approximately four A.M., sir."

How did the murderer get into the room?" asked Lester Leith.

"There, sir," said the valet, "is where the police are baffled. The windows were all closed, and the shutters were all locked on the inside."

"And the murder was committed at just about the time the guards were being changed, eh?" said Lester Leith.

"Yes, sir," said the valet.

"So that either one of the guards might be suspected, eh, Scuttle?"

The valet said: "As a matter of fact, sir, both of them are under suspicion. But they have excellent references."

"Well," said Lester Leith, "did the murderer get the ruby, Scuttle?"

"Well, sir, the ruby wasn't in that bedroom at all. The ruby was kept in a specially constructed safe which was in a secret hiding place in the house. No one knew of the existence of that safe, with the exception of George Navin and the two bodyguards. Also, of course, the secretary. Naturally, after discovering the murder, the men went immediately to the safe and opened it. They found that the stone was gone. The police have been unable to find any fingerprints on the safe, but they did discover something else which is rather mystifying.

"The police are satisfied that the murderer entered through one of the windows on the east side of the room. There are tracks in the soft soil of the garden beneath the window, and there are the round marks embedded in the soil where the ends of a bamboo ladder were placed on the ground."

"Bamboo, eh, Scuttle?"

"Yes, sir. That, of course, would indicate that the murderers were Indian, sir."

"But," said Lester Leith, "how could they get through a steel shutter locked on the inside, murder a man, get out through a window, close the window, and leave the shutter still locked on the inside?"

"That is the point, sir."

"Then," said Lester Leith, "the bodyguards weren't mixed up in it. If they were mixed up in it, they would have let the murderer come in through the door.

"But," went on Lester Leith, "there is no evidence as to how the murderer could have secured the gem."

"That's quite true, sir."

"What are the police doing?"

"The police are questioning all the men. That is, sir, the servants and the bodyguards. Lamont left the house right after talking with Navin, and went to a secret conference with Navin's attorney, a man by the name of During. During had his stenographer there, a young lady named Edith Skinner, so that Lamont can account for every minute of his time."

"Do I understand that the conference lasted all night?"

"Yes, sir. The conference was very important. It had to do with certain legal matters in connection with income tax and publishing rights."

"But that's such an unusual time for a conference," said Lester Leith.

"Yes, sir," said the valet, "but it couldn't be helped. Mr. Lamont was very busy with Mr. Navin. It seems that Navin was rather a peculiar individual, and he demanded a great deal of attention. As soon as the lawyer said that the examination of the records and things would take a period of over eight hours, Navin made so much trouble that Lamont finally agreed to work all one night."

"What time did Lamont leave the conference?" asked Leith.

"About eight o'clock in the morning. They went down to breakfast, and then Lamont drove out to the house in time to get the morning mail ready for Mr. Navin."

"The police, of course, are coming down pretty hard on Blaire and Springer, eh, Scuttle?"

"Yes, sir, because it would have been almost impossible for anyone to have entered that room without the connivance of one of the watchmen. And then again, sir, the fact that the murder was timed to take place when the watchmen were changing their shift would seem to indicate that either Blaire was a party to the crime, and fixed the time so that he could put the blame on Springer, or that Springer was the guilty one, and had committed the crime just as soon as he came on duty so that suspicion would attach to Blaire."

"Rather a neat problem, I should say," said Lester Leith. "One that will keep Sergeant Ackley busy."

"Yes, sir," said the valet, "and it just goes to show how ingenious the Hindus are."

"Yes," said Lester Leith dreamily, "it's a very ingenious murder—save for one thing."

The valet's eyes glistened with eagerness.

"What," he asked, "is that one thing, sir?"

"No, no, Scuttle," he said. "If I should tell you, that would be violating the pact which I have made with myself. I have determined that I wouldn't work out any more academic crime solutions."

"I would like very much, sir," said the valet coaxingly, "to know what that one thing is."

Lester Leith took a deep breath.

"No, Scuttle," he said. "Do not tempt me."

Lester Leith reclined in the long chair, his feet crossed on the cushions, his eyes watching the cigarette smoke.

"Do you know, Scuttle," he said, almost dreamily, "I am tempted to conduct an experiment."

"An experiment, sir?"

"Yes," said Lester Leith. "A psychological experiment. It would, however, require certain things. I would want three fifty-dollar bills and fifty one-dollar bills, Scuttle. I would want a diamond tiepin, an imitation of the ruby which was stolen from Navin's house, and a very attractive chorus girl."

Edward H. Beaver, undercover man who was working directly under Sergeant Arthur Ackley, but who was known to Lester Leith as "Scuttle," surveyed the police sergeant across the battered top of the desk at Headquarters.

Sergeant Ackley blinked his crafty eyes at the undercover man and said: "Give me that list again, Beaver."

"Three fifty-dollar bills, fifty one-dollar bills, a large diamond stick-pin, an imitation of the ruby which was stolen, and a chorus girl."

Sergeant Ackley slammed the pencil down.

"He was taking you for a ride," he said.

The undercover man shook his head stubbornly.

"No, he wasn't," he said. "It's just the way he works. Every time he starts on one of his hijacking escapades, he asks for a bunch of stuff that seems so absolutely crazy there's no sense to it. But every time so far those things have all turned out to be part of a carefully laid plan which results in victory for Leith and defeat for the crooks—and for us."

Sergeant Ackley made a gesture of emphatic dismissal.

"Beaver," he said, "the man is simply stringing you along this time. He couldn't possibly use these things to connect up this crime. As a matter of fact, we have evidence now which indicates very strongly that the crime was actually committed by three Hindus. We've got a straight tip from a stool pigeon who is covering the Hindu section here."

The spy insisted: "It doesn't make any difference, Sergeant, whether or not Hindus committed the crime. I'm telling you that Lester Leith is serious about this, and that he's going to use these things to work out a solution that will leave *him* in possession of that ruby."

"No," went on Sergeant Ackley, "you have overplayed your hand, Beaver. You went too far trying to get him to take an interest in this crime."

"But," protested the harassed spy, "what else could I do? Every time he pulls a job, you come down on him, triumphantly certain that you've cornered him at last, and every time he squirms out of the corner and leaves you holding the sack. As a result, he knows that you have some method of finding out what he is doing all the time. It's a wonder to me that he doesn't suspect me."

"Well," said Sergeant Ackley coldly, "you don't need to wonder any more, Beaver, because he does suspect you. He wouldn't have given you all this line of hooey unless he did."

"If it's hooey," snapped Beaver, "he's spending a lot of money."

"How do you mean?"

Beaver unfolded the morning paper which lay on the sergeant's desk.

"Take a look at the Classified Advertising Section," he said.

"Wanted: A young woman of pleasing personality and attractive looks, who has had at least three years experience on the stage in a chorus, preferably in a musical comedy or burlesque. She must have been out of work for at least eight months."

"And here's another one," said Beaver, and he pointed to another ad.

"Wanted: Ambitious young man to learn detective work at my expense. Must be a man who has had no previous experience and who knows nothing of routine police procedure. I want to train a detective who has a fresh outlook, entirely untrammeled by conventional ideas of police routine. All expenses will be paid, in addition to a generous salary. Preferably someone who has recently arrived from a rural community."

* * *

Sergeant Ackley sat back in his chair. "I'll be—"

"Now, then," said the spy, "if he doesn't intend to do something about that Navin murder, what the devil does he want to go to all this trouble for?"

"It doesn't make sense, Beaver," Ackley said. "No matter how you look at it, it's crazy."

The spy shrugged his shoulders.

"Perhaps," he said, "that's why he's always so successful."

"How do you mean, Beaver?"

"Because his stuff doesn't make sense, Sergeant. It's unconventional and so absolutely unique, there's no precedent to help you."

Sergeant Ackley fished a cigar from his waistcoat pocket.

"Beaver," he said, "the real standard of a good detective is his ability to separate the wheat from the chaff. Now, I'm willing to admit that Leith has done some crazy things before, and they've always worked out. But this is once it won't happen."

"Well," said the undercover man, getting to his feet, "you can have it your own way, but I'm willing to bet he's up to something. I'll bet you fifty dollars against that watch that you're so proud of."

Cupidity glittered in Sergeant Ackley's eyes. "Bet me what?"

"Bet you," said Beaver, "that he uses every one of these things to work out a scheme by which he lifts that Indian ruby, and does it all so cleverly that you can't pin anything on him."

Sergeant Ackley's broad hand smacked down on the top of the desk.

"Beaver," he said, "your language verges on insubordination. Just by way of disciplining you, I am going to take that bet. Fifty dollars against my watch.

"However, Beaver, if he is going to use other means to catch that murderer and hijack the ruby, the bet is off. He's got to do it by these particular means."

"That's the bet," said Beaver.

"And you've got to keep me posted as to everything that he's doing, so that if he should use all of the stuff as a smokescreen and try to get the ruby under cover of all this hooey, we can still catch him."

"Certainly," said the undercover man.

Lester Leith smiled urbanely at his valet. "Scuttle," he said, "this is Miss Dixie Dormley, and Mr. Harry Vare. Miss Dormley is a young woman who is doing some special work for me. She has had rather extensive stage experience, but has recently been out of work. In the position that I want her to fill, it will be necessary that she have some rather striking clothes, and I want you to go around with her to the various shops, let her pick out what clothing she desires, and see that it is charged to me."

The valet blinked his eyes.

"Very good, sir," he said. "What is the limit in regard to price, sir?"

"No limit, Scuttle. Also, I have arranged for Miss Dormley to have the apartment next to us, temporarily," said Lester Leith. "She will live there—the one on the left."

"Yes, sir," said the valet.

"And Mr. Harry Vare," said Lester Leith, "is the fortunate young man who has won the free scholarship in my school of deductive reasoning."

The valet stared at Harry Vare.

Vare met that stare with eyes that were hard and appraising. He narrowed the lids and scrutinized the undercover operative as though he were trying to hypnotize the man.

"Harry Vare," said Lester Leith suavely, "is a young man from the country who has recently come to the city in search of some employment which would be worthy of his talents. He felt that he had outgrown the small town in which he lived. He is possessed of that first essential for detective work—an imagination which makes him see an ulterior motive in every action, a crime in every set of circumstances."

The undercover operative was dignified.

"I beg your pardon, sir," he said, "but as I understand it, sir, most of the real detectives are somewhat the other way. They regard it as a business, sir."

Lester Leith shook his head.

"No, Scuttle," he said. "Sergeant Ackley is one of the shrewdest detectives that I know, and you must admit, Scuttle, that he has one of those imaginations which makes him see a crime in everything."

The girl looked from face to face with a twinkle in her eyes. She was a beautiful woman.

"Mr. Vare," said Lester Leith, "will have the apartment on the right—the one adjoining us. He will be domiciled there temporarily, Scuttle."

"Yes, sir," said the valet. "May I ask, what are the duties of these persons?"

"Mr. Vare is going to be a detective," said Lester Leith gravely. "He will detect."

"What will he detect?"

"That is the interesting part of having a professional detective about, Scuttle. One never knows what he is going to detect. There is Sergeant Ackley, for instance. He detects so many things which seem utterly unreasonable at the time, and then, after mature investigation and reflection, they seem to have an entirely different complexion."

The spy cleared his throat.

"And the young lady, sir?"

"Miss Dormley," said Lester Leith, "will engage in dramatic acting upon the stage which was so well described by Shakespeare."

"What stage is that?" asked the undercover man.

"The world," said Lester Leith.

"Very good, sir," the valet said. "And when do I start on this shopping tour?"

"Immediately," said Lester Leith. "And by the way, Scuttle, did you get me the money and the diamond stick-pin?"

The valet opened a box which he took from his pocket.

"Yes, sir," he said. "You wanted rather a large diamond with something of a fault in it, something that wasn't too expensive, I believe you said."

"Yes," said Lester Leith. "That's right, Scuttle."

"This is sent on approval," said the valet. "The price tag is on the pin, sir."

Lester Leith looked at the diamond pin, and whistled.

"Rather a low price, Scuttle," he said.

"Yes, sir," said the valet. "There's quite a flaw in the diamond, although it doesn't appear until you examine it closely."

"And the money?"

"Yes, sir," said the valet, and took from his pocket a sheaf of bank notes.

Lester Leith gravely arranged them so that the fifties were on the outside. Then he rolled them and snapped the roll with an elastic.

Lester Leith turned to Vare.

"Vare," he said, "are you ready to start detecting?"

"I thought I was going to be given a course of instruction," he said.

"You are," said Lester Leith, "but you are going to learn by a new method. You know, they used to teach law by reading out of law books, and then they decided that that wasn't the proper way to give the pupils instruction. They switched to what is known as the case method—that is, Vare, they read cases to them and let the students delve into the reported cases until they found the legal principles which had been applied to the facts."

"Yes, sir," said Vare.

"That is the way you are going to learn detective work," said Lester Leith. "By the case method. Are you ready to start?"

Vare nodded.

Lester Leith removed the tiepin from his tie, placed it on the table, and inserted the diamond stickpin.

"Very well, Vare," he said. "Get your hat and come with me. You are about to receive the first lesson."

There was the usual crowd in front of the ticket windows of the big railroad station. Everywhere there was noise, bustle, and confusion.

"Now," said Lester Leith to Harry Vare, "keep about twenty feet behind me and watch sharply. See if you can find anyone who looks like a crook."

Vare cocked a professional eye at the crowd.

"They all look like crooks," he said.

Lester Leith nodded gravely.

"Vare," he said, "you are showing the true detective instincts. But I want you to pick out someone who looks like a crook we can pin something definite on."

"I don't see exactly what you mean," said Vare.

"You will," said Lester Leith. "Just follow me."

Lester Leith pushed his way through the crowd, with Vare tagging along behind him. From time to time Lester Leith pulled out the roll of bills and counted them, apparently anxious to see that they were safe. Then he snapped the elastic back on the roll and pushed it back in his pocket.

Leith kept in the most congested portions of the big depot.

Twice he was bumped into, and each time by a sad-faced individual with mournful eyes and a drooping mouth.

The man was garbed in a dark suit, and his tie was conservative. Everything about him blended into a single drab personality which would attract no attention.

Finally, Lester Leith walked to a closed ticket window, where there was a little elbow room.

"Well, Vare," he said, "did you see anyone?"

Vare said: "Well, I saw several that looked like crooks, but I couldn't see anyone that I could pick out as being a certain particular crook. That is, I couldn't find any proof."

Lester Leith put his hand in his pocket, and then suddenly jumped backwards.

"Robbed!" he said.

Vare stared at him with sagging jaw.

"Robbed?" he asked.

"Robbed," said Lester Leith. "My money—it's gone!"

He pulled his hand from his trousers pocket, and disclosed a slit which had been cut in the cloth so that the contents of the pocket could be reached from the outside.

"Pickpockets," said Harry Vare.

"And you didn't discover them," Leith said.

Vare fidgeted uneasily.

"There was quite a crowd," he said, "and of course I couldn't see everything."

Lester Leith shook his head sadly.

"I can't give you a high mark on the first lesson, Vare," he said. "Now let's take a cab and go home."

"Your tiepin is safe, anyway," said Vare.

Lester Leith gave a sudden start, reached his hand to his tie, and pulled out the diamond scarf-pin.

He looked at the diamond and nodded, then suddenly pointed to the pin.

"Look," he said, "the man tried to take it off with nippers. You can see where they left their mark on the pin. I must have pulled away just as he was doing it, so that he didn't get a chance to get the diamond."

Vare's eyes were large; his face showed consternation.

"Really," said Lester Leith, "you have had two lessons in one, and I can't give you a high mark on either. You should have detected the person who was putting nippers on my pin."

Vare looked crestfallen.

Leith said: "Oh, well, you can't expect to become a first-class detective overnight. That's one of the things that training is for.

But we'll go back to the apartment and I'll change my clothes, and you can sit back and concentrate for an hour or two on what you saw, and see if you can remember anything significant."

But a little later Lester Leith returned to the depot—alone. Once more he mingled with the crowd, moving aimlessly about, but this time his eyes were busy scanning the faces of the stream of people.

He noticed the man in the dark suit with the mournful countenance, moving aimlessly about, a newspaper in his hands, his manner that of one who is waiting patiently for a wife who was to have met him an hour ago.

Lester Leith walked behind this man, keeping him in sight.

After some fifteen minutes, Leith shortened the distance between them and tapped the man sharply on the shoulder.

"I want to talk with you," he said.

The man's face changed expression. The look of mournful listlessness vanished, and the eyes became hard and wary.

"You ain't got nothing on me."

Lester Leith laughed.

"On the contrary," he said, "you have got something of mine on you—a roll of bills with some fifties on the outside and dollar bills in between. Also, you have the scarf-pin which you just nipped from that fat gentleman with the scarlet tie."

The man backed away, and turned as though getting ready to run.

Lester Leith said: "I'm not a detective. I just want to talk with you. In fact, I want to employ you."

The pickpocket looked at him with eyes that were wide with surprise.

"Employ me?" he asked.

"Yes," said Lester Leith. "I have been strolling around here all afternoon looking for a good pickpocket."

"I'm not a pickpocket," said the man.

Lester Leith paid no attention to the man's protestation of innocence.

"I am," he said, "running a school for young detectives. I want to employ you as an assistant instructor. I have an idea that the ordinary training of police officers and detectives is exceedingly haphazard. I am looking for someone who can give my students an education in picking pockets."

"What's the pay?"

"Well," said Lester Leith, "you can keep the watch that you got from the tall thin man, the scarf-pin which you nipped from the fleshy man, and you can keep the roll of bills which you cut from my trousers pocket. In addition to that, you will draw regular compensation of one hundred dollars a day, and if you feel like risking your liberty, you can keep anything which you can pick up on the side."

"How do you mean, 'on the side'?"

"By the practice of your profession, of course," said Lester Leith.

The pickpocket stared at him.

"This," he said, "is some kind of a smart game to get me to commit myself."

Lester Leith reached to his inside pocket and took out a well-filled wallet. He opened the wallet, and the startled eyes of the pickpocket caught sight of a number of one-hundred-dollar bills.

Gravely Lester Leith took out one of these hundred-dollar bills and extended it to the pickpocket.

"This," he said, "is the first day's salary."

The man took the one-hundred-dollar bill, and his eyes followed the wallet as Lester Leith returned it to his pocket.

"Okay, boss," he said. "What do you want me to do?"

"Just meet me," said Lester Leith, "at certain regular times and places. Your first job will be to meet me here at nine thirty tonight. I will write a bunch of instructions on a piece of paper, and put that piece of paper in my coat pocket. You can slip the paper out of the coat pocket and follow instructions. Don't let on that you know me at all, unless I should speak to you first."

The pickpocket nodded.

"Okay, he said. "I'll be here at nine thirty. In the meantime, I'll walk as far as your taxicab with you and talk over details. My name is Sid Bentley. What's yours?"

"Leith," Lester Leith told him.

"Pleased to meet you."

After they had finished shaking hands, Lester Leith started toward the taxicab and Bentley walked on his right side, talking rapidly.

"I don't know how you made me, Leith," he said, "but you can believe it or not, it's the first time I've ever been picked up by anybody. I used to be a sleight-of-hand artist on the stage, and then when business got bad, I decided to go out and start work. I haven't a criminal record and the police haven't got a thing on me."

"That's fine," beamed Lester Leith. "You're exactly the man I want. I'll meet you here at nine thirty, eh, Bentley?"

"Nine thirty it is, Captain."

Lester Leith hailed a taxicab. As it swung into the circle in front of the depot, he turned casually to the pickpocket.

"By the way, Bentley," he said, "please don't use that knife. You've already ruined one good suit for me."

As Lester Leith spoke, his left hand shot out and clamped around the wrist of the pickpocket. The light gleamed on the blade of a razor-like knife with which Bentley had been about to cut Lester Leith's coat.

Bentley looked chagrined for a moment, and then sighed.

"You said that it'd be all right for me to pick up anything I could on the side, Captain," he protested.

Lester Leith grinned.

"Well," he said, "I had better amplify that. You can pick up anything you can on the side, provided you leave my pockets alone."

Bentley matched Lester Leith's grin.

"Okay, Captain," he said. "That's a go."

Lester Leith climbed in the taxicab and returned to his apartment.

A vision of loveliness greeted him as he opened the door. Dixie Dormley had adorned herself in garments which looked as though they had been tailored to order in the most exclusive shops.

She smiled a welcome to Lester Leith.

"I kept the cost as low as I could," she said, "in order to get the effect that you wanted."

"You certainly got the effect," complimented Lester Leith, staring at her with very evident approval. "Yes, I think you have done very well, indeed, and we will all go to dinner tonight—the four of us. You, Miss Dormley, Mr. Vare, and, Scuttle, I'm going to include you too."

The spy blinked his eyes. "Yes, sir."

"By the way," said Lester Leith, "did you have the imitation ruby made?"

The spy nodded.

"It's rather a swell affair," he said, "so far as the ruby is concerned.The gold setting is rather cleverly done too. The jeweler insisted upon doing it in a very soft gold. He said that the Indian gold was very yellow and very soft, without much alloy in it. He's duplicated the border design very accurately."

"Quite right, Scuttle," said Lester Leith. "The man knows what he is doing. Let's see it."

The spy handed Lester Leith a little casket, which Leith opened.

The girl exclaimed in admiration.

"Good heavens," she said, "it looks genuine!"

Lester Leith nodded. "It certainly does," he said. "They are able to make excellent imitations of rubies these days."

He lifted the imitation jewel from the case and dropped it carelessly in his side pocket.

"All right, Dixie," he said. "If you'll dress for dinner, we'll leave rather early. I have an important appointment at nine thirty. By the way, I don't want either of you to mention to a living soul that this ruby is an imitation."

At dinner that evening Lester Leith was in rare form. He was suave and courteous, acting very much the gentleman, and discharging his duties as host. It was when the dessert had been cleared away that Leith gravely surveyed Harry Vare's countenance.

"Vare," he said, "you have had your first lesson this afternoon. Do you think that you have profited by it?"

Vare flushed.

"I'll say one thing," he said, "no pickpocket will ever get near you again as long as I'm around."

Lester Leith nodded.

"That's fine," he said. "Now then, I have a rather valuable bauble here that I want to have guarded carefully. I am going to ask you to put it in your pocket."

And Lester Leith slipped from his pocket the imitation ruby and passed it across the table to Vare.

Vare gave a gasp, and his eyes bulged.

"Good heavens," he said, "this is worth a fortune!"

Leith shrugged. "I am making no comments, Vare," he said, "on its value. It is merely something which is entrusted to you for safekeeping, as a part of your training in detective work."

Vare slipped the gem hurriedly into his pocket.

Lester Leith caught the eye of the waiter and secured the check, which he paid.

"I want you folks to take a little walk with me," he said. "Vare is going to have another lesson as a detective, and I would like to have all of you present."

The spy was plainly ill at ease.

"You want me there also, sir?" he asked.

"Certainly," said Lester Leith.

"Very well, sir," said the spy.

Leith helped the young woman on with her wraps, saw that she was seated comfortably in the taxicab, and told the driver to take them to the depot.

The spy stared at him curiously.

"You're leaving town, sir?" he asked.

"Oh, no," said Lester Leith. "We're just going down to the depot, and I'm going to walk around the way I did this afternoon. Vare is going to see that my pocket isn't picked."

There was not as large a crowd in the depot at night, and Lester Leith had some difficulty in finding a crowd of sufficient density to suit his purpose. In his side pocket was a note:

"The young man who is following me around has an imitation ruby in his pocket. He is watching me to make certain that no one picks my pocket. See if you can get the ruby from him, and after you have, return it to me later."

Bentley, the pickpocket, stood on the outskirts of a crowd of people who were waiting in line at a ticket window, and gave Lester Leith a significant glance. Leith gestured toward his pocket.

Leith pushed his way into the crowd, and, as he did so, felt Bentley's fingers slip the printed instructions from his pocket.

Thereafter, Lester Leith wandered aimlessly about the depot, until suddenly he heard a choked cry from Harry Vare.

Lester Leith turned and retraced his steps to the young man, who was standing with a sickly gray countenance, his eyes filled with despair.

"What is it?" asked Lester Leith.

Vare indicated a gaping cut down the side of his coat and through his vest.

"I put that gem in the inside of my vest," he said, "where I knew that it would be safe from the pickpockets, and look what happened!"

Lester Leith summoned the undercover man.

"Scuttle," he said, "will you notice what has happened? This young man whom I was training to be a detective has allowed the property with which I entrusted him to be stolen."

The valet blinked.

"I didn't see anyone, sir," he said, "and I was keeping my own eye peeled."

"Scuttle," Lester Leith said, "I am going to ask you to take Vare back to his apartment. Let him sit down and meditate carefully for two hours upon everything that happened and every face he saw while he was here at the depot. I want to see if he can possibly identify the man who is guilty of picking his pocket."

Vare said humbly: "I'm afraid, sir, that you picked a poor student."

Lester Leith smiled.

"Tut, tut, Vare," he said, "that's something for me to determine. I told you that I was going to give you an education, and I am. You're getting a free scholarship as well as wages. So don't worry about it. Go on to your apartment, and sit down and concentrate."

Vare said: "It certainly is wonderful of you to take the thing this way."

"That's all right, Vare."

As the undercover man took Vare's arm and piloted him toward a taxicab, Lester Leith turned to Dixie Dormley with a smile.

"I've got to meet a party here in a few minutes," he said, "and then we can go and dance."

They continued to hang around the depot for fifteen or twenty minutes. Lester Leith began to frown and to consult his wrist watch. Suddenly Sid Bentley, the pickpocket, materialized through one of the doorways and hurried toward them.

"It's okay," he said.

Leith frowned at him.

"You took long enough doing it," he said.

"I'm sorry I kept you waiting," Bentley said, "but there was one thing that I had to do. You should have figured it out yourself, Chief."

"What was that?"

"I had to go to a good fence and make sure that the thing I had was an imitation," said Bentley.

"Well," Leith said, "there's nothing like being frank."

"That's the way I figure it, Chief," he said. "You know, I've got a duty to you, but I've got a duty to my profession, too. I certainly would have been a dumb hick to have had my hands on a fortune and let it slip."

Lester Leith felt the weight of the jewel in his pocket. He nodded and turned away.

"That's all right, Bentley," he said. "You meet me here tomorrow night at seven o'clock, and in the meantime there won't be anything more for you unless I should get in touch with you. Can you give me a telephone number where I can get in touch with you if I should need you?"

The pickpocket reached in his pocket and took out a card.

"Here you are, Chief," he said. "Just ring up that number and leave word that you'll be at some particular place at some particular time. Don't try to talk with me over the telephone. Just leave that message. Then you go to that place, and I'll be hanging around. If the thing looks safe to me, I'll be there. And if I don't hear from you I'll be here tomorrow night at seven."

"Okay," said Leith.

"Dixie," he said, "I've got something for you to do which is rather confidential. I am going to take you to a night club where there's a chap by the name of Bob Lamont. He makes this night club his regular hangout. He will probably have a companion with him, but, from what I've heard, he has a roving eye. I want you to see to it that his eye roves your way, and that you dance with him. After that, we'll try and make a foursome if we can. If we can't, you can date him up for tomorrow night. Think you can do it?"

"Brother," she said, "in these clothes, if I can't stop any roving masculine eye, I'm going out of show business."

Sergeant Arthur Ackley banged upon the door of the apartment. Bolts clicked back as Harry Vare opened the door and stared stupidly at Sergeant Ackley.

Sergeant Ackley pushed his way into the apartment without a word, slammed the door shut behind him, strode across the room to a chair, and sat down.

"Well, young man," he said, "you've got yourself into a pretty pickle."

Harry Vare blinked and started to talk, but words failed him.

Sergeant Ackley flipped back his coat so that Harry Vare's eyes could rest on the gold badge pinned to his vest.

"Well," he said, "what have you got to say for yourself?"

"I—I—I don't know what you're talking about."

"Oh, yes you do," said Sergeant Ackley. "You're teamed up with this super-crook and you're hashing up a scheme to assist in hijacking a big ruby."

Vare shook his head.

"No, sir," he said, "you're mistaken. I had a big ruby which was given to me to keep but somebody stole it."

Sergeant Ackley let his eyes bore into those of Harry Vare. Then he got to his feet, reached out and thrust a broad hand to the collar of Vare's coat, twisting it tightly.

"Well," he said, "it'll be about ten years for you, and you'd better come along."

Vare stared at Sergeant Ackley with pathetic eyes.

"I haven't done anything," he said.

Sergeant Ackley eyed the man shrewdly.

"Listen," he said, "did you ever hear of George Navin?"

"You mean the man who was murdered?" asked Harry Vare.

Ackley nodded.

"I read something about it in the paper," said Vare.

"All right," said Sergeant Ackley. "Navin was murdered for a big Indian ruby: Bob Lamon was his secretary. Does that mean anything to you?"

"No, sir," said Vare. "Not a thing."

All right," said Sergeant Ackley. "I'll tell you a few things, and you can see how much it means to you. This fellow Lester Leith that you're working for is one of the cleverest crooks this city has ever produced. He makes a living out of robbing crooks of their ill-gotten spoils. He's slick and he's clever, and he usually dopes out the solution of a crime in advance of the police, and then shakes down the crook before we get to him."

"I didn't know that," said Harry Vare.

"Well, maybe you did, and maybe you didn't," said Sergeant Ackley. "That's something for you to tell the jury when you come up for trial. But here's something else that you may like to listen to. Lester Leith picked up this chorus girl, and the two of them went out last night after they left you and picked up Bob Lamont and some other woman.

"Lester Leith is pretty much of a gentleman, and he wears his clothes well, and this chorus girl he had with him looked like a million dollars in a lot of high-priced clothes. The night club was more or less informal, and she gave Bob Lamont the eye. Bob fell for her and started to dance with her, and before the evening was finished they had moved to another table and were having a nice little foursome."

"But," said Harry Vare, gathering courage, "what has that got to do with me?"

Sergeant Ackley studied him in shrewd appraisal.

"So," he said, "they made another date for tonight, and the four of them are going out."

Harry Vare suddenly caught his breath. His eyes grew wide and dark with apprehension.

"Good heavens!" he said.

Sergeant Ackley nodded. "I thought so," he said.

Panic showed in Vare's face.

"You've got just ten seconds to come clean," said Sergeant Ackley. "If you come clean and give me the low-down on this thing, and agree to work with me, there's a chance that we may give you immunity from prosecution. Otherwise, you're going to jail for at least ten years."

Harry didn't need ten seconds. He was blurting out speech almost before Sergeant Ackley had finished.

"I didn't know the name," he said, "and I didn't know it was Lamont until you told me. But Lester Leith hired me to study detective work. He had his pocket picked once yesterday, and then gave me a jewel to carry, and it was picked from my pocket. I felt all broken up about it, but Mr. Leith said that it was all right. I'd have to learn a step at a time.

"He told me that tonight he was going to teach me how to make an arrest. He said that I was to arrest him, just as though he had been a crook. He said that he was going out to a dinner party tonight with another man and a woman, and that they would probably wind up at the man's apartment; that after they got to the apartment, he had it fixed up that Dixie Dormley—that's the chorus girl—was to take the other girl out for a few moments, and that, as soon as that happened, I was to come busting in as a detective and accuse Lester Leith of some crime, handcuff him, and lead him out."

Sergeant Ackley frowned. "That's everything you know about it?"

"Everything," said Harry Vare; "but I get more instructions later."

"Well," Ackley said, "I'm going to give you a break. If you do exactly as I tell you, and don't tell Lester Leith that I was here, I'll see that you get a break and aren't arrested."

"That's all right, officer," Harry Vare said. "I'll do anything you say—"

* * *

Lester Leith handed Sid Bentley, the mournful-faced pickpocket, a one-hundred-dollar bill. "Wages for another day," he said.

Bentley pocketed the hundred and looked with avaricious eyes at the wallet which Leith returned to his breast pocket. "Speaking professionally," he said, "you'd do better to carry your bills in a fold. That breast-pocket stuff is particularly vulnerable."

"I know it," Leith said, "but I like to have my money where I can get at it."

Bentley nodded, his milk-mild eyes without expression. "I," he said, "like people who carry their money where I can get at it."

"Remember our bargain," Leith said.

"What do you suppose makes me feel so bad about getting a hundred bucks?" Bentley asked. "I'm just figuring I made a poor bargain."

"You mean the work's too hard?"

"No, that there are too many restrictions. I'm commencing to think I could make a good living just following *you* around."

Leith lowered his voice. "Where," he asked, "do you suppose I make all this money?"

Bentley said: "Now, buddy, you've got me interested."

Leith said: "We're working on the same side of the street."

"You don't mean you're a dip?"

"No, but I'm a crook. I'm a confidence man."

"What's the game?" Bentley asked.

Leith said: "I have different rackets. Right now, it's sticking a sucker with that imitation ruby. I show the ruby to the man I'm aiming to trim. I tell him I found it on the street, that I don't know whether it's any good or not, that I presume it isn't good, but that even as an imitation, it should have some value. I ask him what he thinks about it.

"If he's a real gem expert, I know it from what he says. He tells me to go home and forget it. I thank him, and that's all there is to it. But if he's a little dubious about whether it's genuine, I gradually let him think I'm a sucker. You see, this ruby is the exact duplicate of a valuable ruby that has been in the newspapers."

Bentley said: "That's what fooled me about it the first time I saw it."

"You recognized it?"

"Sure."

"Well," Leith said, "lots of other people will, too. They'll think it's the genuine priceless ruby. Some of them will want to buy it. Some of them won't. If they guy offers me anything like five hundred dollars for it, I'm perfectly willing to sell."

Bentley said: "I'm still listening."

"The big trouble," Leith said, "is the risk."

"How do you mean?"

"I've got too many of them out," Leith said. "These imitations cost me about fifteen dollars apiece. I've been playing the racket for a week."

"You're afraid some of the suckers have made a squawk?"

"Yes."

Bentley said: "I know just how you feel. When a racket gets hot, you know you should leave it, but there's still coin in it, so you want to hang on."

Leith said: "That's where you come in."

"What do you mean?"

Leith said: "I want you to follow me around from now on whenever I'm going to make a sale."

"What do I do?"

"Just this," Leith said. "A cop can't make a pinch until after I've made a sale. In order to do that, they'll have to plant a ringer on me for a sucker, and have the payments made to me in marked money."

"No, they won't," Bentley said. "You're all wet there, brother. They can *either* have the marked money on you, or they can pinch both you and the sucker and hold the sucker as a material witness."

Leith said: "That last is what I'm afraid of. If that happens, I want you to get the evidence."

"You mean from the sucker?"

"Yes."

"Listen, brother. That evidence will be just as hot as a stove lid. I couldn't—"

Leith took from his pocket a little cloth sack to which was attached a printed tag with a postage stamp on the tag.

"You don't keep it on you for a minute," he said. "You just beat it for the first mailbox, drop it, and let Uncle Sam do the dirty work."

Bentley said: "That's more like it."

"Whenever you do that you get a five-hundred-dollar bonus."

"And that's all I have to do?"

"That's all."

"And my cut is still a hundred bucks a day."

"That's right. You just have to follow me around."

"Lead me to it," Bentley said. "But you'll have to tell me when you're going to make a deal."

Leith said: "In about an hour, Miss Dormley, the young lady who was with me last night, and I are going out to dinner with another couple. I've fixed things up with Miss Dormley so she'll get the other girl out of the way. That will leave me alone with the man. I figure I can put the deal across with him."

"I'll be tagging along."

Leith said: "Carry this mailing sack where you can put your hand on it in an instant. Don't ever be caught without it."

"Listen, buddy," Bentley said, "don't think I was born yesterday. If you think I want to be caught with goods that will hook me up as your confederate, you're cockeyed. And don't pull your stuff in a place where there isn't a mailbox on every corner, because if you do, it's just your hard luck."

Sergeant Arthur Ackley stared reproachfully at Beaver, the undercover operative. "Right under your nose, Beaver," he said, "and you muffed it."

The spy's face colored. "What do you mean, I muffed it? I'm the one that told you he was going after that ruby."

Sergeant Ackley said: "You argued a lot, Beaver, and became personally offensive, but you didn't give me anything constructive."

"What do you mean, constructive?"

"You didn't even smell a rat when he brought that green kid in to act as a detective," Ackley said.

Beaver sighed. "Oh, what's the use. Just don't forget that we have a bet. If all those various things I told you about fit into his plan to get the ruby, I win your watch."

"Not at all, Beaver," said Ackley. "You have overlooked one little fact. It was to have been done so cleverly that I couldn't pin anything on him. You overlooked that little thing, Beaver, and that's going to cost you fifty bucks—because I've already got it pinned on him."

Beaver said: "I suppose you know every step in his campaign."

Sergeant Ackley gloated. "You bet I do."

The spy scraped back his chair and got to his feet.

Sergeant Ackley said: "Don't go to bed until after midnight, Beaver. I'll be calling you some time before then to come down to headquarters. Leith will be booked and in a cell. Then you can have the pleasure of telling him that you helped put him there—and you can pay over the fifty bucks to me."

Beaver lunged toward the door. "You've thought you had him before," he flung back, on the threshold.

Sergeant Ackley laughed. "But this time, Beaver, I *have* got him. I threw a scare into that green kid Vare, and he told me everything."

The four people left the taxicab and walked across the sidewalk to the entrance of the apartment house. Dixie Dormley, attired in soft white, was vibrantly beautiful. The other young woman, although expensively gowned, seemed drab in comparison.

Lester Leith, well-tailored, faultlessly groomed, wore his evening clothes with an air of distinction. Bob Lamont was quick and nervous. He seemed ill at ease.

The four people chatted as they went up in the elevator, and Bob Lamont opened the door of his apartment with a flourish.

It was an apartment which was well and tastefully furnished. As secretary to George Navin, Lamont had drawn a very good salary.

When the two young women were seated, Lamont went to the kitchenette to get the makings of drinks.

Lester Leith gave a significant glance at Dixie Dormley.

She caught the glance, turned at once to the other young woman, and exclaimed, "Oh, my heavens, I left my purse in that taxicab! Or else it may have fallen out on the sidewalk; I don't know which. It seems to me that I heard something drop to the running board as I got out."

The young woman said: "Never mind, Dixie, you can telephone the taxicab company, and they'll have it in the Lost and Found Department."

"Yes," wailed Dixie, "but suppose it dropped to the running board. Then it would have spilled off at the corner."

Lester Leith reached for his hat.

"I'll run down and see."

Dixie Dormley got to her feet quickly and started to the door.

"No, please," she said. "You wait here. I can't explain, but I'd much rather go by myself, unless Vivian wants to come with me."

She flashed the other young woman a smile of invitation, and Vivian promptly arose.

"Tell Bob that we'll be right back," she said.

As the door closed behind the two women, Lester Leith strolled out into the kitchenette where Lamont was taking ice cubes from a refrigerator.

"Well, Lamont," said Lester Leith casually, "you pulled that murder pretty cleverly, didn't you?"

Lamont dropped the ice-cube tray with a clatter, and stared at Leith with bulging eyes. "What the devil are you talking about?"

"Oh, you know well enough, Lamont," he said. "The police were a little bit slow in catching up with you, that's all, but the scheme wasn't really so clever. The guards shut all of the windows and locked the shutters on the inside when they went into Navin's room, but you were the last one in there. It would have been very easy for you to have moved against one of the windows and unlocked one of the shutters. Then you left the room, went directly to the safe, took out the gem, and went to your conference with the lawyer, which gave you your alibi. In the morning you walked in and locked the shutter again from the inside.

"You'd probably been bribed by the Hindus to leave one of the steel shutters unlocked, and had specified that they must break in and do the job promptly at four o'clock, so that the police would be properly confused.

"Where the police made their mistake was in thinking that whoever had committed the murder had also stolen the gem from the safe. It didn't occur to them that they could have been independent acts. And apparently, so far, it hasn't occurred to the Hindus. They thought simply that they failed to find the gem, and that Navin had placed it in some other hiding place.

"But you can't get away with it long, Lamont. The police will be here inside of half an hour."

"You're crazy!" said Lamont.

Lester Leith shook his head.

"No, Lamont," he said, "you're the one who's crazy. You overlooked the fact that, if the Hindus should start to talk, they had you strapped to the electric chair. And that's exactly what happened. The police got a confession out of one of the Hindus about fifteen minutes ago. My paper telephoned me."

Lamont's face was gray. "Who—who are you?" he asked.

"I'm a free-lance reporter," said Lester Leith, "who works on feature stuff for some of the leading papers. Right now I'm assigned to cover the story of your arrest in the Navin case. The newspaper knew it was going to break sometime within the next twenty-four to forty-eight hours. Now if you would like to pick up a little money that would come in handy when it becomes necessary to retain an attorney to represent you, you can give us an exclusive interview. In fact, the only thing for you to do is to confess and try and get a life sentence. If you want to make your confession through my newspaper, we would bring all the political pressure to bear that we could to see that you got off with life."

There was an imperative knock on the door of the apartment.

Lester Leith strolled to it casually.

"Probably the police now, Lamont."

He opened the door.

Harry Vare burst into the room.

"You're under arrest!" he snapped at Lester Leith.

Lester Leith stepped back and eyed Vare with well-simulated amazement.

"What the devil are you talking about?" he asked.

"Your name's Lamont," said Vare, "and you're under arrest for the murder of George Navin. I'm representing the Indian priests who are trying to recover the gem, and I'm going to take you to police headquarters with me right now."

Lester Leith said: "You're crazy. My name's Leith. I'm not Lamont. That's Lamont over there, the man you want. I'm working for a newspaper."

Harry Vare laughed, scornfully.

"I saw you come in here and had the doorman point out the one who lived here. He pointed to you."

"You fool," Leith said, "he made a mistake, or rather you did. He pointed to this man here, and you thought he was pointing me out."

Vare snapped a gun into view, and fished for handcuffs with his left hand.

"Hold out your wrist," he said, "or I'll blow you apart."

Lester Leith hesitated a moment, then held out his wrist, reluctantly. Vare snapped one of the handcuffs to Leith's wrist, locked the other one around his own wrist, and said, "Come on, you slicker, you're going to headquarters."

Leith said: "Listen! You're making the biggest mistake of your life. You're letting the real murderer—"

Bob Lamont laughed.

He turned to Harry Vare and said: "You're quite right, officer, that's Bob Lamont that you've got under arrest, but this comes as quite a shock to me. I've known him for two or three years, and thought he was above reproach."

"No, he wasn't," said Vare. "He was the man who murdered Navin."

Lester Leith groaned.

"Youngster," he said, "you're making a mistake that is going to make you the laughing-stock of the city inside of twenty-four hours."

Vare muttered grimly: "Come along, Lamont."

Lester Leith sighed and accompanied Vare through the doorway to the elevator, down the elevator, across the lobby of the apartment house, and to the street.

"Well," said Leith, "that was pretty well done, Vare. You can let me loose now."

Vare took a key from his pocket and inserted it in the lock of the handcuff only after considerable difficulty. His forehead was beaded with nervous perspiration, and his hand was shaking. He made two attempts to fit the key to the lock. "I can't seem to get it," he said.

Leith glanced at him sharply. "Vare," he said, "what the devil are you trying to do?"

"Nothing."

"Give me that key."

Vare didn't pass over the key but instead looked expectantly back toward the shadows.

The voice of Sergeant Ackley said: "I'll take charge now."

There was motion from the deep shadows of the doorway of an adjoining building. Sergeant Ackley, accompanied by a plainclothes officer, stepped forward.

Leith said to Sergeant Ackley: "What's the meaning of this?"

Ackley said: "You should know more about it than I do, Leith. You've delivered yourself to me already handcuffed."

For a moment there was consternation on Leith's face, then he masked all expression from his face and eyes.

"Didn't expect to see *me* here, did you?" Sergeant Ackley asked gloatingly.

Leith said nothing.

Sergeant Ackley said to Vare: "Give me the key to those handcuffs, young man. I'll slip one off your wrist, and put it on Leith's other wrist."

Vare extended his hand. Sergeant Ackley took the key, clicked the handcuff from Vare's arm, and snapped it around Leith's other wrist.

The rapid *click-clack click-clack* of high heels as two women rounded the corner, walking rapidly, came to Leith's ears. He turned around so that the light fell full on his face.

"Why, Mr Leith!" Dixie Dormley exclaimed. "What's the matter?"

Lester Leith said nothing.

Sergeant Ackley grinned gloatingly. "Mr. Leith," he said, "is being arrested. You probably didn't know he was a crook."

"A crook!" she exclaimed.

From the doorway of the apartment house came a hurrying figure, attired in overcoat, hat, and gloves. He carried a light suitcase in one hand, and crossed the strip of sidewalk with three swift strides. It wasn't until he started to signal for a taxicab that he became aware of the little group.

Sergeant Ackley said to the plainclothesman: "Get that guy."

Lamont heard the order, turned to look over his shoulder, then dropped the suitcase, and started to run.

"Help!" yelled Sergeant Ackley.

Lamont sprinted down the street. He turned to flash an apprehensive glance over his shoulder, and so did not see the figure of Sid Bentley as it slid out from the shadows.

There was a thud, a tangled mass of arms and legs, and then Bentley, sitting up on the sidewalk, said: "I got him for you, officer."

The plainclothesman ran up and grabbed Lamont by the collar. He jerked him to his feet, then said to Bentley: "That was fine work. I'm glad you stopped him."

"No trouble at all," Bentley said.

The officer said: "Come on back with me, and I'll give you a courtesy card which may help you out some time."

Bentley's eyes glistened. "Now, that'll be right nice of you, officer."

The officer pushed the reluctant Lamont back toward the little group which had, by this time, became a small, curious crowd. "Here he is, Sergeant," he said.

Sergeant Ackley said irritably: "All right, Lamont. You'd better come clean."

"I don't know what you're talking about," Lamont said.

Sergeant Ackley laughed. "Come on, Lamont, the jig's up. You killed George Navin and got that ruby. Lester Leith hijacked it from you. Now, if you'll give us the facts, you won't be any worse off for it."

Lamont said: "I don't know what you're talking about. I—I took the custody of the ruby because—"

"Careful, Lamont," Lester Leith said sharply. "Don't put your neck in a noose."

Sergeant Ackley turned and slapped Leith across the mouth. "Keep your trap shut," he said, and to the plainclothes officer: "Go ahead and search him."

"Oh, no," Lamont shouted. "You can't do it. Navin gave it to me to keep for him. I was going to turn it over to the estate."

"Gave you what?" Sergeant Ackley asked.

"The ruby."

Ackley said: "Go head, Lamont, tell the truth. You took the ruby, and then Lester Leith took it from you."

Lamont shook his head.

Sergeant Ackley ran his hands over Leith's coat. Abruptly he shot his hand into Leith's inside pocket and pulled out a chamois-skin bag. He reached inside of that bag, and the spectators gasped as the rays from the street light were reflected from a blood-red blob of brilliance.

"There it is," Segeant Ackley said gloatingly.

Lamont stared, clapped his own hand to his breast pocket, became suddenly silent.

Sergeant Ackley said triumphantly to the crowd: "That's the way we work, folks. Give the crooks rope enough, and they hang themselves. You'll read about it in the paper tomorrow morning. Sergeant Arthur Ackley solves the Navin murder, and at the same time traps a crook who's trying to hijack the East Indian ruby. All right, boys. We're going to the station."

Leith said: "Sergeant, you're making a—"

"Shut up," Ackley said savagely. "I've been laying for you for a long time, and now I've got you."

Dixie Dormley said indignantly: "I think it's an outrage. You've struck this man when he was handcuffed. You won't let him explain."

"Shut up," Ackley growled, "or I'll take you too."

Dixie Dormley fastened glistening, defiant eyes on Sergeant Ackley. "Try to keep me from going," she said. "I'm going to be right there, and complain about your brutality."

Sid Bentley sidled up to the plainclothes officer. "The name's Bentley, Sid Bentley. If you wouldn't mind giving me that card."

The officer nodded, pulled a card from his pocket, and scribbled on it.

"What are you doing?" Sergeant Ackley asked.

"Giving this man a courtesy card. He caught Lamont—stopped him when he was running away."

Sergeant Ackley was in a particularly expansive mood. "Here," he said, "I'll give him one, too."

Sid Bentley took the cards. He stared for a long, dubious moment at Lester Leith, then said: "Gentlemen, I thank you very much. It was a pleasure to help you. Good night."

A police car sirened its way to the curb. Sergeant Ackley loaded his prisoners into the car, and they made a quick run to headquarters with Dixie Dormley, white-faced and determined, following in a taxicab.

Sergeant Ackley said to the desk sergeant: "Well, let's get the boys from the press in here. I've solved the Navin murder, recovered the ruby, and caught a hijacker red-handed."

Dixie Dormley said: "And he's been guilty of unnecessary brutality."

One of the reporters from the press room came sauntering in. "What you got, Sergeant?" he asked.

Sergeant Ackley said: "I've solved the Navin murder."

"Hot dog," the newspaperman said.

The desk sergeant said dubiously: "Sergeant, did you take a good look at this ruby?"

Sergeant Ackley said: "I don't have to. I had the thing all doped out. I knew where it was, and how to get it. That ruby is worth a fortune. There'll be a reward for that, and—"

"There won't be any reward for this," the desk sergeant said, "unless I'm making a big mistake. This is a nice piece of red glass. You see, I know something about gems, Sergeant. I was on the jewelry detail for—"

Sergeant Ackley's jaw sagged. "You mean that isn't a real ruby?"

Lester Leith said to the desk sergeant: "If you'll permit me, I can explain. This was an imitation which I had made. It's rather a good imitation—it cost me fifty dollars. I gave it to a young man who wanted to be a detective to keep for me. His pocket was picked. Naturally, he was very much chagrined. I wanted to get the property returned, so I discreetly offered a reward. The property was returned earlier this evening. What I say can be established by absolute proof."

Sergeant Ackley's eyes were riveted on the red stone. "You didn't get this from Lamont?" he asked.

"Certainly not. Lamont will tell you that I didn't."

Lamont said: "I've never seen that before in my life."

"Then where's the real ruby?" Sergeant Ackley asked.

Lamont took a deep breath. "I haven't the least idea."

"What were you running away for?"

"Probably because of the manner in which you tried to make your arrest," Lester Leith interposed. "You didn't tell him you were an officer. You simply yelled, 'Get him,' and your man started for him with—"

"No such thing!" Sergeant Ackley interrupted.

"That's exactly what happened." Dixie Dormley said indignantly.

The desk sergeant said to Lester Leith: "Why didn't you tell him this was an imitation?"

Dixie Dormley said: "He tried to, and Sergeant Ackley slapped him across the mouth."

Sergeant Ackley blinked his eyes rapidly, then said: "I didn't do any such thing. I didn't touch the man."

Dixie Dormley said: "I thought you'd try to lie out of it. I have the names of a dozen witnesses who feel the same way I do about police brutality, and will join me in making a complaint."

Ackley said savagely: "Give me the list of those witnesses."

Dixie Dormley threw back her head and laughed in his face.

The sergeant said: "You know how the chief feels about that, Sergeant."

Lester Leith said quietly: "I'd like to call up my valet. He can come down here and identify that imitation ruby. It's one which he had made."

The desk sergeant reached for the telephone, but Sergeant Ackley stopped him. "I happen to know there was an imitation ruby made," he said, "if you're sure this is imitation."

The desk sergeant said: "There's no doubt about it."

Sergeant Ackley fitted a key to the handcuffs, unlocked them, said to Lester Leith: "You're getting off lucky this time. I don't know how you did it."

Leith said, with dignity: "You simply went off halfcocked, Sergeant. I wouldn't have held it against you if you'd given me a chance to explain, but you struck me when I tried to tell you that the gem you had was an imitation, that it was my property, that I have a bill of sale for it."

The newspaper reporter scibbled gleefully. "Hot dog," he said, and scurried away toward the press room. A moment later he was back with a camera and a flash bulb. "Let me get a picture of this," he said. "Hold up that imitation gem."

Sergeant Ackley shouted: "You can't publish this!"

The flash of the bulb interrupted his protest.

Edward H. Beaver, the undercover man, was still up when Lester Leith latchkeyed the door of the apartment. "Hello, Scuttle," he said. "Up rather late, aren't you?"

"I was waiting for a phone call."

Leith raised his eyebrows. "Rather late for a phone call, isn't it, Scuttle?"

"Yes, sir. Have you seen Sergeant Ackley tonight, sir?"

"Have I seen him!" Leith said, with a smile. "I'll say I've seen him. You'll read all about it in the papers tomorrow, Scuttle. Do you know what happened? The sergeant arrested me for recovering my own property."

"Your own property, sir?"

"Yes, Scuttle. That imitation ruby. I was rather attached to it, and Vare felt so chagrined about having lost it that I thought it would be worth a small reward to get it back."

"And you recovered it?"

"Oh, yes," Leith said. "I got it earlier in the evening. Sergeant Ackley found it in my pocket and jumped to the conclusion it was the real ruby."

"What did he do?" the spy asked.

Lester Leith grinned. "He covered himself with glory," he said. "He put on quite a show for a crowd of interested spectators, and then committed the crowning indiscretion of inviting them to read about it in the paper tomorrow morning. They'll read about it, all right. Poor Ackley!"

A slow smile twisted the spy's features. "The sergeant didn't give you anything for me, did he, sir?"

"For you, Scuttle?"

"Yes, sir."

"Why, no. Why the devil would you be getting things from Sergeant Ackley?"

"You see, sir, I happened to run into the sergeant a day or so ago, and he borrowed my watch. He was going to return it. He—"

The phone rang and the spy jumped toward it with alacrity. "I'll answer it, sir," he said.

He picked up the receiver, said: "Hello . . . Yes . . . Oh, he did—" and then listened for almost a minute.

A slow flush spread over the spy's face. He said: "That wasn't the way I understood it. That wasn't the bet—" There was another interval during which the receiver made raucous, metallic sounds, then a bang at the other end of the line announced that the party had hung up.

The undercover man dropped the receiver back into place.

Lester Leith sighed. "Scuttle," he said, "I don't know what we're going to do about Sergeant Ackley. He's a frightful nuisance."

"Yes, sir," the spy said.

"And a very poor loser," Leith remarked.

"I'll say he's a poor loser," the spy blurted. "Any man who will take advantage of his official position as a superior to wriggle out of paying a debt—"

"Scuttle," Lester Leith interrupted, "what the devil are you talking about?"

"Oh, another matter, sir. Something else which happened to be on my mind."

Leith said: "Well, get it off your mind, Scuttle. Bring out that bottle of Scotch and a soda siphon. We'll have a quiet drink. Just the two of us."

Beaver had just finished with the drinks when a knock sounded at the door. "See who it is, Scuttle."

Dixie Dormley and Harry Vare stood on the threshold.

Leith, on his feet, ushered them into the room, seated the actress, indicated a chair for Vare, and said: "Two more highballs, Scuttle."

Vare said haltingly: "I'm sorry, Mr. Leith. The way the thing was put up to me, I couldn't have done any differently."

Leith dismissed the matter with a gesture.

Dixie Dormley said: "After you left, a Captain Carmichael came in. He seemed terribly upset, and was pretty angry at Sergeant Ackley. It seems that two of the people who had been standing there were friends of Captain Carmichael, and they telephoned in to him about the brutality of the police."

Leith smiled. "Is that so," he commented idly. "What happened?"

Dixie Dormley said: "Well, Sergeant Ackley had just let Lamont go—figured he didn't have any case against him. Captain Carmichael listened to what Ackley had to report, and was furious. He issued an order to have Lamont picked up again, and a radio car got him within a dozen blocks of the police station.

"They brought him back and Carmichael went to work on him, and in no time had a confession out of him. It seems he'd agreed to open one of the steel shutters for some Hindu priests. They'd paid him for the job. Then he got the idea of doublecrossing them, opened the safe, lifted the ruby, and hid it.

"He had it with him tonight when he was arrested. He swore the plainclothesman must have taken it from his pocket when they were scuffling. The plainclothesman denied it, and then they thought of this man who had first grabbed Lamont.

"So then they figured *he* was the man they wanted, and it turned out the police had not only let him go, *but given him a couple of courtesy cards.* Well, you should have heard Captain Carmichael! Such language!"

Leith turned to Vare.

"There you are, Vare," he said. "A complete education in the detection of crime by the case method. Just observe Sergeant Ackley, do the exact opposite of what he does, and you're bound to be a success."

And the police spy, resuming his mixing of the drinks, could be seen to nod, unconsciously but perceptibly.

THE BLIND SPOT

(1945)

Barry Perowne

Barry Perowne

"Barry Perowne" (1908–) is the pen name of British writer Philip Atkey. One of the very few writers who built a successful career on the revival of a character first developed by another author, Perowne has published some twenty-one novels and story collections featuring Raffles, a crook-with-class first created by E. W. Hornung in 1899. Under his own name, Perowne has written three good mystery novels: Blue Water Murder *(1935),* Heirs of Merlin *(1945), and* Juniper Rock *(1953). He also did the screenplay for the film* Walk a Crooked Path *(1970).*

THE BLIND SPOT

Annixter loved the little man like a brother. He put an arm around the little man's shoulders, partly from affection and partly to prevent himself from falling.

He had been drinking earnestly since seven o'clock the previous evening. It was now nudging midnight, and things were a bit hazy. The lobby was full of the thump of hot music; down two steps, there were a lot of tables, a lot of people, a lot of noise. Annixter had no idea what this place was called, or how he had got here, or when. He had been in so many places since seven o'clock the previous evening.

"In a nutshell," confided Annixter, leaning heavily on the little man, "a woman fetches you a kick in the face, or fate fetches you a kick in the face. Same thing, really—a woman and fate. So what? So you think it's the finish, an' you go out and get plastered. You get good an' plastered," said Annixter, "an' you brood.

"You sit there an' you drink an' you brood—an' in the end you find you've brooded up just about the best idea you ever had in your life! 'At's the way it goes," said Annixter, "an' 'at's my philosophy—the harder you kick a playwright, the better he works!"

He gestured with such vehemence that he would have collapsed if the little man hadn't steadied him. The little man was poker-backed, his grip was firm. His mouth was firm, too—a straight line, almost colorless. He wore hexagonal rimless spectacles, a black hard-felt hat, a neat pepper-and-salt suit. He looked pale and prim beside the flushed, rumpled Annixter.

From her counter, the hat-check girl watched them indifferently.

"Don't you think," the little man said to Annixter, "you ought to go home now? I've been honored you snould tell me the scenario of your play, but—"

"I had to tell someone," said Annixter, "or blow my top! Oh, boy, what a play, what a play! What a murder, eh? That climax—"

The full, dazzling perfection of it struck him again. He stood frowning, considering, swaying a little—then nodded abruptly, groped for the little man's hand, warmly pumphandled it.

"Sorry I can't stick around," said Annixter. "I got work to do."

He crammed his hat on shapelessly, headed on a slightly elliptical course across the lobby, thrust the double doors open with both hands, lurched out into the night.

It was, to his inflamed imagination, full of lights, winking and tilting across the dark. *Sealed Room* by James Annixter. No. *Room Reserved* by James—No, no. *Blue Room. Room Blue. Room Blue* by James Annixter—

He stepped, oblivious, off the curb, and a taxi, swinging in toward the place he had just left, skidded with suddenly locked, squealing wheels on the wet road.

Something hit Annixter violently in the chest, and all the lights he had been seeing exploded in his face.

There there weren't any lights.

Mr. James Annixter, the playwright, was knocked down by a taxi late last night when leaving the Casa Havana. After hospital treatment for shock and superficial injuries, he returned to his home.

The lobby of the Casa Havana was full of the thump of music; down two steps there were a lot of tables, a lot of people, a lot of noise. The hat-check girl looked wonderingly at Annixter—at the plaster on his forehead, the black sling which supported his left arm.

"My," said the hat-check girl, "I certainly didn't expect to see *you* again so soon!"

"You remember me, then?" said Annixter, smiling.

"I ought to," said the hat-check girl. "You cost me a night's sleep! I heard those brakes squeal right after you went out the door that night—and there was a sort of a thud!" She shuddered. "I kept hearing it all night long. I can still hear it now—a week after! Horrible!"

"You're sensitive," said Annixter.

"I got too much imagination," the hat-check girl admitted.

"F'rinstance, I just *knew* it was you even before I run to the door and see you lying there. That man you was with was standing just outside. 'My heavens', I says to him. 'it's your friend'!"

"What did he say?" Annixter asked.

"He says, 'He's not my friend. He's just someone I met.' Funny, eh?"

Annixter moistened his lips.

"How d'you mean," he said carefully, "funny? I *was* just someone he'd met."

"Yes, but—man you been drinking with," said the hat-check girl, "killed before your eyes. Because he must have seen it; he went out right after you. You'd think he'd 'a' been interested, at least. But when the taxi driver starts shouting for witnesses it wasn't his fault, I looks around for that man—an' he's gone!"

Annixter exchanged a glance with Ransome, his producer, who was with him. It was a slightly puzzled, slightly anxious glance. But he smiled, then, at the hat-check girl.

"Not quite 'killed before his eyes'," said Annixter. "Just shaken up a bit, that's all."

There was no need to explain to her how curious, how eccentric, had been the effect of that "shaking up" upon his mind.

"If you could 'a' seen yourself lying there with the taxi's lights shining on you—"

"Ah, there's that imagination of yours!" said Annixter.

He hesitated for just an instant, then asked the question he had come to ask—the question which had assumed so profound an importance for him.

He asked, "That man I was with—who was he?"

The hat-check girl looked from one to the other. She shook her head.

"I never saw him before," she said, "and I haven't seen him since."

Annixter felt as though she had struck him in the face. He had hoped, hoped desperately, for a different answer; he had counted on it.

Ransome put a hand on his arm, restrainingly.

"Anyway," said Ransome, "as we're here, let's have a drink."

They went down the two steps into the room where the band thumped. A waiter led them to a table, and Ransome gave him an order.

"There was no point in pressing that girl," Ransome said to

Annixter. "She doesn't know the man, and that's that. My advice to you, James, is: Don't worry. Get your mind on to something else. Give yourself a chance. After all, it's barely a week since—"

"A week!" Annixter said. "Hell, look what I've done in that week! The whole of the first two acts, and the third act right up to that crucial point—the climax of the whole thing: the solution: the scene that the play stands or falls on! It would have been done, Bill—the whole play, the best thing I ever did in my life—it would have been finished two days ago if it hadn't been for this—" he knuckled his forehead— "this extraordinary blind spot, this damnable little trick of memory!"

"You had a very rough shaking-up—"

"That?" Annixter said contemptuously. He glanced down at the sling on his arm. "I never even felt it; it didn't bother me. I woke up in the ambulance with my play as vivid in my mind as the moment the taxi hit me—more so, maybe, because I was stone cold sober then, and knew what I had. A winner—a thing that just couldn't miss!"

"If you'd rested," Ransome said. "as the doc told you, instead of sitting up in bed there scribbling night and day—"

"I had to get it on paper. Rest?" said Annixter, and laughed harshly. "You don't rest when you've got a thing like that. That's what you live for—if you're a playwright. That *is* living! I've lived eight whole lifetimes, in those eight characters, during the past five days. I've lived so utterly in them, Bill, that it wasn't till I actually came to write that last scene that I realized what I'd lost! Only my whole play, that's all! How was Cynthia stabbed in that windowless room into which she had locked and bolted herself? How did the killer get to her? *How was it done?*

"Hell," Annixter said, "scores of writers, better men than I am, have tried to put that sealed room murder over—and never quite done it convincingly: never quite got away with it: been overelaborate, phony! I had it—heaven help me, *I* had it! Simple, perfect, glaringly obvious when you've once seen it! And it's my whole play—the curtain rises on that sealed room and falls on it! That was my revelation—*how it was done!* That was what I got, by way of playwright's compensation, because a woman I thought I loved kicked me in the face—I brooded up the answer to the sealed room! And a taxi knocked it out of my head!"

He drew a long breath.

"I've spent two days and two nights, Bill, trying to get that idea back— *how it was done!* It won't come. I'm a competent playwright; I know my job; I could finish my play, but it'd be like all those others—not quite right, phony! It wouldn't be *my play!* But there's a little man walking around this city somewhere—a little man with hexagonal glasses—who's got my idea in his head! He's got it because I told it to him. I'm going to find that little man, and get back what belongs to me! I've got to! Don't you see that, Bill? I've *got* to!"

> *If the gentleman who, at the Casa Havana on the night of January 27th so patiently listened to a playwright's outlining of an idea for a drama will communicate with the Box No. below, he will hear of something to his advantage.*

A little man who had said, "He's not my friend. He's just someone I met—"

A little man who'd seen an accident but hadn't waited to give evidence—

The hat-check girl had been right. The *was* something a little queer about that.

A little queer?

During the next few days, when the advertisements he'd inserted failed to bring any reply, it began to seem to Annixter very queer indeed.

His arm was out of its sling now, but he couldn't work. Time and again, he sat down before his almost completed manuscript, read it through with close, grim attention, thinking, "It's *bound* to come back this time!"—only to find himself up against that blind spot again, that blank wall, that maddening hiatus in his memory.

He left his work and prowled the streets; he haunted bars and saloons; he rode for miles on 'buses and subway, especially at the rush hours. He saw a million faces, but the face of the little man with hexagonal glasses he did not see.

The thought of him obsessed Annixter. It was infuriating, it was unjust, it was torture to think that a little, ordinary, chance-met citizen was walking blandly around somewhere with the last link of his, the celebrated James Annixter's play—the best thing he'd ever done—locked away in his head. And with no idea of what he had: without the imagination, probably, to appreciate what he had! And certainly with no idea of what it meant to Annixter!

Or *had* he some idea? Was he, perhaps, not quite so ordinary as he'd seemed? Had he seen those advertisements, drawn from them tortuous inferences of his own? Was he holding back with some scheme for shaking Annixter down for a packet?

The more Annixter thought about it, the more he felt that the hat-check girl had been right, that there was something very queer indeed about the way the little man had behaved after the accident.

Annixter's imagination played around the man he was seeking, tried to probe into his mind, conceived reasons for his fading away after the accident, for his failure to reply to the advertisements.

Annixter's was an active and dramatic imagination. The little man who had seemed so ordinary began to take on a sinister shape in Annixter's mind—

But the moment he actually saw the little man again, he realized how absurd that was. It was so absurd that it was laughable. The little man was so respectable; his shoulders were so straight; his pepper-and-salt suit was so neat; his black hard-felt hat was set so squarely on his head—

The doors of the subway train were just closing when Annixter saw him, standing on the platform with a briefcase in one hand, a folded evening paper under his other arm. Light from the train shone on his prim, pale face; his hexagonal spectacles flashed. He turned toward the exit as Annixter lunged for the closing doors of the train, squeezed between them on to the platform.

Craning his head to see above the crowd, Annixter elbowed his way through, ran up the stairs two at a time, put a hand on the little man's shoulder.

"Just a minute," Annixter said. "I've been looking for you."

The little man checked instantly, at the touch of Annixter's hand. Then he turned his head and looked at Annixter. His eyes were pale behind the hexagonal, rimless glasses—a pale grey. His mouth was a straight line, almost colorless.

Annixter loved the little man like a brother. Merely finding the little man was a relief so great that it was like the lifting of a black cloud from his spirits. He patted the little man's shoulder affectionately.

"I've got to talk to you," said Annixter. "It won't take a minute. Let's go somewhere."

The little man said,"I can't imagine what you want to talk to me about."

He moved slightly to one side, to let a woman pass. The crowd from the train had thinned, but there were still people going up and down the stairs. The little man looked, politely inquiring, at Annixter.

Annixter said, "Of course you can't, it's so damned silly! But it's about that play—"

"Play?"

Annixter felt a faint anxiety.

"Look," he said, "I was drunk that night—I was very, very drunk! But looking back, my impression is that you were dead sober. You were weren't you?"

"I've never been drunk in my life."

"Thank heaven for that!" said Annixter. "Then you won't have any difficulty in remembering the little point I want you to remember." He grinned, shook his head. "You had me going there, for a minute. I thought—"

"I don't know what you thought," the little man said. "But I'm quite sure you're mistaking me for somebody else. I haven't any idea what you're talking about. I never saw you before in my life. I'm sorry. Good night."

He turned and started up the stairs. Annixter stared after him. He couldn't believe his ears. He stared blankly after the little man for an instant, then a rush of anger and suspicion swept away his bewilderment. He raced up the stairs, caught the little man by the arm.

"Just a minute," said Annixter. "I may have been drunk, but—"

"That," the little man said, "seems evident. Do you mind taking your hand off me?"

Annixter controlled himself. "I'm sorry," he said. "Let me get this right, though. You say you've never seen me before. Then you weren't at the Casa Havana on the 27th—somewhere between ten o'clock and midnight? You didn't have a drink or two with me, and listen to an idea for a play that had just come into my mind?"

The little man looked steadily at Annixter.

"I've told you," the little man said. "I've never set eyes on you before."

"You didn't see me get hit by a taxi?" Annixter pursued, tensely. "You didn't say to the hat-check girl, 'He's not my friend. He's just someone I met'?"

"I don't know what you're talking about," the little man said sharply.

He made to turn away, but Annixter gripped his arm again.

"I don't know," Annixter said, between his teeth, "anything about your private affairs, and I don't want to. You may have had some good reason for wanting to duck giving evidence as a witness of that taxi accident. You may have some good reason for this act you're pulling on me, now. I don't know and I don't care. But it is an act! You *are* the man I told my play to!

"I want you to tell that story back to me as I told it to you; I have my reasons—personal reasons, of concern to me and me only. I want you to tell the story back to me—that's all I want! I don't want to know who you are, or anything about you. *I just want you to tell me that story!*"

"You ask," the little man said, "an impossibility, since I never heard it."

Annixter kept an iron hold on himself.

He said, "Is it money? Is this some sort of a hold-up? Tell me what you want; I'll give it to you. Lord help me, I'd go so far as to give you a share in the play! That'll mean real money. I know, because I know my business. And maybe—maybe," said Annixter, struck by a sudden thought, "*you* know it, too! Eh?"

"You're insane or drunk!" the little man said.

With a sudden movement, he jerked his arm free, raced up the stairs. A train was rumbling in, below. People were hurrying down. He weaved and dodged among them with extraordinary celerity.

He was a small man, light, and Annixter was heavy. By the time he reached the street, there was no sign of the little man. He was gone.

Was the idea, Annixter wondered, to steal his play? By some wild chance did the little man nurture a fantastic ambition to be a dramatist? Had he, perhaps, peddled his precious manuscripts in vain, for years, around the managements? Had Annixter's play appeared to him as a blinding flash of hope in the gathering darkness of frustration and failure: something he had imagined he could safely steal because it had seemed to him the random inspiration of a drunkard who by morning would have forgotten he had ever given birth to anything but a hangover?

That, Annixter thought, would be a laugh! That would be irony—

He took another drink. It was his fifteenth since the little man with the hexagonal glasses had given him the slip, and Annixter was beginning to reach the stage where he lost count of how many places he had had drinks in tonight. It was also the stage, though, where he was beginning to feel better, where his mind was beginning to work.

He could imagine just how the little man must have felt as the quality of the play he was being told, with hiccups, gradually had dawned upon him.

"This is mine!" the little man would have thought. "I've got to have this. He's drunk, he's soused, he's bottled—he'll have forgotten every word of it by the morning! Go on! Go on, mister! Keep talking!"

That was a laugh, too—the idea that Annixter would have forgotten his play by the morning. Other things Annixter forgot, unimportant things; but never in his life had he forgotten the minutest detail that was to his purpose as a playwright. Never!

Except once, because a taxi had knocked him down.

Annixter took another drink. He needed it. He was on his own now. There wasn't any little man with hexagonal glasses to fill in that blind spot for him. The little man was gone. He was gone as though he'd never been. To hell with him! Annixter had to fill in that blind spot himself. He *had* to do it—somehow!

He had another drink. He had quite a lot more drinks. The bar was crowded and noisy, but he didn't notice the noise—till someone came up and slapped him on the shoulder. It was Ransome.

Annixter stood up, leaning with his knuckles on the table.

"Look, Bill," Annixter said, "how about this? Man forgets an idea, see? He wants to get it back—gotta get it back! Idea comes from inside, works outwards—right? So he starts on the outside, works back inward. How's that?"

He swayed, peering at Ransome.

"Better have a little drink," said Ransome. "I'd need to think that out."

"I," said Annixter, "*have* thought it out!" He crammed his hat shapelessly on to his head. "Be seeing you, Bill. I got work to do!"

He started, on a slightly tacking course, for the door—and his apartment.

It was Joseph, his "man," who opened the door of his apartment to him, some twenty minutes later. Joseph opened the door while Annixter's latchkey was still describing vexed circles around the lock.

"Good evening, sir," said Joseph.

Annixter stared at him. "I didn't tell you to stay in tonight."

"I hadn't any real reason for going out, sir," Joseph explained. He helped Annixter off with his coat. "I rather enjoy a quiet evening in, once in a while."

"You got to get out of here," said Annixter.

"Thank you, sir," said Joseph. "I'll go and throw a few things into a bag."

Annixter went into his big living room-study, poured himself a drink.

The manuscript of his play lay on the desk. Annixter, swaying a little, glass in hand, stood frowning down at the untidy stack of yellow paper, but he didn't begin to read. He waited until he heard the outer door click shut behind Joseph, then he gathered up his manuscript, the decanter and a glass, and the cigarette box. Thus laden, he went into the hall, walked across it to the door of Joseph's room.

There was a bolt on the inside of this door, and the room was the only one in the apartment which had no window—both facts which made the room the only one suitable to Annixter's purpose.

With his free hand, he switched on the light.

It was a plain little room, but Annixter noticed, with a faint grin, that the bedspread and the cushion on the worn basket-chair were both blue. Appropriate, he thought—a good omen. *Room Blue* by James Annixter—

Joseph had evidently been lying on the bed, reading the evening paper; the paper lay on the rumpled quilt, and the pillow was dented. Beside the head of the bed, opposite the door, was a small table littered with shoe-brushes and dusters.

Annixter swept this paraphernalia on to the floor. He put his stack of manuscript, the decanter and glass and cigarette box on the table, and went across and bolted the door. He pulled the basket-chair up to the table, sat down, lighted a cigarette.

He leaned back in the chair, smoking, letting his mind ease into the atmosphere he wanted—the mental atmosphere of Cynthia, the woman in his play, the woman who was afraid, so afraid that she had locked and bolted herself into a windowless room, a sealed room.

"This is how she sat," Annixter told himself, "just as I'm sitting now: in a room with no windows, the door locked and bolted. Yet he got at her. He got at her with a knife—in a room with no windows, the door remaining locked and bolted on the inside. *How was it done?*"

There was a way in which it could be done. He, Annixter, had though of that way; he had conceived it, invented it—and forgotten it. His idea had produced the circumstances. Now, deliberately, he had reproduced the circumstances, that he might think back to the idea. He had put his person in the position of the victim, that his mind might grapple with the problem of the murderer.

It was very quiet: not a sound in the room, the whole apartment.

For a long time, Annixter sat unmoving. He sat unmoving until the intensity of his concentration began to waver. Then he relaxed. He pressed the palms of his hands to his forehead for a moment, then reached for the decanter. He splashed himself a strong drink. He had almost recovered what he sought; he had felt it close, had been on the very verge of it.

"Easy," he warned himself, "take it easy. Rest. Relax. Try again in a minute."

He looked around for something to divert his mind, picked up the paper from Joseph's bed.

At the first words that caught his eye, his heart stopped.

The woman, in whose body were found three knife wounds, any of which might have been fatal, was in a windowless room, the only door to which was locked and bolted on the inside. These elaborate precautions appear to have been habitual with her, and no doubt she went in continual fear of her life, as the police know her to have been a persistent and pitiless blackmailer.

Apart from the unique problem set by the circumstance of the sealed room is the problem of how the crime could have gone undiscovered for so long a period, the doctor's estimate from the condition of the body as some twelve to fourteen days.

Twelve to fourteen days—

Annixter read back over the remainder of the story; then let the paper fall to the floor. The pulse was heavy in his head. His face was grey. Twelve to fourteen days? He could put it closer than that. *It was exactly thirteen nights ago that he had sat in the Casa Havana and told a little man with hexagonal glasses how to kill a woman in a sealed room!*

Annixter sat very still for a minute. Then he poured himself a drink. It was a big one, and he needed it. He felt a strange sense of wonder, of awe.

They had been in the same boat, he and the little man—thirteen nights ago. They had both been kicked in the face by a woman. One, as a result, had conceived a murder play. The other had made the play reality!

"And I actually, tonight, offered him a share!" Annixter thought. "I talked about 'real' money!"

That was a laugh. All the money in the universe wouldn't have made that little man admit that he had seen Annixter before—that Annixter had told him the plot of a play about how to kill a woman in a sealed room! Why, he, Annixter, was the one person in the world who could denounce that little man! Even if he couldn't tell them, because he had forgotten, just *how* he had told the little man the murder was to be committed, he could still put the police on the little man's track. He could describe him, so that they could trace him. And once on his track, the police would ferret out links, almost inevitably, with the dead woman.

A queer thought—that he, Annixter, was probably the only menace, the only danger, to the little prim, pale man with the hexagonal spectacles. The only menace—as, of course, the little man must know very well.

He must have been very frightened when he had read that the playwright who had been knocked down outside the Casa Havana had only received "superficial injuries." He must have been still more frightened when Annixter's advertisements had begun to appear. *What must he have felt tonight, when Annixter's hand had fallen on his shoulder?*

A curious idea occurred, now, to Annixter. It was from tonight, precisely from tonight, that he was a danger to that little man. He was, because of the inferences the little man must infallibly draw, a deadly danger as from the moment the discovery of the murder in the sealed room was published. That discovery had been published tonight and the little man had had a paper under his arm—

Annixter's was a lively and resourceful imagination.

It was, of course, just in the cards that, when he'd lost the little man's trail at the subway station, the little man might have turned back, picked up *his*, Annixter's trail.

And Annixter had sent Joseph out. He was, it dawned slowly upon Annixter, alone in the apartment—alone in a windowless room, with the door locked and bolted on the inside, at his back.

Annixter felt a sudden, icy and wild panic.

He half rose, but it was too late.

It was too late, because at that moment the knife slid, thin and keen and delicate, into his back, fatally, between the ribs.

Annixter's head bowed slowly forward until his cheek rested on the manuscript of his play. He made only one sound—a queer sound, indistinct, yet identifiable as a kind of laughter.

The fact was, Annixter had just remembered.

THE 51st SEALED ROOM

(1951)

Robert Arthur

Robert Arthur

"Robert Arthur" (1909–1969) was the pen name of the late Robert A. Feder, a noted mystery pulp writer and screenwriter. He specialized in chilling tales of psychological and supernatural terror, had a great talent for stories that were both humorous and scary—a most difficult combination, and was a regular contributor to the late and lamented fantasy magazine Unknown. *In addition, he was a noted ghost-writer (not stories about ghosts, but writing works that appeared under the names of others) and ghost-editor. Indeed, many of the early anthologies that carried Alfred Hitchcock's name were his responsibility. Like several other authors in this volume, his best work still awaits a definitive collection.*

THE 51st SEALED ROOM; OR, THE MWA MURDER

A completely new way to escape from a locked room!" Gordon Waggoner's eyes glowed and he ran an almost translucent hand through hair as silvery as dandelion seed. "Though technically I suppose I should call it a 'sealed room.' The idea only came to me last Friday, the first, and I already have the plot worked out in detail. Think of it, my fifty-first locked-room mystery—and no two alike!"

"Congratulations!" Harrison Mannix said, concealing a stab of envy. "That calls for another drink. Oh, François!"

The small bar of the Fontainebleau, on 52nd Street, was snug against an early September fog that prowled New York like a damp gray alley cat. François, flushed from hurrying drinks to the big, barren room upstairs where a monthly meeting of the Mystery Writers of America was being held, brought a rum-and-cola for Waggoner, Rhine wine and soda for Mannix. The blond, middle-aging writer never touched anything stronger than wine—he prided himself on keeping his head clear even when relaxing. You never knew when a plot idea would pop into your mind, and mystery writing being the highly competitive business it is these days, a man couldn't afford to forget the smallest notion that might be incorporated into a book. At least Mannix, who was finding new ideas harder to come by, couldn't.

They touched glasses. "Skoal!" Mannix said. Then, with just the proper touch of disinterest, "How did you hit on it?"

"You know how these things are," Gordon Waggoner answered. "They come when you least expect it. This one, as it happens, came out of a chance conversation."

He was about to say more when two members from the group upstairs came down, hunting for François, who was muttering to himself as he tried to mix a dozen drinks at once. His black eye-patch giving him the appearance of a genial pirate, Brett Halliday paused, plucked a brandy from the almost-ready tray, and Clayton Rawson, an angular Merlin, reached for a whiskey that vanished in midair before he could get it to his lips. With solemn indignation he demanded and got another, and paid for it with a bill that exploded in bright flame as François took it. The small, stout Frenchman sighed as the two returned upstairs, made a note on a pad, and went on mixing drinks.

Waggoner remained silent after Halliday and Rawson had gone, and Mannix, by way of jogging him, remarked, "I hope you're not going to use a detachable window-frame that looks solid, because John Dickson Carr has already used that."

"Carr!" the little man snorted. "Carr is good, very good, but you don't think I'd repeat anything he's used, do you? Oh, no, when Carr and Queen and the others upstairs read it, they'll wonder why they didn't think of it themselves."

Momentary anxiety clouded Waggoner's puckish features.

"At least, I don't *think* it's been used. But you never can be sure. Especially with Carr. He's written so many stories that even he's forgotten—

"No, I'm sure it's new. I'll have it finished by the end of the month."

"I wish I could plot as easily as you," Mannix said warmly. Flattery was the one thing the shy, introspective little Waggoner responded to. The year round he lived by himself in his rented stone cottage in Connecticut, writing an incredible amount of fiction and carrying on a voluminous and usually acrid correspondence with other mystery writers. These monthly visits to the meetings of the New York chapter of the MWA—Mystery Writers of America—were his only social outings. Usually he simply sat and said nothing, even to colleagues to whom he might have written a five-page letter only the day before. It was sheer luck that he wasn't interested in the lecture on ballistics to which the rest of the MWA membership was listening in the room above, thus giving Mannix a chance to chat with him. Even though they lived only two miles apart, in western Connecticut, Waggoner did not encourage the younger man to drop in.

"Everybody knows you're the best plotter in the business,"

Mannix added—thinking, *If I can get him to tell me the gimmick, then steer him off by telling him it was used years ago—* "I'll certainly be looking forward to reading it."

"I think you'll enjoy it." Waggoner rose to the lure. "I'm going to make my central character a mystery writer—a complete scoundrel who becomes the victim." He cleared his throat. "Ah—I hope you won't mind if he seem a little like you, Harry. Just superficially, of course."

"Why should I?" Mannix asked heartily. "An English setting, I suppose?"

"Oh, no—America. Rural Connecticut, in fact. Country very much like the region where I live."

"I see. An old revolutionary house, then? Big chimney flues—wide floor boards—loose siding on the house—plenty of ways to get out of a locked room."

"Nothing of the sort!" Waggoner crowed. "The murder will take place in a modern cottage. A fireplace, yes, but with a flue so small only a cat could get out. Two doors, both nailed shut by heavy boards across the inside. Three windows similarly barred, the boards being no more than four inches apart. The roof tightly constructed with solid sheathing, insulating paper, and shingles, not one of which is out of place. The floor solid concrete, covered by linoleum. The walls solid stone. No concealed entrances, no Judas windows, no doors sealed shut by gummed paper drawn against the inside cracks by strong suction. How would you get out of a room like that, eh?" he demanded.

"I don't know," Mannix answered. "Are you sure it can be done?"

"Perfectly sure." Waggoner smiled slightly and rose, reaching for his hat, a shapeless black felt. "I have to hurry if I'm going to make my train. I'll start writing it in the morning. . . . You're not coming back to Connecticut tonight?"

"No," Mannix told him. "Matter of fact, I'm flying to Hollywood tomorrow. An eight weeks' contract with Twentieth Century Fox to do a screen treatment. Henry Klinger arranged it."

"Congratulations," Waggoner said. "See you when you get back."

He scuttled for the door, strands of silvery fluff flying where they escaped beneath his hatband. Mannix ordered another Rhine wine and soda and moodily carried it upstairs, where he found a vacant chair at the rear of the crowd. Someone from the New York police department was lecturing on ballistics, with slides, and Mannix regretted he had left the bar.

Many members were making notes, but he saw that Percival Wilde had his eyes closed, while John Dickson Carr was squirming in his seat, as if waiting for an opportunity to contradict the speaker. Rex Stout sat in a rear row, stroking his beard, his expression somehow suggesting benevolent tolerance—the tolerance of a man who has already appeared in print with some of the very material the note-takers around him were so busily recording. Little Helen Reilly, who probably had forgotten more about police procedure than most of the writers present would ever know, gazed longingly into an empty glass and eavesdropped on the whispered conversation which Larry Blochman was carrying on in French with one of the newer MWA members, Georges Simenon, who had transformed himself into a Connecticut squire, thanks to the enviable international success of his Inspector Maigret.

Mannix, eavesdropping himself, found that they were discussing French royalty rates, and ceased to listen. It was true that the official motto of the organization was *Crime Does Not Pay—Enough,* but he sometimes felt that the discussions of royalty rates and contracts which ensued whenever two or more mystery writers met were overdone. This feeling had been growing on him more particularly of late, as his own earnings dwindled.

Abandoning any pretense of giving attention to the speaker of the evening, he slumped in his chair and sipped his drink. He did not bother with such minutiae of mystery writing as ballistics, or even fingerprints. Primarily, he wrote tales of chase and violence, based upon a recipe of rapid action which made clues and explanations not only unnecessary but frequently impossible.

However, he had had a considerable success with a couple of locked-room plots some years before, and as he waited for the meeting to be over he moodily pondered his failure to get Gordon Waggoner to confide in him. He owed his publisher a book, and perhaps, with a little changing around—

He was still brooding when the speaker finally finished and the meeting broke up. The suburbanites hurried homeward. Most of the remainder transferred themselves to a nearby hotel suite where Brett Halliday and Helen McCloy, a husband and wife team who were not collaborators but individually turned out completely different types of mysteries, presided over an auxiliary party that usually lasted until dawn. By the time it broke up, Mannix had forgotten his conversation with Gordon Waggoner.

Some weeks later, in Hollywood, it was violently recalled to him by headlines shouting Waggoner's death.

The writer's body had been found in his Connecticut cottage, seated at his desk, one hand resting on the keys of his typewriter, the other apparently in the very act of moving the spacer arm.

The body had no head.

Gordon Waggoner's head, silvery hair carefully combed, had been found perched on a large beer stein, on top of the bookcase which held a complete set of first editions of his own books.

The room itself had been tightly sealed by having both doors and all three windows nailed shut on the inside by heavy boards.

The world's foremost writer of locked-room mysteries had been rather gaudily murdered—in a locked room.

Mannix pushed his car recklessly along the country road which was the shortest route to Waggoner's cottage. It was silly to be in such a hurry. After all, Waggoner had been killed five weeks before—Mannix had had to finish his Hollywood job before returning East—and the macabre mystery of the writer's death was still unsolved. But now that he was back, Mannix's impatience overcame his logic.

For he knew one fact of which the police were obviously ignorant—the murderer had plainly used Waggoner's own device in sealing the cottage and making good his escape. With that advantage, Mannix felt sure he could find a clue that would unlock the secret for him. And his publisher was pressing him unpleasantly for a new book. If he could puzzle out the escape method, base a mystery on it, and rush it to the publisher, he could cash in on the endless reams of publicity which Waggoner's death had produced.

In his pockets were the notes he had made from the many lurid stories in the papers. Also, and probably more valuable, was a concise report on the murder which he had received from Ed Radin, a fellow MWA member and one of the country's foremost crime reporters.

> Discovery of the murder (Ed had written) was made by rural mail-carrier Jody Pine, who notified owner of the cottage, local farmer named Briscoe. He phoned State Police. Through cracks between

boards that covered windows from the inside, police were able to see Waggoner's body. They broke in with axes to find Waggoner's headless corpse seated before his typewriter. Body was held in place by string, and hands were tied to the typewriter to simulate a man typing. On sheet in typewriter were typed three words: *My Last Mystery*. Experts say they were typed hunt-and-peck, therefore not by Waggoner, and presumably by the murderer.

Waggoner's severed head was sitting on a beer stein on the bookcase, eyes closed. The youngest trooper of the group fainted when a trick of rigor mortis made one eye open and wink at him as he was lifting head down.

Death was apparently caused by strangulation. The head was removed about two hours later, with an old saw. Very little flow of blood. Saw was hanging from a nail over the fireplace.

Newspaper reports of the manner in which the room was sealed from the inside—one-inch boards nailed closely together over both doors and all three windows—were accurate. Killer must have spent several hours preparing the place. When he had finished, a man trapped on the inside without tools would have starved to death before he could get out.

How killer got out, therefore, is driving the authorities nuts. Technical crews found the cottage normal in every respect. Solid floors, solid walls, solid roof, chimney flue only a few inches across, etc.

The saw, boards, nails, and hammer came from the garage, a former barn, where they'd been lying for several years. They were left there after Briscoe, the owner, and a former hired man named Jake built the cottage. Briscoe is noteworthy in the community for lack of energy.

There were no exterior clues such as footprints, and no interior clues as fingerprints, cigarette stubs, or the like.

The murderer's motive is just as baffling as how he got out. Waggoner had no close friends, no enemies, no relatives, and owned nothing of special value. Thus, no imaginable motive exists. And no reason for the elaborate hocus-pocus of the severed head, the sealed cottage, and so on.

The police are reduced to the theory that Waggoner was killed by some screwball, perhaps somebody who had read his books and decided to try his hand at a locked room murder. This theory doesn't satisfy anybody, but it's the only one that makes even halfway sense.

There's no record of any stranger having been seen in the vicinity or of anyone having visited Waggoner. However, the cottage is almost hidden from the road and death occurred at least thirty-six hours before discovery, so half an army might have been around the place by the time State Police arrived.

One odd detail I almost left out: Waggoner's agent reports Waggoner expected to deliver a finished book to him inside of a week. But no sign of any ms. was found. Evidence of a lot of paper burned in the fireplace, but ashes had been stirred and could not be reconstructed.

That's it, Harry, that's all there is, there isn't any more.

But there was more, Harrison Mannix reflected. A great deal more. Waggoner *had* had something of value—the almost finished manuscript of his fifty-first locked-room mystery. The fact that the manuscript was missing could only mean one thing: he had been killed by another mystery writer.

Mannix brought his car to a stop in a tree-lined lane which ran past the cottage. There was a short cut through the trees, which he took at a trot. He emerged from the trees and hurried around the squat stone cottage with its flattish roof and low, overhanging eaves. Then he stopped, cursing.

A large wooden sign was propped up on the lawn:

SEE THE MURDER COTTAGE!
Everything Just As It was Found!
MOST BAFFLING MYSTERY
OF THE CENTURY!!
Adults...*$.50*
Children ....*$.25*
plus tax

Four cars were parked in a field across the main road, and a fat family of father (blue beret), mother (green sun visor), and daughter (12, lollypop) were just filing in the front door.

Standing outside was lanky Willy Briscoe, the farmer who owned the cottage. His features split in a grin.

"Back, eh, Mr. Mannix?" he said. "Come to have alook at th' scene of th' crime?"

Trust a Yankee to turn a dollar, even out of a murder, Mannix thought vexedly. But aloud he said:

"Just thought I'd stop by. After all, I was Waggoner's friend—almost his only friend."

"Eyup," Willy agreed solemnly. "Kept mighty close to himself, he did. But come in, Mr. Mannix—won't cost you nothin', seein' you're a neighbor."

"No," Mannix shook his head. "You're busy now, Willy, and I wanted to talk to you. I'll come by later."

"Okay, Mr. Mannix, got to give my lecture now." Willy Briscoe grinned again. "Goes over mighty well, it does, and I've got th' inside fixed up to give th' folks a real thrill."

Mannix hardly heard him. He was retreating before his deep annoyance made itself visible. These country people were easy to offend, and Willy Briscoe took offense more easily than most. A wrong word and it would have given the shiftless farmer malicious pleasure to bar him from the cottage indefinitely.

The rest of the day he waited impatiently for evening, knowing Willy would not leave the cottage while there was any hope of garnering a last half dollar from the curious. He did not go back on the chance of finding Willy there alone, for he wanted to have the place entirely to himself when he did enter it. He hoped that his first impression of the cottage might tell him something and he did not want to be distracted by Willy Briscoe's gangling presence.

As soon as it was decently dark and he had allowed Willy time enough to eat supper, he drove the two miles to the farmer's run-down establishment, which lay a quarter of a mile from the cottage. Willy's wife directed him to the sagging barn behind the house. He found Willy there, invisible under a jacked-up truck that was so rickety it should have adorned the town dump-heap. After a few moments, Willy crawled out and stood up.

"Evenin', Mr. Mannix." He showed snaggly teeth. "Got to do my fixin' up after dark now. Eyup, keeps me busy showin' folks through th' cottage. You'd be s'prised how much cash money I'm takin' in. Last Sunday forty people come by for a look."

"Willy," said Mannix, "Waggoner was my friend. It was I who persuaded him to come up here to live. I'd like to spend a little time in the cottage, to see if I can discover anything the police missed."

"Figurin' on findin' th' murderer?" The farmer's eyes half-closed in a shrewd grin. "Kind of thought you'd try your hand at it, seein' you write mysteries too."

"I want to see the killer punished," Mannix answered, untruthfully. "But tell me, Willy, you and your hired man built that cottage. If anybody can figure how the murderer got out—"

"Nope." Willy shook his head. "The police asked me that, too, and all I can tell you is what I told them. That there cottage is just a plain, ordinary cottage. More'n that I can't say. If you ask me, th' mystery ain't ever goin' to be solved."

"Just the same, I'd like to spend a couple of days in the cottage,"

Mannix told him. "I'll just sit there and try to figure out the answer. Maybe if I go at it as if I were working out a plot, I'll get the answer."

"I'd like to say yes," Willy answered insincerely, "but right now there's forty, fifty people a day wanting to go through that cottage and— Well, money's money, especially since farming don't pay so good."

Mannix restrained the retort that sprang to his lips. He had anticipated the objection and brought his checkbook. They finally settled that he could have the cottage completely to himself for three days for seventy-five dollars. He made out the check and left.

Mannix's impatience was too great to wait until morning. He drove directly to the cottage. Stumbling along the path to the front door after parking his car, he cursed his lack of foresight in failing to bring a flashlight.

In the darkness he bumped against the blatant sign Willy had erected. Then he found the new door that had been fitted and let himself in with the key the farmer had given him.

The unheated interior was damp and cold. Mannix shivered as he felt for the light switch. He found it, clicked it—and started violently. In the blaze of the light, a man's headless body, the neck-stump crimson, was seated at a desk bending over a typewriter. The missing head, eyes staring at him, rested on a beer stein atop a bookcase.

It took Mannix a moment to realize they were wax, and this was what Willy had meant by saying he had fixed up the interior to give the folks a thrill. Even then his heartbeat returned to normal only slowly, and a feeling of cold repugnance refused to leave the pit of his stomach.

Conquering his revulsion, he picked up the dummy body and flung it onto a sofa. Then he took the trouble to stand on a chair and lift down the head, which he put beside the body, covering both with a small rug from the floor. After that he sat down at the desk and examined the room with a long, careful scrutiny.

Presently he was certain that no detail differed from his memory of the room as he had seen it on his occasional visits in the past. He had hoped something would obtrude upon his attention and give him a clue to the murderer's mode of exit, but he was disappointed.

Discarding the hope, he turned his attention to Waggoner's desk and began going through the papers in the drawers. The police had disturbed them, but seemingly not removed any, and finally he found the dead author's file of plot notes. This he leafed through eagerly.

Once again he was disappointed. There was not a phrase in it anywhere which could have referred to the locked-room plot Waggoner had mentioned at the MWA meeting.

Next he turned his attention to Waggoner's correspondence file. There was just a possibility the little man might have mentioned the plot in a letter—his correspondence had been voluminous, though he had said very little in person.

In the file beginning the first of September—the date Waggoner had mentioned on which the initial idea had come to him—were copies of half a dozen letters, and these Mannix read carefully. One was to Anthony Boucher, in Berkeley, California, and apparently carried on a previous dispute about the 1908 début of a long-forgotten opera star. The next, to Lillian de la Torre, in Colorado Springs, caustically corrected a mistake in the diameter of a hangman's rope in the days of Dr. Sam: Johnson. A third was a bitter note to Lawrence Blochman, castigating him for having his detective, Dr. Daniel Webster Coffee, find a specimen of the murderer's blood in the abdomen of a mosquito killed at the scene of the crime. Waggoner claimed to have conceived this idea first, and to have prior rights to it.

To Hugh Pentecost, Waggoner had written a five-page letter correcting a Pentecostal interpretation in modern psychiatry. Then Mannix found a scrawled note which raised his hopes. It said, *Write Ellery Queen about story.* Eagerly he turned to the letter pinned to it, which began, *Dear E. Q.: I understand that your Sixth Annual Contest for the best detective short story of the year, sponsored jointly by Ellery Queen's Mystery Magazine and Little, Brown & Company of Boston, is closing soon. I very much hope . . .*

Mannix put the letter back and continued going through the file. He found a note to Howard Haycraft, suggesting a revised edition of *Murder for Pleasure,* in which Gordon Waggoner would be acknowledged the dean of the locked-room mystery. A long letter to Bill Roos, half of the husband and wife team that signed itself Kelley Roos, suggested that they collaborate on a mystery musical comedy—Roos to supply the humor, Waggoner the mystery. There was also a complaint to Veronica Parker Johns, of the New York chapter of the MWA, pointing out that the name Gordon Waggoner had been spelled with only one *g* in the last issue of *The Third Degree*—was it too much to hope, Waggoner had written on the very day of his death, that after forty years and fifty volumes, fellow writers would know his name well enough to spell it correctly?

That was all for September. Mannix put the file away and, momentarily at a dead end, stood up and tugged at the boards which still covered all three windows, as well as the door that led to the bedroom. The boards were tightly nailed, so he abandoned further tests—they had been made more skillfully and exhaustively by experts.

The murderer had been in this room. He had got out of it. How he had accomplished this feat had been known only to him and to Gordon Waggoner. Waggoner was now dead. That left the killer in sole possession of the secret which Mannix was determined to uncover.

He could visualize the excitement, six months hence, when his book was published, revealing in fiction form the true story of Waggoner's murder. The publisher's publicity release—the apprehension of the guilty man (Mannix had no intention of having him caught before publication day, if he could prevent it). . . . It was a pleasant daydream and he put it away reluctantly, recognizing the bitter fact that so far the killer's secret was perfectly safe.

No, wait a minute! Waggoner had said the idea had come from a chance conversation. He had even specified the day—Friday, September 1. If it were possible to discover with whom Waggoner had talked that day—and if it were possible to reconstruct the conversations—Mannix might still be able to evolve the whole escape method, just as Waggoner had originally.

But was it possible to check back to the people with whom Waggoner had spoken so many weeks before? Mannix's active mind began to gnaw at the problem. Waggoner had been here in the country at the time. Mentally, Mannix listed the men Waggoner might conceivably have chatted with that day: Jody Pine, the rural mail-carrier; Miss Rorick, the postmistress; Miss Bunce, the librarian; Nahum Brown, manager of the gas station which serviced Waggoner's car; Myron Stuart, the bank manager; McCready, the manager of the grocery. Waggoner came in contact with these people about once a week, and had a chatting acquaintance with them. He saw no one else more than once or twice a month, not even Briscoe, his landlord.

Mannix determined to question all the individuals he had mentally listed. Even if they had talked to Waggoner that Friday, it was unlikely they would remember what had been said. But it was worth a try.

Abandoning temporarily the problem of the killer's escape from the sealed room, Mannix next considered his identity.

He had already decided the murderer must be a mystery writer—probably a fellow MWA member. Only another detective-story writer could have had a motive—the new locked-room plot. Though Waggoner had insisted to Mannix that he hadn't mentioned the plot to anyone else, he *must* have let it slip out at the meeting. Someone else had learned of it, had surreptitiously visited Waggoner, killed him, read the manuscript and burned it, then—

No, he must proceed more slowly, more logically.

First, *would* another writer kill for a plot, however brilliant? It was farfetched, but not impossible. A good plot was money in the bank, and there were several members who might go to great lengths to refurbish their waning reputations. Perhaps one, more desperate than anyone realized—

Mannix paused in his thoughts to consider the roster of possible suspects. There were perhaps 250 writers in the MWA—four-fifths of all the mystery writers in America. Of these, at least 150 belonged to the New York chapter, with sizeable groups located in Chicago, Los Angeles, and San Francisco.

At least 80 writers had been present at that September meeting, and most of them, with the exception of a corporal's guard who had traveled from Boston, Philadelphia, and Washington to be present, lived within two hours' drive of Waggoner's cottage. Many lived closer. There were, for instance, Bruno Fischer and Lawrence Treat, both in northern Westchester, no more than an hour away.

Percival Wilde, Hugh Pentecost, Georges Simenon, the Kelley Rooses, George Harmon Coxe—all lived in Connecticut, within easy driving distance. Others were clustered thickly in the Larchmont-Mamaroneck area—the names of John Dickson Carr, Herbert Brean, Clayton Rawson leaped to his mind. There were more, Mannix knew, if he cared to check. But he could not seriously visualize any of them playing the role of a murderer. All were more than competent enough to create their own plots, and at considerably less risk.

Nevertheless, someone—his leaping thoughts reined up sharply at an obstacle he had not previously envisioned. The whole case had the touch one usually found in third-rate melodramas—the boarded windows, the message on the sheet in the typewriter, the severed head on a beer stein.

From whatever angle you approached the case it reeked of the literary touch, as if a writer had at last discarded paper and typewriter and written his work in deeds, not words. But—and this was the obstacle he could not bypass—if a writer had killed Waggoner for his locked-room gimmick, why had he immediately wasted the idea by translating it into actuality?

Obviously, now, the killer would hardly dare reveal his method of escape by putting it into a book. That would be virtually admitting he was the murderer. Of course he himself hoped to use the idea in a book, but that was different: he had an alibi.

No, the two conclusions were antagonistic: only a mystery writer could be guilty—but no mystery writer would have used Waggoner's locked-room idea as the actual scene of the crime.

Mannix's thoughts revolved fruitlessly, and it was only the opening of the outside door that put a period to them. Startled, he turned. Willy Briscoe was just entering.

"Just come over to make sure I locked up, and seen the light, Mr. Mannix," Willy said apologetically. "Didn't know you was planning to come here tonight."

"I just wanted to get a preliminary impression," Mannix said, annoyed. "But I guess it's time to go now."

"Sure hope you figure it out," Willy told him, nodding his head briskly. "Poor Mr. Waggoner, he might have sat here dead for weeks till I come to collect th'rent, if Jody Pine hadn't had that special-delivery letter to give him."

Mannix stared at him, cigarette frozen in his lips.

"Willy," he said, his tongue strangely thick with tension, "sit down. I'd like to talk to you."

"Sure." Willy Briscoe sat down on an antique ladder-back chair that had been Waggoner's pride. "What about?"

"Willy," Harrison Mannix asked, "you were here at the cottage on September first?"

"Sure, to collect th' rent, like always on the first."

"The rent! Of course. And you talked to Mr. Waggoner? In fact, I think you mentioned an idea for a mystery story to him. Right?"

"You bet I did!" Willy's face flushed, and his lips twisted with the remembered anger. "I been reading his books from th' liberry and I noticed they was always about murders in a room all locked up or nailed shut, or similar. And it come to me I knew a way to get out of a locked-up room he hadn't ever used. So I asked him what th' idea'd be worth to him. He said he'd have to hear it first, so I told him. Right away he said it had been used a dozen times.

"Well, I'd believed him when he said my idea wasn't any good. Then one day I come to fix th' water pump—he'd called up to complain about it—and he was in th' village. But th' door was unlocked. So I come in and see some writin' on his desk and looked at it and there it was—my idea that he'd stole and was usin' in a book!"

The farmer paused, breathing hard, and Mannix felt his heart hammering with excitement. So Waggoner had lied! Not a chance conversation, but a suggestion given to him by an amateur! Every mystery writer had plots suggested to him by amateurs—absurd, impossible plots; but this one hadn't been impossible!

"Then what happened, Willy?" His tone was soothing. "Waggoner came home and you quarreled with him. Right?"

"Yes, blast him!" Willy shouted. "Caught me readin' th' story and lit into me. And I lit into him for stealin' my idea after sayin' it wasn't any good."

"So you killed him," Mannix said, half to himself.

"Yep, I killed him!" Willy said, hands clenching. "He'd said my idea was no good and he lied to me and tried to cheat me, and before I knowed what I was doing I was choking him by the throat. And before I could stop, he was dead."

Willy stopped, as if realizing for the first time what he had said. Mannix nodded reassuringly.

"I understand, Willy," he said. "I'd have done the same thing. But after you killed him you nailed this cottage shut from the inside. Was that to fool the police?"

"No." Willy shrugged. "If I'd wanted just to fool them I'd 'a' took Mr. Waggoner's money and messed up th' house—then it'd look like a tramp done it. But he said my idea wasn't any good. And I knew it was. I couldn't write it in a book, like him, but by thunder I could show it was good! And I did! That's why I fixed the cottage up all nailed shut from the inside, like in the idea I give him."

"And cutting off his head was part of the idea?"

"Sure," Willy told him. "There's always some crazy stuff like that in a mystery story—you know, a crazy statue from Africa or Egypt or somethin'. So I cut off his head to make it interestin', and wrote on his typewriter, *'My Last Mystery.'* I wanted to stab him with a jeweled dagger too, only I didn't have one."

Mannix swelled with triumph. Waggoner *had* been killed by a mystery writer! An illiterate who could only get "published" by acting out his plot in reality.

"Willy," he said, "the more I think about it, the more I think you were perfectly justified in killing Waggoner. So I won't say anything about it to anybody. And I have a proposition to make to you. *I'll* buy your idea. If you'll tell me how you got out of this room I'll pay you five hundred dollars."

Willy Briscoe brightened.

"Honest?" he said. "All right, it's a deal. I'll do better'n tell you—I'll show you."

He rose and came forward with outstretched, work-hardened hands. . . .

Willy Briscoe stood by the fireplace and surveyed the room. The new front door was nailed tightly shut. The windows remained boarded up just as they had been since Waggoner's death.

Harrison Mannix sat erect in the chair just before the typewriter.

Harrison Mannix's head rested on the beer stein on top of the bookcase ten feet away, wide-open eyes surveying the headless body.

The saw which had effected the separation hung above the fireplace.

In all essential respects the room was exactly as it had been the morning Waggoner's body had been discovered—except, of course, for the change in the cast which now put Harrison Mannix in the leading role.

Satisfied Willy turned out the light and, approaching the stone fireplace, climbed upward, using the rough stones of the fireplace for toe holds.

Just a few feet to the left of the chimney was one of the corners of the room. And in that corner there was now an eighteen-inch gap where the roof failed to meet the walls.

Willy wriggled through the gap and dropped to the ground outside.

Then he turned his attention to the sturdy truck-jack, which was now exerting its power against a six-by-six timber, thrust under the corner of the overhanging roof. A turn at a time in the darkness, and Willy eased off the pressure. The roof settled down until once again it rested, with every appearance of solidity, on the walls. The timber which had lifted it started to fall and Willy caught it dexterously.

"Look at a house with a roof on, it looks like a mighty solid piece of building," he muttered aloud. "Easy to forget a roof has to be put on and what can be put on can be took off—or lifted. If'n a real carpenter had builded this house, might not be so easy. But me'n Jake run out of big nails the day we framed this end of th' roof. Always meant to put in a few, but never got around to it. Lucky, way it's turned out."

He carried the truck-jack to a wheelbarrow, tossed it in, and laid the timber across the barrow. Using a flashlight, he made sure there were no significant marks left in the gravel drive where the jack had stood. Then he trundled the wheelbarrow down the road, back to his barn and to the truck that had been in the process of being repaired for two months now.

"Expect they'll be a good lot of excitement when the time Mr. Mannix paid me for is up and I go over to open up th' cottage," he reflected. "But won't nobody think of me. They'll be too excited over th' mystery." Then another thought occurred to him.

"Likely I'll be takin' forty, fifty dollars a week out'n that cottage, showin' it to summer folks the next ten years," he murmured, smacking his thin lips. "That's better'n writin' for a livin' any day!"

THE BIRD HOUSE

(1954)

William March

William March

Law clerk, subpoena server, marine, and corporate vice president, William March (1893–1954) grew up in small sawmill towns of Alabama and Florida. He began writing in 1928 and had his first novel, Company K, *published in 1933—though it was written years earlier. Many of his stories are set in small southern towns and are noted for a skillful handling of eccentric and horrible people. By 1954, he seemed to be reaching the full flowering of his powers. There were works such as* The Bad Seed, *a powerful novel of a psychopathic little girl, and "The Bird House," which suggested an ingenious solution to a real life crime. But then, tragically, he died of pneumonia before being able to capitalize on his newly found fame.*

THE BIRD HOUSE

It was near sunset, and they sat in front of the wide, recessed window that overlooked the park, their drinks arranged on tables beside them. Outside, the red-brick building was covered with lush vines of a peculiar brilliance. They thickened the ledges and the ornate, old-fashioned balconies over which they grew, and so outlined the window itself with dense, translucent foliage that the effect of the small park, seen through it, was the effect of green in an easel of brighter green. Marcella Crosby called attention to the window and the park at once. "Look!" she cried out with soft excitement. "It's like a landscape framed in a florist's wreath!"

She felt warmth in her stomach, a nervous tightening at the base of her neck, and she took a strand of her straight, black hair and brushed it across her lips, nibbling the ends thoughtfully. This was the beginning of a new poem, and she knew that well. She did not, as yet, know precisely what the poem would be, what emotional direction it would take, but she felt that somehow it would concern an old man who, achieving resurrection in his grave, broke through the earth with his hands and sat up in amazement among the stiff floral tributes that others had placed above him.

The idea so excited her that she spoke her thoughts aloud: Most of us see death, when we see it at all, through the long, optimistic window of life, she said: but in her poem the convention would be reversed, for her hero would look forward toward life from the grave, through the most terrible and perhaps truest window of all—the foolish, arranged elegance of a funeral wreath.

The Filipino houseboy came up with a cocktail pitcher. When he had filled the glasses, the guests were silent for a time, staring indolently at the park and the tall buildings beyond. Inside the park, between a flowering syringa and the starched laciness of a ginkgo tree, was a bird house atop a green pole. It was new and elaborate, and it rose upward in setback levels, like the scaled down model of an ancient temple. There were circular holes in each tier, designed so precisely for size that while a bird no larger than a wren could easily enter and find sanctuary, its enemies, because of the very bulk that made them dangerous, were turned back finally, and defeated.

Dr. Hilde Flugelmann gestured with her cigarette holder and said in her ingratiating, foreign voice, "It was not the window that caught my eye: it was the little white bird house." She smiled and inclined her head, exposing obliquely the pink gums above her small, seed-like teeth. "I think the security of the bird house impressed me because I see terror, terror, terror all day long in the poor, insecure minds of my patients. Why, only a moment ago I was thinking to myself that no matter how vulnerable we are, at least the birds are somewhat safe."

For a time they all talked at once, contrasting the security of animals with the security humans know, but at length they turned to Walter Nation, as if some law of courtesy permitted the host the flattery of the final opinion; but he merely sighed and said that all the talk about funeral wreaths and bird houses had put him in mind of a laundryman who had been murdered a few years before. It was an affair which had always interested him, he said, for there was in it mystery, pathos, terror, suspense, and even a touch of that baffling, artistic senselessness which is found in all truly memorable crimes.

He hesitated and glanced expectantly at his guests, but when they said they were not familiar with the case and asked him to tell it to them, he continued: "It happened here in New York, in Harlem to be exact, and the name of the murdered man was Emmanuel Vogel. But let me begin at the beginning, and tell you some of the things the police found out in the course of their investigation: Emmanuel was born in a small Polish village. I've never seen the place, of course, but I've always thought of it as one of those communities Chekhov describes so well: a village consisting of a general store and a collection of houses, surrounded in winter by the traditional sea of mud."

He took a cigarette from a box at his elbow, lighted it, and went on with his story. Emmanuel's father, he explained, had been a poor peddler who went about the countryside with a pack strapped to his back; his mother had been the local laundress. She was a frail woman, and when her son could barely walk, he was already helping her at the washtub. She died when he was seven. Afterwards, he had washed, cooked, and scrubbed for his father, just as she had done; he had even carried on her laundry business as best he could; but three years later his father died too, and he was entirely alone in the little town.

"Oh, I know that place so well," said Dr. Flugelmann. "I have seen it, or its counterpart, many times. At the edge of the village there was an old factory with a rusting iron roof. There was a market place where the farmers came to trade, and about a mile in the distance, set in a grove of handsome trees, was the big house where the local nobility lived." She shook her head, sighed, and continued: "I see Emmanuel so plainly at this instant: I see him delivering a parcel of laundry in a basket almost too big for him to manage, and as he moves down the street, away from his home, he glances back over his shoulder. He has rust-colored hair, a long neck, and a big, jutting nose. I think he cracks his knuckles when he's nervous, and as he waits at the door for the money he's earned, he presses his palms together, or twists one leg anxiously about the other."

"My clearest picture of him is in his home, immediately after his father's funeral," said Marcella Crosby. "He is wearing a ridiculous little black hat: something hard like a derby, but with a very low crown, with mourning crepe sewed over the original band. His suit is too short and too tight for him. He is walking up and down, trying to control his grief, but suddenly he gives in, rests his face against his mother's old washtub, and cries." She brushed back her hair, closed her eyes for concentration, and continued, "He must have felt terror at that moment, knowing he was alone in a world he feared, and which despised him, and a little later, I think he ran to the doors and windows and locked them all securely."

Mr. Nation inhaled, sat farther back in his chair, and said he considered the fantasy of the locking of the doors and windows a most interesting one. Perhaps it really had happened that way; perhaps it was the beginning of Emmanuel's preoccupation with locks and bolts and bars which was, some years later on, to baffle the police so greatly. He crushed his cigarette with a slow, scrubbing motion, and went on with his story:

It seemed that following his father's death, Emmanuel was not only alone, but homeless too, and at once a pathetic, itinerant existence had begun for him, for he became a sort of housewife's helper who rarely spent more than a day or two in any one place: a kind of rustic menial who moved from villager to villager, from farmer to farmer, doing the domestic work required of him in return for his food, his temporary bed, and perhaps even a few coins on occasion. He cooked, he scrubbed, he mended, he baked for his employers—but washing was the thing he did best, and that was the task he was usually called on to do.

But Mr. Nation did not want his listeners to think of Emmanuel as being without ambition during those years. If they did think so, they would be misled, for actually the child had had a positive, if somewhat modest goal that never wavered, and that was to come to America and eventually own a laundry of his own. His task was a difficult one, and to achieve his purpose he had led a life of hysterical penury and deprivation; nevertheless, he had his passage money eventually, and a little besides, and when he was twenty years old he landed triumphantly in New York.

Being a laundryman, he had gone at once to work in a laundry. It was a small establishment, located somewhere on the lower east side, and for the next few years, according to the material the police gathered after his death, he had put in long hours at his washtub, or bending above his ironing board. He had lived entirely to himself, but if the timidity of his temperament had prevented his having friends, it had served equally well to preclude his making enemies. The only relaxation he had had was smoking, and Mr. Nation felt he must make this point sooner or later, since the buying of a pack of cigarettes had figured in his murder.

People who had known him in those years described him as a thin, hairy, shy, eccentric little man with a delicate constitution; and while Mr. Nation found it possible to believe almost anything he had heard about Emmanuel Vogel, he could not bring himself to credit the reports of his physical frailness, since all his life he had performed, as a matter of course, work which would have caused the average, healthy dray-horse to stagger and collapse in the streets.

John Littleton, the lawyer, said: "I know he got his own laundry sooner or later. The question is, how long did it take?"

"It took ten years," continued Mr. Nation. "By that time he'd saved a thousand dollars, and had already found a ground-floor location in Harlem where he hoped to prosper."

In the rear of the living-room, which was already becoming a little dusky, the Filipino houseboy was stuffing broiled mushroom caps with a mixture of crab and lobster meat. He listened with pride to the conversation, smiling and nodding wisely each time Mr. Nation made a point. It was his opinion that his employer was not aggressive enough, that too often he permitted his inferiors to dominate a conversation.

The houseboy placed the mushrooms on circular pieces of thin toast, and added to each a portion of a golden-brown, spiced sauce which he had perfected himself. When he first had come to work for Mr. Nation, he sometimes would put down his tray, rub his hands together, and laugh boisterously at his employer's witty remarks, rolling his eyes and glancing seductively at the guests, as if urging them to appreciate and applaud too; but Mr. Nation had told him finally that such partisanship, while heartwarming and most flattering, was not entirely in keeping with the stricter usages of good form, and he had had to give it up. Now he arranged the mushrooms on a silver platter and moved silently toward the guests, his teeth white and gleaming, and at that instant Mr. Nation was saying:

"It's necessary for me to describe the new place in detail, I'm afraid. Well, to begin with, there was a large front room that faced on the street; behind it, there were two smaller connecting rooms that opened onto a tenement hallway. The one window in the main room looked out on a narrow courtyard at the side.—Have I made myself clear? Do you visualize the layout of Emmanuel's laundry?"

The guests said they did, and he went on: "After taking the place, Emmanuel's first move was to rent the two smaller rooms to an old colored woman who lived alone, and who was content to mind her own business. When the deal between them was made, the connecting door was locked and bolted from the laundry side, but not being satisfied with that, Emmanuel had it nailed securely. He had iron bars put across the window that faced the court, bars so close together that not even a sparrow hawk could have got through them. Afterwards, he had two extra locks and a heavy chain put on the street door, and as a further precaution, the workmen added a strong iron bolt—all, you understand, on the inside."

John Littleton selected a mushroom, bit into it, swallowed, and said, "He'd already invested his capital, so he couldn't have had much loose cash lying around at the time. Then what was he trying to protect? What did he really have to lose?"

Marcella Crosby sat forward excitedly in her chair. It was axiomatic, she said, that those who have the least must guard it the most faithfully. She pointed out that when we love and are loved in return, we leave our riches unguarded for all to accept or destroy; but when love is gone, we see, at last, what has slipped through our fingers, and struggle to keep what we no longer possess.

When we are young and full of life, and have health in profusion, we consider those things our peculiar right, and accept them without gratitude. While we have our treasure, we give no thought to it, as if our very indifference to the things we have in abundance were our assurance they would last forever; but when we are old and ailing, and life has become nagging, painful, and hardly worth keeping, we discover, at length, that it is too precious to be given up, and make the most elaborate efforts to preserve it, to hold on to the unprofitable days we have left.

Marcella confessed that the fable of the barn door and the missing horse had always interested her, not because of its innate truth, but because of its sly, ingenuous falsity. To be accurate, to accord with the perverse nature of man's mind, the moral should be reversed to warn us all that there's no use locking the barn door until we know for certain that the horse is actually gone.

Her voice grew self-conscious, hesitated, and died away.

Phil Cottman, who published her work, who advertised her as the greatest mystic poet since William Blake, and who was embarrassed by her imagery until it was safely between the covers of one of her volumes, looked down at the rug and said, "Perhaps Emmanuel had accumulated more money than the price of his laundry, and the extra cash was hidden somewhere about the place. If that's true, then his precautions were sensible enough."

Outside, the park was now bathed in the soft, full light of the sun, and Dr. Flugelmann, observing it in silence, her eyes half closed and a little sad, waved suddenly in the direction of the bird house and said, "Oh, no, no! It wasn't anything definite, anything real, he feared. The laundry with its locks and bolts and bars was only his little white bird house where he hoped to be safe. Oh, I know the type so well, and have had them in treatment many times. Always, they have a sense of their own doom: they fear they will be robbed, they fear they will be murdered, they fear, beyond the next building, there lurks some terror for them alone."

She turned to Walter Nation, asking him if Emmanuel had expressed his anxieties to others, and if they were now part of the record of his death; but he said that he did not know. A moment later he went on with the details of Emmanuel's life in the new neighborhood. During the months he had lived there, he had not once gone out of the small area from which he drew his living. He had had no assistants. He had continued to work long hours, longer than ever, now that he was laboring for himself alone. He was never known to go to the theater, or even to the movies. He did not read. He did not drink or gamble. He did not have a friend with whom he could talk, or to whom he could confide his ambitions or his fears. He had no sweetheart.

And so Emmanuel lived for a time, and then, after delivering a parcel of laundry to a customer one night, he stopped in the cigar store across the street from his place to buy a pack of cigarettes. It was 10 o'clock at the time, and the clerk, who knew him as well as anybody, asked if he were now going to bed. Emmanuel replied that he'd like to, but could not, as he had at least two hours more work to do that night. Then the clerk watched him cross the street, unfasten his system of locks, enter his laundry, and turn on the lights. Fifteen minutes later, the clerk happened to look across the street again, and seeing the lights in the laundry go out, he said to himself, "Emmanuel didn't do his work after all." He started to turn away, to go back behind his counter, but he had an odd sense of disaster at that moment, a feeling that something was wrong across the street, and he stood irresolute inside his shop, staring at Emmanuel's door.

At about the instant the clerk had seen the lights go out, Emmanuel's tenant, the old colored woman who lived in the adjoining rooms, heard three pistol shots from the interior of the laundry. The sound alarmed her, and she went to the connecting door and called out, "Are you all right? Is everything all right in there?" But she got no answer, and she hurried through the door of the tenement house and onto the sidewalk, bumping into a policeman who was passing. What she told the policeman as she disengaged herself was not known, but the chances were she did not say that she had heard three shots. If she did tell him that, then his assumption that he was dealing with a routine suicide seemed, in Mr. Nation's opinion, almost incredible.

"She was excited at the time," said John Littleton. "Maybe she jumped at the conclusion, and simply told the cop that the laundryman had shot himself. Maybe the cop accepted her theory without question."

Mr. Nation considered this explanation logical. At any rate, neither the policeman nor the old woman had thought murder a possibility as they approached the laundry door. "All this had taken only a minute or so, but already a crowd had gathered, and when the policeman found the door locked, and realized he couldn't get in without breaking it down, he thought of the transom. There was a small boy in the crowd, so the policeman lifted the boy onto his shoulders, and told him to crawl through the transom and open the door from the inside; but the boy found out soon enough that Emmanuel had thought of the transom too, and that it was nailed shut. Then the policeman handed the boy his club, and told him to break the glass with it. The boy did so, and lowered himself into the room. Almost at once the group outside heard him fumbling at the locks and bolts, but he solved them all at last, and the door swung open upon the most beguiling mystery of our time."

The telephone rang just then, and Mr. Nation lifted the receiver. When he replaced it, he went on to say that, in the long, precise wedge of brightness from the policeman's flashlight, Emmanuel Vogel was seen lying in the center of his room, rapidly bleeding to death. There was an expression of horror on his face, as if what he had feared in secret had come true at last, and as the policeman and the crowd watched him, the arm that had rested against his thigh twitched, relaxed slowly, and slid forward to the floor. He moved his lips three times, as if trying to speak, then shuddered and slumped somehow from within. His eyes opened and fixed themselves on the ceiling in the patient, impersonal stare of death, and the obsessed purpose of his harried and insipid life was now fulfilled.

The first thing the policeman noticed was that there was no gun near the body; the next was that the victim had been shot three times—twice in the head, once through the right hand. When the significance of these facts became clear to him, he told one of the people outside to call police headquarters and report a homicide. Then he pushed back the crowd and bolted the door again. He found the light switch and snapped it on, moving forward with nervous caution. He was convinced, at that time, that the murderer was still in the room, but he searched it thoroughly, and there was nobody there. When he couldn't discover the murderer, he determined, at least, to locate the weapon the murderer had used; but he couldn't find the gun either.

By that time the ambulance and the police cars had arrived, and at once the medical examiner settled the question of how Emmanuel had died: he had been shot from a distance of several feet, by a revolver held level with his head. It was murder, he said; it couldn't possibly be anything else. At once the room was filled with specialists testing, measuring, photographing, examining, and asking questions. They found the one window closed, and latched from the inside, the iron bars all in place. The connecting door was still bolted and locked from the inside, still firmly nailed shut.

When the homicide experts saw all this, they looked at one another in astonishment, and shook their heads. Then the policeman repeated his story, and the detectives again questioned the group who had been at the door when it had swung open. They verified each detail of the policeman's story: the door had most certainly been locked on the inside, they said, and after the boy opened it, absolutely nobody had come out of the room. There was no doubt in their minds on this point. They would swear to it anywhere, any time.

The homicide men had then gone back to work in earnest. If the murderer had not left the laundry, obviously he was still in it somewhere; and in the days that followed, they almost dismantled the place as they searched, but without success, for trapdoors, sliding panels, or even holes in the walls and ceiling through which a pistol could have been fired. They followed every clue, exhausted every possibility, and learned nothing. To this day, the mystery of how Emmanuel Vogel was murdered, by whom, and for what reason, was as great as it had been on the original February night of his death.

"How about the boy?" asked Phil Cottman. "He might have picked up the pistol while he was alone in the room. Did anybody think of that?"

"Yes," said Mr. Nation. "Everybody thought of it, including the cop who was first on the scene. When he saw the gun was missing, even before he shut the door again, he searched the child, but there was no gun."

He said he'd like to clear up some of the other points that might be bothering his listeners. To begin with, there were no fingerprints, no strands of hair in the victim's fist, no torn letters to be pieced together, no broken buttons—no physical clues of any sort, in fact. The laundry had not been ransacked. Everything was found to be in order, in its proper place. The glass in the barred window was quite intact, the front door elaborately secured from the inside, as everybody knew by this time. It wasn't likely the murderer could have refastened the bolts and chains after leaving the room, but even if he had been able to do so, he would not have had time. Then, too, he would have had to make himself invisible while doing it, for the cigar clerk had been watching the door from the time the lights went out until the crowd gathered. Afterwards, Emmanuel's life had been traced step by step, from the time he was born, until the time he had died. He had been no famous person in disguise; he had been no secret agent of a foreign government. He had been precisely what he appeared to be—an illiterate, obscure, terrified, eccentric little laundryman who lived alone and who had known almost nobody.

To the west, along Madison Avenue, the cabs sped up and down in a steady, aggressive stream, their bodies flashing yellow, green, and orange in the brilliant, late afternoon light. Farther away, somewhere to the north, an ambulance clanged as it approached East River, and Dr. Flugelmann, listening tensely, as if the warning were a sound most familiar to her, pressed her plump, ringed fingers together and said, "I do not know why, but I assumed that Emmanuel would be killed by a crushing blow, something brutal and entirely primitive. Being killed by a pistol was not at all right for him."

She explained that while Mr. Nation was telling his story, she, too, had been occupied. She had been weaving a fantasy of her own, she said—a fantasy which had concerned Emmanuel and his mother's washtub. As the others no doubt remembered, he had spent his formative years above it, and when he had left his native country at last, what was clearly the most precious thing he possessed? It was the washtub, of course, and she thought it the one thing from his past that he had brought with him to America. He could not have abandoned it if he had tried, for he was tied to the tub in a way that others are tied to the ones they most love: it had become his father and mother, his sister and brother; it had even became a sort of industrious wife to him, a wife who shared his labors, and gave him security against the world he feared so much.

She went on to say that we all want security of one sort or another. It was normal and most natural to want security. But life itself was not at all secure. Life was strong and cruel, and its purpose was not peace, but conflict. If we are just secure enough, we are fortunate indeed, for then we can enjoy the wonderful things that life also has to give us; but if we become too secure, if we give up too much, then we have repudiated life itself. Who can say where the dividing line is? How can we know when we are entirely safe, or are merely not living at all?

She lowered her head with a smiling humility, as if asking pardon for being both trite and tiresome, and said gently: "And now, if you permit it, I will finish my small fantasy of the laundryman and his washtub: now, let us recall that Emmanuel's mother had washed her life away over that tub, and Emmanuel himself, although he did not realize it, perhaps, had really done the same. Then where had the essence of those lives gone? What had become of all that vitality, that energy, that strength and striving? I think the tub had absorbed it."

She turned in her chair, played with the beads about her throat, and went on with her story: she thought that after a while the assimilated lives of Emmanuel and his mother had had their effect on the ancient, wood-and-iron tub—so much so, in fact, that gradually the tub had achieved an awareness of both its own existence and the existence of its tormentors. It had begun to feel a little too; to suffer pain in a sort of primitive, mindless way. Perhaps, during the last months of the laundryman's career, it would sometimes appear to shiver. Perhaps it would manage to slide forward on the bench, as if seeking to escape its oppressor, and Emmanuel, grasping it again with his reddened, soapy hands would sigh patiently and pull it into place once more. Perhaps the tub even resisted him on occasion, and he would feel the tension, the sudden hostility between them.

And then, one night, life itself had originated mysteriously in the tub, just as it had, with an equal mysteriousness, once originated in Emmanuel and his mother, and at that moment the tub understood the bondage the three of them had shared in common; but what it could not know was that the Vogels, being human, and as such almost indestructible, could endure easily what the tub could not. . . . All this had happened on the February night when Emmanuel had bought his cigarettes and crossed the street. Then, as he prepared to do his extra work, the tub had gathered all its strength together, had risen up, struck him, and crushed his skull.

She held her glass forward toward the window, allowing the sunlight to touch it, to bring to life the shattered pinks and greens in the crystal; then, seeing that John Littleton was about to offer an objection to her theory, she smiled and said placatingly, "I know, I know. He wasn't killed by a blow from a washtub. He was shot by a pistol. It makes my story even sillier, doesn't it?"

"Emmanuel Vogel was killed by somebody as real as any person in this room," said John Littleton, "and I think I know how it was done. Now, the first thing is to determine the motive. All right, then: Let's take the commonest motive of all—greed."

He went on to say that the frightened ask for the disaster that so often overtakes them. If Emmanuel had behaved like others, perhaps his neighbors would have thought nothing of him; but with all those bolts and locks, they must have wondered what he had so precious that he must guard it so well; then, since we can understand the minds of others only with the content of our own minds, and since the most precious thing to those who knew him was money, they all must have thought, at one time or another, that the little laundryman was rich, that his wealth was hidden somewhere in his room. Having come to this conclusion, it was only natural that one of them should decide to take the money for himself.

"Now we have a logical motive," said Mr. Littleton; "the next thing is to get the criminal inside the room. That can be done easily between the time Emmanuel left the cigar store and the time the shots were heard. Nobody knows, of course, but I think somebody just knocked on the door, and when Emmanuel asked what he wanted, he said he'd come to pick up a bundle of laundry."

To fear indiscriminately was even more naive, in Mr. Littleton's mind, than to trust without reason. He felt that Emmanuel had so long quieted his terrors with formulas he had established for his protection that he no longer had the power to distinguish between what was dangerous and what was not. The fact that the murderer had announced his intention in a phrase entirely familiar to him, had reassured him, and he had opened the door with no misgivings at all; then, as if to protect both himself and his murderer against a world outside which menaced them equally, he had at once relocked and rebolted his door.

Perhaps the intruder had not planned to kill Emmanuel, had meant only to frighten him into giving up his money; but Emmanuel had gone to pieces when he saw the pistol and had hurled himself at the thief with that despairing, superhuman courage that only the truly timid achieve. No doubt the last thing the robber had anticipated was resistance of such heroic quality. Perhaps he had become frightened, too, and had backed away from the laundryman's hysterical grasp, firing straight at his head. Then he had hurried to the door, but before he could get the locks undone, the crowd was there waiting for him.

"You got him inside the laundry," said Phil Cottman. "Now get him through that locked and watched door—if you can."

To Mr. Littleton's way of thinking, that was the most obvious part of the mystery—so simple, in fact, that perhaps the others would not consider it a solution at all; nevertheless, he was convinced it had happened precisely in the manner he had in mind. He said he could visualize the murderer standing in the dark, his mind working coldly, as he listened to the crowd outside. He knew he was trapped, that if he tried to hide in the room he would be caught. Suddenly he had seen the only way of escape for him, had known what every sleight-of-hand artist takes for granted: that the audience would be so surprised when it saw the laundryman bleeding to death on his floor, so diverted in that first shocking moment of revelation, that no eye could possibly take in anything else.

Realizing this, he had flattened himself against the wall, as close to the door as he dared, and at the instant the door swung inward, he had thrust one foot through the opening, and had planted it on the pavement outside, swaying his body backward as the crowd pressed their bodies forward to meet him. No one had seen him, no one had paid the least attention to him, and in a second, he had ceased to be a murderer trapped in a room, and had become, instead, one of the vanguard of those citizens who sought that murderer. A little later, when the policeman shut the door in the face of the crowd, no doubt he pushed the murderer out with the others.

Phil Cottman laughed. "That situation has its possibilities," he said. "I can see the murderer dusting off his coat where the cop had shoved him, and saying, 'Give these cops a little authority and they think they own the town. Well, I'm a citizen and taxpayer, and I'm not going to stay here any longer and be pushed around by cops!' Then the crowd opened up for him, and he walked away with the murder weapon dangling at his belt."

Marcella Crosby started to speak, but changed her mind. Instead, she sighed and stared intently through the window, her chin cupped in one thin, intense palm. Beyond the park, the buildings cast their precise, wedge-shaped shadows on one another. Two birds came back to the bird house and rested on its upper ledge, ruffling their feathers, stretching their wings to the sunlight. Seeing these things, Marcella leaned forward and touched the dense foliage that framed the window, thinking of the things she had once had, but now had lost; of the things that might have been hers, had she had the courage to take them.

In the park, the last bright rays of the sun lay everywhere as heavy as honey, and sitting quietly back in her chair, she thought: Look at the trees! They take the light, they diffuse it, they drink it up, they change it to fit their shapes, and scatter the patterns of themselves on the grass below. They lean forward to the light, to take the last of it that remains. They cannot live without light, and yet, being mindless, they do not know that light exists.

Suddenly she made a nervous, disavowing gesture and said that while neither of the solutions satisfied her entirely, she was in accord with Dr. Flugelmann's belief that the manner of Emmanuel's death had not been appropriate for him. She, too, felt that it should have been something crushing and overwhelming.

The others laughed at her earnestness, asking what her own explanation was. She said, "Emmanuel never had anything that makes life endurable. He had nothing, I tell you! Nothing! He didn't even know that he'd been cheated of what was rightfully his, and that, to me, is the most dreadful thought of all."

"Perhaps you're right," said Phil Cottman, "but how do you account for the locked door, the non-existent weapon, the vanishing murderer?"

"My explanation is most simple," said Marcella. "I think God happened to be over Harlem on the night of the laundryman's death. I think He glanced down and saw Emmanuel working over his washtub, working fearfully, and with no discernible purpose. I think God looked back in time and saw what Emmanuel's life had been; then He looked forward, to see what the future held for him. When He saw that, he was so moved to compassion, seeing the future held nothing, that He bent down, took Emmanuel's skull between His thumb and forefinger, and crushed it."

BIG TIME OPERATOR

(1970)

Jack Wodhams

Jack Wodhams

Although he has written a novel, Authentic Touch *(1971), Australian writer Jack Wodhams (1931–) is best known for his excellent science fiction short stories such as "The Helment of Hades" (*New Worlds, *1968), "There Is a Crooked Man" (*Analog, *1967), "Split Personality" (*Analog, *1968), and the unforgettable "Whosawhatsa" (*Analog, *1967). The following story should be a refreshing surprise to readers since it was not originally published in a mystery magazine and has never been reprinted. Furthermore we believe it possesses the greatest closing line since T. S. Stribling's "Passage to Benares."*

BIG TIME OPERATOR

Elswick Gansy was in his cups. He chuckled happily. "It's the sweetest." His arm waved in sweeping signal. "Waiter! Waiter! More champagne at this table!"

Seffan smiled. He'd made it his business to get close to Gansy over the past couple of days. Now they were quite good friends. Gansy should soon be right for the payoff. "El, you brag a lot. To hear you talk, you've got your own private gold mine."

"Huh? Huh? Hey, that's good!" Gansy laughed. "You might be right, at that." He smirked at his company. He placed a finger against his nose and winked. "A gold mine." He giggled. Then he threw himself back to roar with merriment. He was in a very good humor indeed.

A fresh supply of champagne arrived. Gansy insisted on doing the pouring, with great exuberance and gaiety, and the girls squealed and the men clinked glasses.

Seffan paid the bill over Gansy's protests. "I'm having a great time," Seffan declared. "To see you happy makes *me* happy. It's not every day we meet a man who knows how to live and enjoy himself."

Gansy was in too cheerful a mood to fight over anything. "Ain't that right, though, ain't that right. If you got it good, enjoy it, hey?" He guzzled some champagne. "Live!" His glass slopped liquid as he gestured. "What's money? Hey?" Archly, he winked again. "What's money? World's full of it, right? Hey," he leaned forward, crooked a finger at Seffan, "here." He put down his glass, dug into a pocket. He produced a few coins, threw them onto the table. "Take a look at those." And he hiccuped.

Seffan deftly reached to beat the scrabblers, took a look. He frowned. "What are they?"

"Huh? What are . . . ? They're guineas, of course, stupid. Golden guineas." Gansy beamed, blinked. "You can have 'em," he said with blithe largess. "Plenty more where they came from." He turned his attention to the female breathing down his neck. "Come on, honeybunch, drink up, or the night's going to beat us to it." He reached for another bottle.

Seffan's lips were curved upwards, but his eyes were shrewd. And his fingers tucked away the gifted guinea.

"What do we know about him?"

"He's from the East. You know Wockskanci, the pusher? He knows him." Seffan very soberly fooled with his guinea. "Petty fraud. Inside he met up with the Brakker gang, and from all accounts was the wheel for them on some of their later jobs." Seffan flipped the coin. "Small stuff. But now he seems to be loning. And doing all right."

"Yes." Mr. Ciano looked very thoughtful. "Most curious. Gold coins, hm-m-m?"

"He's got a bagful in his room, must be a couple hundred. He boasts he can get plenty more."

"Treasure? He's found a hidden hoard?"

"I don't know. When I try to pump him, he starts playing coy." Seffan snatched the coin from the air. "He's onto something. I *know* it. No crime, he says. No proof, he says. Like taking candy from a baby. And he nearly laughs himself sick."

Mr. Ciano smoothed an eyebrow with a finger. "Interesting." He held out his hand for the guinea. Seffan handed it over. Mr. Ciano rolled the coin at his fingertips. "Very interesting. I think we should have a more formal talk with Mr. Gansy, no? To discuss his apparent affluence and, ah . . . perhaps talk over some investment opportunities—"

Elswick Gansy did not much care for the two hard-faced characters who stood at his shoulders. And he did not care for the change in his friend Seffan. And he did not much care to be here confronting Mr. Ciano. Taken all around, he really did not much care for the situation at all.

"We are just curious, Mr. Gansy, that's all." Mr. Ciano was affability itself.

Gansy could not prevent popping sweat. This was too much. His unguarded flamboyance had brought him to the notice of the heavies. "It's nothing," he said. "Just a little sideline of my own. Just to . . . keep me in pocket money, that's all."

"Yes?" Mr. Ciano clipped a cigar, wetted the end for his lips. Seffan produced a light. "We are always looking for new sidelines, bright ideas." Smoke billowed. "Maybe we can help you. We have contacts, outlets. If you have a good thing, we can help you develop it, get the most out of it. You understand?"

Gansy rubbed his damp palms together. "It's nothing. I just . . . struck lucky, that's all. I'm . . . I'm not as rich as I pretend. It's a gag. I've just been putting it on . . . to live high for a while for once in my life."

"Yes?" Mr. Ciano clamped his cigar and tipped the contents of a small sack out onto his desk. "Where did you get these?"

Gansy loosened his collar. "They . . . A legacy. An aunt of mine died and she left them to me."

"Uh-huh." Mr. Ciano poked at the glittering spillage. "These are all British coins, dated in the 1600s. Good condition." His eyes pierced cigar smoke to bore into those of his twitchy guest. "Where did you get them, Mr. Gansy?"

"I . . . I told you, I . . ." Gansy looked up, left, right, at Seffan, back to Mr. Ciano. He found no comfort anywhere. He was out of his league. He'd made a mistake with Seffan. Perhaps . . . Gansy swallowed. He was stuck. Either way he was stuck.

"We want the truth, Mr. Gansy." Mr. Ciano smiled. "You may trust us. What you tell us will be kept in the strictest confidence."

"I . . ." Sweat ran into the corner of Gansy's mouth. Just then he would have liked to have chickened out. "I can't. It's . . . It's a secret." It sounded foolishly lame.

"Mr. Gansy, I am a busy man, so please don't waste my time. You have discovered a source of bullion, and this is very interesting to me. I am a buyer and can give you a good price, but I want to know who I'm dealing with, and know how reliable you are. In other words"—he leaned forward to snap—"I want to know just how hot this gold is!"

"It's not hot at all!" Gansy blurted. "It's—" He stopped. How had he ever got into this? Too late now. He pulled out a handkerchief to dab his face. "It's all legitimate. Honestly."

"Not taken from a sunken ship? Not stolen from a museum, deposit box, some dear old lady you sweet-talked?"

"No. It's straight, I tell you, untraceable."

"Then where did you get it? Did you find it? Dig it up somewhere?"

"No, look," Gansy appealed, "you've got me wrong. Just a few coins, that . . . doesn't mean anything. I . . . collected them, picked them up on my way around."

"Seffan here says that you claimed to know where there was plenty more. And a collector does not throw away handfuls—even when he's drunk. Now one way or another, Mr. Gansy, you are going to cooperate with us." There was menace in Mr. Ciano's tone that made Gansy shiver. "I think it would be better for you to work with us rather than against us. Those who try our patience can get to live short lives of deep regret."

Thus Gansy felt that he had no alternative. He licked his lips. He'd got himself onto this spot through nobody's fault but his own, so now he'd *have* to tell them. He knew nothing else that would sound so plausible. It was crazy, but . . .

"Look, I'll tell you," Gansy said, "but you won't believe it. There's this fellow, see? And—"

The car stopped but the dust cloud didn't, and enveloped them to make visibility bad for a minute or two.

The occupants peered out. "This is the place?" Mr. Ciano did not sound impressed.

Despite the air-conditioning within, Gansy was sticky with sweat. He'd been sweating solid for the last three days, ever since Mr. Ciano had desired to make his acquaintance. He hauled on the handbrake. "This is it." Gansy tried to turn on good cheer. "Well, he should be waiting for us. Like I said, it's up to him."

"I think we might persuade him." Mr. Ciano jerked his head.

The car burst its sides, and the passengers got out. Five men: Seffan, Mr. Ciano, his two henchmen, and Gansy.

They viewed the bleak, shallow canyon, the sparse scrub and dusty rock. They tasted the dry late-afternoon air. They gazed at the squat and ugly cement building that seemed part-buried into the side of a low cliff—very unobtrusive. Hard to spot from the air; remote and unlikely to be found on the surface.

The quiet was broken by the slamming of the car doors.

"Let us go," Mr. Ciano said.

"Sure thing," Gansy said, as lightly as he could manage. He led the way. "There's a door around the side."

Their feet stirred red dust again as they made their way forward. Mr. Ciano had kept his jacket and hat on, his tie tight. The others were down to shirt sleeves and shoulder holsters. There were no windows or apertures in the concrete structure, and the door at the side, when they came to it, was made of steel.

Gansy gave his comrades a nervous smile, met no reciprocation, reached for a raised square plate, and pressed.

They waited.

And waited.

"There's nobody here," Seffan said. It was the most desolate hole he'd seen in his life.

Mr. Ciano said nothing, but his look made Gansy squirm. Way out into the middle of nowhere, to somebody's abandoned atom shelter. Lonely and ludicrous, a chase to a faceless bunker. Mr. Ciano was not prepared to be amused.

Somewhat desperately Gansy pressed the plate again.

Nothing happened.

"Maybe the bell is not working," Moke, a henchman, suggested, his teeth baring unpleasantly. "Or maybe the lady of the house has gone shopping."

"He's here," Gansy protested. "I called him on his special line. I *know* he's here."

The other henchman, Carl, drew his gun from his holster. Gansy's eyes bugged. But the man only turned it around with the intent to use the butt on the door.

But before his first blow could fall there came a sharp *clack!*—as a slot in the door was snapped open. "Hey? Who's that? Who's that?" came an irascible voice. "Coming at all hours. What do you want?" The framed beady eyes lit on Gansy. "Oh, it's you, is it. I might have known." And very tartly, "Brought enough friends with you, haven't you? What do you think I'm running here, a seminar?"

Gansy was self-effacing. "Doctor, these . . . these men are very interested in your project." And he added quickly, "They're willing to pay."

"Hm-m-m. I should think so. D'you think I don't know what they're after? D'you think I'm a fool? Blasted nuisance." The eyes studied them with marked disfavor.

Gansy perspired profusely. "Please, Doctor." There was a wheedling note in his tone. "You wouldn't want this place to become generally known to the authorities, would you?"

The doctor glowered at him. "Bah!" The aperture was slammed viciously shut.

For a moment it looked as though the interview was ended. And then the steel door was dragged open.

The doctor stood aside, scowling, very disgruntled. "If you must, you must—come on then. But be sure you don't touch anything."

The visitors trooped in, the eyes of Mr. Ciano very narrow.

Dr. Leigher had the clipped voice of a teacher who hated to say a thing once, let alone twice. His three-day beard and extremely grubby dustcoat did not detract from his querulousness. "It is not a time-machine but a time-and-space transposer. There is a precise coordination of movement through both time and space, and I am able to move a body from point 'A' to point 'B' as I choose, providing all prior conditions have been fulfilled."

It still sounded like hokum to Mr. Ciano, and yet . . . He looked at the heavy cables snaking across the floor. "What's behind those double-doors—your power plant?"

"Yes." Leigher was wintry. "Would you like to have a look? I'll unlock it for you. You might find the effulgence therapeutic."

"Effulgence?"

"Yes—radiation!" Leigher exploded irritably. "What do you think—I'm hooked to the town supply? What do you think I'm doing here—something that can be run on thirty-two volts and a bicycle?" He snorted. "I need a constant infallible supply without risk of breakdown." He pointed a none-too-clean finger. "It's down there, half-a-mile away, shielded by the earth itself."

"You dig your own tunnel?" Seffan inquired.

Leigher was acid. "Very funny. As it happens, this is an old gold-mining site, and some of the shafts have proved very suitable to my needs."

Mr. Ciano, stepping carefully, circled the transposer chamber.

Again he noted the thickness of the leads trailing to the barred double-doors. "It doesn't seem much," he said. "But it's like an iceberg, eh? Most of it out of sight."

Leigher sniffed. "Hardly an iceberg, but yes, quantitively, that might convey the impression."

"And the power is constant, ready to be tapped at any time?"

"The field is kept open at all times—has to be. To switch off, or close down, would be to break contact. I can't allow that to happen, and there is no provision here for a cut-off switch. So, if you'd like to 'lose' somebody into the past by shutting off the power, you'd have to destroy this entire installation. And believe me, it would not be worth it."

"I was not thinking of anything like that," Mr. Ciano said. "If it really works, the last thing I would wish is to interfere with the power."

"No." Leigher removed his glasses and began to clean them with a filthy handkerchief. "I know what you want," he said bitterly. "The same as the others. Easy pickings."

Mr. Ciano pretended mild shock. "Easy pickings? My interest is primarily historical." He indicated some furniture and bric-a-brac that was piled in one corner. "Although I admit that I have a passing interest in, ah, antiques."

"Oh ha-ha," Leigher said sarcastically. His fingers flicked at the henchmen. "That's why you need your armed guards, I suppose?" he sneered. "And what's in the suitcase? A small arsenal, I shouldn't wonder."

"The suitcase contains items we thought might be useful should certain contingencies arise." Mr. Ciano tried to be crushingly icy. "What weapons you may see are purely for self-defense in case of an emergency."

"Oh ha-ha," Leigher said again. "Do you think I'm an idiot? I know who you are. You're the same as him"—his finger jabbed at Gansy—"a help-yourself crook. Well I don't care. If you shoot somebody dead, they've already been dead for a few hundred years, so it won't make a difference anyway. If you want to help yourselves, you can. But I'm certainly not going to aid you for nothing."

"You've had . . . other friends through here?" Seffan asked.

"I most certainly have," Leigher grated. "Thanks to my own kindness to a dying wastrel I rescued. As it turned out, he was on the run from the police. Since that time I seem to be getting an ever-increasing number of his fellows calling at my door. Most of them making promises that they subsequently fail to keep." He glowered at Gansy.

Gansy was hurt. "I paid, didn't I? One for one. Guineas are worth more than dollars."

Leigher's smile was mirthless. He rammed his glasses back on. "Perhaps. But trying to spend them creates a great deal of unwanted attention, and I am not as familiar as you may be with discreet methods of disposal." He breathed very hard. "If you want to clean out a Seventeenth Century bank, all well and good. But I want to be paid in dollars." And with a touch of fierceness to Mr. Ciano, "And I want to be paid in advance."

Mr. Ciano squinted, sneered in his turn. "How do we know you can do what you say you can do? What if it's a frost?"

"Then that'll be through your own incompetence," Leigher said sharply. "Look, I've had enough of you people coming in here, making grand promises to share what you make, but putting up not a nickel beforehand. And what do I get?" He steamed. "If they *do* come back, they bring me junk." He gestured at the assortment of ancient pieces. "I'm in the furniture business?" His voice was high with indignation. "No! If you've come here to make use of this device, you're unlucky. No more! No more!" His hands swept angry negative. "I've had enough! I'm through!" He seemed very cranky.

Mr. Ciano was quick. "You said, 'if they *do* come back'—does this mean that some of them *don't* come back?"

Leigher glared at him. "It means exactly that. Do you know what it's like in the past? Can't you appreciate the advantages? A modern man there is a king. Armed even with only a .38 he is virtually invincible." Leigher's head nodded. "Oh, yes, I've had some promises. Fat lot of good it's done me. They just throw away their recallers and don't give a damn." He shouted, "I've had enough of it, I tell you!"

Even Mr. Ciano flinched at Leigher's vehemence.

"Take it easy, Doctor, take it easy," Mr. Ciano placated. He clasped his hands in front of him. "You deal with me, and everything will be square. I'm no two-bit punk. I'm here on business. If what I've heard is true, we should be able to come to some arrangement to our mutual advantage. And I can see to it that you are protected and don't get bothered by strangers any more."

Leigher was skeptical. "I've heard such stories before. You people are all the same. Promises," he jeered savagely, "always promises. Well I'm not taking promises any more. You can do what you like. You either pay beforehand, or you get nothing. I'm sick and tired of freeloaders."

"Relax, Doctor, relax," Mr. Ciano soothed. "I represent sound vested interests, and we'll be glad to put up whatever capital you may need."

Leigher was unconvinced. "I'll believe it when I see it. I'm not being taken in again. The purity of your motives and intentions are no concern of mine. You can save your talk. Now it's cash or nothing."

Mr. Ciano pondered briefly. Then he gave Seffan a slight nod.

Seffan opened his valise. He produced one wad of notes. And a second wad of notes. And another, and another. He placed all four bundles upon a small table that could have been designed by Chippendale.

"Your price per man is twenty thousand dollars, I believe," Mr. Ciano said. His eyes were intensely searching. "There is enough on that table to pay for the passage of two. If it is a success, there is more where that came from—you will be paid, no haggling." He waited to let that sink in.

"Hm-m-m." Dr. Leigher strode to the table, picked up the money, riffled it, seemed satisfied. He started to stuff it into his pockets.

Seffan startled him with a cautionary grip on his elbow. "Not so fast, Doc."

"What? Look, what is this? I thought it was a payment?" Leigher was disgusted. "Either it's mine, or it isn't. I'm not going to play games."

Mr. Ciano waved Seffan off. "Go ahead, Doctor, it's yours. But before you send anybody away," he was coolly pragmatic, "we would like to see a demonstration . . ."

Leigher was a trifle ruffled. "A demonstration? What do you have in mind?" He thrust the last bundle of money into a dustcoat pocket, adjusted his glasses, returned his hands to swell the bulges. "If you experience it, it demonstrates itself, surely? What more do you want?"

"First I want you to send one of us." Mr. Ciano raised a considering eyebrow at a henchman. "Carl here, say—and then bring him back. If his report corroborates your claim that you can send people into the past—and recover them—then others of us will go to explore the prospects. Isn't that reasonable?"

Leigher shrugged. "I'm giving no free rides. You want a demonstration, you'll have to pay for it. That will count as one."

"That's pretty tough," Mr. Ciano argued. "We'd only want him to be in the place long enough to confirm that your device *does* work. A half hour, an hour, just to look around and give the O.K."

Leigher was patronizingly cynical. "You can do what you like. You pay for two journeys, and two journeys you can have. I won't take any responsibility for the way that a person may react at the other end."

"What do you mean by that?"

"I've told you. A modern man thinks differently when he gets back there. Even a dumb modern man knows so much more. There is opportunity on every hand, power—you don't realize how tempting it is."

"You mean Carl might want to stay there?" Mr. Ciano's jaw set. "He knows better. He'll do as he's told, or he knows what he can expect."

Leigher was mocking. "Yes? What jurisdiction will you have over him a few hundred years back from now? Would you like to waste time, effort and money sending people to hunt for him in those times? Where are your contacts? Where would you search? And could you find men you could trust not to do the very same thing as the man they were looking for?"

Leigher was sardonic. "I know, I've had some. The past is virtually virgin territory to a modern man. And it's a big world, where it is easy to gain favors from influential people for services rendered. A modern man, *any* modern man, can become somebody. I've had," he thought and mentally counted, "nineteen people come to me to take a so-called 'temporary' trip into the past." He paused, then added with heavy emphasis, "Only three ever came back. And he"—he pointed at Gansy—"was one of them."

"How do you know that they stayed there deliberately?"

"Because they tie their recallers to pieces of junk like that!" Leigher cried, exasperated. "Furniture, knick-knacks. They think it's a joke!" He took a few paces to relieve his irritability. "They seem to think I can operate on thin air. Well, no more. From now on I'm taking no chances."

Mr. Ciano brooded. "Is there no way you can recall them, whether they want to come, or not?"

"Arbitrarily? No. The recaller must be worn properly. It is not all that comfortable, and looks odd, so it is generally taken off. Thus I dare not recall anyone unless I get the correct signal." He shook his head in despair. "And when I do get the signal, it so often has turned out to be something like that unfinished statue from medieval Florence." Leigher stared at Mr. Ciano. "You must know what you're doing. It's not quite as simple as it looks."

Mr. Ciano dug out a cigar to help him think. He nipped the end, tasted, frowned, took a light from Seffan. His unblinking contemplation of him made Carl uneasy.

Mr. Ciano broke to study his smoke with seeming concentration. "So," he said, "is there no way that we can be sure that a traveler will return . . . will *want* to return?"

"There is." There was a devilish light in Leigher's eye. "I have given the matter some thought, and I *do* have one solution." He walked over to his Queen Anne escritoire, opened a drawer, brought forth a tube. "This." He tapped the plastic. "One of these pills will kill in six hours. Allowing an hour beforehand for it to be fully assimilated into the system, and one hour afterwards for a safety margin, that will leave four hours in-between when the volunteer can make examination of the past. But, if he lingers overtime he will die, for the antidote is here."

Mr. Ciano halted in mid-puff. "Well." He liked it. "That sounds like a good idea."

Carl shot a glance between the pair. It did not sound such a good idea to *him*. "I'm taking no poison," he warned.

"Carl!" Mr. Ciano was sternly abrupt. "You will come to no harm. You will get back here after two or three hours, take the antidote, and that's all there'll be to it."

"Yeah? I'm taking no poison," he repeated. "Supposing something should happen? Suppose I got knocked on the head? Suppose I lost this recall thing? No. I'm sorry, Mr. Ciano, but that's *out*." Mr. Ciano was grieved. He went a little red, but he could see that Carl was adamant. He filed this intractability for future reference. "Very well, Carl. Then it will have to be Moke. Moke?"

Moke was checking the magazine on his pistol. He did not raise his eyes. "I don't think I'd like it either, Mr. Ciano. It'd be sorta against my religion. Fooling around with poison, I mean, a man could get killed. It'd be easy to make a mistake, wouldn't it?"

Mr. Ciano became tense. He was unused to such flagrant insubordination. Way out here, they suddenly thought they could do as they pleased. He came within an ace of losing his temper. "Seffan?" It came out very tight-wound.

Seffan relished the thought of imbiding some toxic substance no more than did the others, but he was more slyly diplomatic. "Surely it would be best to send someone experienced, someone who knows all about it and who would, therefore, be less likely to make an error?"

The others followed the direction of his gaze.

"Huh?" And Gansy jerked to quick attention.

"Now wait a minute! I've been there before," Gansy said. "Why send me? I've already told you what it's like."

"Perhaps we would like you to tell us again," Mr. Ciano silkily replied. "To personally show us how it works."

"Huh? Look . . ." Gansy took in the circle of faces. "Be reasonable, I've been already. *I* know it's all right. What's the point of me going again? What'll it prove?"

"We wish to witness the sequence, the procedure. I think you might satisfactorily play this role."

Gansy's hands fussed at his belt. "I don't see it. It would be better for Seffan to . . . to check. You can take my word for it—you've got that already. It . . . needs somebody else."

"We're not calling you a liar, Mr. Gansy," Mr. Ciano reproved him. "We believe you. Why be so troubled about going again? It will only be for a few hours."

Gansy wiped at his face. "It doesn't make sense." He smiled weakly. "*I've* been. It'd be better for someone else to go." He appealed to Dr. Leigher. "Wouldn't it be more logical for . . . for Carl, or Seffan to go? I mean . . ."

"I couldn't care less, quite frankly," Leigher informed him crisply. "You can sort it out amongst yourselves. And when you have decided you can let me know."

Gansy did a re-take of his "friends." "Well," he wasn't really happy, but he gave in, "I think it's crazy. But if that's the way you want it, it's O.K. by me. But," he made a firm stand, "I'm taking no poison."

"But you must," Mr. Ciano said pleasantly. "It guarantees your safe return."

"I don't need it!" Gansy began to pop sweat all over again at the thought of what he was doing. "I . . . I came back last time, didn't I? It doesn't affect me. I don't *want* to stay in the past."

"In that case to come back for the antidote will put little strain on your wishes, even should you meet a fair damsel," Mr. Ciano observed. "It is an innocent precaution against temptation—for your own security. I don't see that you can have any objection."

"I refuse to take poison!" Gansy said loudly.

There came disagreeable *cluck-snack* noises from a couple of handguns in the room, and Mr. Ciano's henchmen eased out to give Gansy meaningful attention.

Gansy slowly rubbed his hands over his hip pockets. "No," he protested feebly. "No."

But he was outvoted.

The recall outfit was a light metallic band that fitted over the forehead, with leads trailing to a button-signaler strapped tightly to the chest. A few more leads led to thin metallic anklets. The unfortunate Gansy was ready to be positioned in the space/time-transposer chamber.

"The polarity is important," Leigher was saying. "The frequency differential between the composition of these metals is known, and is unique. They don't look much, perhaps, but they form the identity location marker in time and space." He took Gansy's elbow. "Come."

They stepped into the tubular chamber. Gansy shone with perspiration.

"Now. In the center, near enough. Feet together, stand upright. The distance between the contact bands is important," Leigher explained to his audience. "Around the ankles below, or even worn stirrup-fashion. And on the head worn," he smiled bleakly, "like a laurel wreath. The distance between the two is vital. On no account, when being sent or recalled, should one set, or the other, be held in the hands. And neither should the body be bent in a position to bring the head and feet closer together. This would foreshorten the field, with possibly disastrous results. No one seems to have tried it so far, and it is not recommended that anyone do so.

"These bands are tougher than they look, and collapse to quite a small package that can be carried in a pocket with no inconvenience. This," Leigher pointed to the small matchbox-size button-box, "is the recall signaler. On arriving at the destination, open the front and press the button once. This will indicate intact arrival, and that circumstances are satisfactory. Pressing the button twice will indicate that the time and/or place of arrival is inopportune, at which the traveler may be immediately carried forward to another date and alternative venue.

"After arriving satisfactorily, the double signal may be employed in order to jump from one week to the next. But if more than three such jumps are attempted, there will be an extra fee to pay, and the fourth double signal will be interpreted as a triple signal—the recall advice."

Critically Leigher looked Gansy over, and found everything wanting but his equipment. "To press the button three times in succession is the triple signal that requests recall. Be sure that the bands are in place and that the bodily stance is that of one standing at attention—thus to keep well within the bounds of safety. That way there is nothing to fear."

Leigher produced a small oxygen mask, gave it to Gansy who, without enthusiasm, tied it over his nose and mouth.

"There is some risk of breathlessness on the journey, although it doesn't take long in subjective time. To counter this there is this mask and miniature oxy-tube, which is more than adequate to serve its purpose. It is not absolutely essential, and if it gets lost, recall without it should not be a serious threat. Everything is here to resuscitate the needy in the unlikely event that a mishap should occur."

"Right, Mr. Gansy, you are ready? Good. Come, gentlemen, stand clear of the chamber, please."

Leigher moved out and over to his console. With its cover removed, it was a gleamingly impressive long, low computerlike instrumentation. Leigher threw switches, and a light bleeped red-red-red. He scanned his illuminated inlay chart of the counties in South-east England, brought in a blowup of North Middlesex. *Flick, flick, tuck, tock, tock, tock.* Unhesitating, efficient, sure of himself. In went the main power gate.

Sss-sook. The curved door to the transposer-chamber slid closed, shutting off Gansy's damp and rigidly upright figure, and from somewhere came a hum that rose to become hard for human ears to bear.

Leigher was absorbed in his function, checking this dial and that, making an adjustment here, moderating there, flicking switches, closing a second power gate. He raised his eyes and screwed around to regard the festoon of insulators and boosters worn like a crown by the high dome of the chamber. He saw the flash, the confirming trigger, and he closed the major circuit.

There was a *bang!* that made everybody but Leigher jump, and the humming dropped sharply to become a steady purr.

Mr. Ciano gawked at the time-indicator that he had found, saw the day-wheel become a blur, the month-indicator flipping by, the year slot jitter to: 1948 — 1947 — 1946 — 45 — 44 — 43 — 42 — 41 —, faster and faster, in seconds to become a blank shimmering with speed.

Leigher had half his attention on the Southern Counties map, bringing a small bright dot to the north of Middlesex, cutting to the blowup again, tuning a dial with one hand, sliding a knob through a gradated slot with the other, keeping an eye on the pre-selector, quick of movement, certain.

The date-recorder slowed, slowed, rapidly — 1683 — 1682 — December — November — October — September — August — 22 — 21 — 20 — 19 — 18 — 17 — 16 — . . .

Leigher's hands flew, *click, tuck, tuck, poomp, poomp.* August 3rd crept over to become August 2nd. Moments hung poised. Leigher slammed over a lever. His eyes went to a thick and oddly coiled aerial at the back of the console. Its tip burst into a bright orange glow. Once. Twice.

"Damn!" Leigher re-opened the channel, re-tuned the locator, made fresh adjustments.

Mr. Ciano saw the date revolve—August 3rd, 4th, 5th, through to 10th. Again Leigher slammed the lever to positive.

He watched for the orange light. It came. Once.

"Ah." Leigher relaxed. "Good." He went over his bank of buttons, cutting-out, locking-on, setting the recall on auto.

Sssss-sook, the curved door of the transposer-chamber slid open.

Seffan went over to take a look. There was a peculiar smell. There was no sign of Gansy. Seffan felt his skin prickle. It was queer. He shook off the feeling and went over to listen-in on some of the technical data that Mr. Ciano was gleaning from Leigher.

Gansy got mud on his shoes. His feet were soaking wet and even his pants cuffs were soggy. Mud. He'd get it on the rest of his clothes. He swore silently to himself. He didn't like this poison-antidote business. If something went wrong . . . He didn't entirely trust Leigher.

Four whole hours poking around—what was he supposed to do? This coat he'd got was not a very good fit. Still it was better than nothing—this place was like a freezer. He looked about him. What a great century to be in. Anything was possible here. These people would believe anything. There was a fortune to be made.

Four hours. Not much longer. Four. Old Ciano worried him. It *would* have been nice not to have to show up to see *him* again. Dr. Leigher could have him. For keeps.

Gansy squirmed his toes. He'd have to get back shortly.

"You can see what straits I'm under." Leigher had mellowed somewhat, had his guests drinking coffee from assorted not-very-hygienic drinking vessels. "By the time my initial, ah, appropriations came to an end, the bulk of my work here was finished—that is to say, the installation. But lately lack of funds has been most aggravating. There is equipment I need in order to bring about refinements, and I must admit that I'm glad to see some real cash at last. The other fellows that have been here seemed to think this place was a free soup kitchen. Promises, nothing but promises."

"Who were they?" Mr. Ciano inquired. "Do you remember their names?"

"I have a list somewhere," Leigher said. "I can't remember them all. William Clayfield, I think, and, uh, Sydney Finebaum was one. And then there was a fellow called Gatniche, and, ah, that escaped prisoner, what was his name? Felch? Or Velch?"

"Sidney Winebaum?" Mr. Ciano was surprised. "So this is where he's been!"

"Mr. Winebaum? Yes. I did a special routing for him, to pre-Revolution France." Leigher curled a disdainful lip. "My reward for my services was those two Louis XIV chairs over there."

"And Willy The Chopper," Carl asked, "what happened to him?"

"Willy The Who?"

"Clayfield, Willy Clayfield. Where did he go?"

"Oh, yes, him. He was the one that wanted a hiding place. Till the, ah, 'heat was off', was the way he put it, I think."

"What about his roll, did he take that with him?"

"He *did* have a bag with him. He was one of the few who gave me some recompense. He swore on oath that he would return in a couple weeks and pay me the balance, but he never did."

"Where did he *go?*"

"To somewhere around 1350. He's still there."

"Tell me," Mr. Ciano said, "I've been thinking—why do we have to wait the time here the same time that a person has there? Like Gansy, why can't you just pick him up four hours ahead and bring him straight back?"

"I don't know," Leigher confessed. "It's one of the problems I'm working on. It would seem simple, but there is an unavoidable and inseparable relationship between the passage of subjective time for the transposer and for its user. Thus, to enjoy four hours there means to wait four hours here. This is one thing I wish to research further. Another is to obtain greater precision that I might not merely strike the correct month in the right year, but the very exact right minute upon a certain defined day. And in exactly the right place."

Leigher's eyes began to glow. "I need a lot more autocontrols and relays. And I need fully variable wall charts of the entire world, with a delineation-enlarger capacity that any point may be brought to at least one-to-ten, with full gravitational compensation and terrain evaluation, with the known characteristics at any period.

"The possibilities are tremendous, Mr. Ciano." Leigher for a moment had the shining vision before his eyes. He had the radiance of a dedicated fanatic. "A man could see the last stone being placed upon the pyramids, stand on the heights and see Rome burn, watch the Huns sacking and looting, see Michelangelo himself put the finishing touches to his David, see the Battle of Waterloo, see Prince Ferdinand assassinated. So many things, to be there, to see the things that made history! On the spot, authentic, no time wasted! To be there, just for the few minutes!"

Leigher paused, his face flushed, his glasses full of eyes.

There was an impressive silence.

Leigher became aware that they were all looking at him in the same strange manner. His radiance faded and died, and his face reverted to its acid cast.

Seffan sipped his dubious coffee. "Sounds like it could be a sound commercial proposition," he said.

Ssss-sook, the chamber door closed. The orange light pulsed one-two-three. Five seconds. One-two-three—Five seconds. One-two-three—

Leigher went to the console, busied himself verifying that the auto-recall cycle was perfect. The date began to climb: 1690—1691—1692—93—94—

The constant hum that had been with them again began to rise in pitch. The high whine sang inside their skulls and squinched their eyes . . . then mercifully descended the scale, like a jet engine being throttled back.

The sound died to a low throb, a green flasher ticked. All eyes turned to the chamber door.

Flash, flash, flash. The suspense mounted as they waited for the door to open.

A long minute went by. A second minute started.

"What's going on?" Mr. Ciano cried. "Why doesn't it open up?"

"When going back into the past, arriving at a precise second is not essential," Leigher said, "but on recall it is vital to connect with the exact split second of present time. To be out of phase causes disturbance. It is something like an elevator slowing to match floor levels. Ah!"

Sssss-sook. The door opened.

Gansy tore off his face mask. He looked relieved. He couldn't limp out of the chamber fast enough. "The antidote, give me the antidote. I'm getting dizzy."

They gave Gansy a Louis XIV chair, and he slumped into it. Dr. Leigher calmly prepared the hypodermic.

Mr. Ciano keenly looked Gansy up and down, noting what looked like grass stains on his knees, the strange coat he was wearing, and the wide-brimmed hat with the droopy plume. Mr. Ciano himself stooped to wipe a finger along Gansy's shoes. The mud was still moist. Gansy, in fact, was quite damp; his hat quite heavy with soaking. He smelt of rain—and other things.

"You've been drinking!" Leigher accused. "You fool, if you'd got drunk, you might have passed out!"

Gansy struggled out of the coat to offer a bare arm. "It was cold there." he groused. "You dropped me in some kind of field, and it was raining on and off. I had to walk a mile before I met anybody."

Leigher dabbed alcohol on the presented arm, inserted the needle, emptied the syringe.

"I hope you're in time." Gansy sounded somewhat anxious. "I don't feel so good."

"You're all right," Leigher said. "What else have you brought back?"

"What else? I wasn't there long enough to get organized. What did you expect? When you got poison, you shouldn't get excited."

Coat and hat to one side, Leigher helped Gansy remove his traveling harness. "Didn't you see anything, do anything?"

"I didn't have time, did I?" Gansy retorted. "What was I supposed to do? It takes a day or two to settle in, find the best places, pick the best targets." He rubbed his knee. "And I caught a bench and nearly broke my leg."

Seffan went through the pockets of the coat—lace handkerchief, copper snuff box, a battered nosegay that had lost most of its fragrance, a large iron key, a tinderbox, some beads, two crumpled letters, loose pennies and a money pouch containing ten-and-a-half guineas and some silver.

"What's this?" Leigher tugged.

"Go easy! It's loaded, I think." Gansy freed the snag and removed the flintlock pistol from beside the more modern version in his belt. "I didn't want to take it off him, but you know how it is. I didn't want to have to shoot him just to borrow his coat for a spell. It was wet, man."

"I'm sorry." Leigher turned to Mr. Ciano with a shrug. "That's another thing I wish to correct, to select the most climatically propitious times. My work." He held out his hands. "There is so much to do!"

Mr. Ciano nodded. "I can see." But there was a new gleam in his eye.

They dickered about who would go next. Gansy went out to hide the car under a camouflage sheet.

No one would take on the poison trick. It was generally agreed that a few days would have to be spent in order to reconnoiter the ground and orientate to the past surroundings.

It was first thought that Seffan and Carl should go together. They were willing. But Mr. Ciano thought twice, and three times, and four times, and gnawed his lip. He did not trust Seffan, and began to trust him even less. And Carl had disappointed him recently. Seffan and Moke? Moke and Carl? The more he thought about it, the less he liked the combinations.

"Three days should be sufficient," Seffan said. "We can stake out the best prospects, get everything set for what the market will take—which should be plenty. They'll be wide open for anything. With our know-how we should be able to move in and mow the hay."

Mr. Ciano wriggled his fingers, tapping ash. He made his decision. "Carl and I will go. You will stay and keep an eye on things here."

"What?" Seffan was surprised. "You are going yourself?"

"This is big," Mr. Ciano said. "I want to see for myself, firsthand. I want no foul-ups, and I want no mistakes. There seems need to establish some positive form of control at the reception end." He spat fragments of cigar. "The only way I can be sure that there is no deviation is to attend to the matter personally."

"But, Mr. Ciano . . ."

"No 'buts'. *I* will come back." He turned to the inventor/discoverer. "Dr. Leigher, you can send Carl and myself to some suitable place where we might study the conditions for a permanent rendezvous area?"

"You anticipate a regular traffic to one particular era? Ah." Leigher raised his eyebrows. "If someone remained to provide a permanent fix, yes. The continuity-gap remains constant. I can send any number of persons to match a current past-contact on the board." He played with a pen. "This is perhaps one reason why absconders invariably return their recall harness—it makes it extremely difficult to find them again."

"Well," Mr. Ciano mashed out his cigar, "you won't see my recall-harness without me in it. So—let's get going, shall we?"

"As you wish. I think you will find that 1640 was a very interesting year in London. Ah, two of you wish to travel together?"

"That's right, just me and Carl."

"Good," Leigher said. "That'll be another twenty thousand dollars, please . . ."

"Carl's has got a corner missing—will it make any difference?"

"No, it's only a casing. In here now, gentlemen."

And stiffly back-to-back, Carl and Mr. Ciano were put in darkness as *sssss-sook,* the chamber door sealed.

Primed to readiness, came the hum to shiver the nerve ends of their teeth, the closing of contacts. And at the key moment the throwing-in of the major circuits.

Bang! like the crack of doom, and the hum dropped to a steady pulsing, and Carl and Mr. Ciano were on their way.

One day passed, and another. And another.

Gansy was sent to town to get some supplies, and to order a heap of special components that Leigher desired. Leigher spent most of his time shut away in his workroom fooling around with a cabinetful of complicated wiring. Seffan and Moke played cards, Gansy joining them as available from his chores.

There was much private thinking, much silent pondering and speculation upon the whereabouts and doings of the couple who had departed. There was some temperamental disparity in the group remaining. Moke had the limited outlook of a hired gun, Seffan the devious mind of an intriguer. Gansy was now more or less a supernumary, a small man who'd found himself a good thing but was a degree nervous of his new-found "partners." Leigher lived in a world of his own.

Towards the end of the third day, the orange light blipped once, twice, three times. Seffan hastened to fetch Leigher, but Leigher had a relay to his workroom and was already on his way.

Sssss-sook. Leigher went through his own planned drill.

The drag of idle waiting was swept away, and in two minutes the tension had hearts pounding and breath hanging shallow.

Come on, come on!

It seemed ages before *sssss-sook,* the chamber door slid open.

There was no one there.

Leigher ran forward, but Seffan beat him. On the floor of the chamber was a single harness and, attached to it, a letter.

Seffan scooped up the bundle, tore the letter free, opened it. The paper felt gritty. He read the inky scrawl: "Doc Layah, you were right. Mr. Ciano had bad luck, is at the bottom of river. Send nobody else. Don't follow me. Everything be O.K.—C.M."

Seffan was bewildered. "What . . .? What . . .?"

Leigher took the letter from his hands, read.

Seffan looked at the harness. Yes, it was Carl's all right, the recaller-button case had a chipped corner.

"M'yah." Leigher handed the letter back. He seemed not the least perturbed. "That's the way it happens. The good old days are really good—being there, we know that the future is assured. It is known that the world will not end tomorrow, and the good things of life are plentiful."

"Mr. Ciano at the bottom of the river." Seffan was stunned. "Carl wouldn't dare do a thing like that."

"It may have been an accident," Leigher said. "Or perhaps he didn't want competition. Or perhaps didn't like being told which apple to pick in an overloaded orchard."

"Yeah?" Seffan snarled. "Well he won't get—" He stopped. And truly Carl was beyond his jurisdiction.

"If you'd like to go back to his time, I still have a fix on Mr. Ciano's recaller. Carl may have thought, erroneously, that the water would destroy its efficiency."

"Can you bring Mr. Ciano back?"

"Not if he had the recaller in his pocket. I can override the safety guard, but all we might get could be just a portion of his jacket, say."

"Carl!" Seffan threw aside the harness. "He'll pay for this!"

"While Mr. Ciano's recaller is locus operable, we can at least know where Carl is in time, if not in place."

"Ah." Seffan smote his fist. "Yes." His sense of fidelity and loyalty had been outraged. The Code had been broken. What would other Chiefs have to say about this?

Seffan took respite to reflect. Yes, what *would* the Chiefs have to say about this? Would they believe him? Yes. Would they? What if they didn't? Mr. Ciano had been his boss. Seffan's mind came up with a skitter of awkward questions. Blame. Fault. Carl scot-free. They wouldn't like that.

Seffan went cold. He swung on Leigher. "Look what you've done!" Could he take Moke, a spare harness, bring Carl back, alive or dead? How reliable would Moke be? "Blast you!" This was a job for the organization. How many to send back? How trustworthy the enforcers, with no living network to keep them in line?

Seffan stamped. He saw trouble ahead. With his patron, guide and mentor gone, his security was shattered. Questions, too many questions to answer. And Carl, at peace forevermore, laughing at them.

Moke spoke. "Thinking of going after him?"

"No," Seffan said. He thought of Elaine. Never satisfied, everlastingly wanting things. He'd already thought about the chances of losing her, half-seriously. No more Elaine. Or Charlotte, either.

Women tired a man. A fresh start. Why not? Others appeared to revel in it. If Carl could prefer it, choose it, find it so plainly desirable . . . "No," Seffan repeated, "I'm going back to a different time." It was obvious. It would be refreshing, exhilarating, a brand-new life. With his brains . . .

"Huh? What about me?"

"You can suit yourself."

Seffan got the valise, came to drop it at Leigher's feet. "My passage money is in there." He stooped, retrieved the bag, opened it to remove two boxes of cartridges. "I might need these." He dropped the bag again. "Doc, I want to go back someplace. Make it around." he guessed at a number, "1773."

"Now hold it," Moke said grimly. "You ain't going nowhere. You're not leaving *me* here to carry the baby."

"Oh? Well, I don't want *you* where I'm going. You make your own arrangements."

"Yeah?" Moke's gun was loose in his hand. "I'm as entitled to that passage money as you are."

Leigher, perhaps mollified by his increased income, or sensitive and fearful that a shooting match might damage his equipment, interrupted, "Please! There is no need to fight. Under the circumstances I shall be willing to accommodate both of you for the single fee." He sighed. "I understand the situation only too well. It is happening all the time." Leigher kicked the valise to one side. "I shall do my best for you both." He sounded weary suddenly. "If you would just tell me where you would like to go . . ."

Seffan stuck with his random selection of 1773. Moke opted for a nearer era—he wanted to go back only as far as Prohibition, a great time to be alive.

In due course they each in turn entered the transposer chamber, and so dropped into history.

Gansy lived like a king—Leigher was quite indulgent with him. Gansy was one who always came back.

The Mob tagged Gansy, twisted his arm. Gansy was forced to talk. He introduced other high-ranking officers to pester Dr. Leigher. The good doctor's equipment became more sophisticated. Leigher professed unhappiness at the service he was obliged to afford persons who owned not the least of altruistic motives—but they did pay promptly, and in cash, without fussing over minor details such as receipts and tax-duties. And they were discreet.

But all good things come to an end.

Much of the folding money that Gansy got to spend while living it up in Miami turned out to be part of the ransom that had been paid to the much-wanted kidnaper of Bernice Bernousie. Which little thing brought Gansy very smartly to the notice of the law. And from there it was but a step to making everything legal.

"A time-and-space transposer. Fantastic." Federal Agent Dixel surveyed the plant. The batteries of dials, screens, knobs, and switches, gleamed and winked back at him. "What a project!"

His fellow agent, Gordon, stepped gingerly into the transposer chamber. "You said it. What a racket, sending hoods into the past." He mulled the thought. "One way of getting rid of them, I guess."

Dixel shook his head, marveling at the intricate machinery. "Wired every piece himself. The man was a genius."

"He'd have been better if he'd used his talents to serve society." Gordon mulled *this* thought over. "Maybe he did, at that. Another one and he'd have had a round forty taking his escape trail. From as low as five thousand bucks. That's a small price to pay to raise hell sometime else. Hey! don't touch anything! I don't want to go any place!"

Dixel laughed. "Take it easy, Johnny, the power's off." He came over to the chamber. "This place is sealed, right? And if we want to go anywhere, we'll have to do it in our own time."

"My wife would miss me," Gordon said simply, "and the way this thing works she might have trouble collecting the insurance."

Dixel peered. "Is that an inspection hatch up there?"

"Huh? Yes, it looks like it." Gordon tested the rings of radiation bars. "Wouldn't grab these when they're hot. It must have been like an oven in here." But cold, he found that they made a serviceable ladder.

Gordon climbed. He tested the hatch, found that it moved easily to one side. He poked his head up through, and a hand with a flashlight.

"What's up there?" Dixel asked. "A valvo transistorium?"

"Uh-huh." The torch beam played.

Satisfied, Gordon descended. He did not feel comfortable in the chamber and felt that he had overcome his reluctance sufficiently for this investigation.

"Well? What did you see?"

"An air-bed, a refrigerator, a hose and a couple buckets, a clothes closet and spare harness things, and a paperback library." Gordon stepped out and dusted his hands. "Friend Gansy's hideaway." He scanned the laboratory. "Beautiful. A time machine. He could afford it. Tin, flashbulbs, and imagination." He turned to gaze somberly at the floor of the chamber. "And a trapdoor over the deepest abandoned mine in the state of Arizona . . ."

THE LEOPOLD LOCKED ROOM

(1971)

Edward D. Hoch

Edward D. Hoch

A full time writer since 1968, Edward D. Hoch (1930–) is the most prolific producer of mystery short stories since Erle Stanley Gardner. Indeed, with over 600 published, he is one of the very few writers in any branch of literature who has made his living primarily through short fiction. His stories, which first began to appear in 1955, feature more than a dozen series characters, including the popular Nick Velvet and the grim but always interesting Captain Leopold. Because he has written relatively few novels he does not enjoy the critical acclaim due him. Short story collections include City of Brass and Other Simon Ark Stories *(1971),* The Spy and the Thief *(1971), and the wonderful* The Thefts of Nick Velvet *(1978).*

THE LEOPOLD LOCKED ROOM

Captain Leopold had never spoken to anyone about his divorce, and it was a distinct surprise to Lieutenant Fletcher when he suddenly said, "Did I ever tell you about my wife, Fletcher?"

They were just coming up from the police pistol range in the basement of headquarters after their monthly target practise, and it hardly seemed a likely time to be discussing past marital troubles. Fletcher glanced at him sideways and answered, "No, I guess you never did, Captain."

They had reached the top of the stairs and Leopold turned in to the little room where the coffee, sandwich, and soft-drink machines were kept. They called it the lunchroom, but only by the boldest stretch of the imagination could the little collection of tables and chairs qualify as such. Rather it was a place where off-duty cops could sit and chat, which was what Leopold and Fletcher were doing now.

Fletcher bought the coffee and put the steaming paper cups on the table between them. He had never seen Leopold quite this open and personal before, anxious to talk about a life that had existed far beyond the limits of Fletcher's friendship. "She's coming back," Leopold said simply, and it took Fletcher an instant to grasp the meaning of his words.

"Your wife is coming back?"

"My ex-wife."

"Here? What for?"

Leopold sighed and played with the little bag of sugar that Fletcher had given him with his coffee. "Her niece is getting married. Our niece."

"I never knew you had one."

"She's been away at college. Her name is Vicki Nelson, and she's marrying a young lawyer named Moore. And Monica is coming back east for the wedding."

"I never even knew her name," Fletcher observed, taking a sip of his coffee. "Haven't you seen her since the divorce?"

Leopold shook his head. "Not for fifteen years. It was a funny thing. She wanted to be a movie star, and I guess fifteen years ago lots of girls still thought about being movie stars. Monica was intelligent and very pretty—but probably no prettier than hundreds of other girls who used to turn up in Hollywood every year back in those days. I was just starting on the police force then, and the future looked pretty bright for me here. It would have been foolish of me to toss up everything just to chase her wild dream out to California. Well, pretty soon it got to be an obsession with her, really bad. She'd spend her afternoons in movie theaters and her evenings watching old films on television. Finally, when I still refused to go west with her, she just left me."

"Just walked out?"

Leopold nodded. "It was a blessing, really, that we didn't have children. I heard she got a few minor jobs out there—as an extra, and some technical stuff behind the scenes. Then apparently she had a nervous breakdown. About a year later I received the official word that she'd divorced me. I heard that she recovered and was back working, and I think she had another marriage that didn't work out."

"Why would she come back for the wedding?"

"Vicki is her niece and also her godchild. We were just married when Vicki was born, and I suppose Monica might consider her the child we never had. In any event, I know she still hates me, and blames me for everything that's gone wrong with her life. She told a friend once a few years ago she wished I were dead."

"Do you have to go to this wedding, too, Captain?"

"Of course. If I stayed away it would be only because of her. At least I have to drop by the reception for a few minutes." Leopold smiled ruefully. "I guess that's why I'm telling you all this, Fletcher. I want a favor from you."

"Anything, Captain. You know that."

"I know it seems like a childish thing to do, but I'd like you to come out there with me. I'll tell them I'm working, and that I can only stay for a few minutes. You can wait outside in the car if you want. At least they'll see you there and believe my excuse."

Fletcher could see the importance of it to Leopold, and the effort that had gone into the asking. "Sure," he said. "Be glad to. When is it?"

"This Saturday. The reception's in the afternoon, at Sunset Farms."

Leopold had been to Sunset Farms only once before, at the wedding of a patrolman whom he'd especially liked. It was a low rambling place at the end of a paved driveway, overlooking a wooded valley and a gently flowing creek. If it had ever been a farm, that day was long past; but for wedding receptions and retirement parties it was the ideal place. The interior of the main building was, in reality, one huge square room, divided by accordion doors to make up to four smaller square rooms.

For the wedding of Vicki Nelson and Ted Moore three-quarters of the large room was in use, with only the last set of accordion doors pulled shut its entire width and locked. The wedding party occupied a head table along one wall, with smaller tables scattered around the room for the families and friends. When Leopold entered the place at five minutes of two on Saturday afternoon, the hired combo was just beginning to play music for dancing.

He watched for a moment while Vicki stood, radiant, and allowed her new husband to escort her to the center of the floor. Ted Moore was a bit older than Leopold had expected, but as the pair glided slowly across the floor, he could find no visible fault with the match. He helped himself to a glass of champagne punch and stood ready to intercept them as they left the dance floor.

"It's Captain Leopold, isn't it?" someone asked. A face from his past loomed up, a tired man with a gold tooth in the front of his smile. "I'm Immy Fontaine, Monica's stepbrother."

"Sure," Leopold said, as if he'd remembered the man all along. Monica had rarely mentioned Immy, and Leopold recalled meeting him once or twice at family gatherings. But the sight of him now, gold tooth and all, reminded Leopold that Monica was somewhere nearby, that he might confront her at any moment.

"We're so glad you could come," someone else said, and he turned to greet the bride and groom as they came off the dance floor. Up close, Vicki was a truly beautiful girl, clinging to her new husband's arm like a proper bride.

"I wouldn't have missed it for anything," he said.

"This is Ted," she said, making the introductions. Leopold shook his hand, silently approving the firm grip and friendly eyes.

"I understand you're a lawyer," Leopold said, making conversation.

"That's right, sir. Mostly civil cases, though. I don't tangle much with criminals."

They chatted for a few more seconds before the pressure of guests broke them apart. The luncheon was about to be served, and the more hungry ones were already lining up at the buffet tables. Vicki and Ted went over to start the line, and Leopold took another glass of champagne punch.

"I see the car waiting outside," Immy Fontaine said, moving in again. "You got to go on duty?"

Leopold nodded. "Just this glass and I have to leave."

"Monica's in from the west coast."

"So I heard."

A slim man with a mustache jostled against him in the crush of the crowd and hastily apologized. Fontaine seized the man by the arm and introduced him to Leopold. "This here's Dr. Felix Thursby. He came east with Monica. Doc, I want you to meet Captain Leopold, her ex-husband."

Leopold shook hands awkwardly, embarrassed for the man and for himself. "A fine wedding," he mumbled. "Your first trip east?"

Thursby shook his head. "I'm from New York. Long ago."

"I was on the police force there once," Leopold remarked.

They chatted for a few more minutes before Leopold managed to edge away through the crowd.

"Leaving so soon?" a harsh unforgettable voice asked.

"Hello, Monica. It's been a long time."

He stared down at the handsome, middle-aged woman who now blocked his path to the door. She had gained a little weight, especially in the bosom, and her hair was graying. Only the eyes startled him, and frightened him just a bit. They had the intense wild look he'd seen before on the faces of deranged criminals.

"I didn't think you'd come. I thought you'd be afraid of me," she said.

"That's foolish. Why should I be afraid of you?"

The music had started again, and the line from the buffet tables was beginning to snake lazily about the room. But for Leopold and Monica they might have been alone in the middle of a desert.

"Come in here," she said, "where we can talk." She motioned toward the end of the room that had been cut off by the accordion doors. Leopold followed her, helpless to do anything else. She unlocked the doors and pulled them apart, just wide enough for them to enter the unused quarter of the large room. Then she closed and locked the doors behind them, and stood facing him. They were two people, alone in a bare unfurnished room.

They were in an area about thirty feet square, with the windows at the far end and the locked accordion doors at Leopold's back. He could see the afternoon sun cutting through the trees outside, and the gentle hum of the air conditioner came through above the subdued murmur of the wedding guests.

"Remember the day we got married?" she asked.

"Yes. Of course."

She walked to the middle window, running her fingers along the frame, perhaps looking for the latch to open it. But it stayed closed as she faced him again. "Our marriage was as drab and barren as this room. Lifeless, unused!"

"Heaven knows I always wanted children, Monica."

"You wanted nothing but your damned police work!" she shot back, eyes flashing as her anger built.

"Look, I have to go. I have a man waiting in the car."

"Go! That's what you did before, wasn't it? *Go, go!* Go out to your damned job and leave me to struggle for myself. Leave me to—"

"You walked out on me, Monica. Remember?" he reminded her softly. She was so defenseless, without even a purse to swing at him.

"Sure I did! Because I had a career waiting for me! I had all the world waiting for me! And you know what happened because you wouldn't come along? You know what happened to me out there? They took my money and my self-respect and what virtue I had left. They made me into a tramp, and when they were done they locked me up in a mental hospital for three years. Three years!"

"I'm sorry."

"Every day while I was there I thought about you. I thought about how it would be when I got out. Oh, I thought. And planned. And schemed. You're a big detective now. Sometimes your cases even get reported in the California papers." She was pacing back and forth, caged, dangerous. "Big detective. But I can still destroy you just as you destroyed me!"

He glanced over his shoulder at the locked accordion doors, seeking a way out. It was a thousand times worse than he'd imagined it would be. She was mad—mad and vengeful and terribly dangerous. "You should see a doctor, Monica."

Her eyes closed to mere slits. "I've seen doctors." Now she paused before the middle window, facing him. "I came all the way east for this day, because I thought you'd be here. It's so much better than your apartment, or your office, or a city street. There are one hundred and fifty witnesses on the other side of those doors."

"What in hell are you talking about?"

Her mouth twisted in a horrible grin. "You're going to know what I knew. Bars and cells and disgrace. You're going to know the despair I felt all those years."

"Monica—"

At that instant perhaps twenty feet separated them. She lifted one arm, as if to shield herself, then screamed in terror. "No! Oh, God, no!"

Leopold stood frozen, unable to move, as a sudden gunshot echoed through the room. He saw the bullet strike her in the chest, toppling her backward like the blow from a giant fist. Then somehow he had his own gun out of its belt holster and he swung around toward the doors.

They were still closed and locked. He was alone in the room with Monica.

He looked back to see her crumple on the floor, blood spreading in a widening circle around the torn black hole in her dress. His eyes went to the windows, but all three were still closed and unbroken. He shook his head, trying to focus his mind on what had happened.

There was noise from outside, and a pounding on the accordion doors. Someone opened the lock from the other side, and the gap between the doors widened as they were pulled open. "What happened?" someone asked. A woman guest screamed as she saw the body. Another toppled in a faint.

Leopold stepped back, aware of the gun still in his hand, and saw Lieutenant Fletcher fighting his way through the mob of guests. "Captain, what is it?"

"She . . . Someone shot her."

Fletcher reached out and took the gun from Leopold's hand—carefully, as one might take a broken toy from a child. He put it to his nose and sniffed, then opened the cylinder to inspect the bullets. "It's been fired recently, Captain. One shot." Then his eyes seemed to cloud over, almost to the point of tears. "Why the hell did you do it?" he asked, "Why?"

Leopold saw nothing of what happened then. He only had vague and splintered memories of someone examining her and saying she was still alive, of an ambulance and much confusion. Fletcher drove him down to headquarters, to the Commissioner's office, and he sat there and waited, running his moist palms up and down his trousers. He was not surprised when they told him she had died on the way to Southside Hospital. Monica had never been one to do things by halves.

The men—detectives who worked under him—came to and left the Commissioner's office, speaking in low tones with their heads together, occasionally offering him some embarrassed gesture of condolence. There was an aura of sadness over the place, and Leopold knew it was for him.

"You have nothing more to tell us, Captain?" the Commissioner asked. "I'm making it as easy for you as I can."

"I didn't kill her," Leopold insisted again. "It was someone else."

"Who? How?"

He could only shake his head. "I wish I knew. I think in some mad way she killed herself, to get revenge on me."

"She shot herself with *your* gun, while it was in *your* holster, and while *you* were standing twenty feet away?"

Leopold ran a hand over his forehead. "It couldn't have been my gun. Ballistics will prove that."

"But your gun had been fired recently, and there was an empty cartridge in the chamber."

"I can't explain that. I haven't fired it since the other day at target practise, and I reloaded it afterwards."

"Could she have hated you that much, Captain?" Fletcher asked. "To frame you for her murder?"

"She could have. I think she was a very sick woman. If I did that to her—if I was the one who made her sick—I suppose I deserve what's happening to me now."

"The hell you do," Fletcher growled. "If you say you're innocent, Captain, I'm sticking by you." He began pacing again, and finally turned to the Commissioner. "How about giving him a paraffin test, to see if he's fired a gun recently?"

The Commissioner shook his head. "We haven't used that in years.

You know how unreliable it is. Fletcher. Many people have nitrates or nitrites on their hands. They can pick them up from dirt, or fertilizers, or fireworks, or urine, or even from simply handling peas or beans. Anyone who smokes tobacco can have deposits on his hands. There are some newer tests for the presence of barium or lead, but we don't have the necessary chemicals for those."

Leopold nodded. The Commissioner had risen through the ranks. He wasn't simply a political appointee, and the men had always respected him. Leopold respected him. "Wait for the ballistics report," he said. "That'll clear me."

So they waited. It was another 45 minutes before the phone rang and the Commissioner spoke to the ballistics man. He listened, and grunted, and asked one or two questions. Then he hung up and faced Leopold across the desk.

"The bullet was fired from your gun," he said simply. "There's no possibility of error. I'm afraid we'll have to charge you with homicide."

The routines he knew so well went on into Saturday evening, and when they were finished Leopold was escorted from the courtroom to find young Ted Moore waiting for him. "You should be on your honeymoon," Leopold told him.

"Vicki couldn't leave till I'd seen you and tried to help. I don't know much about criminal law, but perhaps I could arrange bail."

"That's already been taken care of," Leopold said. "The grand jury will get the case next week."

"I—I don't know what to say. Vicki and I are both terribly sorry."

"So am I." He started to walk away, then turned back. "Enjoy your honeymoon."

"We'll be in town overnight, at the Towers, if there's anything I can do."

Leopold nodded and kept on walking. He could see the reflection of his guilt in young Moore's eyes. As he got to his car, one of the patrolmen he knew glanced his way and then quickly in the other direction. On a Saturday night no one talked to wife murderers. Even Fletcher had disappeared.

Leopold decided he couldn't face the drab walls of his office, not with people avoiding him. Besides, the Commissioner had been forced to suspend him from active duty pending grand jury action and the possible trial. The office didn't even belong to him any more. He cursed silently and drove home to his little apartment, weaving through the dark streets with one eye out for a patrol car. He wondered if they'd be watching him, to prevent his jumping bail. He wondered what he'd have done in the Commissioner's shoes.

The eleven o'clock news on television had it as the lead item, illustrated with a black-and-white photo of him taken during a case last year. He shut off the television without listening to their comments and went back outside, walking down to the corner for an early edition of the Sunday paper. The front-page headline was as bad as he'd expected: *Detective Captain Held in Slaying of Ex-Wife.*

On the way back to his apartment, walking slowly, he tried to remember what she'd been like—not that afternoon, but before the divorce. He tried to remember her face on their wedding day, her soft laughter on their honeymoon. But all he could remember were those mad vengeful eyes. And the bullet ripping into her chest.

Perhaps he had killed her after all. Perhaps the gun had come into his hand so easily he never realized it was there.

"Hello, Captain."

"I—Fletcher! What are you doing here?"

"Waiting for you. Can I come in?"

"Well . . ."

"I've got a six-pack of beer. I thought you might want to talk about it."

Leopold unlocked his apartment door. "What's there to talk about?"

"If you say you didn't kill her, Captain, I'm willing to listen to you."

Fletcher followed him into the tiny kitchen and popped open two of the beer cans. Leopold accepted one of them and dropped into the nearest chair. He felt utterly exhausted, drained of even the strength to fight back.

"She framed me, Fletcher," he said quietly. "She framed me as neatly as anything I've ever seen. The thing's impossible, but she did it."

"Let's go over it step by step, Captain. Look, the way I see it there are only three possibilities: either you shot her, she shot herself, or someone else shot her. I think we can rule out the last one. The three windows were locked on the outside and unbroken, the room was bare of any hiding place, and the only entrance was through the accordion doors. These were closed and locked, and although they could have been opened from the other side you certainly would have seen or heard it happen. Besides, there were one hundred and fifty wedding guests on the other side of those doors. No one could have unlocked and opened them and then fired the shot, all without being seen.

Leopold shook his head. "But it's just as impossible that she could have shot herself. I was watching her every minute. I never looked away once. There was nothing in her hands, not even a purse. And the gun that shot her was in my holster, on my belt. I never drew it till *after* the shot was fired."

Fletcher finished his beer and reached for another can. "I didn't look at her close, Captain, but the size of the hole in her dress and the powder burns point to a contact wound. The Medical Examiner agrees, too. She was shot from no more than an inch or two away. There were grains of powder in the wound itself, though the bleeding had washed most of them away."

"But she had nothing in her hand," Leopold repeated. "And there was nobody standing in front of her with a gun. Even I was twenty feet away."

"The thing's impossible, Captain."

Leopold grunted. "Impossible—unless I killed her."

Fletcher stared at his beer. "How much time do we have?"

"If the grand jury indicts me for first-degree murder, I'll be in a cell by next week."

Fletcher frowned at him. "What's with you, Captain? You almost act resigned to it! Hell, I've seen more fight in you on a routine holdup!"

"I guess that's it, Fletcher. The fight is gone out of me. She's drained every drop of it. She's had her revenge."

Fletcher sighed and stood up. "Then I guess there's really nothing I can do for you, Captain. Good night."

Leopold didn't see him to the door. He simply sat there, hunched over the table. For the first time in his life he felt like an old man.

Leopold slept late Sunday morning, and awakened with the odd sensation that it had all been a dream. He remembered feeling the same way when he'd broken his wrist chasing a burglar. In the morning, on just awakening, the memory of the heavy cast had always been a dream, until he moved his arm. Now, rolling over in his narrow bed, he saw the Sunday paper where he'd tossed it the night before. The headline was still the same. The dream was a reality.

He got up and showered and dressed, reaching for his holster out of habit before he remembered he no longer had a gun. Then he sat at the kitchen table staring at the empty beer cans, wondering what he would do with his day. With his life.

The doorbell rang and it was Fletcher. "I didn't think I'd be seeing you again," Leopold mumbled, letting him in.

Fletcher was excited, and the words tumbled out of him almost before he was through the door. "I think I've got something, Captain! It's not much, but it's a start. I was down at headquarters first thing this morning, and I got hold of the dress Monica was wearing when she was shot."

Leopold looked blank. "The dress?"

Fletcher was busy unwrapping the package he'd brought. "The Commissioner would have my neck if he knew I brought this to you, but look at this hole!"

Leopold studied the jagged, blood-caked rent in the fabric. "It's large," he observed, "but with a near-contact wound the powder burns would cause that."

"Captain, I've seen plenty of entrance wounds made by a .38 slug. I've even caused a few of them. But I never saw one that looked like this. Hell, it's not even round!"

"What are you trying to tell me, Fletcher?" Suddenly something stirred inside him. The juices were beginning to flow again.

"The hole in her dress is much larger and more jagged than the corresponding wound in her chest, Captain. That's what I'm telling you. The bullet that killed her couldn't have made this hole. No way! And that means maybe she wasn't killed when we thought she was."

Leopold grabbed the phone and dialed the familiar number of the Towers Hotel. "I hope they slept late this morning."

"Who?"

"The honeymooners." He spoke sharply into the phone, giving the switchboard operator the name he wanted, and then waited. It was a full minute before he heard Ted Moore's sleepy voice answering on the other end. "Ted, this is Leopold. Sorry to bother you."

The voice came alert at once. "That's all right, Captain. I told you to call if there was anything—"

"I think there is. You and Vicki between you must have a pretty good idea of who was invited to the wedding. Check with her and tell me how many doctors were on the invitation list."

Ted Moore was gone for a few moments and then he returned. "Vicki says you're the second person who asked her that?"

"Oh? Who was the first?"

"Monica. The night before the wedding, when she arrived in town with Dr. Thursby. She casually asked if he'd get to meet any other doctors at the reception. But Vicki told her he was the only one. Of course we hadn't invited him, but as a courtesy to Monica we urged him to come."

"Then after the shooting, it was Thursby who examined her? No one else?"

"He was the only doctor. He told us to call an ambulance and rode to the hospital with her."

"Thank you, Ted. You've been a big help."

"I hope so, Captain."

Leopold hung up and faced Fletcher. "That's it. She worked it with this guy Thursby. Can you put out an alarm for him?"

"Sure can," Fletcher said. He took the telephone and dialed the unlisted squadroom number. "Dr. Felix Thursby? Is that his name?"

"That's it. The only doctor there, the only one who could help Monica with her crazy plan of revenge."

Fletcher completed issuing orders and hung up the phone. "They'll check his hotel and call me back."

"Get the Commissioner on the phone, too. Tell him what we've got."

Fletcher started to dial and then stopped, his finger in mid-air. What *have* we got, Captain?"

The Commissioner sat behind his desk, openly unhappy at being called to headquarters on a Sunday afternoon, and listened bleakly to what Leopold and Fletcher had to tell him. Finally he spread his fingers on the desktop and said, "The mere fact that this Dr. Thursby seems to have left town is hardly proof of his guilt, Captain. What you're saying is that the woman wasn't killed until later—that Thursby killed her in the ambulance. But how could he have done that with a pistol that was already in Lieutenant Fletcher's possession, tagged as evidence? And how could he have fired the fatal shot without the ambulance attendants hearing it?"

"I don't know," Leopold admitted.

"Heaven knows, Captain, I'm willing to give you every reasonable chance to prove your innocence. But you have to bring me more than a dress with a hole in it."

"All right," Leopold said. "I'll bring you more."

"The grand jury gets the case this week, Captain."

"I know," Leopold said. He turned and left the office, with Fletcher tailing behind.

"What now?" Fletcher asked.

"We go to talk to Immy Fontaine, my ex-wife's stepbrother."

Though he'd never been friendly with Fontaine, Leopold knew where to find him. The tired man with the gold tooth lived in a big old house overlooking the Sound, where on this summer Sunday they found him in the back yard, cooking hot dogs over a charcoal fire. He squinted into the sun and said,"I thought you'd be in jail, after what happened."

"I didn't kill her," Leopold said quietly.

"Sure you didn't."

"For a stepbrother you seem to be taking her death right in stride," Leopold observed, motioning toward the fire.

"I stopped worrying about Monica fifteen years ago."

"What about this man she was with? Dr. Thursby?"

Immy Fontaine chuckled. "If he's a doctor I'm a plumber! He has the fingers of a surgeon, I'll admit, but when I asked him about my son's radius that he broke skiing, Thursby thought it was a leg bone. What the hell, though, I was never one to judge Monica's love life. Remember, I didn't even object when she married you."

"Nice of you. Where's Thursby staying while he's in town?"

"He was at the Towers with Monica."

"He's not there any more."

"Then I don't know where he's at. Maybe he's not even staying for her funeral."

"What if I told you Thursby killed Monica?"

He shrugged. "I wouldn't believe you, but then I wouldn't particularly care. If you were smart you'd have killed her fifteen years ago when she walked out on you. That's what I'd have done."

Leopold drove slowly back downtown, with Fletcher grumbling beside him. "Where are we, Captain? It seems we're just going in circles."

"Perhaps we are, Fletcher, but right now there are still too many questions to be answered. If we can't find Thursby I'll have to tackle it from another direction. The bullet, for instance."

"What about the bullet?"

"We're agreed it could not have been fired by my gun, either while it was in my holster or later, while Thursby was in the ambulance with Monica. Therefore, it must have been fired earlier. The last time I fired it was at target practise. Is there any possibility—any chance at all—that Thursby or Monica could have gotten one of the slugs I fired into that target?"

Fletcher put a damper on it. "Captain, we were both firing at the same target. No one could sort out those bullets and say which came from your pistol and which from mine. Besides, how would either of them gain access to the basement target range at police headquarters?"

"I could have an enemy in the department," Leopold said.

"Nuts! We've all got enemies, but the thing is still impossible. If you believe people in the department are plotting against you, you might as well believe that the entire ballistics evidence was faked."

"It was, somehow. Do you have the comparison photos?"

"They're back at the office. But with the narrow depth of field you can probably tell more from looking through the microscope yourself."

Fletcher drove him to the lab, where they persuaded the Sunday-duty officer to let them have a look at the bullets. While Fletcher and the officer stood by in the interests of propriety, Leopold squinted through the microscope at the twin chunks of lead.

"The death bullet is pretty battered," he observed, but he had to admit that the rifling marks were the same. He glanced at the identification tag attached to the test bullet: *Test slug fired from Smith & Wesson .38 Revolver, serial number 2420547.*

Leopold turned away with a sigh, then turned back.

2420547.

He fished into his wallet and found his pistol permit. *Smith & Wesson 2421622.*

"I remembered those two's on the end," he told Fletcher. "That's not my gun."

"It's the one I took from you, Captain. I'll swear to it!"

"And I believe you, Fletcher. But it's the one fact I needed. It tells me how Dr. Thursby managed to kill Monica in a locked room before my very eyes, with a gun that was in my holster at the time. And it just might tell us where to find the elusive Dr. Thursby."

By Monday morning Leopold had made six long-distance calls to California, working from his desk telephone while Fletcher used the squadroom phone. Then, a little before noon, Leopold, Fletcher, the Commissioner, and a man from the District Attorney's office took a car and drove up to Boston.

"You're sure you've got it figured?" the Commissioner asked Leopold for the third time. "You know we shouldn't allow you to cross the state line while awaiting grand jury action."

"Look, either you trust me or you don't," Leopold snapped. Behind the wheel Fletcher allowed himself a slight smile, but the man from the D.A.'s office was deadly serious.

"The whole thing is so damned complicated," the Commissioner grumbled.

"My ex-wife was a complicated woman. And remember, she had fifteen years to plan it."

"Run over it for us again," the D.A.'s man said.

Leopold sighed and started talking. "The murder gun wasn't mine. The gun I pulled after the shot was fired, the one Fletcher took from me, had been planted on me some time before."

"How?"

"I'll get to that. Monica was the key to it all, of course. She hated me so much that her twisted brain planned her own murder in order to get revenge on me. She planned it in such a way that it would have been impossible for anyone but me to have killed her."

"Only a crazy woman would do such a thing."

"I'm afraid she was crazy—crazy for vengeance. She set up the entire plan for the afternoon of the wedding reception, but I'm sure they had an alternate in case I hadn't gone to it. She wanted some place where there'd be lots of witnesses."

"Tell them how she worked the bullet hitting her," Fletcher urged.

"Well, that was the toughest part for me. I actually saw her shot before my eyes. I saw the bullet hit her and I saw the blood. Yet I was alone in a locked room with her. There was no hiding place, no opening from which a person or even a mechanical device could have fired the bullet at her. To you people it seemed I must be guilty, especially when the bullet came from the gun I was carrying.

"But I looked at it from a different angle—once Fletcher forced me to look at it at all! I *knew* I hadn't shot her, and since no one else physically could have, I knew no one did! If Monica was killed by a .38 slug, it must have been fired *after* she was taken from that locked room. Since she was dead on arrival at the hospital, the most likely time for her murder—to me, at least—became the time of the ambulance ride, when Dr. Thursby must have hunched over her with careful solicitousness."

"But you *saw* her shot!"

"That's one of the two reasons Fletcher and I were on the phones to Hollywood this morning. My ex-wife worked in pictures, at times in the technical end of movie-making. On the screen there are a number of ways to simulate a person being shot. An early method was a sort of compressed-air gun fired at the actor from just off-camera. These days, especially in the bloodiest of the Western and war films, they use a tiny explosive charge fitted under the actor's clothes. Of course the body is protected from burns, and the force of it is directed outward. A pouch of fake blood is released by the explosion, adding to the realism of it."

"And this is what Monica did?"

Leopold nodded. "A call to her Hollywood studio confirmed the fact that she worked on a film using this device. I noticed when I met her that she'd gained weight around the bosom, but I never thought to attribute it to the padding and the explosive device. She triggered it when she raised her arm as she screamed at me."

"Any proof?"

"The hole in her dress was just too big to be an entrance hole from a .38, even fired at close range—too big and too ragged. I can thank Fletcher for spotting that. This morning the lab technicians ran a test on the bloodstains. Some of it was her blood, the rest was chicken blood."

"She was a good actress to fool all those people."

"She knew Dr. Thursby would be the first to examine her. All she had to do was fall over when the explosive charge ripped out the front of her dress."

"What if there had been another doctor at the wedding?"

Leopold shrugged. "Then they would have postponed it. They couldn't take that chance."

"And the gun?"

"I remembered Thursby bumping against me when I first met him. He took my gun and substituted an identical weapon—identical, that it, except for the serial number. He'd fired it just a short time earlier, to complete the illusion. When I drew it I simply played into their hands. There I was, the only person in the room with an apparently dying woman, and a gun that had just been fired."

"But what about the bullet that killed her?"

"Rifling marks on the slugs are made by the lands in the rifled barrel of a gun causing grooves in the lead of a bullet. A bullet fired through a smooth tube has no rifling marks."

"What in hell kind of gun has a smooth tube for a barrel?" the Commissioner asked.

"A home-made one, like a zip gun. Highly inaccurate, but quite effective when the gun is almost touching the skin of the victim. Thursby fired a shot from the pistol he was to plant on me, probably into a pillow or some other place where he could retrieve the undamaged slug. Then he reused the rifled slug on another cartridge and fired it with his home-made zip gun, right into Monica's heart. The original rifling marks were still visible and no new ones were added."

"The ambulance driver and attendant didn't hear the shot?"

"They would have stayed up front, since he was a doctor riding with a patient. It gave him a chance to get the padded explosive mechanism off her chest, too. Once that was away, I imagine he leaned over her, muffling the zip gun as best he could, and fired the single shot that killed her. Remember, an ambulance on its way to a hospital is a pretty noisy place—it has a siren going all the time."

They were entering downtown Boston now, and Leopold directed Fletcher to a hotel near the Common. "I still don't believe the part about switching the guns," the D.A.'s man objected. "You mean to tell me he undid the strap over your gun, got out the gun, and substituted another one—all without your knowing it?"

Leopold smiled. "I mean to tell you only one type of person could have managed it—an expert, professional pickpocket. The type you see occasionally doing an act in night clubs and on television. That's how I knew where to find him. We called all over Southern California till we came up with someone who knew Monica and knew she'd dated a man named Thompson who had a pickpocket act. We called Thompson's agent and discovered he's playing a split week at a Boston lounge, and is staying at this hotel."

"What if he couldn't have managed it without your catching on? Or what if you hadn't been wearing your gun?"

"Most detectives wear their guns off-duty. If I hadn't been, or if he couldn't get it, they'd simply have changed their plan. He must have signaled her when he'd safely made the switch."

"Here we are," Fletcher said. "Let's go up."

The Boston police had two men waiting to meet them, and they went up in the elevator to the room registered in the name of Max Thompson. Fletcher knocked on the door, and when it opened the familiar face of Felix Thursby appeared. He no longer wore the mustache, but he had the same slim surgeon-like fingers that Immy Fontaine had noticed. Not a doctor's fingers, but a pickpocket's.

"We're taking you in for questioning," Fletcher said, and the Boston detectives issued the standard warnings of his legal rights.

Thursby blinked his tired eyes at them, and grinned a bit when he recognized Leopold. "She said you were smart. She said you were a smart cop."

"Did you have to kill her?" Leopold asked.

"I didn't. I just held the gun there and she pulled the trigger herself. She did it all herself, except for switching the guns. She hated you that much."

"I know," Leopold said quietly, staring at something far away. "But I guess she must have hated herself just as much."

VANISHING ACT

(1976)

Bill Pronzini
and
Michael Kurland

Bill Pronzini and Michael Kurland

So far we have limited our anthology to locked room stories only, but we thought this would be a good opportunity to introduce the impossible crime story which is usually considered part of this subgenre because it investigates the same problem—how could a seemingly uncommittable crime have been committed?

Bill Pronzini (1943–), the first author, is a good young mystery writer who is quietly becoming great. He has always written brilliant stories such as "Peekaboo," "Sweet Fever," and "The Man Who Collected 'The Shadow'," but now he is producing them more frequently and consistently.

Michael Kurland (1938–), the second author, has written (and collaborated on) several science fiction novels, and won an Edgar Allan Poe Scroll from the Mystery Writers of America for A Plague of Spies *(1969).*

VANISHING ACT

The three of us—Ardis, Cedric Clute and I— were sitting at a quiet corner table, halfway between the Magic Cellar's bar and stage, when the contingent of uniformed policemen made their entrance. There were about thirty of them, all dressed in neatly pressed uniforms and gleaming accessories, and they came down the near aisle two abreast like a platoon of marching soldiers. Most of the tables that front the stage were already occupied, so the cops took over the stack of carpet-covered trunks which comprise a kind of bleacher section directly behind the tables.

I cocked an eyebrow. "Most saloon owners would object to such an influx of fuzz," I said to Cedric. He owns the Cellar, San Francisco's only nightclub devoted solely to the sadly vanishing art of magic.

"Policemen have a right to be entertained," he said, smiling. "Their lot, I understand, is not a happy one."

Ardis said speculatively, "They look very young."

"That's because they're most of the graduating class of the Police Academy," Cedric told her. "Their graduation ceremony was this afternoon, and I invited them down as a group. Actually, it was Captain Dickensheet's idea." He indicated a tall, angular, graying man, also in uniform, who was about to appropriate a table for himself and two other elder officers. "I've known him casually for a couple of years, and he thought his men would enjoy the show."

"With Christopher Steele and The Amazing Boltan on the same bill," Ardis said, "they can't help but enjoy it."

I started to add an agreement to that—and there was Steele himself standing over the table, having appeared with that finely developed knack he has of seeming to come from nowhere.

Christopher Steele is the Cellar's main attraction and one of the greatest of the modern illusionists. I don't say that because I happen to be his manager and publicist. He's also something of a secretive type, given to quirks like an inordinate fascination for puzzles and challenges, the more bizarre the better. Working for and with him the past five years has been anything but dull.

Steele usually dresses in black, both on stage and off, and I think he does it because he knows it gives him, with his thick black hair and dark skin and eyes, a vaguely sinister air. He looked sinister now as he said, "The most amazing thing about Phil Boltan, you know, is that he's still alive. He does a fine job on stage, but he has the personal habits and morals of a Yahoo."

Ardis' eyes shone as they always did when Steele was around; she's his assistant and confidante and lives in a wing of his house across the Bay, although if there is anything of a more intimate nature to their relationship neither of them has ever hinted at it to me. She said, "You sound as though Boltan is hardly one of your favorite people, Christopher."

"He isn't—not in the least."

Cedric frowned. "If you'd told me you felt that way, I wouldn't have booked you both for the same night."

"It doesn't matter. As I said, he *is* a fine performer."

"Just what is it that you find so objectionable about Boltan?" I asked as Steele sat down.

"He's a ruthless egomaniac," Steele said. "Those in the psychological professions would call him a sociopath. If you stand in his way, he'll walk over you without hesitation."

"A fairly common trait among performers," I said blandly.

"Not in Boltan's case. Back in the '40's, for example, he worked with a man named Granger—"

"The Four-Men-in-a-Trunk Illusion?" Ardis said immediately.

"Right. The Granger Four-Men-in-a-Trunk Illusion premiered at the Palladium before George the Fifth. That was before Boltan's time, of course. At any rate, Granger was getting old, but he had a beautiful young wife named Cecily and an infant son; he also had Phil Boltan as an assistant.

"So one morning Granger awoke to find that Boltan had run off with Cecily and several trunks of his effects. He was left with the infant son and a load of bitterness he wasn't able to handle. As a result, he put his head in a plastic bag one evening and suffocated himself. Tragic—very tragic."

"What happened to the son?" Cedric asked.

"I don't know. Granger had no close relatives, so I imagine the boy went to a foster home."

Ardis asked, "Did Boltan marry Cecily?"

"No. Of course not. He's never married any of his conquests."

"Nice guy," I said.

Steele nodded and leaned back in his chair. "Enough about Phil Boltan," he said. "Matthew, did you have any problem setting up for my show?"

"No," I told him. "All your properties are ready in the wings."

"Sound equipment?"

"In place."

"Ultraviolet bulbs?"

"Check," I said. The u.v. bulbs were to illuminate the special paint on the gauze and balloons and other "spook" effects for Steele's midnight seance show. "It's a good thing I did a precheck; one of the Carter posters fluoresced blue around the border, and I had to take it down. Otherwise it would have been a conspicuous distraction."

Cedric looked at me reproachfully. "I suppose you'd have removed the Iron Maiden if that had fluoresced," he said, meaning the half-ton iron torture box in one corner.

"Sure," I said. "Dedication is dedication."

We made small talk for a time, and then Cedric excused himself to take his usual place behind the bar; it was twenty past ten. I sipped my drink and looked idly around the Cellar. It was stuffed with the paraphernalia and memorabilia of Carter the Great, a world-famous illusionist in the '20's and '30's. His gaudy posters covered the walls.

The stage was rather small, but of professional quality; it even had a trapdoor, which led to a small tunnel, which in turn came up in the coatroom adjacent to the bar. The only other exits from the stage, aside from the proscenium, were curtains on the right and left sides, leading to small dressing rooms. Both rooms had curtained second exits to the house, on the right beyond the Davenport Brothers Spirit Cabinet—a privy-sized cubicle in which a tarot reader now did her thing—and on the left behind a half-moon table used for close-up card tricks.

At 10:30 the voice of Cedric's wife Jan came over the loudspeaker, announcing the beginning of Boltan's act. The lights dimmed, and the conversational roar died to a murmur. Steele swiveled his chair to face the stage, the glass of brandy he had ordered in one hand. He cupped the glass like a fragile relic, staring over its lip at the stage as the curtain went up.

"Oh, for a muse of fire . . ." he said softly, when The Amazing Boltan made his entrance.

"What was that?" I whispered, but Steele merely gave me one of his amused looks and waved me to silence.

The Amazing Boltan was an impressive man. Something over six feet tall and ever so slightly portly, he had the impeccable grooming and manners of what would have been described fifty years ago as a "born gentleman." His tuxedo didn't seem like a stage costume, but like a part of his personality. It went with the gold cuff links and cigar case, and the carefully tonsured, white-striped black hair. He looked elegant, but to my eyes it was the elegance of a con man or a headwaiter.

Boltan's act was showy, designed to impress you constantly with his power and control. He put a rabbit into a box, then waved his hands and collapsed the box, and the rabbit was gone. He took two empty bowls and produced rice from them until it overran the little table he was working on and spilled in heaps onto the stage floor. He did a beautiful version of an effect called the Miser's Dream. Gold coins were plucked out of the air and thrown into a bucket until it rattled with them; then he switched to paper money and filled the rest of the bucket with fives and tens. All the while he kept up a steady flow of patter about "The Gold of Genies" and "The Transmutations of the Ancients of Lhassa."

When he was finished with this effect, Boltan said to the audience, "I shall now require an assistant. A young lady, perhaps. What about you, miss? That's it—don't be afraid. Step right up here on stage with me." He helped a young, winsome-looking blonde girl across the footlights, and proceeded to amaze her and the rest of the audience by causing sponge balls to multiply in her closed hand and appear and disappear from his.

He excused the girl finally and asked for another volunteer: "A young man, perhaps, this time." I could tell by the pacing of the act that he was headed toward some impressive finale.

A bulky bearded man who had just pushed himself to a table at the front, and was therefore still standing, allowed himself to be talked into climbing onto the stage. He was dressed somewhere between college casual and sloppy: a denim jacket, jeans, and glossy black shoes. He appeared to be in his late twenties, though it wasn't easy to tell through his medium-length facial hair.

"Thank you for coming up to help me," Boltan said in his deep stage voice. "Don't be nervous. Now, if you'll just hold your two hands outstretched in front of you, palms up . . ."

The bearded man, instead of complying with this request, took a sudden step backward and pulled a small automatic from his jacket pocket.

The audience leaned forward expectantly, thinking that this was part of the act; but Steele, who apparently felt that it wasn't, jumped to his feet and started toward the stage. I pushed my own chair back, frowning, and went after him.

Boltan retreated a couple of steps, a look of bewilderment crossing his elegant features. The bearded man leveled the gun at him, and I heard him say distinctly, "I'm going to kill you, Boltan, just as someone should have done years ago."

Steele shouted something, but his words were lost in the deafening explosion of three shots.

Boltan, staggering, put a hand to his chest. Blood welled through his fingers, and he slowly crumpled. A woman screamed. The uniformed police cadets and their officers were on their feet, some of them starting for the stage. Steele had reached the first row of tables, and was trying to push between two chairs to get to the stage. The bearded man dropped his weapon and ran offstage right, disappearing behind the curtain leading to the dressing room on that side.

The entire audience knew now that the shooting wasn't part of the show; another woman screamed, and people began milling about, several of them rushing in panic toward the Cellar's two street exits. Blue uniforms converged on the stage, shoving tables and civilians out of the way, leaping up onto it. Steele had made it up the steps by this time, with me at his heels, but his path toward the stage right curtain was hampered by the cadets. Over the bedlam I heard a voice shout authoritatively, "Everyone remain calm and stay where you are! Don't try to leave these premises!"

Another voice, just as authoritative, yelled, "Jordan, Bently, Cullen—cover the exits! Let no one out of here!

I could see the stage area exit beyond the Spirit Cabinet, the one from the dressing room area stage right to the club floor; in fact, I had kept my eyes on it from the moment the bearded man had run off, because that was the only other way out of that dressing room—but no one appeared there. Steele and the cops pushed their way through the stage right curtain just as several other cadets reached the exit I was watching. Any second now they would drag the bearded man out, I thought, and we could start to make sense out of what had just happened.

Only they didn't emerge, and I heard shouts of surprise and confusion instead.

"He's got to be in here somewhere."

"He's not here, damn it, you can see that."

"Another exit . . ."

"There isn't any other exit," Steele's voice said.

"Well, he's hiding in here somewhere."

"Where? There's no place for a man to hide."

"Those costume trunks—"

"They're too small to hold a man, as you can plainly see."

"Then where the hell is he? He can't have vanished into thin air!"

Subsequently, it appeared that the man who had shot The Amazing Boltan in full view of more than thirty cops had done just exactly that.

Half an hour later I was again sitting at the corner table, along with Steele, Ardis, a harassed-looking Cedric, and Ced's slender and attractive wife Jan. The contingent of police had managed to quiet the frightened patrons, who were now all sitting at the tables or in the grandstand, or clustered along the walls, or bellied up to the bar for liquid fortification; they looked nervous and were mostly silent. Blue uniforms and business suits—the cadets and their officers, and several regular patrolmen and Homicide people—stood guard or moved about the room examining things and asking questions and doing whatever else it is cops do at the scene of a violent crime.

A number of things had occurred in that half hour.

Item: Bolton had died of the gunshot wounds, probably instantaneously.

Item: The gun which the murderer had dropped, a Smith & Wesson

M39, had been turned over to the forensic lab men. If they had found any fingerprints on it, we hadn't heard of it yet.

Item: The police cadets who had covered the Cellar's two street exits immediately after the shooting swore that no one had left.

Item: The entire stage area and the remainder of the club had been thoroughly searched without turning up any sign of the bearded killer.

Conclusions: The Amazing Boltan had been shot to death by a man who could not have left the Magic Cellar, was therefore still here, and yet, seemingly, was not here at all.

All of us were baffled, as we had said to each other several times in the past few minutes. Or, rather, Ardis and Cedric and Jan and I had said so; Steele sat in silence, which was unusual for him, and seemed to be brooding. When I asked him how he thought it had been done, since after all he was a master illusionist and a positive fanatic when it came to "impossible challenges," he merely gave me a meditative look and deigned comment.

We had considered, of course, the trapdoor in the stage, and had instantly ruled it out. For one thing, it was located in the middle of the stage itself—right behind where Boltan had fallen, as a matter of fact—and all of us had seen the killer exit stage right through the side curtain; there was no trap in that dressing room area. The tunnel leading from under the stage trap to the coatroom had been searched anyway, but had been empty.

I dredged my memory for possible illusions which would explain the bearded man's vanishing act, but they all seemed to demand a piece of apparatus or specific condition which just wasn't present. Houdini once vanished an elephant off the stage of the Hippodrome, but he had a large, specially made cage to do it. What did seem clear was that the murderer knew, and had applied, the principles of stage magic to come up with a brilliant new effect, and then had used it to commit a cold-blooded homicide on the stage of the Magic Cellar.

Captain Dickensheet approached our table and leaned across it, his palms hard on the edge. "Everybody," he said pointedly to Cedric, "has to be somewhere. Don't you have *any* ideas where the killer got to—and how?"

Cedric shook his head wearily. "There's just no other way out of that dressing room besides the curtain onto the stage and the curtain next to the Spirit Cabinet," he said. "The Cabinet is solid down to the floor, and the other walls are brick."

"No gimmick or gizmo to open that Cabinet's back wall?"

"No, none."

"Even if there were," Steele said, "it woud merely propel the killer into the audience. The fact is, Captain, he could not have gotten out of the dressing room unseen. You have my professional word on that."

Dickensheet straightened up, glaring. "Are you telling me, then, that what we all saw couldn't have happened?"

"Not at all." Steele stood abruptly and squeezed past my chair to the aisle. "I can assure you that what you saw is exactly what happened. Exactly." Then, nodding to the table, he headed back to the stage left dressing room.

Dickensheet lowered his lanky frame into the aisle chair and stared across at the Carter the Great poster on the wall facing him. It depicted Carter astride a camel, surrounded by devils and imps, on his way to "steal" the secrets of the Sphinx and the marvels of the tomb of old King Tut. "Magicians!" the captain said, with feeling.

Cedric asked, "How much longer will you be holding everyone here?"

"I don't know just yet."

"Well, can't you just take all their names and addresses, and let them go home?"

"That's not up to me," Dickensheet said sourly. "You'll have to talk to Lupoff, the homicide inspector in charge of the investigation."

"All right." Cedric sighed, and got up to do that.

I decided to leave the table too, because I was wondering what Steele was up to backstage. I excused myself and went into the left dressing room where I found Steele sitting in front of the mirror, carefully applying his stage makeup.

"What are you doing?" I demanded.

"It's twenty till twelve, Matthew," he said. "I'm on at midnight."

"You don't think they're going to let you do your show *now*, do you?"

"Why not?"

"Well, they just took Boltan's body off the stage fifteen minutes ago."

"Ah yes," Steele said. "Life and death, the eternal mysteries. My audience is still here, I note, and I'm sure they'd like to be entertained. Not that watching the police poking and prying into all the corners big enough to conceal a man isn't entertaining."

"I don't understand why you'd even *want* to go on tonight," I said. "There's no way you can top the last performance. Besides, a spook show would hardly be in good taste right now."

"On the contrary, it would be in perfect taste. Because during the course of it, I intend to reveal the identity of the murderer of Philip Boltan."

"What!" I stared at him. "Do you mean you know how the whole thing was actually done?"

"I do."

"Well—how? How did the killer disappear?"

"The midnight show, Matthew," he said firmly.

I looked at him with sufferance, and then nodded. Steele never does anything the easy way. As well, here was an opportunity to put on a kind of show of shows, and Steele is first and foremost a showman. Not that I objected to this, you understand. My business is publicity and public relations, and Steele's flair for drama is the best kind of both. If he named the killer during his midnight show, and brought about the capture of the bearded man, the publicity would be fantastic.

"All right," I said, "I'll use my wiles to convince the cops to allow you to go ahead. But I hope you know what you're doing."

"I always know what I'm doing."

"Ninety percent of the time, anyway."

"Ask Ardis to come in here," Steele said. "I'll have to tell her what effects we're doing now, and in what order."

"You wouldn't want to give me some idea of what's going on, would you?"

Steele smiled a gentle, enigmatic smile. "It is now quarter to twelve, Matthew. I would like the show to begin at exactly midnight."

Which meant that he had said all he intended to say for the time being, and I was therefore dismissed. So I went back out into the club where Captain Dickensheet was still sitting at our table with Jan and Ardis; Cedric had also returned, and had brought with him the dark, intense-looking inspector-in-charge, Lupoff.

When I got to the table I told Ardis that Steele wanted to see her.

Immediately, she hurried to the stage left dressing room. I sat down and put on my best PR smile for Lupoff and Dickensheet.

"I have a request from Christopher Steele," I said formally. "He wants to be allowed to do his midnight show."

Both cops frowned, and Lupoff said, "I'm in no mood for levity."

"Neither is Steele. He wants to do the show, he says, in order to name the murderer and explain how the vanishing act was done."

Everyone at the table stared at me, Cedric and Jan looking relieved. Lupoff and Dickensheet, on the other hand, looked angrily disbelieving. The inspector said, "If Steele knows how and who, why the hell doesn't he just come out here and say so?"

"You have to understand him," I said easily. "He's an artist, a showman. He thinks only in threatrical terms." I went on to tell them about Steele's idiosyncracies, making it sound as though he were a genius who had to be treated with kid gloves—which was true enough. "Besides, if he solves the case for you, what can it hurt to let him unmask the killer in his own way?"

"The murderer *is* still here, then?" Cedric asked.

"I think so," I said. "Steele didn't really tell me much of anything, but that's what I would assume." I returned my gaze to the two cops. "You've got the Cellar sealed off, right? The killer can't possibly escape."

"I don't like it," Lupoff said. "It's not the way things are done."

I had to sell them quickly; it was nearing midnight. I decided to temporize. "Steele needs the show in order to expose the guilty man," I said. "He's not sure of the killer's identity, but something he has planned in the show will pin it down."

"How does he know it will work?" Dickensheet asked. Then he scowled. "He wouldn't be wanting to do this show of his just for publicity, would he?"

"Listen, Captain," I said, "the publicity won't be very good if he blows it. I'd say Steele's pretty sure of himself."

Cedric nodded eagerly; he knew, as I did, that if Steele came through as usual, it would turn a possibly harmful blow to the Cellar's image into a potential drawing card. He said, "I've known Christopher Steele for a long time, and I'll vouch for what Mr. Booth says. If Steele claims to know what happened here tonight, then he does know. I think you ought to go along with him."

Lupoff and Dickensheet held a whispered conference. Then they both got up, told us to wait, and went backstage, no doubt to confront Steele. Three minutes later they came out again, still looking dubious—but knowing Steele as I did, I could tell even before Dickensheet confirmed it that they had given him the go-ahead.

Midnight; and the civilian audience had been fidgeting in their seats for a couple of minutes, since Cedric had announced to them over the loudspeaker that Steele was going to do his midnight show. The contingent of police were also fidgeting, owing to the fact that none of them had any idea, either, of what was about to happen. I was alone at the table, Jan having gone back to the bar and Cedric off to work the light board.

The house lights dimmed, and the curtain rolled up. Steele stood motionless at center stage, the rose-gelled spots bathing him in soft light; his work clothes, a black suit over a dark turtleneck, gave him a sinister-somber look. He bowed slightly and said, "Good evening."

The last murmur died away among the audience, and two hundred people silently watched for whatever miracle Christopher Steele, Master of Illusion, was about to perform.

"We have, all of us," he said, "just witnessed a murder, and a murder is a horrible thing. It is the one irremediable act, terrible in its finality and inexcusable in any sane society. No matter how foul the deeds or repugnant the actions of another human being, no one has the right to take from him that which cannot be given back: his life.

"But the murder itself has been overshadowed by the miraculous disappearance of the killer, seemingly before our very eyes. He ran into that dressing room—" Steele gestured to his left, "—which has only two exits, and apparently never came out. The room has been thoroughly searched, and no human being could possibly remain concealed therein. A vanishing act worthy of a Houdini."

Steele's eyes peered keenly around at the audience. "I am something of an authority on vanishing—"

Suddenly the lights went out.

There was an immediate reaction from the audience, already edgy from the past hour-and-a-half's happenings; no screams, but a nervous titter in the dark and the sound of chairs being pushed back and people standing.

Then the lights came back on, and Steele was still there, center stage, facing the audience. "Accept my apologies," he said. "Please, all of you be seated. As you can see—" he indicated the two police officers standing one on each side of the stage, "—there is nowhere I could go. As well, the lights were off then for a full five seconds, which is much too long for an effective disappearance. A mere flicker of darkness, or a sudden burst of flame, is all that is needed.

"I shall now attempt to solve this mystery, which has so completely baffled my friends on the police and the rest of us. I'm sure you will forgive me if, in so doing, I create a small mystery of my own."

Steele clapped his hands together three times, and on the third clap there was a blinding flash of light—and the stage lights went out again—and came back on almost instantly.

Steele was gone.

In his place stood the beautiful Ardis, in her long white stage gown, her arms outstretched and a smile on her lips. "Hello," she said.

The audience gasped. The thing was done so neatly, and so quickly; Steele had turned into Ardis before their eyes. Someone tentatively applauded, as much in a release of tension as anything else, but there was no doubt that the audience was impressed.

Ardis held up her hands for silence. "What you have just seen is called a transference," she said when the room grew still again. "Christopher Steele is gone, and I am here. And now I, too, in my turn, shall leave. I shall go into the fourth dimension, and you shall all observe the manner of my going. Yet none of you will know where I have gone. Thus—farewell."

There was another bright flash, and the lights once more went out; but we could still see Ardis before us as a kind of ghostly radiance, her white dress almost glowing in the dark. Then she dwindled before our eyes, as though receding to a great distance. Finally, the lights came on to stay, and the stage was empty, and she was gone.

There was a shocked silence, as though the audience was collectively holding its breath. In that silence, suddenly, a deep, imperious voice said, "I am here!"

Everybody turned in their seats, including me, for the voice had come from the rear of the room.

Incredibly, there stood the murderer—beard, denim jacket, and all.

Several of the policemen started toward him, and one woman shrieked. At the same time, the bearded man extended his arm and pointed a long finger. "I," he said, "am you."

He was pointing at one of the young police cadets standing near the Iron Maiden.

The cadet backed away, startled, looking trapped. Immediately, the bearded man hunched in on himself and pulled the denim jacket over his head. When he stood up again, he was Steele—and the apparition that had been the murderer was a small bundle of clothing in his hand. Even the jeans had been replaced by Steele's black suit trousers.

"You are the murderer of Philip Boltan," Steele said to the cadet. "You—"

The cadet didn't wait for any more; he turned and made a wild run for the nearest exit. He didn't make it, but it took three other cops a full minute to subdue him.

Some time later, Steele, Ardis, Cedric, Jan, and I were sitting around the half-moon table waiting for Inspector Lupoff and Captain Dickensheet to return from questioning the murderer of Philip Boltan. The Cellar had been cleared of patrons and police, and we were alone in the large, dark room.

Steele occupied the seat of honor: an old wooden rocking chair in the dealer's spot in the center of the half-moon. He had said little since the finale of his special midnight show. All of us had wanted to ask him how he knew the identity of the killer, and exactly how the vanishing act had been worked, but we knew him well enough to realize that he wouldn't say anything until he had the proper audience. He just sat there smiling in his enigmatic way.

When the two officers finally came back, they looked disgruntled and morose. They sat down in the two empty chairs, and Dickensheet said grimly, "Well, we've just had an unpleasant talk with Spellman—or the man I knew as Spellman, anyway. He's made a full confession."

"The man you knew as Spellman?" I said.

"His real name is Granger. Robert Granger."

Cedric frowned, looking at Steele. "Isn't that the name of Boltan's former partner, the one you told us committed suicide?"

"It is," Steele told him. "I had an idea that might be who the young cadet was."

"You mean he killed Boltan because of what happened to his father?" I asked.

"Yes," Lupoff said. "He decided years ago that the perfect revenge was to kill Boltan on stage, in full view of an audience, and then disappear. He's planning it ever since, mainly by studying and mastering the principles of magic."

"Then he intended from the beginning to murder Boltan in cirumstances such as those tonight?"

"More or less," Dickensheet said. "He wanted to do the job during one of Boltan's regular performances, and the invitation to the Academy graduating class tonight convinced him that now was the time. It was only fitting, according to Granger, that Boltan die on stage under an aura of mystery."

Jan said bewilderedly, "But why would a potential murderer join the *police* force? It's incredible!"

"Spellman, or Granger, is mentally unstable. We try to weed them out, but every once in a while one slips by. He believes in meting out punishment to those who would 'do evil,' in his words just now. God only knows what he might have done if he'd gotten away with this murder and gone on to become an officer in the field." Dickensheet shuddered at the possibility. "As if we don't have enough problems . . ."

"I don't understand how Granger could join the force under an assumed name," Cedric said. "I mean, if his real name is Granger and you knew him as Spellman—"

"Spellman is the name of the family who adopted him out of the orphanage he ended up in after his father died. As far as our people knew, that was his real name. I mean, you usually don't check back past a kid's sixth birthday. We might never have known he was Boltan's partner's son if he hadn't admitted it himself tonight."

"What else did he say?" I asked.

"Not much. He talked freely enough about who he was and his motives, but when we started asking him about the details of the murder, he closed up tight."

So we all looked at Steele, who continued to sit there smiling to himself.

"All right, Steele," Lupoff said, "you're on again. How did Spellman-Granger commit the murder?"

"With a gun," Steele told him.

"Now look—"

Steele held up a placating hand. "Very well," he said, "although you must realize that I dislike explaining any illusion." He began to rock gently in the chair. "Granger used a clever variant on an illusion first used by Houdini. As Houdini did it, the magician rode into an arena—this was a major effect only done in stadiums and arenas—on a white horse, dressed in flowing Arabian robes. His several assistants, clad in red work suits, would grab the horse. Houdini would then stand up in the saddle and fire a gun in the air, at which second a previously arranged action of some type would direct all eyes to another part of the arena. During that instant, Houdini would vanish; and his assistants would then lead the horse out."

Dickensheet asked, "So how did he do it?"

"By a costume change. He would be wearing, underneath the Arabian robes, a red work suit like his assistants; the robes were specially-made breakaway garments, which he could get out of in a second, roll into a ball, and hide beneath his work suit. So he became one of the assistants and went out with them and the horse.

"Spellman's vanishing act was worked in much the same way. He probably donned his breakaway costume and false beard in the men's room just prior to Boltan's act, *over* his police uniform, and made sure he was picked from the audience by being there standing up when Boltan did the selecting. After he shot Boltan and ran into the dressing room through the curtain, he pulled off his breakaway costume and false hair, rolled them into a bundle and stuffed them into one of the costume trunks. Next he backed against the side of the curtain, so that when the first cadets dashed through, he immediately became one of them."

"But we looked in all of the trunks . . ."

"Yes, but you were looking for a man hiding, not for a small bundle of denim and hair stuffed in toward the bottom."

Lupoff shook his head. "It sounds so simple," he said.

"Much magic works like that," Steele said. "You could never in a lifetime guess how it's done, but if it's explained it sounds so easy you wonder how you were fooled. Which is one reason magicians do not like to explain their effects."

Ardis said, "You knew all along it had to be one of the cadets, Christopher?"

"By the logic of the situation," Steele agreed. "But I had further confirmation when I remembered that, despite his somewhat scruffy appearance, the murderer was wearing well-shined black shoes—the one item he wouldn't have time to change—just as were all the other graduating cadets."

"But how did you know which of the cadets it was?"

"I didn't until I was on stage. I had found the costume and the beard right before that, and I saw that the guilty man had fastened his face hair on with spirit gum, as most professionals do. It must have been very lightly tacked on so he could rip it off effectively, but the spirit gum would leave a residue nonetheless."

"Of course!" I said. "Spirit gum fluoresces under ultraviolet light."

Steele smiled. "Not very much, but enough for me to have detected the outline of a chin and upper lip when looked for them in the darkness."

Lupoff and Dickensheet seemed baffled, so I explained that there were u.v. bulbs in some of the spots because they were necessary for Steel's spook show effects.

They nodded. Lupoff asked Steele, "How did you manage *your* disappearance?"

"The stage trap. I dropped into it, and Ardis popped out of it. Then she kept the audience's attention long enough for me to crawl to the coatroom, put on the breakaway costume, and approach the audience from the rear. When the lights went out again and she disappeared, I looked again for the outline of chin and upper lip, to make sure I would be confronting exactly the right man."

"And now your disappearance, young lady?" Dickensheet asked Ardis.

She laughed. "I walked off the stage in the dark."

"But we saw you, ah, dwindle away . . ."

"That wasn't me. It was a picture painted on an inflated balloon which was held over the stage for our show. I pulled it down with a concealed string while the lights were out, and allowed it to deflate. So you saw the picture getting smaller and seeming to recede. The method's been used for many years," Ardis explained.

Dickensheet and Lupoff exchanged glances. The inspector said, "All of this really is obvious. But now that we know just how obvious magic tricks are, at least, we'd never fall for anything like them again."

"Absolutely not," the captain agreed.

"So you say," Steele said. "But perhaps—"

Suddenly Ardis jumped up, backed off two steps, and made a startled cry. Naturally, we all looked around at her—and she was pointing across the table to Steele's chair.

When we looked back there again, after no more than a second, the chair was rocking gently and Steele had vanished.

Dickensheet's mouth hung open by several inches. Lupoff said in a surprised voice, "He didn't have time to duck through the curtain there. Then—where did he go?"

I know most of Steele's talents and effects, but not all of them by any means. So I closed my own mouth, because I had no answer to Lupoff's question.